CAT'S EYE GREEN

CAT'S EYE GREEN

A Gideon Griffin Mystery

Lisa Dornell

⊙ CONSTRUCTIVE INSOMNIA

CAT'S EYE GREEN
A Gideon Griffin Mystery

Copyright © 2023 by Lisa Dornell

All rights reserved. No part of this publication may be reproduced in any form or by any electronic or mechanical means, including information and retrieval systems, without permission in writing from the copyright holder.

This story is fictional. All of the characters in this publication are fictitious and any resemblance to actual events, locales, or persons, living or dead is purely coincidental.

Production and book design by Forrest Dylan Bryant

A work of Constructive Insomnia

ISBN: 978-0-9846984-2-4

For Forrest. For everything.

*In memory of Cipher,
the original Catullus*

*With special thanks to all my friends who asked,
"Where's your damn book?"
Here it is. It's all your fault.*

"And a man's foes shall be they of his own household."

—Matthew 10:36

Chapter 1

"I say, Griff, do you have any bullets? My brother just died."

I put down the knife and fork with which I was excavating the last bit of pink, flaky goodness from a particularly fine Scottish salmon and regarded the man looming over my table.

Lord Valentine Hatton-Haxley, concern spread across his rather pale face, threw himself down in the chair opposite me and gave a terribly posh sigh filled with equal quantities of anxiety and exhaustion. Only with more anxiety.

"Hello, Val. Sorry about your brother. No bullets, I'm afraid. Will a 9-iron do?"

Val shook his head, unable to answer due to the rather large potato filling his mouth—a potato he'd snagged from my plate.

I moved the plate a little farther from my best friend and a little closer to me.

"So," I asked, "why and which one?"

"Why what and which who?"

Val signaled for Gustav, the Austrian headwaiter who had been presiding over the dining room of the Icarus Club since Cromwell's day, and ordered lunch, a nice pinot noir, and three aspirin.

As he turned back to me, he caught sight of himself in the long mirror that lined one wall of the members' dining room. Being harmlessly vain, he ran a taming hand through his disobedient hair. Val was the same age as me, which was thirty-one, and we were often mistaken for brothers. In fact, I looked more like him than most of his family did.

Which meant, of course, that he was equally as handsome as I. Only I was slightly more handsome. We both had rather square faces, dark brown hair with a tendency to be unruly, and pleasingly regular features thanks to our respective parents. The one difference was our eyes. His were blue. Mine were, and are, blue. And brown. One of each.

"Why do you need bullets? And which brother?"

"Oh. Erasmus," he replied, answering the second question first.

"I'm sorry. He was like an acquaintance to me."

"And I need bullets so I can protect myself, because if Erasmus is dead then it means I'm next."

"Next in line to inherit?"

"Next in line to die."

"Oh," I paused to arrange the cutlery on my now-empty plate. "Well, that's unfortunate. I've always rather liked you."

"Yes, I agree it's unfortunate," Val said. "I do have a revolver, though. Souvenir of the trenches and all that."

"You were never in the trenches," I pointed out. "I was."

"I could have been in the trenches," Val protested.

"And I could have discovered Tutankhamun's tomb if I'd been an Egyptologist. Or if I wasn't allergic to sand."

"You aren't allergic to sand."

"You spent your war in Budleigh Salterton," I observed. "You used a stapler, not a gun."

"Well, even so they gave me one. And I had to leave the stapler on the desk when I left, but I got to keep the gun." He paused while one of Gustav's staff opened the wine and poured for his approval. Val sipped, nodded, and returned to the subject of his imminent demise.

"Anyway, with Erasmus gone, that just leaves me."

"Just leaves you where?"

"Just leaves me as the last brother. Poor old Erasmus." He drank and sighed.

"What happened to him?" I asked, enjoying the way Val's pinot noir clashed with my glass of Chablis.

"Oh, he was murdered," Val replied casually. He must have noticed the widening of my eyes at this revelation, as he quickly added, "All of my brothers have been murdered. I'm the only non-murdered brother left. Have I never mentioned this before?"

"No, you've never mentioned this before. What are you talking about? Didn't your brother Druscilla die on the Somme?"

"It's Drausinus, and he drowned. Drogo died at the Somme."

"Well, that's not exactly murder, is it? And what the hell kind of names are Drogo and Drausinus anyway?"

"I think Drogo would disagree with you. I think he'd say he was murdered. I mean, somebody else killed him, after all. I'm pretty sure he didn't run voluntarily into a bullet."

I pondered this with another sip of wine. "That's rather the definition of war, isn't it? Running voluntarily into bullets? And what about Drausinus drowning, then? That sounds like an accident, not murder."

"Nope. Murder. And if any of us brothers were to survive, I would have put money on Drausinus."

"Why?"

"St. Drausinus is the patron saint of invincible people."

"Do invincible people need their own saint?"

The arrival of Val's lunch distracted him before he could answer. He took a moment to appreciate the artistic arrangement of beef, carrots, and boiled potatoes before continuing.

"Drausinus couldn't drown without some help. He swam like a lobster."

"I don't think lobsters swim," I observed.

"Certainly, they swim!" Val protested. "They live in the ocean. They've got to swim. How do they get around if they don't swim?"

"I'm pretty sure they walk. They just hang around on the bottom, walking."

"Fine," he huffed. "Drausinus swam like something that swims for a living. He couldn't possibly drown in three feet of water. He was six feet tall."

"He could have had a cramp."

"Nope. Murder. He had bruises on his neck and back like he'd been held underwater."

"Bruises do sound suspicious," I admitted. "But who would want to murder your brother?"

"Brothers," Val corrected. "Plural. Except for Drogo being shot by some German soldier, all my brothers were probably murdered by Uncle Sally and Aunt Jim."

"You have an Uncle Sally and an Aunt Jim?"

"That's the part you question? Their names?"

"It's the easiest thing to latch onto after a heavy lunch. My body is too busy digesting salmon to digest all this for dessert."

"If you must know, their names are really Sulpicius and Jemima Hatton-Haxley, known as Sally and Jim."

"You have an uncle named Suspicious?"

"Sulpicius."

"I see. And you're suspicious of Sulpicius?"

"Yes." Val paused to cut a potato into neat fourths. "And he's the patron saint of ugly people."

I shook my head, fuzzled by two different kinds of wine and too many non sequiturs.

"Your Uncle Suspicious is the patron saint of ugly people?"

"No. Saint Drogo was."

There was a moment of silence while Val tucked into his lunch, and I wondered why he and I were friends. Against my better judgment, I asked the obvious question.

"There's a patron saint of ugly people?"

Val nodded.

"And your parents named your brother after him?"

Val nodded again.

"Good lord, why?"

"Well, we were all named for saints. There was Medard, he was the oldest. Then the twins, Servatius and Erasmus. Then Drogo, Drausinus, and finally me. Saint Valentine."

"Forgive me for saying this," I observed, "but your parents were decidedly odd."

"*Your* name is Gideon Plantagenet Griffin." He made it sound like an accusation. "Wasn't one of them a saint? Anyway, don't throw stones."

"I'm not throwing stones. I'm stating an opinion. And my considered opinion is that your parents were weird. Besides, Gideon liberated Israel and the Plantagenets were kings. Either is a better namesake than the patron saint of ugly people."

"Fair point," Val admitted.

"Besides," I continued. "My name looks impressive on the covers of books."

"I suppose it does. Did you become a mystery writer just to see your name in print?"

"No, I became a mystery writer because I'd be a horrible coal miner." I helped myself to more of Val's wine. "So, tell me what happened to brother Saint Erasmus. And why don't you seem more upset?"

"Brother Saint Erasmus was found in his bathtub."

"Another drowning?"

"Sort of."

"How does one *sort of* drown?"

"Well, nobody is sure whether he drowned or whether he choked on a marble."

"A marble?"

"A marble."

"The kind one plays with or the kind one carves?"

"The former, of course. A cat's-eye green bumboozer."

I began to wonder if this was what having a stroke felt like. "A what?"

"A cat's-eye green bumboozer."

"What in the name of your dead sainted brother is a cat's-eye green bumboozer supposed to be?"

"It's a marble."

"We've already been there. Repeating the same few nonsense words over and over is not the same thing as an explanation."

"Sorry." He didn't look it.

"Let me make it easier for you. A bumboozer is a…? And if you just say it's a marble again, you may not outlive your brother for long."

Val looked up from his plate. "A *bumboozer*." He said it as if it should be patently obviously to any moderately intelligent lamp. "A cosher. A goom. A bumbo."

"Stop making up words and explain!" My voice rose to such an inappropriate level that Gustav, sitting at the other end of the room, cleared his throat. A sure sign that I was about to be in trouble.

"You know, the big one. That you shoot with."

"Why don't you just call it a shooter?"

"Because we always called them bumboozers."

"For the sake of my sanity, can you just call it a shooter?"

"Why?" Val seemed honestly perplexed.

"Because this whole conversation borders on the imbecilic and it doesn't help things when you say your brother may have been killed by a bumboozer. It sounds like some kind of Cockney slang for a drunken harlot."

He chewed and sat for a moment with an air of confusion. I was fond of Val's perplexed expression, which I saw often. It gave him an endearing look, rather like a befuddled spaniel.

"Fine. He may have choked on a cat's-eye green shooter. Does that make more sense?"

"Not in the least," I replied.

"Perhaps I should start again."

"For the love of God, no," I pleaded. "How about if I ask questions and you answer them?"

"If you prefer."

"I do." I took a breath and tried to find something to latch onto. "So, brother Saint Erasmus was found dead in his bathtub?"

"Yes, he—"

"No, please, just let me keep asking questions."

"Go ahead." He inclined his head gracefully, as if offering the royal blessing.

"And he may have died from drowning in the bathtub. Or by choking on a large marble?"

"Yes."

"And you think he's just the latest of your late brothers to die of murder?"

"Yes."

"I was wrong," I admitted. "This isn't any better."

"But that's not the weirdest bit," he commented.

"I'm afraid to ask, but what could possibly be stranger than a grown man choking on a marble while taking a bath?"

"He was *reading*." The phrase was uttered with a tone of such ominous satisfaction I half-expected him to add: "*...and the bathtub was full of exploding piranhas.*"

I was beginning to believe myself doomed to live the rest of my life in a state of wild confusion. All I could do was repeat dumbly, "He was reading."

"Yes. And that is decidedly odd, because Erasmus didn't read much. He wasn't what you'd call an intellectual. Not like me."

"Like I," I murmured, remembering our adolescent English

classes. Val had very nearly flunked out when he refused to believe in apostrophes.

"And what he was reading was odd, too," he added.

Rather than ask another question that would only lead to a non-answer, I expressed my query through the skillful use of eyebrows.

"He was reading *The Gospel of Nicodemus*."

"He was reading what?" I couldn't have heard that right.

"*The Gospel of Nicodemus*," he replied. "It's a—"

"I know what it is," I stopped him. "*Nicodemus* is one of the apocryphal gospels."

"I keep forgetting you're my smart friend," he observed around a mouthful of beef. "Well, it's incredibly weird because I can't recall Erasmus ever reading anything that wasn't either light and fluffy or some sinister book he illegally smuggled in from France. Why would someone whose favorite author is 'Anonymous' be reading early Christian theology?"

"Maybe he was trying to broaden his horizons?"

"A man who reads books like *The Confessions of a Naughty Novitiate* does not casually pick up *The Confessions of Saint Augustine* for some relaxing bath time page-turning. But a copy of the text was found floating on the water. *The Gospel of Nicodemus*!" He flailed a hand. "Who brings a book like *The Gospel of Nicodemus* into the bath? If *The Gospel of Nicodemus* isn't a sign of foul play, then I don't know what is."

"That is a bit suspicious. And, by the way, congratulations on winning the award for most mentions of 'Nicodemus' in one minute. But why in the world would you suspect your Uncle Louise and Aunt Arthur of killing your brother?"

"Uncle Sally and Aunt Jim. And I don't suspect them, I know they're behind it. They're behind all the others, too."

"Except for Saint Brother Ugly."

"Hey!"

"Sorry," I said, only halfway sincere. "I just can't get over the ugly bit. But tell me, why do you think—"

"*Know*," Val corrected.

"How do you *know* they killed your brothers?"

"Because they want the money."

"What money?"

"*The* money. The Hatton-Haxley money. Good lord, now it's *my* money!" Val stared at me, aghast. He put down his knife and fork and I seized the opportunity to steal a potato, making up for the one he'd snagged from me.

"Don't your aunt and uncle have money?"

"Not as much as we do. After all, dearly departed papa *was* the Earl of Haxley. Uncle Sally was the younger brother. He has some money, mostly due to beastly Aunt Jim and her horrid family. But he's the world's tightest tightwad and he will never have enough money to satisfy. He's always been upset that he wasn't the eldest. Although they treat the house like they own it."

"What house?"

"Our house," Val said in the patient tones of an expert trying to explain photosynthesis to a crab puff.

Meanwhile, I felt rather like a crab puff trying to grasp the concept of photosynthesis. I shook my head in a futile attempt to land any one of the three dozen thoughts in my brain into the slot marked "*comprehension*." Failing, I resorted to the eyebrow maneuver again.

Val sighed heavily. "It's quite simple, old fish. You take an ancient family curse, add an uncle and aunt with all the morals of the mayor of Gomorrah and his lady wife, and you get our family. They are evil. They are greedy. They are completely unscrupulous, and now they have run through all my brothers so that I am the only thing that stands between them and the Earldom and the Hatton-Haxley fortune."

I was silent. What could one say to a statement like that?

"And to make things worse," Val continued, "now I must walk into the lion's den. Tower Field Hall, the ancestral pile. I have to bury Erasmus and they'll be right there, waiting for me with hemlock-laced porridge and a hidden knife in the feather bed."

"Don't you think you might be overreacting a smidge?"

"Does a soldier overreact to going over the top?"

"We've already established that you were never in the trenches."

"Well, I feel like I am now. I've got to go down tomorrow."

"Ah yes, to lovely old… what is it? Hatrack-Under-Towel?"

"Hatton-Under-Tower."

"Whatever."

"Griff, come with me!"

"To Hatrack-Under-Towel?" I asked incredulously.

"Yes, come with me to Hatrack-Under-Towel. It's been years since you've come to stay. I think the last time was when we bagged those pheasants, and you broke a tooth on the buckshot."

"Hardly the sort of memory that makes me want to visit the old place again."

"Perhaps not, but I could really use your help. With you watching my back, maybe I'll survive the funeral. I'd really prefer not to die this weekend. I've got a date with one half of the most gorgeous twins in London. The Throgmortons."

"Ah, yes," I said, "the lovely Hyacinth and… what is it? Howard? Harold?"

"Homer. Anyway, we're going to the premiere of *Socks Off, Sailor* at the Empress next Friday. I've been trying to arrange this date for donkey's years. I think I'm in love."

"How could you possibly be in love with a Throgmorton?" There was really no response to this, so Val didn't respond. I went back to what little of the narrative I was able to comprehend. "If you're afraid of this weekend, why don't you just… *not go?*"

"How would it look if I missed the funeral of the last brother I'll ever have?"

"Were you there?"

"Where?"

"There. At the Hall. Were you there when it happened?"

"No, I was in the middle of nowhere in Scotland. Best Man for George Maitland. He married this smashing girl whose father owns a lot of hilly bits. I only got back to town yesterday."

"So, what exactly happened?" I asked.

"I honestly don't know anything beyond the facts of the bath, the book, and the—"

"Please," I begged, "for the love of God, don't say 'bumboozer.'"

"Why not? You just did."

I may have actually growled.

"Anyway," he continued, "I think we'll have to wait for more information until we get to the Hall. I was planning on being there this weekend, anyway, even without the funeral. For my great-grandfather's birthday."

"Your great-grandfather is still alive?"

"Oh no, he died donkey's ages ago, but under the terms of the old reprobate's will, the entire family is required to gather once a year on his birthday to drink to his memory and keep their place in the line of succession. It's mandatory."

"I hate to ask, but for the sake of curiosity, what was his name?"

"Adjutor."

"Adjutor?"

"Patron saint of swimmers."

"Hmm… maybe if Saint Brother Drausinus had been named after your great-grandfather he wouldn't have drowned."

"Would you want to go through life as an Adjutor?" Val asked.

"Not particularly. Val, what does your family have against normal names?"

"What's wrong with Remigius?"

"Who or what is a Remigius?"

"My grandfather."

"And does your grandfather play any role in any of what you've been talking about?"

"No."

"Then why bring him into it?"

"I just like the name."

Thinking that silence was probably the safest course, I went that way.

"You see," Val explained, "my family has always named their sons after saints."

"Why? Don't they like them?"

"Who, saints?"

"No, their sons."

"Oh no, I'm sure they like their sons a suitable amount. No, all those saints' names are there as an attempt to counteract the family curse."

"Ah yes, you did casually drop a family curse into the whole indigestible buffet of dead brothers a few minutes ago. I was hoping to ignore that. So there actually is a curse?" I paused. "What am I saying? Of course, there's a curse. And I'm assuming this curse is a worse fate than being named something like Egregious or Fornicatus."

"Fornicatus is not a name," Val protested.

"Until a minute ago, I didn't think Remigius was a name."

"Well, it is. And no, the names are not the curse."

"That might be a matter of opinion. You know, Val, I'm not sure if your family story is a Greek tragedy or a Shakespearean comedy."

"I prefer Shakespeare. *Much Ado About Erasmus* maybe."

"Or perhaps *Drausinus Andronicus*." I paused. Hard thinking always made me hungry. "I'm going to order some oysters."

"How can you eat those things?"

"What's wrong with oysters?"

"Hey, look! I found a rock with snot in it. Let's eat it!"

I changed my mind about the oysters. "All right then, order another bottle of wine and tell me about it." I didn't think the wine would help, but I felt I was earning it.

Val signaled for Gustav, settled himself casually in his chair, and began to tell me about his family curse.

Chapter 2

"In 1642," Val said, "around the time of the Civil War, the Hatton-Haxleys were happy, prosperous, and curse-free."

"Whose side were they on?" I asked.

"Cavaliers."

"Of course. Silly of me to ask."

"When the war began, Edward Hatton-Haxley, the 3rd Earl of Haxley, was engaged to the daughter of a very rich neighbor. Her name was Mary Anne Theodore and her father, George Theodore, owned a whiskey distillery. Rich, but not at all aristocratic."

"But a good man to have for a father-in-law."

"He might have been. But the marriage never took place."

"Why not?"

"The two families came out on opposite sides of the war."

"And that was enough to prevent the banns?"

"Well, they didn't particularly like each other to begin with."

"Who?" I asked, "Edward and Mary Anne?"

"No, Edward and George. They didn't like each other very much. But Edward and Mary Anne liked each other a little too much."

"How much is too much?"

"'Congratulations, it's a boy' too much," Val explained.

"Yes, I think we can all agree that is just a bit too much. So what happened?"

"Unfortunately for all concerned, before they knew there was going to be a baby, Edward and George had words over politics. Harsh enough that no rapprochement was possible. So Edward turned around and abruptly married one Lady Agnes Mills whose family was suitably blue-blooded. But a month after Edward and Agnes were wed, poor Mary Anne discovered she was with child."

"Oh dear."

"It gets worse."

"Of course."

"Mary Anne died in childbirth and the baby died, too."

I grimaced. "This is a horrible story. Why are you telling me this horrible story? And why is my wine glass empty while you make me listen to this horrible story?"

"It gets worse again."

"It would, wouldn't it."

"By the time Mary Anne died, Lady Agnes was three months pregnant."

"How does that make it worse?"

"Mary Anne's mother, Una, was Scottish, and rumor had it she was what used to be known as a wise woman."

"You mean she was a witch?"

"Well, that's one way of putting it."

"Is there another way?" I asked.

"Yes. She was a wise woman."

"Right."

"Apparently, the loss of Mary Anne and her baby pushed Una the Witch around the proverbial bend. She cursed Edward, Agnes, their unborn son, all future sons, and every generation of sons forevermore with horrible luck and early death. She vowed that no eldest son would ever inherit the title or property associated with the Earldom of Haxley."

"Nice. Good curse. Very *King Lear*," I observed.

"Is there a curse in *King Lear*?"

"No idea. Please continue."

"Well, Una the Witch was apparently very good at the curse stuff. It has proven true in every single generation since, for nearly three hundred years."

"You're joking."

"I only wish."

"No eldest son has ever inherited?"

"Not a one. The baby that Lady Agnes was carrying died in infancy. They had two more sons before Agnes herself died at the age of thirty. Both boys died before the age of eighteen and the title passed to Edward's younger brother, Thomas."

"Should I be taking notes?"

"Thomas's eldest son, Arthur, died when he was just twelve and when Thomas himself died the title passed to his second son, Godfrey. It was Godfrey who started the tradition of naming boys after saints. When his first son was born, like all fathers in our family, he looked forward to the day when his son would die young in some tragic or gruesome fashion. So, he named the boy Jude for protection."

"Jude as in lost causes?"

"Exactly."

"I take it Saint Jude didn't help the boy."

Val shook his head, sadly. "No, Jude died when he about nine years old. The eventual heir was his younger brother, Francis."

I waggled my finger at Val, "See? It is possible to name your child after a saint without resorting to Wendleburt or Grammarian."

"Well, there's an odd tradition in our family."

"You mean another one?"

"The Hatton-Haxleys don't reuse names. Every child born since the origin of the curse has had a unique name. The usual ones were used up long ago. There's a massive book in our library we use to find new ones, but pretty soon we'll have to start consulting the dons at Oxford."

"What about the girls?"

Val nodded. "The girls, too. Remind me to introduce you to my cousins Quiteria, Hedwig, and Margaret of Cortona."

"Margaret of Cortona?"

"The homeless and the mentally ill," Val explained.

"Fitting for your family. But Margaret of Cortona? Is 'of' really her middle name?"

"No that's just to tell her apart from another cousin, Margaret the Virgin. She hates that name."

"You astound me. Pray continue."

"Well, my father—"

"I'm sure I'll regret asking, but what was his name again?"

"Gummarus."

"Really?"

"Patron saint of bad marriages."

"What does your family have against the patron saints of good stuff? Ugly people? Bad marriages? Do you have a cousin named for the patron saint of pus-filled boils? Perhaps an Uncle Tiny Bladder or Great-great-grandfather Pox?"

"Now, don't be facetious, Griff. Father was Lord Gummarus Balthasar Pius Hatton-Haxley, the 15th Earl of Haxley."

"That's a large amount of name."

"Yes. Poor old stick, he never quite lived up to it."

"I'm guessing he was a younger son?" Was I actually beginning to follow this madness?

"Right. His older brother, my uncle Columbanus, fell out of a church steeple during bell-ringing practice and died at the age of seventeen."

"That is definitely odd."

"Aren't all curses odd?" Val asked.

"You have a point," I agreed, "But I was talking about the

bell-ringing. I never could understand the attraction. And I can't even imagine a healthy seventeen-year-old boy taking up bell-ringing as a hobby. Not while the earth is full of healthy seventeen-year-old girls."

Val was silent. The whole club was quiet now, as we'd talked clear through luncheon and well into the afternoon.

"Tell me something," I said. "If your family has this horrible curse, why would your parents, with malice aforethought, keep having sons? And if people keep dying even with the weird saint names, then obviously the names aren't working. So why keep inflicting an already afflicted family with such outlandish monikers?"

"Why do you keep harping on our names?"

"Perhaps because it's the only part of your insane story I can follow. I don't know what to do with curses and dead brothers. But weird names are always suitable for some good-natured mocking. So, I'm mocking you, good-naturedly."

"Well, whatever their names, the eldest sons always die. Accidents. Plague. Dozens of would-be inheritors living to the ripe old age of 'died in infancy.' Sometimes a whole branch will die out and the title passes to a cousin. That's what's going on with me and my brothers. My eldest brother—"

"Mad Dog."

"Medard."

"Whatever."

"Anyway, poor Medard was born with a target on his back and my family spent most of his childhood waiting for him to die."

"What a lovely memory," I observed. "Tea in the nursery, playing soldiers in the woods, and waiting for your older brother to pass on."

"Which he did."

"I figured that. Drogo drowned, so is Medard the one who was electrocuted?"

"You're mixed up. Drausinus drowned. Medard's the one who had a gargoyle fall on his head."

I looked around the room to make sure I wasn't in some mad new country called Lunacyland. But the familiar arrangement of tables and chairs overseen by dull portraits of past Icarus Club presidents suggested I was still in reality. With my friend. Talking about his many dead brothers. And now there was a lethal gargoyle to boot.

"Please tell me you're joking about the gargoyle," I pleaded.

"Not in the least. It happened a week before his sixteenth birthday. So, when my father finally turned up his toes, the title went to my brother Servatius."

"Who was... Let me guess. Attacked by a bear?"

"Avalanche," Val replied, dismally.

"Avalanche."

"He went hiking in Scotland with some friends. Never came back. They found him later, buried in snow," Val said, sadly.

"An avalanche?" I asked again. He nodded. "In Scotland?" He nodded again. "Right. Scotland. Totally normal. Go on."

"And now," Val concluded, "may dear Saint Valentine protect me, I'm the new Earl."

"Um, congratulations?"

"No," Val corrected. "Condolences. Because if I'm the new Earl, I'm already a dead man."

Chapter 3

The afternoon moved along, as afternoons do. Eventually the hovering Gustav indicated in the politest and least ignorable way that luncheon was well and truly over, and we had to clear out so he could ready the dining room for dinner.

Val and I took our conversation to the small library, which was empty except for Colonel Wilkinson, who was always there and always asleep. There was a rumor that the Colonel had in fact died some years earlier, but nobody was brave enough to check on him. He looked so comfortable.

The small library was far friendlier than the Icarus Club's formal library. In the latter space, silence was strictly observed, and members were expected to read things. The walls were lined with shelves and the tables well supplied with everything from the *Times* to the *Sporting News*.

The small library, on the other hand, was a cozy space with oak paneling, a thick red carpet that one sank in almost to the ankles, and three large, arched windows that let in the sunlight.

It wasn't much of a library. The sole bookshelf held the works of Shakespeare, Dickens, and a notoriously bad poet named Edmund Gilbert-Rodmere, who had been a member of the Icarus Club and bequeathed them a complete set of his works. So there, on display amid never-read copies of *Titus Andronicus* and *The Old Curiosity Shop* and far from the eyes of the club's regular readers, resided such unappealing titles as *An Ode to*

Steam Power, *Fifty Love Poems About Love*, and *Seventy Sonnets from Somerset*. Pride of place was held by Gilbert-Rodmere's collection of war poetry, a magnum opus called *My Butler's Son Died of Dysentery at Ypres*.

Ignoring the possible corpse that was Colonel Wilkinson, we grabbed chairs in the farthest corner of the room, underneath a portrait of one of the club founders. I always thought the subject looked like he was sitting on something extremely painful but was doing so in front of Queen Victoria, so instead of springing up and screaming, "*Gadzooks! I am sitting upon something extremely painful*," he grimaced and bore it in the finest English tradition.

We ordered coffee and now sat drinking the inky fluid, secure in the knowledge that only a possibly dead colonel could overhear our surreal conversation.

"You don't have any brothers, do you, Griff?"

"No."

"Very wise. I don't think you should get any. They just die and make your life miserable."

"Thanks for the advice. The next time I talk to my dead parents, I'll try to persuade them not to give me a little brother for Christmas." I sipped my coffee, feeling like I'd have done better with a stiff Scotch, and plowed on. "Right. Well, we've had the family curse. Shall we move on to Uncle Eleanor and Aunt Roger?"

"Uncle Sally and Aunt Jim," corrected Val.

"They, as well. Walk me through it. What makes you think they've murdered your many sainted brothers? And why would they want you to pass into eternity?"

"The oldest of motives."

"Because you stole fire?" I hazarded.

"Not that old," Val explained. "Greed. Envy. Greed and envy."

"Ah, two of my favorite sins."

"You know, now that I think about it, they could win a Deadly Sin contest. They have most of them." He counted them off on his fingers: "Greed, envy, gluttony—"

"Aren't those all rather the same thing?"

Val continued as if I hadn't interrupted, "They're also pretty angry, disgustingly snobbish, and full of sloths."

"Sloth," I corrected. "Sloth. Singular. Sloths are animals. Sloth is sitting around doing nothing."

"That too. They're unscrupulous—"

"Not a Deadly Sin, surprisingly."

"And they don't like me."

"That's also not a Deadly Sin, although I take offense on your behalf."

"Well, whatever number of sins they have, their favorite is greed. They want the Hatton-Haxley family bankroll and are using the curse to their benefit. Now I'm all that stands between Uncle Sally and our coffers of gold."

"What exactly is a coffer?" I asked.

"It's something you put gold into."

"You don't actually have one, do you?"

"One what? A coffer or a fortune in gold?"

"Either."

"Neither," Val replied, shortly. "But at the moment I'm more concerned about coffins than coffers."

I sighed and wondered, not for the first time, why my friends always seem to be two bottles ahead of me.

"So, there's your Uncle Betty and Aunt Ralph, being greedy," I said. "And that's enough to make you think they're out to murder you? That's leaping it a bit, isn't it?"

"May I remind you of *The Gospel of Nicodemus* and the cat's-eye green marble? And angels didn't throw a gargoyle down onto Medard's head."

"You actually think your Uncle Sally and Aunt Jim—"

"Aha!" Val pointed a triumphant finger at me. "See, you *can* get their names right!"

"And you think they've been killing off all your brothers, one by one."

"Yes. Although it might have been fitting had the twins gone together. They were inseparable."

"Yes, poor planning on their part," I agreed.

Val continued, "You see, Uncle Sally has always been a nasty, greedy rat. Aunt Jim is even worse. She's brittle and sour. And I just know that underneath those prim black dresses she wears, she's simply *striped* with varicose veins. I hate varicose veins." He gave a little shudder.

"Are her varicose veins integral to this story?"

"No. They just disturb me. Every time I look at her, I think about those varicose veins. It makes it damned difficult to look her in the face at breakfast. She doesn't have them on her face, though. Thank God."

"Val, can we just ignore your aunt's veins for now?"

"That's just the problem! I can't ignore them. They're always there…" He faded off and shuddered again. "Anyway, she's also one of those insufferably righteous people who quotes the Bible in public. It's rather fascinating how readily she can quote from the Bible without ever actually following it. She's quite an accomplished sinner. But in the most superlatively pious way possible."

"Oh, are we back to the Seven Deadly Sins?"

"Sort of. She has an insane pride in her horrible sons. She's wildly judgmental towards everyone she considers to be her inferior, which is everyone. And I won't use the word 'theft' but quite a lot of valuable family pieces have ended up in her room or have just plain disappeared. She's vengeful, vicious, and cunning. In sum, she's just plain nasty."

"Sounds like a lovely woman," I observed.

"Oh, she is, she is. I've spent my whole life watching Uncle Sally and Aunt Jim hate each other with excessive gentility."

"We all need a hobby. You know, I've got to say I'm finding all this a little hard to swallow."

"I suppose it does sound mad," Val admitted. "But it's true. My family seems to be made up of murderers and murder victims."

"Saints and sinners," I observed.

"And this isn't the first time, either."

"It's not?"

"Oh no, if you look into the old family tree, you'll find quite a few branches that were cut off with the family axe."

"I honestly have no idea what that means."

"It means that over the years, more than one Hatton-Haxley has helped themselves into the line of succession. More than one firstborn son has been done unto death by a greedy younger sibling. And Uncle Sally is hardly the first Hatton-Haxley uncle to displace a hapless nephew."

I looked around the room, wondering if my time might be better spent trying to check the Colonel for signs of life. But Val's earnestness couldn't really be ignored.

"You really mean this, don't you?" I asked. "You honestly believe that your aunt and uncle want to kill you and have, in fact, already killed your brothers."

"I do. And now I've got to go home for Erasmus's funeral and they're going to come after me with strychnine and stabby things." He swallowed heavily. "Have you ever thought of how many ways there are to kill someone at a weekend house party?"

"As a matter of fact, I have," I answered. "I do write mystery novels for a living, you know. But that's fiction. Here on Planet Earth, the only cause of death I run into in an average country weekend is boredom."

"But think about it. They can put a thistle under your saddle so that when you mount up your horse bucks you off. They can slip a poison mushroom or two into your soup. There's the old iron balanced on the door that biffs you one when you open it, or a well-placed rusty nail that's been smeared with plague and left to be stepped on."

"*Smeared with plague?*"

"Well, you know what I mean. The Hall is basically one big murder weapon. It's just like all those ingenious books you write that everyone thinks are so clever."

"Everyone?" I asked. "But not you."

He shifted uncomfortably, "I must confess that I haven't gotten around to reading all of them."

Since I had achieved a certain level of success with my series of mystery novels featuring Zoltan Szabo, the most brilliant Hungarian detective in all of London, I naturally assumed my best friend had read my work. But if he thought smearing a nail with plague resembled any of my plots, I wasn't so sure.

"Just how many of my books have you read?" I asked.

"Well, once when I was stuck in Rome during a railroad strike, I did pick up *Zoltan Szabo and the Lost Hippo of Hippocrates*. But then I had to put it down again."

"Why?"

"The strike ended."

"I see. By the way, Val, *Zoltan Szabo and the Lost Hippo of Hippocrates* is not the title of one of my books. Nor anyone else's, to my knowledge."

"Oops."

"Speaking of names, for the sake of my tiny plebeian mind—"

"Are you still harping on about our Christian names?"

"No, actually. Now I'm harping on about your surname. Or surnames. You're a Hatton-Haxley. But once you become the Earl, then you're just a Haxley? What happens to poor old Hatton?"

"Oh, we pawn that name off on the next in line. He becomes

the Viscount Hatton-Haxley, though we generally call him Lord Haxley. It's less confusing."

"Huh." I thought for a second. "No, that's more confusing. So, let's get back to a more important question. You've never actually read *any* of my books?"

"No. But if you come down this weekend, I promise I'll read them all. I'll even buy them. I won't cadge free copies off you."

"Oh good, the ten shillings in royalties I receive from your generous offer should more than compensate me for risking a weekend that sounds like an executioners' fun fair."

"It's not an appealing prospect," Val admitted. "But I can promise you excellent dinners, an outstanding wine cellar, and the exciting possibility of watching your friend suffocate in a broom closet."

"If you're in a broom closet, I won't be able to watch you."

"I am aware of that; it's a metaphor."

"No, I don't think it is." I sighed, "Look. Why me?"

"Because I also want you to help me prove that Erasmus was murdered."

"I repeat. Why me?"

"Because you were in intelligence during the war."

"Yes, where I worked with the Belgian resistance. I wasn't a bodyguard. And I'm not a detective, even if I do write about one."

"Well, you're the closest thing to both, as least that I know. And if you come, I'll make sure you sit next to the Honorable Miss Daphne Ferguson at dinner."

"Who," I asked, "is the Honorable Miss Daphne Ferguson? Another murderer?"

"A distant cousin, on my mother's side. Red hair, beautiful blue eyes. Just your type."

"Does my type have red hair and beautiful blue eyes? What color blue?"

"What do you mean, what color blue? *Blue*-blue."

"No, I mean what shade? A dark-nearing-purple blue? Off-the-coast-of-Corsica blue? Royal Faberge Egg blue?"

"God, I hate it when you talk like a writer. Her eyes are pretty much the same color as mine."

"Oh, then you're right. She does have beautiful blue eyes."

"I'm going to ignore the fact that you just said you think I have beautiful eyes and finish my recitation of the superior qualities possessed by the Honorable Miss Daphne. She reads for pleasure, knowns a great many filthy limericks, and honestly enjoys fishing."

"Is that relevant?"

"No. Just throwing that in."

"You're not about to throw in the fact that she looks like Edna May Oliver, are you?"

"Not at all," Val asserted. "I suppose she's quite pretty. Which is surprising, considering her parents are two of the homeliest people in Britain."

"I must say, Val, that it'll take more than a girl who likes to fish to make a weekend at Murder Hall sound enjoyable."

"I know, but it's all I have. Please come with me. I really need your help."

"What do you want me to do? Follow you around like a squire? Shall I bring a sword? Do I get a title, too?"

"Just keep an eye on me, and on the aunt and uncle. Make sure I'm never alone with them. Maybe follow them if you see them walking into my bedroom with a scorpion in a jar."

"Val," I said. "If you honestly think your brother has been murdered, why don't you go to the police? Why haven't you told them about *Nicodemus* and the cat's-eye green whatsit."

"Bumboozer," Val supplied.

"Shooter," I corrected.

"You know," he said, "usually when one's talking about murder, the word 'shooter' means something different."

"Usually when one's talking about murder, the word 'murder' means something different," I retorted.

"Like?"

"Like a gunshot wound or a sliced throat. Something nicely definitive. Instead, all you've got is a child's toy and a water-logged gospel."

I looked aimlessly out the window for a moment, taking in the growing dark of the afternoon and trying to sort out the threads of Val's mad story. Val stared at Colonel Wilkinson's inert form, perhaps to see if he could discern any movement in the tweed-clad chest.

"I do wonder, though," I said slowly, "if there's some sort of connection between the gospel and the marble."

"See!" Val pointed at me in triumph. "That's why I need you. You've probably read *Nicodemus*!"

"I haven't. If detailed knowledge of *The Gospel of Nicodemus* is what is needed to solve this potential crime, then you don't need me, you need the Pope."

"I don't know him. And even if I did, I'm not sure I could entice him to come to Tower Field Hall for the weekend."

"I'm still not sure you can entice *me*," I replied.

"You see," Val said, "if Erasmus was killed, the killer had to be somebody in the family. Or at least somebody in the Hall. But I can't just waltz up to the police and say, '*please arrest my family.*' For one thing, being an English aristocrat means I have a highly developed abhorrence of scandal. That's why I don't want to go to the police until I'm pretty sure which one of my appalling relatives might be guilty. That's still an appalling scandal, but to have the entire household under investigation would be so much worse."

"Who else lives at the Hall these days? I only remember your immediate family."

"Oh, a few old loyal family retainers and some appalling

cousins. Uncle Sally and Aunt Jim have three ghastly sons, all of whom are just as eager for the inheritance as their parents."

"Athos, Porthos, and Aramis?"

"Nicodemus, Wulfstan, and Theobald."

"Hang on," I said. "You have a cousin named Nicodemus?"

"Yes."

"As in *The Gospel of…*?"

"As in the Gospel of what? Oh!" I watched the light slowly dawn. "Huh."

"Huh, indeed. Coincidence? Confession?"

"You know, surprisingly, that never occurred to me," Val said.

"I'm not at all surprised, to be honest. But it does add yet another layer of absurdity to your story. Do you have any suspects that aren't related to you?"

"I suppose there are a few other suspicious characters in the village," Val added. "Will you come?"

I hesitated.

"Please?"

I still hesitated. But Val had known me for a long time. "You're intrigued, aren't you? Aren't you? I can see it in your eyes. Admit it!"

I refused to admit it. But I didn't deny it, either.

Chapter 4

As far as I was concerned, the one benefit to going down to Hatstand-Under-Towel, or whatever it was called, was a chance for a drive in the country. With Lucille the Lagonda purring like a well-fed kitten, Val and I left damp and drizzly London for the countryside, where the sun was shining, the grass was green, and the drinks and motives would be plentiful. It was one of the first days of Spring, and I was happy to be out in the world.

My other well-fed kitten, Catullus, was happily napping in his carrier on the back seat. Wherever I went, Catullus went. Val was less than pleased about bringing a cat along but was far more relaxed now that he wouldn't have to face the weekend alone.

I didn't share Val's confidence. What the heck was I doing? I wasn't Sherlock Holmes, or even Zoltan Szabo. I had no qualifications for solving a mystery, unless I'd written the clues and created the suspects myself. I just hoped the weekend would pass with nothing more upsetting than a weak martini or a lumpy bed.

But I was also curious. Could I solve a real murder? And was it, in fact, murder? To find out, I'd need a hell of a lot more information than just a bathtub, a pair of Nicodemuses, and a cat's-eye green marble.

"Tell me, what did Erasmus's body look like when it was found?" I asked.

Val, who had been staring at the passing scenery while quietly singing one of the more pornographic versions of *Mademoiselle from Armentières*, ceased the *parlez-vous*-ing and shot me a curious look.

"What do you mean? It looked like Erasmus."

"I mean how did he appear?"

"Wet and naked, I suppose. And dead."

I sighed and tried again. "Did he have any bruises? Cuts? Evidence of someone holding him underwater?"

"Oh. Huh." Val paused, "I don't know. I haven't seen him myself and haven't really thought about it."

"Well, think about it now. Is it likely that Erasmus would sit quietly in his bathtub while someone shoved a marble in his mouth and dropped a book in his lap?"

"No," he admitted. "It is not likely."

"So how are you imagining this actually happened?"

"What do you mean?"

"I mean, explain your theory of his death. You say it was murder. So, was he drugged? Was there more than one person involved? Did Uncle Shirley hold him down while Aunt Edgar popped the marble in his mouth? Did he drown? Did he choke? Would an autopsy show a lunch full of marbles in his stomach? Or might it prove he started his bath with a nice relaxing cup of cyanide?"

"These are all excellent questions," Val said with unflattering surprise. "And I can't answer any of them."

"At the moment, I'm not looking for answers, I just want your opinion. You are convinced your aunt and uncle killed your brother. If we accept this theory, what do you think they did? How did they do it?"

The humming started up again.

"Val, *Mademoiselle from Armentières* is not an answer to my brilliant and insightful question."

"I know. I just don't know."

"You know, but you just don't know," I repeated. "You do realize that you make absolutely no sense for more than half of your life."

"That's an extremely disrespectful thing to say to the 17th Earl of Haxley."

"Perhaps," I agreed. "But it's a perfectly reasonable thing to say to someone I once convinced to eat a piece of chalk."

"I think we've been friends long enough," he said. "Please go away now."

"I can't go away. You're in my car. If I go away, you go away too, which would defeat the whole going-away-ness of your plan."

"And you say I don't make sense," Val complained.

"You don't," I replied. "Now, seriously, I feel like your assertion that this was a murder is going strictly on instinct and a hatred of your uncle and aunt, even if well-deserved. But step back for a moment. Is there any real evidence?"

"I guess we'll find out when we get there."

"Considering this happened a week ago, I doubt there's any evidence left to find." I gave him an arch look. "But maybe we'll get lucky, and I'll catch Uncle Virginia in the act of pushing you down the stairs."

"Oh yes," he said with dismal sarcasm. "That would be ever so lucky."

* * *

THE QUIET VILLAGE of Hatton-Under-Tower was one of those picturesque towns among green hills that seem designed for the express purpose of being painted. Old stone cottages lined a crooked High Street. There was a tea shop, an antique store, and a small grocery that doubled as the post office, displaying fruit and bread in elegant bow windows. Nearby was a dignified little church, which I recalled came complete with a delightfully scatty vicar and his plump, reassuring wife. The village also boasted two comfortable and welcoming pubs.

Despite my mockery, I had to admit a fondness for the place. I liked the scent of hay and roses, and the fat brown cows with their big eyes and soft coats. I approved of the quiet air of placid eternity, as if the village had always been there and ever would remain. And I enjoyed the colors of Hatton: the wide green and golden fields and the darker green of the woods that curled around the village like an embrace, the gray-faced cottages made of local stone, and the deep blue sky and scudding clouds that one only sees in the country.

Val, however, saw none of this simple beauty. His mind was fixed on the imagined dangers of his family home. After a good ten minutes or so of silence, he suddenly intruded into my musings on local beer and pastoral pleasures.

"See those cows over there?" Val said abruptly. "I bet they've all been poisoned."

"What's that? Who would want to kill the cows?"

"They want to kill *me*, remember? Picture it. Dinner tomorrow night, a nice juicy steak on my plate, and *boom*! Just like that. Poisoned. Dead."

"You really haven't thought this through," I commented.

"Well, maybe not. But I'm new at all this. Say, have I told you about Aunt Elsie?"

I thought for a moment. "No, I don't think you have. Does she want to murder you, too?"

"Oh, no, she just likes telling people how they're going to die."

"Excuse me?"

"Aunt Elsie thinks she's psychic, you see, and she loves things like séances and Ouija boards. One of her hobbies is letting people know how they are going to die. She thinks it's nice to be warned beforehand."

"I don't want to be warned beforehand."

"No," Val agreed sadly, "nobody does. But she doesn't believe it when people say, '*please don't tell me how I'm going to die.*' She considers it a kindness to be told that you're going to go in a flu epidemic or a railroad accident."

"That's not kind, that's disturbing." I made a mental note to work that into a book sometime.

"Yeah, it is."

"So has she told you that Uncle Maud and Aunt Frank are going to kill you, or is she not in on the family plot?"

"Please don't say 'family plot,'" Val pleaded.

"Sorry."

"No, according to Aunt Elsie my end will come from some mysterious illness that will baffle the doctors."

"That's wonderful!"

"I'm so glad you think so," Val said sarcastically.

"Sorry," I backtracked. "I just meant that perhaps you have nothing to fear. Your aunt and uncle are hardly likely to infect you with a mysterious disease, after all. You should take some comfort from that."

"I don't," Val replied, shortly.

"Why not?"

"Because Aunt Elsie has never once been right in any of her predictions. She told Erasmus that he was going to die in bed at the age of one hundred and six. And she was certain that Drogo would fall from a hot air balloon."

"Oh."

"But the upside is that if Aunt Elsie tells you that you're going to burned at the stake, you can be pretty sure it won't happen."

"I'm already pretty sure it won't happen. Predicting people's deaths? What an interesting hobby."

"Her other hobbies are making herbal remedies that give the recipient diphtheria and rewriting her will."

"Oh, dear."

"Indeed. If you have a headache and she offers you anything besides aspirin, run."

"Good advice. And what's this about rewriting her will?"

"She concocts a new one every six months or so."

"Does she have much to bequeath?"

"Practically nothing."

"But she visits a solicitor twice a year?"

"Oh no, she doesn't bother with that. She just writes something on a piece of notepaper and gets a couple of the maids to witness it."

"I see. Just out of curiosity, is Aunt Elsie your mother's sister or your father's?"

"I have no idea."

"Of course, you don't. Why don't you ask her how many of her male relatives are still alive, that should give you a clue."

"To tell you the truth, I have no idea how she's related to us. She might not be."

"But you're not sure."

"No, not really. She just appeared one day when I was about six years old. My parents said she was going to live at the Hall and that we should call her Aunt Elsie. That's really the last time anyone talked about her. Since then, she's just been there, living on the third floor, growing hemlock in the kitchen garden, making herbal medicines that you need to pour down the sink, and stealing sugar cubes from the tea table."

"Sugar cubes?" That comment about growing hemlock would have to wait.

"Yeah. She sort of collects them. She'll dump a whole bowl into this ridiculous purse she always carries with her. Even around the house. We're not sure what she does with them."

"Maybe she has an army of sugared-up mice somewhere, ready to do her bidding."

"Don't joke. When you say things like that, my mind instantly goes to images of my soon-to-be-dead body staked to the ground like Gulliver and covered by homicidal mice. Little tiny mouse feet running over my chest. Tiny mouse teeth going for my throat. Mice in a gang with little knives and big grudges."

"Nice image."

"It's your own fault," he accused.

"Sorry."

"I have to admit," Val said, "I'm almost looking forward to watching you tackling my herd of cousins."

"Herd?"

"Flock. School? What *do* you call a couple of cousins?"

"Incest, I think."

Val laughed and hit me in the arm.

We didn't speak for the rest of the drive, so I listened with pleasure to the purr of Lucille's engine. Val probably spent the time calculating how much it would hurt to be shot in the head with an arrow.

* * *

I HADN'T BEEN to Val's place since I was fourteen years old, but I recognized everything instantly. Spotting a break in the hedgerows up ahead, I turned Lucille off the road and into a long, narrow lane bordered on both sides by ancient yew trees. We had on-again, off-again glimpses of the Hall through the gaps, until the view suddenly opened, revealing the ancestral pile in full.

Tower Field House was once a low, square box made of local gray stone. But generations of dead and saintly Hatton-Haxleys had added onto it so that it now appeared to have been built by a feuding committee. The symmetry of the original Palladian front had given way to a pustulant façade of irregular angles, curves, and a fussy overabundance of eaves. The guilty parties hadn't even bothered to match the stone, it seemed, because the extended wing on the left was made of a much darker hue than the rest of the house and the stone on the right wing was a dusty tan color. Compounding the offense, the house sported a parade of mismatched windows. Some were leaded, some weren't. Some were square-framed, others were arched. There were round windows, rectangular windows, protruding windows, and recessed windows. There was even one made of stained glass, depicting either the Battle of Hastings or the Adoration of the Magi.

But I wasn't really thinking about the house as I pulled to the front portico. Glancing at Val's greenish face, I wondered if things could really be as bad as he feared. Was I in for a normal weekend of tennis and bridge or an ordeal of sharp words and blunt objects?

There was no time to discuss the matter. The door to the Hall was already open and a host of footmen in dark green livery approached to snap up the luggage before I could even turn off the ignition. Watching over them was Lydgate, the Hatton-Haxleys' impeccable butler, who stood with eerily perfect posture upon the front step.

My stomach clenched a little. I had taken an instant dislike to Lydgate in my childhood visits to Tower View Hall. He bore an uncanny resemblance to my godfather, an interfering old windbag who pinched and lectured me across the map of my childhood. Lydgate had that same superior air and suck-lemon twist to his lips.

Val sighed and delivered the only Shakespearean quote he could remember, *"once more unto the breach, dear friends."*

"Welcome home, your lordship," Lydgate said in his best sepulchral tones. He turned to me. "And welcome back to the Hall, Mr. Griffin."

I saw Val's gaze scan across the exterior of the Hall, as if looking for loose gargoyles or other booby traps. "Thank you,

Lydgate," he said at last. "Good to see you again. And how is Mrs. Lydgate?"

Mrs. Lydgate was as magical as her husband was stern. She was easily one of the best cooks in the county, if not all England. She produced such masterpieces from the vast Tower View kitchen that stories were told about them in the town, and for several towns beyond. She had no known first name. When she first came to the house, about fifteen years earlier, she had been only as Mrs. Colbert. Presumably Lydgate knew her Christian name, but he kept it a marital secret.

"She's very well, thank you, my lord. You'll find Viscount and Viscountess Hatton-Haxley in the day room. I believe they have been waiting tea for your arrival."

"Thank you, Lydgate. Where have you put Mr. Griffin?"

"He's in the Amber Room, sir. Shall I show him up?"

"No, thank you, just bring up the bags. We'll go straight in for tea. Oh, and not the Amber Room, Lydgate. Is there anybody in either Oak or Cypress?"

"No, my lord, both rooms are currently unoccupied."

"Good. Put Mr. Griffin in Cypress."

"Those rooms are both in the family wing, my lord."

Lydgate managed, with the skill of a consummate actor, to subtly convey both surprise and disdain in words pronounced without any outward emotion. He made me feel guilty, as if I'd committed some sin against the household. I felt as if I should refuse the very idea of the family wing and beg to be allowed the favor of sleeping in the Amber Room.

"Yes, Lydgate, I do recall," Val responded wearily. "I was only born here, you know. But Mr. Griffin has a morbid fear of sleeping in rooms not named after trees, so please put him in Cypress."

"Of course, my lord. I shall have Cypress prepared." Lydgate glided away, leaving me with my guilt. He was my godfather reincarnate. I wondered if he would pinch my ear or lecture me first.

One of the footmen moved to take our luggage and I slipped a pound coin into his hand with whispered instructions to see that Catullus was happily set up in my room. I whispered instructions to Catullus as well, in Latin: "*Dormies bene, cattus.*" Val overheard and shot me an exasperated look. "Why do you insist on talking to that animal in Latin?"

"Remember all those painful hours in Professor Kalkman's Latin class? I didn't spend months memorizing verb endings only to forget everything later. Speaking with Catullus keeps my Latin in tune."

"The only things I remember from that class are his awful jokes," Val admitted.

"They were pretty bad," I agreed. "Although there was one that I thought was funny."

"I'm afraid to ask."

"A Roman legionnaire walks into a bar, holds up two fingers, and says '*I'd like five beers, please.*'"

Val groaned and looked appraisingly at Catullus, who was busily washing his face.

"I'm not sure that your cat does speak Latin."

"He doesn't speak English, either, Val. He's a cat."

Val shot me a dirty look, called "*Caveat emptor*" to Catullus, and led me into the house.

Compared to the flurry of activity out front, the interior of the house felt eerily silent. Our steps echoed like heartbeats as we crossed the tall foyer. Avoiding the grand staircase that dominated the space, we headed towards the back of the Hall, where the day room looked out on a vista of velvet lawns and hideous fountains.

"You know, I'd managed to forget that with Erasmus dead, Uncle Sally became the Viscount Hatton-Haxley," Val said. "He and Aunt Jim must be thrilled to finally be titled. So plebeian to be merely Honorable, you know." Val took a deep breath to gather his courage and opened the day room door.

I followed him with some hesitation. Surely, I thought, this couldn't be real. People don't actually murder each other in settings like this, do they? In books, perhaps, but not in real life. This was the natural habitat for stilted conversations and repressed emotions, not massacres and alibis.

Or was it? When I got my first look at Val's aunt and uncle, a strange tingle started in the pit of my stomach.

Uncle Sally and Aunt Jim looked like two people who were very much capable of homicide to get what they wanted, and glared at Val as if he was the only thing standing in their way.

Chapter 5

I tried to concentrate on the elegant room instead of its weird occupants.

The day room should have been a relaxing, welcoming place, with its pale green walls and soft cream sofas and chairs. There were flowers and a tea set laid out on the tables, scenes of Venice on the walls, and peach-colored draperies held back with ties of gold braid and fat tassels that looked like dead canaries. In short, it was lovely and civilized. Nothing bad could happen in a pleasant room like that, could it?

Unfortunately, anyone wishing to luxuriate in that gentle ambiance would be thwarted the moment they caught sight of Aunt Jim. Val's descriptions had been unsettling enough, but they seemed inadequate now that I got a look at this woman in the flesh. Such as it was. She was decidedly skeletal. Even seated, I could tell she wouldn't break five feet in height or one hundred pounds on a scale. Everything about her was little, but in the worst possible interpretation of the word. And I found the incredible whiteness of her skin disturbing. She looked like a shrunken, antiseptically clean polar bear.

She had squinty little eyes and a tiny, pinched mouth further marred by a garish slash of carnation-pink lipstick. Should she ever smile—a horrifying thought—I had no doubt that she'd have a mouthful of tiny teeth. Tiny, terrifying rabbit teeth. Her compact white head teetered atop a scrawny white neck and was crowned with a helmet of blonde hair that looked as if it could repel shrapnel.

Avoiding the glare of those tiny, sharp eyes, I saw a pair of diminutive hands folded across a brittle body, an impeccable black dress that unfortunately was fifty years out of date, and neat little-girl feet in neat little-girl shoes. She emitted an odor of old roses and sanctity. Her entire air was menacing and hard. A grim, tight, humorless woman. I decided that Val was right to fear her varicose veins.

Beside her sat an immense, extremely unpleasant-looking man. If a thumb and a weasel had a child, it would look like Uncle Suspicious. He had to weigh at least two hundred and fifty pounds and towered over the wee bird-skeleton woman at his side. And yet I got the impression that his was the less dominant personality. There was an immovable aura around Aunt Jim that was missing in her husband. Despite all that size, he radiated weakness.

He was more upholstered than dressed, his massive torso tightly wrapped in a florid brocade waistcoat across which stretched a pastoral scene of maidens and deer. I wasn't entirely sure what the maidens were doing with the deer and didn't want to know.

Neither relative rose as we entered the room.

"Good afternoon, Valentine," Uncle Sally said, although his tone indicated the opposite.

"Hello, Uncle. Good afternoon, Aunt." Val's voice was oddly tight. "How are you both?"

"Well, thank you," his aunt answered. She had a surprisingly mannish voice for so petite a woman.

"This is my good friend, Gideon Griffin. Griff, this is my uncle Sulpicius and aunt Jemima, the Viscount and Viscountess Hatton-Haxley."

I stepped forward and suppressed a wince as Val's uncle tried to strangle my hand. Perhaps not so weak as he appeared, then. I then moved to his aunt, who presented a twig-like bundle of tiny fingers. "How do you do, Viscount, Viscountess. I'm sorry to meet under such sad circumstances."

"To what sad circumstances do you refer?" Aunt Jim asked.

I looked at Val, confused. "To the death of your nephew… Erasmus?" I wasn't sure why I framed the name like a question, but it seemed like maybe they didn't remember his name.

"Oh, yes. Very sad." She managed a properly somber tone, only to ruin the sentiment with a judgmental sniff and sudden wave of her hand, as if she were dismissing a moth that had dared interrupt dinner with the king.

She'd said, "very sad," but what I heard was: *I am experiencing great ennui and cannot fathom why I should be polite to this completely unimportant and obviously dull stranger.*

Meanwhile I stood there feeling completely unimportant and obviously dull. The previous day, I honestly hadn't believed a word Val told me about these two, but thirty seconds in their company was enough to make me think my friend wasn't much longer for this world.

Uncle Sally cleared his throat and parroted his wife: "Yes, very sad, Mister… *Griffin.*" Saying my name seemed to leave a bad taste in his mouth.

As if the atmosphere wasn't awkward enough, Val's aunt interrupted him. "*The Lord is close to the brokenhearted and saves those who are crushed in spirit.* Psalm 34."

Nobody had a response to that.

"Take a pew, Griff," Val mumbled, indicating the two chairs facing the sofa. I sat, slowly, so as not to startle the elders.

Aunt Jim's raised eyebrow seemed to be the only offer of tea we were going to get, and Val responded to the signal. "Cream and one sugar for me, Aunt Jim." He looked questioningly at me.

"Oh, the same for me, please," I answered, then we all sat in uncomfortable silence while she begrudgingly performed the part of Mother. Once the tea, sandwiches, and silent judgment had been passed around, conversation finally began. Or, rather, conversation could no longer be avoided.

"How have you been keeping, Uncle?" Val asked, politely.

"Well enough," Sally replied shortly, followed by another silence that indicated that was all the answer Val was going to get.

"And you, Aunt Jim?" Val plowed on, gamely.

Casting a look at her nephew that managed to convey the impression he had stood up in the House of Lords to raise the topic of her bowel habits, she replied with a single word: "Well." She turned her accusatory glare to the tray of sandwiches, as if they too had somehow offended her.

Fun group, I thought. I counted the slow ticks of the mantle clock and wondered how soon we could escape.

"Where is Aunt Elsie?" Val asked. "Doesn't she usually join you for tea?"

"She is rarely on time," Jim observed.

Uncle Sally muttered something under his breath. It sounded like "crazy old bat."

As if hearing her cue, the door opened, and Aunt Elsie walked in.

"Floated" might be a better description for how Aunt Elsie moved into a room. She was a surprisingly tall woman, but thin as a willow. She wore an ancient, floor-length dress that hid her feet, so she appeared to hover rather than walk. And she did so in a cloud of sandalwood perfume so strong that she smelled like a Catholic church.

Adding to the waterfall of flounces and flourishes were at least three different scarves and what must have been the entire contents of her jewelry box. And possibly also a junk drawer. Four or five necklaces, rings on every finger, rows of bracelets jingling on her arms, and two very large and very ugly earrings:

one a large gold hoop that put me in mind of Long John Silver, and the other a dangling monstrosity that seemed to be either a small chandelier or a large dung beetle. On her head was a crown of what appeared to be dandelions woven into a circlet. She looked like the Ghost of Ophelia Past.

However, good manners override personal shock, so Val and I got to our feet. Uncle Suspicious, I noticed, did not.

"Hello, Aunt Elsie, how are you? May I introduce my dear friend, Mr. Gideon Griffin." Val nodded toward me.

Elsie turned her soft brown eyes my way and squinted a little, as if short-sighted.

"Oh, but we've met already," she cooed—really, it was the only word for that odd little purr of a voice.

"We... we have?" I replied, confused. "Please forgive me Miss... uh..." I scrambled, knowing her only as "Aunt Elsie." Thankfully, Val leaned over and whispered, *"Armistad."* Before pulling away he added something that sounded like, "good luck."

"...Miss Armistad, but I'm afraid that I don't recall..."

She laughed. It was a bubbly, startlingly girlish sound from a woman on the back side of seventy. And she simpered. I had never quite known what that word meant until that moment. It was one of those words that you hear or read, and have some vague notion of what it is, but aren't entirely sure. Aunt Elsie gave a weirdly affected smile that made me completely clear on the definition of simpering.

"Oh, but it was a *very* long time ago, my dear," she twinkled at me. "Don't you remember? At the Court of Louis XIV. That New Year's Ball. We danced the whole night together and you looked so handsome in your blue uniform. And I in pale gold. You told me I looked like a goddess, remember?" And then, to my horror, she simpered again.

I swear the temperature in the room rose about fifty degrees in ten seconds. My shirt collar became inordinately tight, and

I felt about to burst into a ball of perspiration. Like all good Englishmen, I loathe acknowledging the existence of emotions, and Aunt Elsie very much looked the emotional sort. But really, *Louis XIV*?

"Of course, before that," she continued, "you were my favorite boatman, and I was the beloved daughter of the Pharaoh." She tilted her head back, a frightening look of nostalgic ecstasy on her pale face. "Moonlight on the Nile, the smell of jasmine in the air, ahh…" she faded off, clasping her hands across her bosom like an overly dramatic soprano.

I looked to Val in a state of near panic, having no idea how to respond to any of this.

"Of course, the last time we were together," she said sadly, "I waved you off to Waterloo, and you never returned." Aunt Elsie pulled a lacy handkerchief from her sleeve and dabbed at her eyes. Why were old ladies always putting handkerchiefs up their sleeves?

"Uh… I'm sorry?" I floundered.

"Oh, I'm sure it wasn't your idea to die heroically on the field of battle. But you *did* get a medal."

"Yes," Val commented drily, "I'm sure Griff has never once had the idea that he'd like to die heroically on the field of battle."

He winked at me. I shot him a look that couldn't be repeated in polite company, though it had been well-known to the men of my unit when things got tense on the Western Front.

"Besides," she continued, "I already knew you wouldn't come back. I always know."

"You do?" I was beginning to feel a bit queasy at the direction the conversation was taking, and yet it had a morbid fascination.

"Oh yes," she smiled. "Why, by the time I was your age, the *first* time I was your age, I mean—"

"Aunt Elsie," Val interrupted gently, "when you were my age, all you were was exactly the same age as I am now."

She ignored him. "I'd already lost seven lovers. And I *always* knew. Just as I knew all those centuries ago that poor, dear Gwillym would be crushed by a rock when that huge rainstorm made the ground all soggy, just as we were about to raise—"

"Elsie!" Aunt Jim hissed. "Do sit down. The tea is getting cold, and we do *not* need to hear the story of how you built Stonehenge again."

Actually, I rather wanted to hear that story.

Showing no sign of offense, Aunt Elsie floated over to the sofa and accepted a cup of tea with—I counted—six sugar cubes. She then picked up the sugar bowl and tipped the remaining cubes into a small purse she'd retrieved from somewhere amid the layers of scarves and skirts.

Over the next half an hour, Sally had to ring twice for the footman to replenish the sugar bowl as Elsie somehow put away eight sandwiches, three scones, four more cups of tea, and a thick slice of seed cake. Where they all went on that skinny frame was a mystery. I could only assume that living so many lives required a constant intake of food.

"Have you started plans for the funeral, Uncle?" Val asked.

"Of course, we waited for you to make the most important decisions regarding dear Erasmus," Sally replied with great insincerity. "After all, you are the Earl of Haxley now." He said the latter with a mouth clenched so tightly that it seemed as if his lips were glued together.

Aunt Jim continued, "We've spoken with the vicar, of course. We think '*Lead, Kindly Light*,' and '*Abide with Me*' would be suitable for the music." I had a vision of Aunt Jim leading the bass section in the church choir.

She sniffed again. I would come to learn that sniffing was a conversational tool for Aunt Jim. "And I believe a reading from Romans would be appropriate. '*For the wages of sin is death*' seems fitting."

I shot Val a look. His Aunt Ferdinand was a fun woman. An absolute delight.

"Also," his uncle continued, "we've put a notice in the *Times* and the *Morning Trumpet* about the service. And notified the staff about the arrangements, the food, and such. We've also given instructions to the gardeners about flowers, and we've spoken to Lydgate about arranging for the stone cutters to come in and attend to the family mausoleum. And, of course, we've seen to the... that is... to Erasmus."

"And of course," Aunt Jim sniffed, "we've invited all the *appropriate* people."

I couldn't help but wonder who she considered to be the inappropriate people. I also wondered what exactly was left for Val to do if this was what they considered leaving things to him. Then again, I wondered what Uncle Sally meant by "seeing to Erasmus." Embalming, I assumed. And I wouldn't put it past them to do it themselves, probably using an old family recipe.

"So, what exactly is left for me to do?" Val asked, as if reading my thoughts.

Another sniff before his aunt informed him that there was still one more hymn to choose.

"Tell me, Mr. Griffin," Sally said, turning abruptly to face me, "did you know our nephew, Erasmus?"

"Why yes, I did. I have stayed here before. Perhaps you weren't aware?" I left a questioning pause, but nobody answered.

"Griff and I were at school together," Val explained. "He spent a few holidays here when we were younger, but I believe that was when you were all at the London house. However, he got to know all the brothers."

"Yes. And again, I'm terribly sorry for your loss," I said.

Aunt Jim took this as a cue to remember to look as if she were in mourning which, in her case, involved wiping non-existent tears from her pinched little face and sniffing a couple more times.

"Thank you," Uncle Sally replied. "Yes, such a loss. Dear... um... Erasmus..."

He trailed off in a way that suggested he couldn't quite remember just which of his numerous dead nephews was which. I supposed with so many deaths in the family, it might be easy to lose track.

"Yes, the poor lad," Aunt Elsie commented around a mouthful of sandwich. "But how comforting to know he was reading something uplifting when it happened."

"I'm afraid I just can't picture Erasmus reading anything, let alone *The Gospel of Nicodemus*," Val observed.

"But he was," she insisted. "I saw him!"

"You *saw* him?" Val asked.

"Oh, yes. It was so comforting to see him pass on while reading a dear, sacred text." She swallowed and reached for the jam, then paused and then looked around, blushing a little. "Oh, I didn't see him in the *bath*, of course, because that would be most immodest! It was in a vision. In my crystal."

"Elsie, please..." Sally interrupted, much to everyone's relief.

"When is Eldridge coming down, Uncle?" Val asked, deftly completing the save.

I wondered vaguely if this Eldridge person was sane or if he was another relative.

"He'll be here by evening," the uncle said. "And he'll stay the weekend, of course. I imagine with you being the..." He cleared his throat, which was obviously his version of Aunt Jim's sniffing. "...*The heir*, he'll need to spend some time holed up with you discussing details. I'm afraid your friend is in for a dull weekend."

"Oh, don't worry about me," I said. After this display, I could hope for nothing better than a weekend being ignored by every member of the Hatton-Haxley clan. "I've always admired your library, so I shall be quite all right." It made as good an excuse as any, and I could hardly say that I planned to spend my time trying to catch them out for murder. I met Val's amused glance with a raised eyebrow that meant: "*If you say anything, I shall throw a scone at you.*"

"Well, you shan't be on your own for the entire weekend," Aunt Jim explained. "We shall have several guests down for the service and for Adjutor's birthday."

It had only been a day, yet I had to scrape my memory to associate the word "Adjutor" with "*dead great-grandfather with an absurd will*." These names were going to be the death of me.

"Isn't it just like Erasmus to be so considerate?" Elsie piped up with a smile. "To die just in time for us to have a funeral and a birthday toast on the same weekend, so everyone only needs to gather once. Such a thoughtful boy."

Aunt Jim sniffed, looked even more displeased, and said to me in a tone of complete boredom, "Tell me, Mr. Griffin, do you live in London?"

"I do, Lady Haxley, although my people come from Kent." Five minutes in her presence, and I was already talking like the Archbishop of Canterbury.

"How nice," she sniffed. "And what do you do in London?"

Val jumped in before I could respond. "We are entertaining a celebrity. Griff is Gideon Griffin, the mystery writer."

Aunt Jim looked at me and sniffed with her eyes.

"Oh, my goodness!" Aunt Elsie exclaimed. "You wrote that lovely book, *The Woman in White*!"

"Um... No, no I didn't, Miss Armistad."

"Yes, you did!" She clasped her hands in front of her, dislodging a waterfall of sandwich and cake crumbs. "Oh my, this is *such* a thrill."

"Griff didn't write *The Woman in White*, Aunt Elsie. That was... uh... Dickens?" Val tried, lamely.

"Wilkie Collins," I corrected.

"Yes, Wilkie Collins," he repeated.

Patiently, as if explaining to a child, Aunt Elsie said, "Yes, but what if he *was* Wilkie Collins?"

Thankfully, Aunt Jim marched right on past Aunt Elsie's diversion and continued the previous conversation. "Of course, the boys will be here," she said to me. "Our sons, you know, Nicodemus, Wulfstan, and Theobald. Such dear things," she said, in the first expression of real affection I'd heard.

Sally added, "Nicodemus is quite a wizard in finance. And investing. *International* finance."

"And *disreputable* investing," Val muttered under his breath.

"He's with Sheffield Commercial. The bank, you know."

"Oh, I hadn't realized he was with *the* bank," Val said.

"Yes, he's much talked about in important banking circles, and great things are expected from him." Uncle Sally paused and lifted the delicate teacup to his oversized mouth. I watched, fascinated, and tried to calculate whether he could fit the entire thing inside.

"Yes, with his experience and reputation, I wouldn't be at all surprised to see Nicky taking his place as a Cabinet minister or as a financial advisor to the right kind of people."

I was pretty sure "*the right kind of people*" did not include me. For which I was grateful.

"We're so proud," Jim continued, "and yet he's so very modest about it all. My Nicky doesn't believe in blowing one's own horn, you see."

I wondered how she knew so much about him if he never talked about himself. Instead, I inquired after her other sons. She waved them off with quick disinterest. It was easy to see who her favorite was.

"Oh," she waved vaguely, "Wulfstan is also interested in politics, and he's a poet as well. You probably know him, since you're both writers."

She made it sound like being a writer was rather like being a Freemason. The minute you publish your first story, they teach you the secret handshake.

"And Theo is away at St. Gordon's, my husband's old school," she continued. "They think very highly of him on the football pitch, I hear."

"And very little of him anywhere else," Val mumbled.

Uncle Sally cleared his throat, breaking the flow of the conversation, and steered us back to praise of their golden firstborn son.

"Why, Nicodemus is a financial genius. And he's got guts, like his father. You've got to have guts to make it big in this world. As I've always told him, there are no big gains without big chances."

I had to admit, if anybody knew about big guts, it was surely massive Uncle Sally. "I look forward to meeting them all," I lied.

"And there will be a few distant cousins here this weekend, one or two old friends. And the Bishop, of course."

"The Bishop?" I asked, without thinking, and then cursed myself for helping to keep the conversation going. It was like a train wreck, impossible to turn away from.

"Oh yes, of course," Aunt Jim intoned. "The vicar might be acceptable for a small prayer gathering in our chapel here at the house. But an Earl deserves the honors befitting his station. Naturally, the Bishop will preside at the church in town."

"Naturally," agreed Uncle Suspicious.

"You have a chapel?" I asked Val in a whisper.

Val whispered back something shocking. I was glad his aunts couldn't hear it.

"He's such a nice man for a cleric, our Bishop," Aunt Elsie observed. "So many religious people are really rather horrid, have you noticed?"

"*Elsie!*" Aunt Jim rapped out.

"Well, they are," she insisted. "I remember one time when Cardinal Richelieu—"

Val took this as a sign that I had been tortured enough.

"This has been a wonderful tea, Aunt Jim, thank you. But Griff and I had a rather early start and I think we'd both like to go to our rooms, if you'll excuse us."

"By all means," replied Jim, who sounded just as eager for us to go as we were to leave. "We shall see you at dinner, I suppose, Mr. Griffin. Drinks are at seven o'clock in the west drawing room. Ring for a maid if you need anything."

"Ta-ta, James," said Elsie. "We'll catch up later."

James? Who in the hell was James?

Chapter 6

I closed the door behind me with an audible sigh of relief and turned to Val in a mixture of confusion, amusement, and sense of having been sandbagged.

"That's your family?"

Val nodded. "Afraid so."

"I can see why you wanted my company. And I agree that they're out of the ordinary. I suppose I can imagine them as killers. Or victims. They're a little… a little…"

"Odd."

"I'm sorry, but yes."

"I'm sorry, too," Val said, "but you're wrong. They're not a little odd, they are extremely odd. They go beyond odd into insane."

"That Aunt Herman is like Dracula's mother," I observed.

"Did Dracula have a mother?"

"Naturally, he did. Where do you think he came from?"

"I don't know. Maybe they just crack open a new coffin, like an egg, and out comes a bouncing, baby vampire."

I ignored that. "And your Aunt Elsie…" I faded out.

"She's also insane, but in a more interesting way. Congratulations, by the way, on your medal at Waterloo. Sorry you died."

"Thanks. I always wanted to do the family name proud. She's quite… unique."

"But basically harmless. Which is more than could be said for Sally and Jim." Val led the way up the stairs.

"I like how your Aunt Angus resents your presence in your own house," I said. "So gracious."

"Oh, no," he moaned, stopping mid-stair. "You're right. This *is* my house now. Good God, I'm doomed."

"And that sense of fatalism is why *you* did not get a medal at Waterloo. But don't worry about that now, let's get back to your family. I found their favoritism to be fascinating."

"Ah, yes. I've never quite figured out whether they truly believe Nicky is a genius, or just like to say so. But he and Uncle Sally have similar flavors of unscrupulousness. My uncle is just as much of a hustler, but with better taste in clothing and a higher standard of sinning. Uncle and Nicky bond over their mutual and abiding love for large sums of money, particularly the kind you don't have to work for."

"And does Aunt Boris share that love?"

"Oh, she most definitely likes the finer things in life. But she has money of her own."

"At the risk of being gauche, how much?"

"Quite a lot, I understand. Aunt Jim's father was a warm and fluffy character named Edgar Faringdon, who my mother once called the most repellent man she'd ever met. Aunt Jim might act like one of Victoria's ladies-in-waiting, but her family fortune comes from underwear."

That I had not expected. "Underwear?"

"Remember Faringdon's Flannels?"

"Oh God, yes. That horrible winter stuff that itched like the devil."

"Well, that's her family. Old Faringdon had one of those nasty, old-fashioned minds that believes men are wise simply by virtue of being men while women are irrational children who need a man's guiding hand."

"And children need to be kept stifling hot and itchy all winter, apparently. So not exactly the modern type."

"Hardly. Jemima—that's Aunt Jim—was his only child and he never got over his disappointment that she wasn't a son. When he died, he put his money in trust, overseen by a fleet of lawyers. Jim doesn't get control of it until her husband dies. Until then, she gets a generous quarterly allowance. But if she divorces him, all the money reverts to the trust and goes to charity."

"What is it with this family and weird wills?" I mused aloud.

"It's been something of an ongoing problem," Val continued. "Uncle Sally is so cheap that Aunt Jim has to use her allowance to cover most of the family expenses."

"I imagine that doesn't go down well with her."

"Nope. They've argued over money for as long as I can remember. My aunt has always found it terribly unfair that her sons should have to economize simply because Uncle Sal needs a locksmith to pry open his wallet."

Val had turned to the right at the top of the stair and ambled slowly down the richly carpeted hallway of the family wing. Up here the drab walls were enlivened with portraits of Hatton-Haxleys past, many of them presumably cursed and/or murdered. They were not, overall, a handsome family. One particularly striking portrait featured a woman as tall and thin as weird Aunt Elsie, but sporting a towering, powdered wig and a nauseous green dress seemed to be wearing her, rather than the other way around. She had a face like a trout and a slack-jawed expression to match.

Most of the male subjects were painted in extreme youth, which made sense. If your family's sons have a habit of dying young, better paint them while you have the opportunity.

"By the way," I said, turning away from all the postmortem portraits, "you didn't tell me I'd be dining with a Bishop. I wish I'd had more warning. Being around the clergy always makes me feel guilty."

"Believe me, there will be others at dinner who are more guilty than you could ever be."

"That should make for interesting dining table conversation."

"Sorry," Val said shortly.

"And if you make me sit next to your Aunt Elsie, I may challenge you to a duel."

"Don't worry, I already promised to sit you next to the only normal guest who will be here this weekend. The most normal and the most charming."

"Oh yes, the Honorable someone."

"The Honorable Miss Daphne Ferguson. Her mother and my mother were some sort of distant cousins. Aside from my brothers, she and her parents are the only likeable relations I have. I think everyone hoped she'd be the next Countess of Haxley."

"She and Erasmus were an item, then?"

"Oh, no. Never a spark. But the families always wanted Daph to marry one of us. They'll probably try to throw her at *me* now."

"Throw?" I asked. "Any woman that has to be thrown at a series of men doesn't sound very charming."

"Quite the contrary. She's rather something, really. But to us she's been like a little sister. Besides, she's too smart and has too much taste to marry into this lunatic asylum."

"As long as she doesn't claim we used to be Romeo and Juliet or Victoria and Albert, I'm sure I'll enjoy her company."

"Romeo and Juliet weren't real," Val noted.

"I'm not sure your family is."

"They are. Unfortunately for me."

Val stopped at a door. "You're three down from here," he said, pointing. "This is mine, and I'd appreciate it if you'd come in and help me look around."

"Help you look around your room?"

"Yes."

"Do you not know your own room? Maybe need help finding the light switch? Shall I check under the bed for monsters?"

"Yes," he said. "Yes, you should. Monsters, ghouls, and I need help checking for booby traps."

I wanted to laugh, but one look at my anxious friend had me swallowing the sound. "You're serious, aren't you?"

"Well, yes. I thought you knew that." I'd never seen his face, normally so carefree and handsome, look so grave. "Now," he said, "will you help me or not?"

I think that was the exact moment when I truly understood that Val wasn't mad or joking. As outlandish as it sounded, with family curses and dozens of dead brothers, he sincerely believed his aunt and uncle weren't merely loathsome, they were actually murderers. And now he was counting on me to not only confirm this belief but, if possible, to find the proof. All while acting as bodyguard so he wouldn't manage to get *himself* murdered over the weekend.

I nodded. "I'll help. After all, I came here for you, not for the pleasure of dining with a Bishop or finding out how I died at Pompeii."

"Volcano, probably," Val muttered, as he opened the door and led me inside. He paused, looking around as if expecting to find a firing squad or a hungry alligator.

A thought occurred to me. "A thought just occurred to me," I said. "Where in the family love parade do the other two brothers fall? Wolfrick and Theo? You didn't mention them."

"Theo is unmentionable. As for Wulfstan, he is and has always been second-best in his parents' eyes."

I regarded the room, which I remembered well from my previous visits. It was comfortably furnished in steel-gray tones with accents of maroon and dark blue. There was the requisite enormous bed, a dressing table and chair, and an exquisitely crafted Hepplewhite cupboard that I recalled, with some chagrin, stashing myself in during a game of hide and seek when we were about twelve years old. A tall walnut dresser of Jacobean ugliness seemed out of place, but useful. Across from that, a large Bokhara rug and a pair of comfortable-looking chairs were arranged in front of the fireplace. It looked like a nice place for reading on a dark and stormy night, with thunder echoing through the house.

On the other hand, a dark and stormy night in a house full of oddities and potential murderers seemed like a bad idea.

With nary a storm in sight, the room was light and airy, thanks to three tall windows letting in the afternoon light. Maroon draperies framed a view of the same hideous fountains I'd seen from the day room. I wasn't sure if the nearest one was Leda and the Swan or the Wreck of the Hesperus.

The one truly bizarre feature of Val's room was a large, pseudo-Baroque painting of Zeus and Europa, with an overblown Europa wearing nothing but sandals and a bored-looking Zeus wearing nothing but Europa.

"I think we should search the suite," Val said, breaking me out of my reverie. He squared his shoulders and assumed the agonized expression of an early Christian martyr. "You start in here. I'll start in the dressing room."

I stopped him as he made a move to walk away. "What are we looking for?"

"A hidden weapon, or a trap. You know, anything that could kill me. All it takes is one well-placed rusty nail in my bed—"

"Smeared with plague, perhaps?" I joked.

"An ordinary one would do, but it would be easy to hide. Then suddenly my jaw is locked, and nobody has the key. You're the writer, use your imagination!"

"Very well. We shall banish all rusty nails." Calling forth my inner Zoltan Szabo, I began to poke aimlessly around the room.

I went first to the hideous Jacobean dresser. Drawers would

make lovely hiding places for an Egyptian asp, I mused. Or, given a big enough drawer, a rampaging hippo. Unlikely, perhaps, but no crazier than anything else I'd heard since the previous day.

I pulled out each drawer delicately, as if piles of cordite and lit matches might be balanced inside. Most were empty, but some contained items that Val likely kept ready for visits such as this. I found a pair of pajamas, a few ancient sweaters, some collars and socks. One heavy bundle wrapped in a towel looked suspicious until I unwrapped it and found a bath brush and soap. Aside from an unframed photograph of Clara Bow lounging with a stuffed tiger, I found nothing of interest. I closed the last drawer with a forcefulness that Val obviously heard from the next room.

"Anything?"

"Just Clara Bow."

"I say," Val commented, "I've just had the best idea I've ever had. Why don't you take this room for the weekend, and I'll stay in yours?"

"Yes, you're right, that *is* the best idea you've ever had. And it is a horrible idea."

"No, it's perfect!" Val stood in the doorway, looking so proud of his own brilliance. "We won't tell anybody. We'll even let them see us go to our assigned rooms. Then, when the house quiets down, we can switch."

"I've got a better idea," I countered. "Why don't you write all this out and then I can circle all the words that mean *no*."

"But they'd never expect it, so it's a brilliant way to catch them in the act, don't you agree?"

"If I agreed with you, then we'd both be wrong."

"Coward," Val muttered.

"How can you say that? I won a medal at Waterloo, remember. And I was the first guy to jump out of the horse at Troy. Really, just ask your Aunt Elsie."

"I apologize. You are noble and wise. Folk tales will be sung about your brave deeds in saving me from the family curse."

"Not if you keep calling me a coward."

Val shot me a mischievous look and returned to the dressing room. I gave up on the drawers and tried the cupboard.

"If you're that scared," I called out, "why not scurry to some hidden box room or corner of the attic and hide in there for the night? Nobody would find you."

"That's what I'm afraid of."

"What?"

"That nobody would find me. Like for eighty or ninety years."

"Val, I promise that if you ever vanish for eighty years, I'll start looking for you." I heard a snort from the other room.

"Of course, you're welcome to stay in my room." I added. "There must be a sofa or chaise longue in there."

"You'd be willing to sleep on the sofa?"

"No, I'd be willing for *you* to sleep on the sofa. I'm taking the bed, thank you."

He didn't respond to that.

The cupboard held a few shirts, some hunting clothes, and a garishly orange dressing gown that I would rib him about later. But no spring-loaded daggers or nests of poisonous wasps presented themselves.

"You know, Val, searching your room right now is a waste of effort."

"What do you mean? We need to search," he objected.

"I agree. But searching it *now*, before you're ready for the night, is pointless. Just because we may not find a booby trap now doesn't mean one won't be planted after we've cleared the room. There's plenty of time."

Val was silent, which I took to mean: "*You have a good point, but I don't want to admit it.*"

I continued, looking at the bed. "I mean, if we strip off the sheets and find that your bed is entirely scorpion-free, that does not mean it will *remain* scorpion-free."

More silence.

"Tell me something," I said. "Just for the sake of argument, if your brother was murdered—"

"He was."

"Fine, he was. Obviously, you've cast Uncle Lucy and Aunt Arnold as First and Second Murderer. But stretch your mind a bit. If it's not them, who else might be capable?"

Val appeared in the doorway again, holding a small wooden box decorated with carved acanthus leaves and bearing a stain of what looked like bright yellow paint.

"Well, certainly the cousins would have a motive."

"Athos, Porthos, and Aramis?"

"You've already used that joke."

"Forgive me. I'm so focused on looking for hidden blow guns that my witty repartee is off par."

"I think I found something," Val said, holding up the box.

"What is it?"

He lifted the lid, and I peered inside, warily.

"That's a razor," I said.

"I know it's a razor."

"Well, what's wrong with it?"

"It's a *straight* razor," Val said in a tone that declared the whole thing should be perfectly obvious and I was an idiot to not see it.

"Yes, that is a straight razor. So?"

"So?" Val was incredulous. "Don't you read your own books?"

"You don't, so why should I?"

"The straight razor is universally recognized as a notorious murder weapon! Don't you think it's highly suspicious to find a straight razor hidden in my dressing room?"

"I don't know," I replied. "It depends on whose razor it is."

"It's mine."

"I see." I did not see. "I'm sorry, *what's* wrong with it? And where do you usually keep it?"

"In there," Val gestured with his head to the dressing room where he'd found the box.

"And has it always been there?"

"Well, of course. But I switched to a safety razor ages ago."

"Then why do you find it suspicious that *your* razor is in *your* dressing room where, presumably, *you* put it?"

Without a word, Val clapped the box shut, spun on his heel, and returned to the dressing room.

"Is it even sharp?" I called after him.

"Stop making fun of me and look for the monsters under the bed," he yelled.

Feeling like an idiot, I looked under the bed and found nothing, save the fact that the Tower Field Hall servants did an admirable job of keeping the rooms clean. Then, feeling like an even bigger idiot, I moved on to examine counterpane, duvet, and sheets, all the while making a silent apology to the Hatton-Haxleys' hard-working chambermaids. I found no sign of insectival invaders, poisoned thorns, or explosive devices.

Plunking myself down in one of those inviting chairs by the fireplace, I opened a small tin at my elbow and caught the scent of gingersnaps. I grabbed one and nibbled.

"Don't eat that!" Val yelled.

He startled the unchewed cookie down my throat and I began to choke. I reached for the carafe of water on the table, but Val snatched it from my hand. Great, biscuit lodged in throat and no water. And then Val again, slapping me on the back as if trying to dislodge a rib. It worked, but painfully.

"What the hell was that?" I asked. My voice was rough, and my eyes watered profusely.

"We have no idea what's in that cookie. Or in the water. You could be lying there dead by now."

"I nearly was, thanks to you!"

"I may have just saved your life, my friend."

"By startling me into choking on a gingersnap?"

"By keeping you from ingesting something terrible, like strychnine, or cyanide, or rubella."

"Rubella isn't a poison," I croaked.

"Belladonna, then. We have no idea how they plan to get rid of me or when they'll try. So we must be on guard, every second of every minute of every day of the—"

"I get it, I get it. But wouldn't it be awfully suspicious if you suddenly turned up dead only days after your brother died mysteriously? And with the people with the biggest motive to kill both of you right here in the house, pouring your tea?"

Val was silent for a moment. "You might have a point. I can see that going after me here and now might point the finger at them. But I also know that they're ruthless."

"Is anyone ever ruthful?" I wondered.

"What?"

"Ruthful. Full of ruth. What is ruth, anyway?"

"Griff!" Val snapped. "Focus!"

"Sorry."

"Can we please concentrate on my imminent demise?"

"Well now, there's a sentence I've never heard before."

"Griff…" There was a warning tone to Val's voice.

"I know. I'm sorry. I think choking half to death has cut off the supply of oxygen to my brain. In fact, I'm pretty sure it just got rid of everything I ever knew about the Battle of Hastings."

"Well, just don't lose Waterloo. I'm sure Aunt Elsie will want to reminisce later."

"Aces," I said, sarcastically. "So, I've examined your room. See? I even demolished your nicely made bed. No rabid bunnies in the bedclothes. No dynamite under the bed. But we don't really know what we're looking for. In fact, I'm not entirely convinced I'm here this weekend. I think I may be in my flat, suffering from some tropical fever I picked up while searching for lost treasure in the jungle."

"You've never been to the jungle."

"Are you sure? Perhaps you should ask your Aunt Elsie. Maybe we were intrepid explorers searching for the source of the Nile. Yes, in fact I think you were one of our bearers."

"And now I'm just a potential murder victim."

"You always have been," I countered.

"What's that supposed to mean?"

"If you're convinced that Uncle Jane and Aunt Fred have been killing off your brothers for decades, then you must also accept that they could have gone for your throat at any time. They could have poisoned your nursery cocoa or pushed you off your training pony when you were six. Why wait until you were an adult? If they really wanted your entire family dead, then they could have pulled the trigger at any point of your life."

"That's a horrible thing to say!" Val was appalled.

"It's logical, isn't it?"

"Well... Yes. But it's still a horrible thing to say."

"Val, you're the one who brought me here to be your own personal Sherlock. Your Aunt and Uncle being unpleasant is a long way from them being murderers. But if you're right, if I'm going to solve a possible crime and keep you from becoming an ex-friend, then I have to be realistic about things. And so do you."

"I need to sit down." Val fell heavily onto the mess that I had made of his bed. "My God, you're right. My whole life I've been living on borrowed time."

I pulled a silver flask from my jacket pocket. "Care for a bolt? I brought it with me, so I can promise you it's safe."

Val took a swig. The neat Scotch knocked him back into shape in something under five seconds. I took my own sip and let the alcohol numb my sore throat. Then I looked at the flask before putting it away. I'd picked it up in a London pawn shop shortly after the war, solely for the enigmatic message engraved on the front:

I'M JUST HERE FOR THE CHEESE

"So, what's our plan for the weekend?" I asked. "I consider you a good friend, Val, but I draw the line at tasting your food at every meal and hiding behind the curtains to spy on your family."

"That's fair," Val agreed. "You know, I haven't thought this out completely. I'm not exactly sure what the best way to go about this is."

"I'm still not certain I understand any of this. What exactly is going on with your family that makes murder your weekend party game?"

"What is going on is my great-grandfather was a scheming, self-important demigod, my grandfather was a ridiculous moron, and my greedy family has no morals."

"That's all been established, but it still doesn't add up. There needs to be a reason for multiple murder, and I'm simply not seeing it."

Val reached for the flask and took another pull.

"Have you ever heard of a tontine?"

"I don't suppose that's a French dessert?"

"Get comfortable, Griff, this will be a long story."

Chapter 7

"A tontine," Val began, "is a kind of legal trust. All the members have a share, and each shareholder's payout increases as the other shareholders die off. Winner takes all."

"That's a terrible idea. I sincerely hope that you're not going to tell me that one of your insane ancestors set up something like that and now your uncle is killing off all the other shareholders so he can cop the lot."

"One of my insane ancestors set up something like this and now my uncle is killing off all the other shareholders so he can cop the lot," Val confirmed.

"And it's working?"

"And it's working."

"Why?"

"Why is it working?" Val asked.

"No, why would anyone do this? I mean, you already have some hideous family curse. What sadist would add a murder sweepstakes to the mix?"

"Well, my Great-grandfather Adjutor's—"

"The fellow whose birthday you're all celebrating this weekend, yes? He's the one with the ridiculous will?"

"*Celebrating* is a bit much," Val corrected. "But yes, he's the reason we have to be here. The *other* reason I mean, after Erasmus. Adjutor was a horrible man who admired himself enough to compensate for the fact that everyone else loathed him."

"Not including your great-grandmother, presumably?"

"Especially her! They were married for over sixty years but only spent ten of those years in the same house. As soon as she'd produced enough heirs for the family line to continue, curse and all, she got the hell out of Tower Field Hall and fled to the south of France."

"How did Great-grandfather Adjutor handle that?"

"By starting a rumor that his wife was insane. He said she wasn't really in France; he'd had her committed to an asylum. She was obviously mad because she'd left him, and he was perfect, you see. They never saw each other again and he kept himself occupied with a series of ever-younger mistresses. The last one turned thirty a week before his eightieth birthday."

"You certainly keep up on the family dirt."

"Only so I don't end up *under* the family dirt."

"So, after a lifetime of apparent joy and kindness, the angels come to take Sainted Narcissist Adjutor and then… what?" I asked. "Are you saying the *same* crazy will that stipulated everyone has to sing Adjutor's praises each year also set up this… what did you call it? A *tontine*? What was the point? Why make things so difficult for your grandfather?"

"My grandfather, Blaise, had two brothers and one sister. All the brothers were idiots. Seriously. Adjutor's eldest son, Linus, didn't even have to wait for the family curse to find him. He died at age twelve when he tied a firecracker to the tail of his father's horse. The horse bucked and landed one right on Linus's forehead."

"Serves him right. What horrid little tick!"

"Wasn't he? And my grandfather once lost £5 Christmas money by giving it to a boy at school who was developing an invisibility potion. Said he'd spilled some on the note by mistake and then it got all over the bottle, so both were lost forever."

"So, brains weren't in abundance in that generation."

"Nope. The exception was the sister, Matilda, my great-aunt. She married for love, moved away, and never spoke to anyone in the family ever again."

"Wise lady."

"Indeed. Anyway, with intelligence being conspicuous by its absence, Adjutor decided that the Hatton-Haxley fortune was probably doomed to be squandered at the racetrack or in an Antarctic diamond mine if any of his heirs got it. Instead, he played a fast one. Grandfather was given the use of the money through a trust that was overseen by Adjutor's solicitors. When grandfather died, the dosh would be doled out through a tontine among his sons and grandsons. Rather like Aunt Jim's money, come to think of it."

"Does your entire family use the same lunatic solicitor? Sir Gordon Oddly-Vindictive, Esquire?"

Val laughed. "I never thought of that. I think old Adjutor hoped that by the time my generation came 'round, there might be someone with brains enough to handle the whole fortune."

"At the moment," I said, "I'm sorry to say I don't have Adjutor's faith in your generation's brains. Or his own, for that matter. This all sounds like dribbling madness."

"It does, doesn't it?" Val sighed.

"And it's all true, isn't it?"

"I'm afraid it is."

We let that sit as we traded the flask back and forth.

"So, the last living members of Saint Adjutor Death Club are you, Uncle Suspicious, and…?"

"My three hideous cousins," Val finished. "You've got it. And I object to the name 'Saint Adjutor Death Club.' A club is something one joins, and I most decidedly did *not* sign up to join this."

"But now you're the Earl. And if they manage to kill you off, then…"

"Then Uncle Suspicious—damn, you've got me doing it now—Uncle Sulpicius takes the title, the last survivor of the tontine is guaranteed to come from that branch of the family, and thus his gruesome brood gains complete control of the fortune forever."

"Hmm..." I thought for a moment. It seemed like that would give all the cousins pretty good motives for homicide, too, not just Uncle Murgatroyd and Aunt Bruce. But Val was frightened enough already. I chose a friendlier question. "What happens when you marry?"

"Oh, I won't ever marry."

"Why not?"

"Well... I mean... Suppose I were to marry."

"We *are* supposing you're married," I observed.

"Well, I'd marry a woman," he paused.

"That's usually how it goes, yes."

"Naturally, she'll want children."

"That's also usually how it goes."

"Well... I can't!"

"You can't?"

"I can't have children!" Val all but shouted.

"Is this a medical thing?"

"No, of course not!" He sounded offended. "It's a moral thing. I can't father a son who will be born with a big, target-shaped birthmark on his forehead."

"This screwy trust business is insane enough, but you really believe in the curse, too, don't you?"

"Absolutely. If I were to have a son, he'd die before he could become my heir. I don't want that. Presumably I'd be fond of my hypothetical wife, and I wouldn't want to do that to her, either."

"On behalf of your non-existent future progeny, I applaud your compassion. On behalf of myself, I think you're nuts."

"Well," Val asked, "would *you* marry me?"

"Gosh, Val, this is so sudden."

"Shut up."

I gave the flask a shake and we drank again.

"Well, at least your rooms are clear," I said. "For now, anyway. But if I'm to be your personal knight errant, I think a good next step would be for you to take me on a tour of the house."

I knew my way around some of it, of course, but a grand house like Tower View Hall is full of attics and backstairs, whole wings the guests never see. I wondered what else might be hidden away. Priest holes? Hidden staircases? Maybe a secret cupboard full of dead and gone ancestors?

Val seemed to read my mind. "Did you know there's a hidden door between the study and the library? I'll show you."

"We also need a list of everyone in the house. Not just family, but dinner guests and staff."

"Staff?"

"Sure. Even if your uncle wants you dead, who says he'd do the dirty work himself? Why not slip a few quid to one of the grooms to tamper with your saddle or bribe a chambermaid to slip something into your morning tea?"

"You're not making me feel any better, you know."

"If you really are under threat, then we need to be smarter than the enemy."

"That shouldn't be too hard. Everyone in my family, except for me, is a moron."

I snagged another gingersnap, and this time Val didn't stop me. He was busy trying to look like the smartest person in the house. I'm not sure he succeeded, but he looked smarter than the gingersnap, at least.

"I don't think we have anything to fear in the way of criminal masterminds among the cousins," he said. "The three of them combined couldn't find their way out of a paper bag. Not even if the bag was open at both ends."

"Noted," I said. "Oh, and we'll need a second list, of everyone who was here when Erasmus died. If there's someone here *this* weekend who wasn't around *last* weekend, we might be able to write them off."

"Unless we're talking about multiple murderers."

"True. You've ruled the cousins out as power behind the dead throne, but would they be willing to break a few laws and one or two commandments to do their parents' bidding?"

"Undoubtedly. They're all ghastly. They're vicious, greedy, unscrupulous, bad losers, and all three of them have terrible taste in footwear."

"Is that important?"

Val looked aghast. "Good footwear is always important!"

"I meant important to any supposed plot to kill you."

"Oh. No, it's just one more reason why I think they're all detestable. Trust me, they're awful."

"You don't have to convince me. I'm quite prepared to hate them on sight, if not sooner." I paused before adding, "There. I just went ahead and hated them in anticipation. Does that help?"

"Yes," Val said, deadpan. "Everything is fine now. I am no longer in fear for my life because you've joined me in hating my sickening cousins."

"Glad I could help. By the way, this great-grandfather's birthday gathering is going to complicate things. Absolutely everyone has to come?"

"Everyone. No exceptions. During the war, Drogo had to get special permission from the solicitors to miss it because there was no provision in the trust for a potential heir being posted to the Western Front."

"No foresight, old Saint Adjutor." I shook my head. "By the way, these solicitors. Who are they?"

"Ah, the old family firm of Eldridge, Baker, Armstrong, and Eldridge."

"And which one is your guy?"

"It used to be the first Eldridge, Harold. But he died, so now it's the second Eldridge, Edmund."

"And is this second Eldridge Edmund trustworthy or is he in Uncle Suspicious's pocket?"

"Oh, he's as innocent as a newborn fawn. There's a lot of corruption in this family, but none of it applies to the firm of Eldridge, Baker, Armstrong, and Eldridge. There is nary a blot on the old family escutcheon due to them," Val asserted.

"What exactly is an escutcheon?" I asked.

"No clue. It's either some sort of family crest or it's another word for esophagus."

"Right. Can you enlist Eldridge Junior to help keep you alive this weekend? Does he share your views about your aunt and uncle?"

"Eldridge Junior is about five steps from ninety years old. But he's still sharp." Val paused for a moment, thinking. "I don't honestly know how he feels about my aunt and uncle. We've never discussed them. We've never discussed anything other than business, really. He's *all* business. Impassively correct, never voices an opinion on anything. But that's an idea, Griff. Maybe I should talk to him."

"What about your Aunt Elsie?" I asked. "Do we need to worry about her?"

"Not at all. Like I said, she's mad, but harmless. She's not a factor in the inheritance bingo, so she has no motive. And she loved Erasmus. Besides, she didn't predict him dying that way."

"But her predictions are always wrong, you said."

"True. But I just can't see Aunt Elsie walking in on Erasmus's bath and murdering him in cold blood. I mean she may be crazy, but she's not insane."

I snorted and looked around the room, realizing that all we'd managed to do was create a mess. "Well, I'm going to my room now," I said. "If you find an assassin in your biscuit tin, feel free to come hide under my bed."

Val shot me an unprintable look.

I started to leave and then stopped myself. "Say, where is Erasmus, anyway?"

Val gaped. "What do you mean, where is he? He's dead!"

"I know he's dead. But where's his body? You haven't held the funeral yet."

"Oh. He'd be in the chapel. That's where family members usually lie in state until they join the ancestors."

"I want to see him."

"Good lord, why?"

"To see if he has any marks or bruises."

"But he's already been embalmed, surely," Val objected.

"Yes, but we still might find something. If you don't want to come, I'll understand."

He didn't, so I followed his labyrinthine directions to the ancient chapel, hidden away in the oldest, coldest part of the house. After what seemed like an hour, I eventually found it. I opened the door, gave out a small yelp, turned around, and headed straight back the way I'd come.

No matter how he felt, Val needed to see this.

Chapter 8

"I hate looking at dead people," Val protested as we traversed the long, low hallway leading to the chapel.

"Don't worry," I said. "You won't have to."

We reached an arched oaken door of Gothic design that looked as if it had been carved, slowly and painstakingly, by monks. I'd expected it to let loose a dramatic creak the first time I opened it, perhaps followed by an outpouring of bats, but instead it slid noiselessly on oiled hinges, allowing us into a stately and surprisingly large chapel complete with pews, embroidered kneelers, and an altar of heavy wood covered with a white linen cloth.

A huge crucifix dominated the apse, holding an unusually muscular Christ who looked surprisingly happy to be there. Crude statues of the Virgin Mary and an unidentified saint flanked the apse, with Mary sporting an impressive bosom and a decidedly un-ecclesiastical neckline.

There was a sort of column or plinth placed in the middle of the aisle, draped in purple velvet. And there, flanked by two white candles and two vases of lilies and white roses, sat the urn which held Erasmus's ashes.

With a flourish, I presented this scene to Val, who appeared even more confused than usual. "Where... where *is* he?" Val asked in the hushed and reverent tones one always adopts when confronted by religion.

I gestured to the urn. "I rather think he's in there."

"What?" Poor Val looked totally flummoxed. "What's he doing in there?"

"Not much, I imagine."

"He's been cremated!" He turned with sudden alarm and grabbed my lapel. "Why would he be cremated?"

"I was going to ask you."

"Why cremated?" Val repeated. He slid into a pew as if his legs had stopped working.

I took the pew in front of my friend. "I assume this comes as a surprise to you."

"I'd have been less surprised to find him upright and doing a tap dance."

"Cremation isn't a family tradition?"

"*Never*," he whispered, aghast. "Everyone else is safely dressed in their Sunday best and resting comfortably in the vault. No Hatton-Haxley has ever been cremated. Not even Great-great-great-uncle Vedast who, legend has it, spontaneously burst into flame at the age of ninety-seven."

I ignored Uncle Vedast. "So, you didn't authorize this? You didn't know?"

"Of course not! I assumed he'd been embalmed, was intact, and you were going to come in here and find a clue."

"I think the fact that he isn't intact *is* the clue."

"What do you mean?"

"I mean, maybe somebody didn't want the body examined. Didn't want to leave any evidence."

"Well, that could only be Uncle Sally and Aunt Jim. They said they'd arranged everything."

I nodded. "I agree. It had to be them. Nobody else would have the authority."

Val sighed and pulled a silver cigarette case from his pocket, absently holding it out in offer to me.

"Val! You can't smoke in here. It's a church!"

"It's a chapel," he corrected.

"Nevertheless. It's still a consecrated place of worship."

"A consecrated place of worship? Who says things like that? And what would you know about either consecrations or places of worship? I've never seen you anywhere near a church."

"I learned quite a lot while researching for *Zoltan Szabo and the Case of the Cardinal's Claw*."

"Where do you come up with those titles?"

"In the bathtub, mostly," I admitted.

"I meant... Oh, never mind." He lit his cigarette. "I'm going to hate myself, but what's this about a Cardinal's claw?"

"Well, it takes place at the Vatican. Zoltan Szabo is there to receive the Pope's Medal of Gratitude for recovering the priceless Chalice of the Holy Ox in a previous book."

"The Pope reads your books?"

"You see, there's this counterfeit priest with a hook for a hand who's going around killing prostitutes and—"

"For the love of God, stop! Isn't *this* story weird enough for you? Ten minutes ago, my brother had a body and now he doesn't. I lost a whole body in ten minutes! I rather think I've suffered enough."

He offered me his cigarette case again. Now that he'd set a precedent, I shrugged and took one.

It was quite a lovely space despite our desecrating smoke, one of the finest in the house. "Do you know who built this chapel?" I asked. "Your family isn't terribly religious, is it?"

"Not anymore. It was built by the either the 1st Countess of the 2nd Earl or the 3rd Countess of the 5th. Whoever she was, she was Catholic."

"It's a Catholic chapel?"

"I doubt it. She was the only Catholic in the family, as far as I know. It probably switched allegiance to the old C of E the day after she met her Catholic maker. But I don't know if it was officially re-sanctified or whatever they call it."

I spied a plaster shield on the wall bearing the Hatton-Haxley coat of arms. It depicted a lion and a… goat? Perhaps a camel? The beasts regarded each other dubiously over what looked like an eel or possibly an elongated duck. Two crossed axes completed the ensemble. What *did* this family have against art?

I'd seen those arms several times before, but this was the first time I'd ever noticed the motto underneath: *Praestst esse secundus primo.* I burst out laughing. "Is your family motto really, *'It is better to be second than first?'*"

Val nodded. "Appropriate, isn't it?"

I returned to the previous subject. "Who uses the chapel now? Does anyone say mass in here?"

"Not in ages. My grandmother was devout, so the local vicar would come on special occasions to lead a service. We've had a few funerals and at least one wedding in here since she passed on. Aunt Jim talks about coming down here but never does. It's mostly used as a place for poor dead relatives to await burial. All my brothers have had their time here, except Drogo, of course. But there was a memorial for him a few days after we learned he'd been killed."

He pointed to two white marble tablets set into side arches, bearing a long list of dead and gone Hatton-Haxleys. "I'll have to get Erasmus's name added."

"If he isn't buried, what becomes of him?"

"I suppose he'll be interred here. Well, not *here*." He gestured around the chapel. "I mean in the family mausoleum at the other end of the grounds. It's a Gothic monstrosity full of cherubs and sanctity. You'll love it."

I nodded to the misshapen pair of statues at the front of the church. "Who's the saint?"

Val gave a thin smile. "We have no idea."

"Really?"

"Really. He's been here since the foundation, as far as I know. But there's no record of who he is."

"Given your family history, he's probably Saint Vindictivus, the patron of dysentery."

"What do you think of Our Lady of Décolletage over there? She's always been popular."

"She's quite the healthiest Madonna I've ever seen."

"Family lore has it that she was modeled after the mistress of a previous Earl."

"That sounds like something you'd go to Hell for," I said.

"Well, family lore also has it that the same Earl was also a member of the Hellfire Club, so I imagine commissioning bad sculpture was the least of his sins."

"You know, somebody really needs to write a book about your family."

"You're the writer. After this weekend I fully expect your next bestseller to be *Zoltan Szabo and the Family that Killed Itself to Death*."

"Actually, my next bestseller will be coming out next month. It's called *Zoltan Szabo and the Corsican Canary*."

"You made that one up!"

"I make all of them up, it's my job."

"The Corsican Canary?"

"Yes, it's about a group of crooks searching for a fabulous jewel-encrusted statuette that once belonged to Napoleon."

"That's a ridiculous plot," he said.

"Remind me again why we're friends," I said.

He let out a windy sigh. "Well, the whole cremation thing certainly puts an incinerated spoke in our wheel of clues."

"Indeed."

"I was just hoping we'd learn something."

"We have. Between this and the marble, I'm convinced."

"The marble?"

"I could convince myself Erasmus had a heart attack or something if it weren't for that damned marble in his mouth. But that clearly demonstrates that someone besides Erasmus was there. A shooter—sorry, *bumboozer*—is too big to swallow and choke on. And he didn't spit it out in the throes of death. No, it was *placed* in his mouth. And now... this."

"This," agreed Val.

I looked at my cigarette. "We need to go."

"Why?" Val asked.

"Because my cigarette ash is about to drop off and I have just enough fear of Hell that I'd rather avoid leaving ashes here."

"Whoever had Erasmus cremated didn't share your fear," he noted. "What do we do next?"

"What you do is your own affair. I'm going to settle into my room, check on my cat, and get ready to meet the rest of your family."

"Trust me, you'll never be ready enough for that."

Chapter 9

My appointed room was tastefully decorated, which came rather as a shock. Tones of green and gold created a pleasing sense of restful comfort. A soft bed and a good reading lamp promised a serene end to the day, and instead of the usual pile of boring and improving books one expects to find in country houses, I found *Murder in the Second Act,* a popular new mystery written by one of my most annoying competitors, one Mortimer O'Malley. A collection of Poe stories and what looked like an interesting biography of Lord Curzon sat ready if, or rather when, O'Malley disappointed.

Catullus had already made himself at home, curled up like a comma in a cozy chair under a conveniently placed sunbeam. His green eyes opened briefly as I entered and interrupted his difficult job of napping. I stroked the little brown tabby and urged him not to work too hard. *"Non laborare nimis,* Catullus." Contrary to what I'd told Val, I had forgotten nearly all my Latin. In speaking to Catullus, I often threw random Latin words together. But my cat was good at keeping secrets and wouldn't tell.

A carafe of water gave me pause. I lifted the overturned glass that served to keep it fresh and took a cautious sniff. I wouldn't have known how to detect poison, but it seemed the thing to do. No whiff of death laid me low, so I poured myself a glass.

A small tin of gingersnaps matched the one in Val's room.

I picked one up and ate it. It tasted like a gingersnap. I didn't die. Two points for me.

My bags had already been unpacked by the household staff, so I picked up the O'Malley and settled in beside the fireplace. A silver box full of French cigarettes and a rather fetching female figurine that seemed to be either Cleopatra or Theda Bara dressed as Cleopatra stood at hand.

I lit a cigarette, saluted Cleo, and spent an enjoyable hour snickering at O'Malley's tortured prose. He really was a terrible writer. By the fourth chapter, I'd already figured out that the ingenue was guilty of dropping the sandbag on the leading lady, and why. It was with absolutely no reluctance that I put the book down and prepared for dinner.

I was shaved, dressed, and ready to go when the gong rang for cocktails at seven. A moment later, Val knocked on my door and we headed down together.

"How's your room?" Val asked, playing the good host.

"Very comfortable, thank you. It's rather nice to be in the family wing. Where's the guest wing from here?"

"Opposite end." He indicated direction with a movement of his head. "Keeping the guests far away from the main rooms makes it easier to conduct illicit affairs without detection. You're in Drogo's old room. I need you nearby in case of emergency."

"They're going to think *we're* having an illicit affair," I said, archly. "It's a good thing I didn't bring along the collected works of Oscar Wilde or my lavender velvet waistcoat."

"Do you own a lavender velvet waistcoat?"

"Thankfully, no. But it does raise a point. What am I *doing* here, anyway?" Val stopped and looked at me quizzically.

"What do you mean what are you doing here? You're here to save my life."

"Yes, yes. But what are you telling your family about why I'm here? One doesn't usually invite old school friends to family weekend funerals and ceremonial dinners. Won't they think it's strange that I'm here? I'm amazed Uncle Petunia and Aunt Elmer haven't confronted us about it already."

"They might if they ever thought about it, but they do very little of that. Thinking, I mean. I doubt they'll say anything. You see, if they *are* guilty then they know they are guilty and if they know they are guilty then they wouldn't be surprised to learn that *I* know they are guilty and wouldn't be surprised that I brought along re-enforcements to *prove* that they're guilty."

I tried to digest that but got lost around the third "guilty."

"You know, Val, I just realized: I don't care. I will hopefully never see the rest of your family again and I'm not bothered by what they think. I'll just keep my fingers crossed that they don't see me as an obstacle to be removed."

"I think you'll be safe," Val said, with a disturbing lack of conviction. "Hatton-Haxley murders are generally confined to members of the family. Besides, you're too famous to kill off. It would make the papers and draw unwanted attention."

"Lucky me."

"Plus," Val added, "having you as a guest will give them a certain cachet. Everybody likes knowing famous people."

"They've never even heard of me," I observed. "It was obvious this afternoon that Uncle Heidi and Aunt Horatio had no clue who I was. And your Aunt Elsie thinks I'm Wilkie Collins."

I heard voices as we approached what was, no doubt, the west drawing room, and prepared to meet the rest of Val's strange clan.

* * *

WITH ALL THE talk of death, I had forgotten how welcoming and lovely Tower Field Hall could be. The drawing room was luminous, with rich gold wallpaper glowing in the rays of the setting sun.

Aunt Elsie sat right in the center of the room, which would

not have been noteworthy if that was where the Hatton-Haxleys kept their chairs. But the rest of the chairs were grouped over by the fireplace, leaving Elsie isolated, an island unto herself, adrift upon a beautiful Kashmiri rug. She had changed into a hectic garment of clashing purples and reds, with a succession of necklaces ornamenting her bosom. One of these necklaces displayed a sapphire of impeccable perfection while another consisted of an acorn pierced with a piece of string.

Horrid Aunt Jim and appalling Uncle Sally were already there, the latter standing with a delicate sherry glass in his ham hand and leaning against the mantelpiece as if waiting for his cue. Aunt Jim had selected a stiff-backed, bare wooden chair that appeared to be the only uncomfortable piece of furniture in the room. Indeed, it may have been the worst seat in the house, and her rigid position further proclaimed her self-inflicted martyrdom.

Two men sat on the sofa facing her, and there could be no doubt these were Nicky and Wulfie. They took after their parents, which is to say they were not attractive specimens. But where their mother's tight, tiny features were proportionate to the rest of her diminutive person, the boys' squinty eyes and thin lips just made it seem as if they had an excess of head and insufficiency of face. Huge sand dunes of skin ranged over their foreheads and cheeks, requiring the viewer's eye to make long-distance treks from eyebrow to mouth.

The cousins rose with grudging politeness as we entered.

"Hello, cousins," Val said with audible reluctance. He made no false attempt at a "good to see you again" or "you're looking well," instead skipping straight to the introductions.

I learned that the taller of the two was Nicodemus, the supposed financial genius and favorite of Uncle Sally and Aunt Jim. I couldn't guess at the size of his portfolio, but he had the most enormous Adam's apple I'd ever seen. It looked like he'd tried to swallow a cricket ball. But he oozed an atmosphere of self-impressed perfection and regarded me with a combination of easy disdain and anticipatory boredom. His condescending gaze told me I was beneath his notice, but since there was no one more suitable around, he might as well acknowledge my existence. He wore an impeccable evening suit, but I got the impression that he would have preferred something loud and, unfortunately, checked.

I turned to Wulfstan—the alleged politician-poet who was consigned to second-favorite status—and stifled a cough. He was just plain repulsive. But my eyes were mercifully distracted from his face by his sickly-pink sweater. It lacked the cheerful pink vibrancy of a rose or the soothing pink softness of a sunset. It was more like the hideous pink of a baby rat. Set against this was a rather traumatic tie in multiple shades of clashing yellow. Lowering my gaze still further, I noticed a disreputable pair of baggy trousers that didn't even have the goodness to be honestly disreputable. They were, in fact, of exceeding fine quality, but given rough treatment—clearly a conscious attempt to make Wulfie appear negligently indolent and thus more "poetic."

Making true my promise to Val, I hated both cousins on sight.

"Where's Theo?" Val asked his aunt.

"He'll be here tomorrow. There was a rather important game against Eton today and the team wouldn't hear of him missing it."

"I should think not," Sally added. "He's their best striker."

I accepted a sherry, a drink which I hate with a passion, from a passing tray carried by an impeccable footman. That got me thinking about the household staff, and especially old Lydgate. He'd been the butler there for decades, and likely been witness to many disputes. Did he feel loyalty to one side of the family over the other? Could he be a possible ally? I made a mental note to talk to Val about who might help us if it came to it.

With the drinks passed, we all settled into our seats for an interminable stretch of stilted conversation and uncomfortable silence. But before the misery set in, Lydgate stepped through the door to announce the arrival of Sir Lawrence and Lady Margaret Ferguson, along with the Honorable Miss Daphne Ferguson.

And with that, the evening suddenly became a good deal more interesting.

Chapter 10

Sir Lawrence Ferguson was one of those hearty old county types, stuffed with only a slight bulge into an ancient dinner jacket and brimming with friendly humor. He had the broad, homely face of a camel, and seemed well suited to his wife—one of those "comfortable" women you could tell had never been a beauty but had always been charming. Her joyful, plump little figure was showcased in a somewhat old but still serviceable blue gown. She had a bright smile, and an air of befuddled good humor that made her endearing.

Their daughter, the Honorable Miss Daphne Ferguson, was something else entirely.

Daphne had glorious masses of curly red-gold hair and sparkling blue eyes that twinkled as if everything amused her, as if she was ever on the edge of mirth. She wore a marvelously adventurous dress in layers of green ranging from pale moss to deep emerald, which complimented her delicate hands and feet.

The introduction of pleasant, apparently normal people into the room made things instantly more bearable. The Honorable Miss Daphne and her parents were so obviously free of any homicidal impulse that the whole atmosphere lifted, and my sense of impending doom was dispelled.

More of the detestable sherry was passed, polite talk was made, and everyone became more familiar. It could almost pass for a typical country weekend. Of course, the family was entertaining on the weekend they were going to bury someone, and that was a bit odd, but nobody seemed bothered about it.

The arrival of Mr. Edmund Eldridge, the family solicitor, reminded us all why we were there.

Even without knowing Mr. Eldridge's profession beforehand, I would have been able to guess it. He pleased me exceedingly by looking so exactly like the respectable family solicitor one might see in a movie. A small, rather round man with a long face, he had the pale skin indicative of one who hasn't been out of doors for eighty or ninety years and the type of spectacles that are forever slipping down the nose and being pushed up by one finger.

All in all, he conveyed an aura of complete dispassion. He moved as if his joints had never been oiled, and I found it impossible to picture him ever laughing or losing his temper or falling in love. I sincerely hoped he wasn't married and pitied any woman who had to be tied to him for life. Then again, if a woman was to be with him, she would know exactly what she was getting into, fully documented and notarized.

Val introduced him to me and, upon discovering we both lived in London, Eldridge launched into a lengthy dissertation about the recent changes to Charing Cross station. Rapidly losing focus, I attempted to concentrate on the movement of his thick lips, only to discover Eldridge's unfortunate habit of getting his mustache caught in his mouth when he spoke. Lydgate effected a rescue by coming back into the drawing room and announcing dinner.

As promised, Val had me seated next to the lovely Honorable Miss Daphne, who proved to be a charming dinner companion. But he broke another promise by placing Elsie on my opposite side, and her elaborations on our shared history hampered both my conversation with Daphne and my digestion.

Still, I was greatly relieved to learn that there were previous lives where Elsie and I *weren't* doomed lovers. We'd been siblings in Ancient Rome, business partners in Renaissance Florence, and soldiers of the King during the American Revolution. There may have been more, but Elsie overheard Sir Lawrence talking about golf and turned to tell him she'd been there when the game was invented. Thus, I was free to talk with Daphne, unencumbered.

"Val tells me you all sort of grew up together?" I said in one of my less brilliant conversational openers.

She smiled, "Yes, although some of us grew up more than others."

"Meaning Val?"

"Meaning no matter how old they got, I never lost sight of the brothers as ten-year-old boys trying to push me into the river or convince me the Hall had a ghost." She sighed. "I'm going to miss Erasmus. I can't believe he's gone."

"I'm sorry for your loss," I replied automatically. The words were trite, but none the less sincere.

"Thank you. I think most of the truly joyous memories of my childhood were made here. Christmases, and a few weeks every summer. I'm an only child, and I always wanted a brother or sister. But whenever I was here, I had plenty of brothers."

Daphne paused, blinked, and stared at my face. I smiled.

"Yes, I have bi-colored eyes."

I appreciated that she didn't blush or pretend she hadn't been staring, "Oh, how lovely!" She enthused. "I've heard about that, but I've never met anyone who had them before. Except for Charlie. He belongs to Don, one of the stable boys here, and he has one brown eye and one blue, just like you. Oh," she added, belatedly, "Charlie's a cat."

"I wondered," I said drily.

She looked casually around, then leaned in and whispered, "Tell me, Mr. Griffin, which one of them do you think did it?"

My jaw dropped. "Um…" I had no idea how to respond.

Seeing my confusion, she added, "I'm sorry. It's just that I know Val thinks his horrible aunt and uncle are guilty of killing off his brothers, so I assumed he'd discussed it with you and that's why you're here." She looked me right in my bi-colored eyes. "That *is* why you're here, isn't it?"

"Well… um… Yes," I admitted, dropping into a whisper myself. "I can't believe how calm you two are about this theory that half the family is made up of murderers. You both act like it's not an outlandish concept."

She considered for a moment, and we sipped at the soup, a delicious creamy-tomatoey-spicy blend that deserved our full attention. The kitchen staff was obviously as skilled as I remembered from childhood. Only after my first spoonful did it occur to me to wonder about the safety of the food. But it had been ladled into the bowls from a communal tureen, and as there was no sign of poison or plague smeared on said bowls, I decided it was safe and kept going.

"I suppose it does sound crazy to someone who hasn't been around this family all their life," she observed, voice low enough not to carry. "But to Val and me it makes perfect sense. I mean, family curses aside, it *is* rather unusual for an entire family to die young, and in so many suspicious ways. And Sally and Jim are truly awful people."

"How so?" I mumbled. I looked around, but conversations were going on around us and nobody seemed to be listening to Daphne and me. "They do seem dashed unpleasant, but I've barely met them."

"They're greedy," she answered quietly between spoonfuls of soup. "Dishonest. Unscrupulous. Heartless. Uncle Sally cares only for money and status. He's a bully with delusions of grandeur who thinks bulldozing the local gentry into electing him Captain of the Hunt makes him Napoleon. And Aunt Jim wants everyone in the world to fawn over her perfect life and her brilliant, devoted sons. They're neither, of course, but she really *does* think there's something magnificent about them. Nicky, especially. God knows why."

"What are the sons like?"

"As greedy as their parents, but entirely lacking in brains or effort. Sally uses intimidation to get what he wants. Aunt Jim goes for manipulation. The boys have ambition, but don't see any need to exert themselves for it."

"I thought one was an investor in London and the other just out of Oxford."

She laughed. "Nicodemus is a bank clerk! He's no financier, he's just the man who hands over your money when you cash a check. And he only got that job because Aunt Jim's godfather is president of the bank. Nicky loves money, but he's a drowned eel; wet, slimy, and utterly unappetizing. And if you were a woman, I'd also advise you to watch out for wandering hands and dark corners. That earned him a black eye last weekend."

I put down my spoon. "I think I just lost my appetite."

"Yes, talking about the boys does tend to have that effect."

I took the opportunity to glance around the table again. We were still being ignored, even by Elsie, who was deep into predicting Sir Lawrence's future.

"So. Nicky sounds like a winner," I whispered. "What about the other one?"

"Oh, Wulfie scraped through Oxford, that's true, but only by the skin of his nasty, pointed teeth. He's hardly a scholar. As it happens, I have a friend who was in his college and the truth is that Wulfie blackmailed an acquaintance into taking his finals for him."

"Charming," I observed.

"Oh, he's a pretentious, lying little hypocrite."

"Hypocrite?"

"His latest pose is being a communist. And like all good communists, he draws a monthly allowance, owns a flat in Soho, and enjoys gambling for high stakes in continental casinos."

"Ah yes," I observed, "*Chemin de fer*, the opiate of the people."

"By the way, watch out for Wulfie."

"You think he might be dangerous?"

"No. I mean yes," she corrected, "but only because he has some ridiculous idea that he's a writer. Once he learns who you are, he'll probably try to make you his new best friend."

"Oh!" I wasn't sure what to say. "So, you know I'm a writer."

"Of course. I once spent an entire rainy weekend eating exquisite pastries and reading *Zoltan Szabo and the Phantom Pilgrim*. It was great."

"Thanks. But it wasn't as good as *The Woman in White*."

"Excuse me?"

"Aunt Elsie thinks I may have been Wilkie Collins."

Daphne laughed again. It was a good laugh.

"She would. Anyway, if you're not careful, Woeful Wulfie will try to finagle you into an introduction with your publisher."

The conversations around us seemed to be dying out, so by unspoken consent we moved on to less slanderous topics. Daphne was a delightful dining companion, witty and engaging with intelligent opinions about books, current events, and travel. We discovered a mutual interest in history and were chatting amiably about the Wars of the Roses when I became aware of Val, on the other side of the table, trying to be subtle about catching my attention.

I gradually became aware that Aunt Jim and Mr. Eldridge were discussing the family curse. I couldn't hear much of it, but it sounded like the aunt was a believer.

Unfortunately, they were drowned out by the drone of Uncle Sally lecturing Nicodemus about how you can always tell a true gentleman by his punctuality, followed by Elsie holding forth on the importance of mulch to a thriving garden. Then Wulfstan gave what could only be described as a lecture on the unfair distribution of wealth, all the while stuffing his face with partridge and washing it down with a rather nice claret. And when he finally shut up, Nicky enthralled us all with a loud, long, and pointless story about how he'd advised the Director of his bank to look into Turkish drachmas and how grateful the Director was in return. I doubted both sides of this alleged exchange.

* * *

THE END OF dinner promised blessed relief, until I realized the Hatton-Haxley clan kept to the ancient ritual of men and women going their separate ways. Val and I were herded toward brandy and cigars in the billiard room; Daphne, her mother, and the aunts drifted back in the direction of the west drawing room for whatever went on there.

Val caught my elbow before we left the dining room.
"Well?"
"Well, what?" I asked.
"Did you see anything suspicious?"
"You mean other than *Uncle* Suspicious?"
"Stop calling him that," he hissed.
"No, Val, I saw nothing suspicious."
"Did Daphne say anything?"
"Many things. She's a charming girl. And she agrees with you. She thinks your brothers were murdered and the horrid Hatton-Haxley gang is responsible."
"Yes, I know. We've discussed this before. But she hasn't had any more luck proving it than I have."
"Any instructions for the next part of the evening? Should I stick close to anybody or just float around hoping to overhear your uncle saying, *'remember that time I killed my nephew?'*"

"Just keep your eyes and ears open. And your mind, too. Oh, and there'll be a costume party up in my room tonight at one. Be there."

"A... did you say a costume party?"

"Yes."

"Let me try this again. You're holding a *costume party*?"

"You'll see. Just come over to my room. One o'clock."

With that, we entered the masculine domain of the billiard room. I soon engaged Nicodemus in a game of snooker, to get a better idea of the kind of man he was.

It didn't take long to figure out that there wasn't much to find out. He was a lousy snooker player, too, constantly choosing risky shots and failing to hit them.

As he missed and missed again, I learned that Nicodemus Hatton-Haxley was shallow and remarkably self-centered. He'd ramble on about his supposed genius for money, how he was being groomed to join his bank's executive board, or how he was dating no fewer than three beautiful daughters of rich, titled fathers. But I'd have had more luck trying to engage one of the snooker balls in conversation than getting him to talk about Erasmus.

Even when talking about himself, I sensed a furtive air about him. When asked the most innocent of questions, he'd become restless and defensive. For instance, when I asked, "I heard you had a black eye last weekend. What happened?"

"Uh..."

I waited.

"Horse," he said.

"Horse?"

"Horse."

"Huh... horse."

He then changed the subject, throwing out hints that he was in early on several can't-miss schemes and, with a pretended reluctance that wouldn't have fooled a child, he offered to advise me on investing.

I decided to quiz him a bit to test his knowledge, but I know less about investments than I know about Old Norse limericks. I tried a generic question about foreign currency.

Nicky mumbled something about it being hard to explain to the ignorant public, implying I was clearly a member of that class, and steered back to the can't-miss investment potential of South American mining.

I then remembered a phrase I'd seen in all the papers lately and asked about the scandalous collapse of the Megatherium Trust. And at that moment something interesting happened.

But first, I must digress. In December of 1917, I found myself in a very small boat off the coast of Holland with a Captain Geoffrey Belt. The winds were cold, the water choppy, and we were within sight of a German encampment. Belt was recovering from an over-enthusiastic farewell party and a dinner of beef stew that was just shy of going off. I remember him sitting in a shaft of wet light, his face displaying the most fantastic play of colors I'd ever seen, like a beautiful sunset, or one's first glimpse of the northern lights. Ruddy brown faded into a pale gold, and then into cream. Then the cream curdled into the green of fresh asparagus, until the asparagus were drowned in the pale-yellow hollandaise sauce of true nausea.

Nicky turned that same color.

The Megatherium Trust scandal, that golden fleece that fleeced a thousand gold-diggers, was clearly a sore point for Nicky the Genius.

He suddenly asked when my next book was coming out, which was the first time all night he'd shown interest in anything but himself. I was shocked into an inane answer and the moment was lost.

Still rattled, Nicky missed a shot that a blind flounder could have made, and I finally put him out of his misery. He proved as poor a loser as a player, pouting like a child and claiming that he'd been put off his game by worrying about instability in the international gold market.

"Yes," I commiserated, "I often find myself unable to sleep at night because of the instability of the international gold market."

I replaced my cue and ambled over to Val, who was conversing with his corpulent uncle.

"I assume you're planning on moving down here now that you're the... *ahem*... Earl." Once again, he managed to make the word *Earl* sound like a deadly insult.

"I don't know what my plans are," Val replied. "It's all too soon to think about, don't you think? After all, I just lost my brother."

Reminded that there had just been a tragic death in the family, Uncle Suspicious attempted a sad face. He was no better an actor than his son was a snooker player.

"Oh, yes. Poor... um... Erasmus."

"Forgive me, Viscount," I interjected, politely, "but the new Earl and I were surprised to discover that poor... um... Erasmus has been cremated."

Like father, like son, I thought. *So Uncle Sally can turn that color, too!*

He cleared his throat a few times.

"Oh, uh... Just following orders, you know," he stammered.

"Orders? From whom?" Val asked. I must admit, I was proud of him for the "whom."

"Well... uh... that is..." He paused for some more throat clearing before strangling out an answer. "Um... from Erasmus, of course."

"Erasmus!" Val squeaked in his surprise.

"Erasmus ordered you to have him cremated?" I asked.

"Oh... uh... no, not *orders* of course. No. Figure of speech. But he told us that's what he wanted done." This statement was followed by one more clearing of the throat and a reach into his pocket for a handkerchief with which to mop his perspiring brow. Sally really was hopeless under pressure.

I began to ask, "What did he—" When Uncle Sally pulled out a pocket watch with great enthusiasm and yelled that it was time to rejoin the ladies. He all but ran from the room.

I had hoped to fall back for a quiet word with Val, but I was accosted by Cousin Wulfstan instead.

"Valentine tells me that you were in the war," Wulfstan said. He made it sound like an accusation.

"Yes, I was."

"I'm against war," he said, smugly.

"Oh. Are you a pacifist?"

"Absolutely. And a communist." His smugness increased.

"Can you be both?" I asked. Behind me, I heard Val snicker.

"Why not? I'm in favor of revolution. But I object to war." This time it was more of a sneer than a smug.

"It's just that I think there might need to be a modicum of war if you want a revolution. In fact, I believe it's required. I mean, if you want to overthrow the system but don't believe in war, then it's not much of a revolution, is it? It's more of a temper tantrum."

"Spoken like a true member of the bourgeoisie," he sneered yet again. I had to admit, he was good at sneering.

Remembering what Daphne had said about Wulfstan's Oxford career, I said, "You know, Wulfie, I've never actually understood what the term bourgeoisie means. I bet you're just the man to explain it to me. And what exactly is the difference between the bourgeoisie and the proletariat?"

It turned out the whole Haxley family could turn that unusual color. Captain Belt would be proud.

"Uh… It's difficult to explain to a layman," he said, parroting Nicky's earlier evasion. But Wulfie had just a sliver more spine.

He glared at me suddenly. "You strike me as being hostile to me and my brothers," he said.

"Well, I haven't met Theo yet."

"No, not them. My brothers in arms. My comrades. The oppressed army of workers."

"Oh. Them."

"You'll be a lot less superior when society finally wises up. Wasn't it Marx who said, '*When we hang the capitalists, they will sell us the rope we use.*'"

"No."

"No? What do you mean, no?" He demanded. "Are you arrogantly negating my commitment to the struggle? Is that what you mean by no?"

"I mean 'no,' it wasn't Marx. It was Stalin." I smiled.

Wulfie's drink suddenly became fascinating to him. He stared at it intently.

I continued, enjoying myself out of all proportion. "I'd love to hear your views on philistinism versus materialism."

"Well, there's a lot of nuances to both," he threw out, vaguely.

"I imagine you and Nicky often trade opinions on economic determinism around the old billiard table, don't you?"

"Sorry," he said, backing away. "You just reminded me of something important. I need to go talk to Nicky before we join the ladies."

Recalling the immortal words of Shakespeare, I murmured under my breath: "*Exit, pursued by a bear.*"

Val joined me then, shaking his head. "I thought he'd given up on communism. I suppose that explains the clothing. Would it surprise you to know that I recently overheard that so-called communist asking his father for money to buy a sailboat. I kid you not, a sailboat! He asked for five hundred quid."

"Val," I said, "I'm surprised at you. Don't you know all the top communists have sailboats nowadays?"

"How do you know so much about communism, anyway? Stalin quotes and all that?"

"I had to do a lot of research for *Zoltan Szabo and the Murder at the People's Revolutionary Fête.*"

"What?"

"Joke," I replied. "By the way, why was your Aunt Elsie sitting alone in the middle of the room earlier?"

"Oh, that's just another one of her hobbies." He made it sound commonplace. "She likes to rearrange furniture."

* * *

THE LADIES SAT scattered about the drawing room in decorative poses reminiscent of an Impressionist painting, and the room itself seemed open and bright compared to the atmosphere of dark paneling and pretense we had just left.

Val and I were the last men to enter, and we made our way over to Daphne, who sipped coffee while Elsie, sitting beside her, dumped the contents of the sugar bowl into her bright yellow purse.

"Hello," Daphne smiled. "Did you men enjoy talking about shooting, cricket, and piston engines?"

I laughed. "Is that what you think men talk about?"

"I can only imagine," she replied. "But I've had to listen to Aunt Jim talking about how wonderful Wulfie is and how the world is falling into sin because we don't all read the Bible for fun anymore."

"You know, dears," Elsie said, "I hate to speak ill of anybody. But she really is rather a hypocrite, you know. Always has been. And her saintly sons are a pack of no-good swindlers."

"Any orders for what we should be doing?" Val asked.

"Well, I tried tackling Uncle Sally about the circumstances of Erasmus's cremation…" I began.

"Erasmus has been cremated?" Daphne exclaimed. "Why?"

"According to Uncle," Val said, "it was Erasmus's own wish."

"Bosh!" Elsie said. "He'd have hated that. Why didn't you stop it, dear?" She looked sharply at Val.

"I didn't know!"

"Oh. Well, that's different then. In that case, I forgive you." She smiled gently.

"Forgive me for what?" Val asked, confused.

"For having Erasmus cremated."

"But I didn't."

"I know that, dear," Elsie explained patiently, "and that's why I forgive you."

"I also forgive you, Val." I smiled.

"Shut up."

I looked over and saw Sally and Jim in private conference by the fireplace. "Come on, I want to broach the subject again."

I should have been more explicit about my invitation, because both women took this as an opportunity to join me and Val in our quest.

"Ah… uh… Valentine." Val's uncle had a definite problem remembering the names of his nephews.

The new Viscountess sniffed a greeting. I was scrambling in my mind for a way to approach the subject when Elsie dove in headfirst. "We want to know why you had Erasmus cremated, because none of us believes it was his idea."

"Thank you, Aunt Elsie," Val murmured. "Very tactful."

"Oh, bother tact," she waved the idea away, as if it was an insect. "Did Alexander the Great waste his time being tactful?"

"What does Alexander the Great have to do with anything?" Daphne asked. "I don't get the connection."

"*I* am the connection, dear," Elsie replied as if it should be obvious. "They both knew me, didn't they?"

"It's just that news of Erasmus's cremation came as a surprise to us all," I said, sparing everyone Elsie's reminiscences of ancient Macedonia. "According to Val, he never expressed any desire for it."

A sniff announced Aunt Jim's entry into the conversation.

"Oh, but he did, Mr. Griffin. He most certainly did." She gave me another of those pinched looks she did so well.

"When?"

"Oh... uh... well..." Uncle Sally stammered with his usual eloquence. But that was as far as he got. Aunt Jim, who was obviously the brains of the family, kept going.

"It was only two months ago, when poor old Sir Benjamin Monk passed on."

"Who?" I whispered to Val.

"Local gentry. Ancient. Sat next to Moses in nursery school."

Sniff. "Dear Erasmus, the Viscount, and I represented the family at the services and at dinner that evening, Erasmus commented that the funeral had been very tasteful, but that he didn't want to be buried or put into the family vault when it was his time. 'I'd prefer to be cremated,' he said, 'it seems so much more hygienic.'"

"Yes. Yes. Hygienic. Very hygienic," Uncle Sally said with undue enthusiasm. "You know how Erasmus was always so concerned with... uh... hygiene."

"Was he?" I asked Val.

"Not that I ever noticed."

"Nor I," Daphne concurred.

"Of course not," Elsie objected. "What a stupid thing to say: *Erasmus was always so concerned with... uh... hygiene.*" It was a bang-on impersonation.

"Really, Elsie!" Jim protested.

"I must say, Elsie..." Sally began. "I mean, I really must say." But he left it there, leaving whatever must have been said, unsaid.

At this moment, Aunt Jim lifted her arm and, with a gesture that would have summoned a dozen taxis, waved the nearest son into her orbit. Nicky responded with the alacrity of one who knows which parent holds the power.

"Son," she addressed him with a sniff, "do you remember dinner the evening after Sir Benjamin's funeral?"

Nicky nodded. "You mean when Erasmus said he wanted to be cremated after death because it was so hygienic?"

I blinked. Did they think anyone was going to believe this? Testing a theory, I took a few steps away to the fireplace, where Wulfie was lurking and trying to look communistic; appearing displeased with everything and conveying an unspoken certainty that life would be so much more fun if everyone agreed with him. I interrupted his plans for peaceful revolution and quietly asked him to join us.

"Tell me, Wulfstan," I said. "Did you ever hear Erasmus talk about cremation?"

"Sure," came the prompt reply. "It was after old Crawford's funeral," he recited. "Erasmus said he didn't want to be buried because cremation was more—"

"*Hygienic*," Val, Daphne, and I said in unison.

Chapter 11

At one o'clock, I peeked around the corner of my bedroom door, feeling like a fool. The house was silent, the corridors empty, the death traps nonexistent. I knocked quietly on Val's door, still wondering what coded message he'd tried to convey by calling this meeting a "costume party." I soon found out. Val opened the door wearing a ridiculous cowboy hat with an oversize crown and a fake feather in the band.

Dumbfounded, I looked past him and was surprised, but pleased, to see Daphne. She sat on the floor by the fire with a steaming mug in her hand and a Napoleonic officer's hat on her head. I wondered in passing whether it had once been mine.

Val ushered me in, with Catullus trotting at my heels. I heard Val mutter "*amo, amas, amat*" at the cat.

Daphne smiled. "Who is this?"

As I made the introductions, Catullus paused to claim the room with a quality of righteous ownership. He then assumed the cat's privilege of crawling into her lap and looking cute. I envied him.

"Cocoa?" Daphne offered, gesturing towards a tray on the hearth.

"Of course," I said, joining her on the floor. "Just what every secret discussion about murder needs. Cocoa."

"It's a little-known fact that Sherlock Holmes's drug of choice, after cocaine, was cocoa," she said with a smile. "Speaking of which…" She reached into the old carpet bag at her side and withdrew an old-fashioned deerstalker hat, plopping it onto my head as Val handed me a mug of the chocolate brew.

"When we were children," Daphne explained, "we would have costume parties up in the nursery." She smiled at the memory.

"We had this wonderful governess, Miss Cain," Val added. "One weekend, the family held a big masquerade ball downstairs, and the children were upset at being left out. So she organized another party up here, just for us. From then on, costume parties became a regular thing. We'd have cocoa and play games. She'd let us stay up late and never tell."

"Miss Cain was a lovely person," Daphne continued. "When we get together now, we have cocoa in her memory and hide away from the older generation. And the cousins."

"I thought you were a cousin," I observed.

"Other side, remember," she said, shortly. "We're second cousins, or third cousins once removed, or something."

"How exactly does one remove a cousin?" I asked.

"I think the horrid Hatton-Haxleys could actually answer that," she replied. "I believe they've been removing their cousins quite effectively for years. And if we don't want dear Val to join the ranks of the removed, we need to do something."

"Such as?" Val asked. "I'm all in favor of me not dying. Capital idea. But I honestly have no idea how to stop it. Daph, you were here when Erasmus died. What happened?"

"Oh, thank goodness!" I sighed. "Details at last."

"Details?" Daphne asked.

"So far all I know for sure is that Erasmus died. Val wasn't here. I'm dying to know what really happened."

"Don't say 'dying,'" Val pleaded.

"Sorry. So, *you* were here that weekend?" I asked.

"Oh, yes. I was here for the wedding of an old family friend. Montague Mortlake."

"Montague Mortlake?" I turned to Val. "With a name like that he must be a relative."

"Nope, no relation," Val said. "But his new wife, Dwynwen, is a distant cousin of some sort."

"Dwynwen? How do you spell that?"

"With six W's and a silent 'th.'"

"By any chance, was Dwynwen a saint?"

"Patron saint of lovers."

"Well, that's better than being the patron saint of ugly people."

"Poor Drogo," Daphne sighed.

"Let's get back to your more recently deceased brother. What happened, Miss Ferguson?"

The fire popped and crackled while she sipped and gathered her thoughts. She stalled a bit, rifling through the mysterious bag and pulling out a long, purple ribbon, which she tied around Catullus's neck. Catullus, strangely enough, let her live. "He was the only one not in costume," she explained.

Finally, she got around to telling her version of events.

According to Daphne, on the morning of the wedding she and Erasmus had gone riding. He'd been in a good mood, and they were looking forward to seeing old friends at the wedding. They'd returned to the Hall around ten o'clock, had some tea, and then Erasmus went into his study for a bit to work. At about noon, he instructed his valet to draw his bath and lay out his suit. The valet, Sutherland, asserted afterwards that everything in the bath was as normal and Erasmus was his usual self. He also asserted that Erasmus was not currently reading any book, and certainly not *The Gospel of Nicodemus.*

"I honestly cannot picture Erasmus reading for pleasure," Daphne said. "The idea of him perusing apocryphal Christian theology is outrageous."

"Yes," Val agreed. "That alone is enough to make his death suspicious. If they wanted the world to think that he was reading in his bathtub, they should have given him *Punch* or some ridiculous murder mystery."

"Like one of mine?" I asked.

"Yes," Val said. "I mean, no, of course not!"

"Or *What the Maid Saw Through the Keyhole*," Daphne added.

"Daphne!" Val exclaimed in a scandalized tone.

"What? I was sixteen when I found Erasmus's secret library. It was most educational." She gave a sly smile.

"You don't mean to say you read them?" Val was aghast.

"I did. My favorite was the one where the stable boy and Lady Ursula were—"

I had, unfortunately, just taken a sip of cocoa and began to laugh and choke at the same time.

"Are you alright?"

"Fine," I replied. "Fine. I just got something stuck in my escutcheon." I traded looks with Val.

"Your what?" Daphne looked amused.

Wanting to get the proceedings back on track, I just shook my head and asked, "What about Uncle Suspicious and Aunt Fred? Did you see them that day?"

"Uncle Suspicious and Aunt Fred!" Daphne gave out a hoot of laughter. "Yes, I saw them at breakfast, and they were their usual dismal selves. No muttered threats over the toast and marmalade, no secret hand signals, no venomous glances."

"Right," I said. "Erasmus goes to get ready for the wedding. Then what?"

Daphne explained that she was staying in her usual room and passed the time chatting with Mary, one of the housemaids, while dressing.

"I've known Mary for ages," she said. "I remember we were laughing about something Aunt Elsie said. Just the day before, Elsie had enlisted Mary and one of the other maids, Lily, to witness her new will. For about the tenth time. And Aunt Elsie took that occasion to inform Mary that she was going to be shipwrecked. We were laughing about it when we heard noises from the other wing."

"What kind of noises?" I asked.

"It was Sutherland shouting for help, though we didn't realize it at the time."

"Could you hear what he was saying?"

She just shook her head. "My room is at the end of the opposite wing. I couldn't really tell what the commotion was."

"And then what?"

"Naturally, we were curious," she said. "This is not a house where you hear a great deal of shouting. When Mary and I got to the family wing, Sutherland was standing in the corridor outside Erasmus's room. He was almost incoherent. He said something about an accident, and I just assumed Erasmus had sprained his ankle getting out of the tub or something. I was worried we might be late to the wedding. But then…"

She stopped, her eyes filling with tears, and grabbed Val's hand, uniting them in grief. With all the gothic absurdities of the family history, it was easy to forget that these two had just lost someone they loved.

I let them have a few minutes and then, as gently as I could, asked her to go on.

"Who explained to you what happened?"

"Sutherland. I think he said, 'He's dead, miss, he's dead,' but I didn't understand any of the words. I heard voices from the bath and tried to go in, but he stopped me. He said it wasn't a fit sight for ladies. I never saw Erasmus *in situ*, as it were. Not that I really wanted to, of course."

"Of course not," Val said.

"You said you heard voices from the bath," I asked. "Who was in there? Was the uncle there? Or the aunt?"

"No, it was just the staff. Sutherland did say that someone

had gone to get Sally, but I was the first member of the family to arrive."

"Who was with Erasmus, then?" Val asked.

"I heard Lydgate and Gregory. He's one of the footmen," she explained to me. "Oh, and Fitzhugh."

"Fitzhugh? Are you sure? That's odd."

"Why? Who's Fitzhugh?" I asked.

Val exchanged a glance with her before answering. "Gilbert Fitzhugh. My horrible uncle's equally horrible valet."

"What's so odd about him being there?" I asked.

"Just him being at the scene is intriguing," said Val. "If Uncle Sally wanted to kill someone, he'd most likely get Fitzhugh to do the dirty work."

"I agree," Daphne said. "The man's creepy. I wouldn't trust Fitzhugh as far as I could kick a piano."

"If you both dislike him so much, he must be a real gem. What's he like?"

"He's the type of man novelists like you refer to as a dangerous character," Val said. "Regular army before the war, Sergeant, invalided out after he took some shrapnel in the leg at Ypres. It left him with a limp and a bad attitude."

Val turned to me and added, "Remember Geoffrey Fowler?"

I thought for a moment, "Tall fellow, big nose, bowled for Sadler House."

"That's the one. He served in the same regiment as Fitzhugh. Called him an angry man. Very angry. Bullied the ranks. He once punched a kid for crying when his best mate got his arm blown off. Broke the guy's jaw."

"Sounds like a prince," I said. "Anything else?"

"Oh sure. He said Fitzhugh gambled a lot, was rumored to cheat at cards, was known to be a thief, participated in illegal boxing matches, had little respect for authority, and may have killed a German prisoner."

"Really? You never told me that," Daphne said.

I nodded. "The higher-ups eventually cracked down on ill treatment, but there were a lot of complaints from prisoners of war about rampant theft," I recalled. "Wedding rings, cigarette cases, money, even boots."

"Precisely," said Val. "Well, according to Fowler, word had it that Fitzhugh tried to take a prisoner's watch. The prisoner objected and Fitzhugh shot him. That's the rumor, at least."

"Do you think it's true?" I asked.

"If you know Fitzhugh, it seems plausible. That's enough to make me suspicious of his lurking near the bath right after Erasmus died."

The fire popped and crackled as we were all silent for a moment. I found myself staring again at the hilarious spectacle of Zeus and Europa on Val's wall.

"Um, Val…" I started. "Why does Zeus have three hands?"

"Who? What?"

"That painting. Zeus has two right hands."

"No, he doesn't!"

I walked over for a closer look. "Yes, he does," I confirmed.

Catullus meowed in protest as Daphne jumped up to join me. "See?" I pointed out. "He's got his right arm around Europa's waist, and his left hand is over here. So, what's this hand doing on her shoulder?"

She laughed. "Oh my God. You're right. How have I never noticed this before?"

Val stood and examined the painting closely. "Three hands," he murmured. "No wonder they stashed it in the attic."

"It's a truly horrible painting," Daphne said.

"I know. But I found it up there when I was about fifteen and it had a naked woman in it, so I brought it down here. I've been looking at that painting ever since and never saw the third hand. I guess I was too busy looking at the naked people."

"You know," I said, "in some ways that makes me like it more."

Our moment of art appreciation lifted some of the heaviness from the room, so it was with some reluctance that I went back to more relevant topics.

"I'm curious about this family curse of yours," I said. "Do your aunt and uncle also believe in it?"

"I have no idea," Val answered. "We've never discussed it."

"Never discussed it?" I was almost amused. "There may be a fatal curse haunting your family and you've never even had a conversation about it?"

"Can you blame me?" Val protested, "That would just plant ideas in their heads. But I think I heard Aunt Jim mention it at dinner. I tried to signal you."

"I saw that. Very subtle. And I overheard a little of it, but I couldn't catch the gist."

"She believes," Daphne said. "I'm not sure about Sally."

"Really?" Val asked. "What makes you think dear auntie is a believer?"

"Well, she absolutely adores Nicky," she answered. "Years ago, I think it was after Drausinus drowned, she said she was grateful that Nicky wasn't the heir, because it would break her heart if anything ever happened to him."

"She has a heart?" Val asked.

"She does where Nicky is concerned. You know that."

"True," Val said. "The only time she ever displays anything so gauche as an emotion is when she talks about her amazingly perfect sons."

"Anyway," Daphne continued, "another time I heard her mention to Val's mother how relieved she was that none of her sons were the heir because it would be terrible to know your eldest son was doomed from the start. But then she consoled herself by saying, 'Of course, my second son would also be an exemplary Earl.'"

Val snorted, and then let out with a whoop of laughter when Daphne finished her story by adding, "And then Aunt Jim quoted the family motto. *Praestst esse secundus primo.* And all that."

"What a lovely woman," I said.

"We highly suspect her of feeding poisoned pablum to local babies," Val commented.

I turned to Daphne. "Is *your* side of the family this odd?"

"Oh no, everyone is distressingly normal. Although I do have one cousin, Maurice, who likes to go mushroom picking in the nude."

"Interesting hobby," Val observed around a laugh.

"And my parents are wonderful." She smiled.

"Yes," Val agreed. "They are."

"My father has always treated me as a princess."

"That's sweet," I said.

"Isn't it? When I was just fourteen, he married me off to a fifty-year-old stranger so we could strengthen our ties with the Hapsburgs."

We all laughed, but soon another question occurred to me.

"When was the marble found? Was it right away?"

"No, the doctor found that," Daphne explained. "I was with the aunts, downstairs. Lydgate had taken charge and rang for Doctor Ridgeway. I don't really know how long everyone was upstairs. I was in rather a state of shock."

I nodded and she continued, "Eventually, Doctor Ridgeway came down with Uncle Sally and explained that it appeared Erasmus had drowned, but there was one oddity."

"The marble," I said.

She nodded. "The marble."

"What did you think when you heard about it?"

She took a sip of cocoa before answering. "I'm not sure I understood at first. I mean, it was unbelievable that he was dead. But to have a marble in his mouth? I know this might sound strange, but I was... well... offended. On his behalf. It just seemed cruel, somehow."

"What exactly did he say?" Val asked.

"I'm not sure what you mean," she said.

"The doctor," he explained. "Did he ask if Erasmus regularly sucked on marbles while taking a bath? Or maybe: *'Did the deceased have any strange hobbies, like juggling knives or snacking on rocks?'*"

"Valentine Dunstan Jarlath! That's a horrible thing to say."

"*Valentine Dunstan Jarlath?*" I laughed. That *is* a horrible thing to say."

Val shot me a dirty look. "I was just wondering how the doctor phrased it."

"Valentine Dunstan Jarlath?" I repeated.

"No," Daphne said, ignoring me. "He didn't say anything like that. He just said he'd found something odd, and that Erasmus had a marble in his mouth. That's all."

"Valentine Dunstan Jarlath?"

"Will you shut up!"

I let it drop and turned to Daphne. "Did the doctor, or anybody else, mention *Nicodemus* at this point?"

They both looked confused for a moment. Then Daphne caught my meaning.

"You mean the book, not the financial wizard? Yes. After the marble, Doctor Ridgeway mentioned Erasmus's book was floating in the bath and likely ruined."

"That's another thing," I said. "Can either of you see any significance to the *Gospel of Nicodemus*? It's not a confession from Cousin Nicky's subconscious or anything?"

"No," declared Val. "For one thing, I seriously doubt Cousin Nicky has any subconscious... ness. Sub-conscientious-ness."

Daphne took pity on his grammar, and broke in, "I've been

thinking about that all week, and I can't honestly think of a single reason for it."

"But at this point, the phrase 'foul play' would probably have come to mind for a competent investigator," I observed.

"It certainly did to me," she said. "It was all too weird."

"Yes…" I said, slowly. "It *is* too weird. That's the problem."

"What do you mean?" Daphne asked.

"Unexpected deaths happen. A seizure or heart attack, some tragic accident. But when you stuff a marble in the victim's mouth and give him a gospel he would never read, that rather rules out a tragic accident. It's suspicious."

"Very," Val agreed.

"And that's why it's a problem. The first objective of every successful murderer, after committing the deed itself, is to get away with it. So why make it look so obviously fishy? Why hand us reasons to suspect Erasmus was murdered?"

"Good question," Daphne said. "It's pointless. And stupid."

I thought for a moment. "Miss Ferguson, do you know if Erasmus's bathroom showed any signs of a struggle?"

She shook her head, "No idea. Sutherland could tell you."

"How about the body? Were there bruises, or signs he was held down?" Val hadn't been able to tell me, but surely Daphne knew more.

She shrugged. So much for that.

"Did the authorities conduct an autopsy?" I pressed. "Check to see if he'd been drugged?"

"Authorities? What authorities?"

"Well, the local police. Surely, they—"

"No," Val replied. "The police weren't involved."

"Why not?"

Daphne answered, "Doctor Ridgeway said there was no reason to. He's the local coroner, as well as the family physician.

He declared that the cause of death was accidental drowning, wrote out a death certificate, and that was that."

"And nobody even looked into the possibility?"

Val shook his head. "Nope. Nobody questioned it, at least as far as I'm aware."

I pondered that.

"So, if you two are suggesting that this Fitzhugh character had something to do with it—"

"We are," Daphne interjected.

"Then are we to assume that Erasmus sat calmly in his bath while furtive Fitzhugh skulked into the bathroom carrying a copy of an apocryphal gospel and a giant marble? And then kept sitting there, calmly, while the man shoved the marble into his mouth and held him under the water until he peacefully passed away? No struggle? No fight? Nothing to arouse the interest of your so-called doctor? I don't buy it."

"You're right," Val agreed.

"And that applies to whoever else we may suspect of killing him. Look, it's all very well for us to sit here and play Holmes and Watson."

"Ooh, can I be an Irregular?" Daphne said in an exaggerated Cockney accent. "I've always wanted to be an Irregular, guv."

"Can one be both Honorable and Irregular?" I asked.

"You've just described the royal family," Val replied.

I laughed. "My point is we're woefully ill-equipped for this job. Val, you know less about being a detective than you know about most things. And you know very little about most things. And my sole claim to detective experience is solving fictional crimes that I essentially plan and commit myself. I know the murderer, motive, and all the clues from page one. This is totally different."

"Well, what would Zoltan Szabo do?" Daphne asked. "Isn't this like the murder in *Zoltan Szabo and the Windmill of Death*?"

"Good lord!" Val exclaimed. "You've actually read his books?"

"Could you possibly say that with less astonishment?" I asked with feigned offense. "But no. In *Windmill of Death*, the Swiss ambassador was shot by the fake opera singer using a poison dart and a blowgun. I'm not seeing a parallel to Erasmus."

"Oh," she said. "Sorry. Wrong book. Which is the mystery where that Chinese butler was found dead inside an ancient Egyptian sarcophagus?"

"*Zoltan Szabo and the Pharaoh's Pagoda*."

"Oh yes," she paused. "And now that I think about it, finding a Chinese butler in an Egyptian sarcophagus isn't very much like drowning in your bathtub with a marble in your mouth and a book in your lap, either."

"Now that you mention it though," I said, "it *is* a bit like the murder in *Zoltan Szabo and the Copper Ballerina*."

"Right! Where the priest is found in the confessional stabbed through the heart with the butter knife."

"I'm sorry," Val interrupted, "but people *buy* these things? And why does every single one of your books have to start with your detective's name? Do you think people are going to forget who he is? Who could forget a name like Zooey Whoozits? Why is he Hungarian, anyway? You've never even been to Hungary. Why not someplace you've been to, like Belgium? Why not a Belgian detective?"

"It's been done," I said.

"Don't pick on Griff," Daphne said. "His books are great fun. You should read *Zoltan Szabo and the Ghost Fox of Skye*. There's an exotic dancer in that one, you'd probably like it."

"Yes," I said. "The least you can do is read one of my books. After all, I am trying to solve your brother's murder *and* keep you alive."

"Fine," he said. "Fine! I'll read *Zigfried Zeppo and the Case of the Lithuanian Death Rabbit*. Now can we please get back to the business at hand? Do any of your ridiculously named books have any bearing on what happened to Erasmus?"

"Yes," Daphne said. "He already said it's like *Zoltan Szabo and the Copper Ballerina.*"

"Where the fake Chinese priest is killed by an exotic dancer with a blowgun hiding in the sarcophagus of the ruddy Swiss Ambassador," Val said.

"I don't want to be friends anymore," I said.

"Okay, okay, I'm sorry," Val said. "Now, please. Explain!"

"Well, in *Zoltan*—" I started.

"For the love of God, please don't say the name of the book again," he pleaded.

"Right. Well, in that story the actual killer *wanted* it to look like murder so he could frame someone else for the crime. Murdering the priest wasn't really the point. The killer wanted a particular person to be arrested, tried, and hanged for the crime."

"You think someone went to all the trouble of killing Erasmus just to frame someone else for it?"

"Perhaps," I said.

"I take it back," Val said. "I'm not going to read *Zelda Zigzag and the Case of the Monkey's Bloomers*. That's an absurd idea."

"Do you have a better one?" Daphne asked.

"Well, no," he admitted. "But think about it. Who exactly would be framed by those clues? A cat's-eye green bumboozer and a book?"

"Nicodemus, perhaps," I said. "But then the murderer would have to think that *we'd* think Nicky was confessing at the scene, and we've been over that. Makes no sense."

"What in the world is a *bumboozer*?" Daphne asked.

Val looked exasperated. "What's the matter with you two? Didn't either of you play marbles as a child?"

"I was never a child," Daphne replied. "I emerged fully formed, like Venus." She struck a glamorous pose.

"Apparently Valentine Dunstan Jarlath and all his sainted brothers called shooters a bumboozer," I explained. "Madness."

"Well, there's your motive, right there," she said.

"Hey!" Val objected.

"Sorry," she said.

"Back to murder," I said, turning to Val. "I realize I've asked this twice before, but you'll have to keep explaining until it makes sense. *Why* don't you just go to the police?"

"I don't want to. Not just yet. I need to have more information before we go to the authorities."

"But why?" I asked.

"Well, I might want to hush things up."

Daphne turned to him. "That doesn't make sense. We all know it was murder. And you may be in danger. Why wouldn't you want to catch the guilty party?"

Val sighed heavily. "Look, what if it's Aunt Elsie? If she killed Erasmus, wouldn't it be better to deal with it privately, in a good hospital? Or what if... what if it was *suicide*? Would we want to tarnish Erasmus's reputation?"

"You can't honestly think dear old Elsie killed Erasmus," Daphne argued. "And Erasmus would never..." She shook her head, unable to say the word.

"Maybe. I don't know. I'm ninety-nine percent certain he was murdered by Sally and Jim. And Fitzhugh. But there's still this one percent doubt in my mind. I'd just feel better if we could get rid of that doubt before we go to anyone else with this. It's just something that I need to do."

"Huh. I think I sort of agree," I said.

"Exactly how much agreement is a *sort of*?" Val wondered.

"Well, all we really have so far is a bunch of odd circumstances. We have no proof of foul play, the death certificate says it was an accident, and now Erasmus has been cremated. If we go to the local constabulary with only a hunch, they might do a cursory investigation or they might laugh in our faces. But if we can find some real evidence, something solid, then the police will have to take our concerns seriously. So yes, I suppose I agree with Val. No police… yet."

"That rather leaves us at a loss," Daphne sighed.

"Yes, it does," I agreed. "It would be so much simpler if we could ask for an autopsy."

"Autopsy…" Val murmured. "When you think about it, doesn't autopsy mean operating on yourself?"

"What?" I asked.

"Oh, just wondering out loud. But doesn't the prefix 'auto' mean doing something by yourself?"

"What the hell are you on about? Sorry, Honorable Miss."

Val plowed on. "You know, like an autograph means signing your name. So technically, shouldn't performing an autopsy mean doing your own operation?"

I looked over at Daphne. She whispered, "We love him, but he really can be thicker than a whale omelet at times."

"No," I said. "That is not what autopsy means."

He shrugged. "I guess it doesn't really matter since we can't have one anyway."

Daphne sighed, "I'm getting discouraged."

"I'm too busy being stunned to learn that Val knows the word 'prefix' to be discouraged. But now that I think about it, I'm discouraged, too. And the more we discuss it, the less confidence I have in my ability to investigate a possible crime. Val, you have berefted me of my confidence to investigate."

"How can I bereft you? You were in Intelligence during the war," he reminded me.

"Which had nothing whatsoever to do with solving country house murders. In a war, it's obvious why people are killing each other. I highly doubt Erasmus was killed because somebody broke a treaty or assassinated an Archduke."

"See?" Val said, "You can do it. You've already eliminated two motives."

"Yes," I said. "That *does* narrow it down."

"Well," Daphne said, "I bet he wasn't killed because he broke his oath to a secret criminal society."

I nodded. "No doubt. And I also think we can write off the idea that his murder was in retribution for the role your family played in the War of Jenkins' Ear."

Val burst out laughing. "Is that the title of one your books? *Zebulon Zebedee and the War of Jenkins' Ear?*"

"No, surprisingly, it's a real thing. Against Spain. Either the tenth or eleventh time England and Spain have tried to kill each other."

"Wait, somebody's ear went to war?"

"No."

"So, somebody went to war *because* of an ear?"

"I'm not clear on the details. All I know is that some bloke named Jenkins lost his ear and then someone else put the word 'war' after it."

"You know the oddest things."

Daphne laughed. "Tell us more odd things, Uncle Griff!"

"Daph, for the love of God, don't encourage him. I'm not strong enough to hear about the time we went to war with France for crimes against snails."

I yawned, finished off the last of my cocoa, and stood up to leave. "Look. It's very late. And it's been a wildly bizarre day. Let me sleep on things. I might be smarter in my sleep than I am awake."

"Doubtful," Val observed.

"But one more thing I would like to know," I said, turning to Daphne. "I asked Val who was in the house the day Erasmus died. He started making a list, but then it turned from possible suspects into a list of his favorite ties."

"I was organizing!" Val protested.

"So please, Honorable Miss, who exactly was in the house the day that Erasmus died? Aunt Conrad and Uncle Maryanne, Aunt Elsie…?"

"And Nicky and Wulfie."

"What were they doing here?" I asked.

"I'm not entirely sure," she said. "Wulfie was probably down here for the horse races at Bloomfield, like a good communist. He never misses an opportunity to prove he has no idea how to pick a winner. I think Nicky was just here for the free food and drink. He often shows up to dine on the family dollar. But he and Sally did spend a lot of time behind closed doors. Maybe he had another of his ridiculous schemes."

"Interesting," I yawned. "Val, your family is exhausting. Present company excluded, of course. I'm for bed."

"Okay," Val said. "But before you both leave, can we give this room another going over?"

Ten minutes and one room search later, I staggered back to my chamber and readied for bed. My last thought before falling asleep was, *I wonder what I did at Waterloo to earn a medal.*

Chapter 12

I DIDN'T GET much sleep that night. Ideas tumbled through my mind in fascinating confusion. For half the night, I fixated on Val's insane family, curses, and the general lunatic goings on at Wombat-under-Toast. Then, thoroughly softened up, my brain began stringing nonsense syllables together to invent new saint names. They were almost as lunatic as the real ones.

By the time I finally drifted off at about three in the morning, I had worked out most of the plot to *Zoltan Szabo and the Curse of Saint Thrumnipple*. Finally, Catullus decided he'd enough and curled up on top of my head, a feline nightcap whose warm purr lulled me to sleep at last.

* * *

BREAKFAST WAS A help-yourself affair with hot dishes on the sideboard and, best of all, a continually refilled toast rack.

I love toast. I could eat an entire loaf for breakfast. Skip the eggs. Hold the sausages. And I cannot face any form of fish first thing in the morning. Give me endless toast and coffee, fresh butter, and strawberry jam, and I am a happy man.

That morning, I was a happy man.

I was on my eighth or ninth piece of toast when Daphne came in. I stood politely, checking my chin for breadcrumbs under the guise of a scratch.

"Good morning, Miss Ferguson."

Her blue eyes twinkled. "Good morning, Mr. Griffin."

She made the rounds of the chafing dishes and returned with a plate of eggs and bacon, taking the seat opposite mine.

"Coffee or tea?" I asked, indicating the pots at my right hand.

"Coffee, please." She held out her cup for me to fill. "Thanks. Tea isn't enough to start the morning when you know it will be a tough day."

"Do you know it'll be a tough day?"

She nodded. "Bound to be. First of all, we're burying… um, laying Erasmus to rest tomorrow, and I can hardly think of anything else. But we'll need to start investigating. We can't just sit on the sidelines and speculate. Today, we must start talking to people and looking for clues."

"And what," I asked, "do you think a clue looks like?"

"You know… a clue," she asserted, as if it were obvious. "A bloody fingerprint."

"There was no blood," I countered.

"A muddy footprint, then," she replied.

"It happened inside."

"A pile of cigar ash?"

"Ah yes," I said portentously, "The infamous clue of the cigar ash. Luckily, I have written a monograph on that very subject. The non-existent cigar ashes in this case prove that the killer was left-handed man who has spent some time in India, has a wooden leg and a cocker spaniel, and is probably a Freemason. Elementary!"

"Oh, do shut up, Mister Holmes."

"But of course, Miss Adler," I said with a smile.

"Well, without the police here we are somewhat hampered," Daphne observed. "But in the plus column, we know more about the victim and the possible suspects than the police ever could. I think we need an official council of war. Figure out our plan of attack."

"You sound like a general."

"I think I'd make a great general," she stated. "And as a general, I think that we need to sit down and come up with some practical work we can do. Make a list of staff members to interview, perhaps, or conduct a thorough search of Erasmus's room. Something like that. We're three intelligent people, so we should be able to come up with a plan."

"Well, you and I are obviously intelligent, but I have my doubts about Val. Remember, I went to school with him. There was many an occasion where his brains were conspicuous by their absence. Ask him who won the Wars of the Roses."

She laughed in anticipation. "Do tell?"

"Once, when we were studying Roman history, Val was napping or daydreaming and when the Classics master asked Val what he knew about Julius Caesar, Val answered that Julius Caesar was a character in a play who died. That was it."

Nicky oozed into the room with a supercilious air and too much Brilliantine in his hair. It wasn't even the good stuff. It was the cheap kind that always made me think of darts players and the sort of people who say, "*no offense, but—*" right before offending you.

"Good morning, Daphne." He gave her an oily smile before sending the briefest of glances in my direction. I watched as he loaded up a plate with great quantities of pretty much everything. Except toast. One more reason for me not to like him. I also found his suit appalling. It was funereal black, but there was a strange, artificial shininess to it that matched his hair. He looked like a greased mortician.

"Good morning, Nicky," said Daphne politely, rolling her eyes behind his back.

"Where's Val?"

"I believe he's in the study," I said.

"Do either of you know anything about the arrangements

for the funeral? I'd like to know when I can get out of here and back to London. I've important business there." He made it sound like he had an urgent meeting with the Chancellor of the Exchequer.

Did he actually think anybody believed his charades? Nicky combined the innocent stupidity of a not-very-bright-sheep with the untrustworthiness of a Borgia.

"Ah, yes," I said with fake brightness, "your mother said you were something to do with high finance in the City. Where do you work?"

He got a pinched, sort of bad-taste-in-the-mouth look. "Sheffield Commercial. Venerable institution, one of the finest."

"And what do you do there?"

"Uh... Temporarily learning from the ground up, I'm afraid. They require all their Directors to spend time working in a branch position." He stopped bragging long enough to shovel in some eggs, then spoke around them. "At the moment I am advising our, uh... less-wealthy clients."

"People like me," Daphne said. "I'm very less wealthy."

"Oh!" I said, picking up the newspaper I had folded by my plate. "I'm sorry, this must be yours. I'm sure you'll want to check the headlines."

I passed him the day's *Financial Record*. With a look of extreme distaste, he had no choice but to take it. "Thanks. I'll... read it later. Always like to savor it over the second cup of coffee, you know."

"Look here, even more public outcry about that Megatherium Trust crash," I observed, testing the subject that had shut him up the previous evening.

To my fascinated delight, he again took on a lovely, mottled greenish-white shade. He swallowed so deeply that his prominent Adam's apple bobbled at me like a conductor's baton. "Um... ahem..."

I continued: "As a financial outsider, I simply don't understand all the details. Perhaps you could explain. I'm sure Miss Ferguson would be as fascinated as I to get your *expert* opinion."

As Nicodemus squirmed, Val walked in.

"Good morning, all," Val said, sailing over to the sideboard to gather his breakfast. He sat down, oblivious to the awkward silence and Nicky's discomfort, and smiled at us. "Where's cousin Wulfie?"

"Val," Daphne said, "you know you can't expect Wulfie to show his face before the clock hits double digits."

"Actually, he already left," Nicky said around a mouthful of sausage.

"Left?" Val asked. "Has he returned to London already? He's not staying for the funeral?"

"No." Nicky changed things up by speaking with his mouth full of bacon this time. "He went up to Tacker's Farm. They're having their monthly pig races."

"On the morning of Erasmus's funeral?" Daphne exclaimed.

I choked a bit on my food, but still somehow managed to swallow before speaking, "Your brother likes pig races?"

"Not particularly," Nicky smiled snidely. "He likes gambling. Pigs. Horses. Dogs. If there were hippopotamus races, he'd bet on those. Plus poker and roulette, of course."

"Hippo racing is a dangerous hobby. Is he usually lucky?"

The snide smile turned into a snide laugh. "Only when he's able to hide from his bookmakers!"

The rest of the meal was excruciatingly polite. We commented with tiresome predictability on the weather, gardening, and the plot of "*A Toucan in the Teacup*," the latest West End hit that none of us had seen but all of us discussed as if we had.

Nicodemus, still seemingly rattled, lost the ability to even pretend to be interested. "Uh… excuse me," he said at last. "I really need to… uh… check the markets."

"It's Saturday," I observed.

"In Zurich," he called over his shoulder.

"Am I reading too much into it," I said once the sound of his footsteps had faded, "or did we just get two potential motives out of Nicky?"

"I don't think you're reading too much, but you may be reading the wrong book. Nicky didn't say anything," Val said.

"Oh, but he did," Daphne argued. "He reminded us Wulfie has a gambling problem and is often in debt to the brotherhood of the turf. He could be really in need of money. But that's only one motive." She looked at me.

"Did you see his face when I mentioned the Megatherium crash? And that's the second time. What are the odds he sunk a packet into that swindle?"

"High," Val said after thinking for a moment. "Very high. If he's a financial genius, I'm Louise Brooks."

"Hi, Louise. Tell me, do you think Nicky might be speculating with someone else's money?"

"I'd bet on it," Daphne replied. "I know he thought the Megatherium deal was a sure thing. He said as much to me a few months ago. He acted like he was giving me a hot tip as a favor, but I could tell he was really hitting me up for cash. And I'm not exactly rolling in it."

"Interesting," I pondered for a moment.

Val asked, "Well, what do you think?"

"I think we should divide and conquer."

"Oh? Who's being divided and who's being conquered?"

"We three are dividing up the work and conquering all the suspects."

"Excellent! I can talk to the servants," Daphne offered. "I've known most of them since I was a little girl. And since I'm not a member of the Hatton-Haxley family, they might open up to me. Less need for formality."

"Good idea," Val said.

"Oh," Daphne recalled, "I was chatting with Mary when she brought my morning tea earlier, and she informed me that the constable in the village actually *was* called when Erasmus died. I guess I didn't see him."

"Did Mary tell you what the police did? If anything?" I asked.

"Unfortunately," she explained, "the nearest proper police station is miles away, in Danforth. Hatton-Under-Tower is under the somnolent eye of Constable Dunn. Who is commonly referred to as Constable Undone. I don't think he's investigated anything more complicated than the crime spree that occurred when Mrs. Ramsey's dog got loose and ran through the village stealing washing off the lines. As I recall, he was upset to learn he couldn't arrest the dog."

"Then I suppose we shouldn't expect any help from that quarter. If Miss Ferguson—"

"Daphne," she corrected. "If we're going to be partners in anti-crime, we should at least be on a first-name basis."

"*His* name is Gideon Plantagenet," Val said snidely. Daphne turned a snort of laughter into a cough.

"Is it really?"

"Sadly, yes. But please, call me Griff."

"I'd rather call you Plantagenet. You look like a Plantagenet. Don't you think he looks like a Plantagenet, Val?"

"No," Val replied. "I think he looks more like an Irving. Or maybe a Zebadiah. Yes, definitely. Zebadiah."

"Absolutely not," I asserted. "Being called Zebadiah would give people the impression that we're related. And then someone might try to kill *me*. And that would be a real tragedy."

"Why would your impending death be more tragic than mine?" Val asked.

"Because I have a cat to feed."

Val started to reply, but a sound from somewhere had caught

my ear. I signaled for silence and tiptoed to the door, then yanked it open.

"Just checking," I said. "It occurs to me that we should be more cautious discussing our suspicions in the house. A family who enjoys a little light murder would hardly balk at listening through keyholes."

"Good point," Daphne agreed.

"Can you actually hear anything through a keyhole?" Val asked. "I mean, have either of you ever tried it? They're awfully small, aren't they?"

"Val," I said. "We're trying to find a murderer. Why are you nattering on about keyholes?"

"Sorry, that's just how my mind works," he replied.

"Are you certain that it *does* work?"

"Whether or not you can hear anything through a keyhole," Daphne interjected, "Griff is right about eavesdropping. We're toying with fire. Let's go into the garden and talk where we can't be overheard."

But first, we went upstairs for more appropriate shoes. Before entering my room, I walked over to Val's door and put my ear to the keyhole.

I heard him humming.

Chapter 13

Our garden walk was enjoyable but brought us no closer to a plan. We soaked up a beautiful morning. The sky was a clear, Renaissance blue, and the air was filled with the comforting smells of old roses and new-cut grass. It was hard to believe, on such a glorious day, that we were surrounded by mystery and murder and family secrets.

At the southern end of the property was a small pond, where Val and Daphne engaged in a rock skipping contest. Never having been able to skip rocks, much to my childhood shame, I sat down and let my mind wander. And had a rare moment of brilliance.

"Drake!" I called out.

Val did a hilariously balletic turn as I startled him mid-skip. "What the hell, Griff?"

"Drake," I repeated.

Daphne looked up at the sky and then looked at me. "Are you trying to warn us about ducks?"

"No," I explained. "Inspector Hugo Drake, CID. We served together during the war. He helps me out from time to time when Zoltan has a question that I can't answer."

"You mean Zoltan Szabo isn't all-seeing, all-knowing?" Val asked.

"Oh, he is. The problem is that I'm not."

"True."

"Ignoring that," I said, "I think I might be able to convince Hugo Drake to give me some unofficial help if I need it."

"Does he owe you a favor?" Val asked.

"Well, I did save his life once, so I think he might be agreeable to giving us some assistance."

"Was this in the war?" Daphne asked, intrigued.

"It was, but I didn't save him in the way you might think."

"So how did you save his life?" Val asked.

"I talked him into breaking up with a malevolent harpy named Christine Peterson. He thought he was in love with her. I convinced him he wasn't."

"That's horrible!" Daphne flamed at me.

"No, it wasn't. She was only with him because his family has money."

"You can't be sure of that," she scolded.

"Oh no, I can. She admitted it. Hugo Drake is the son of Sir Winfield Drake, the art collector. Lots of lovely old family money. I overheard Miss Peterson talking to a friend once. She apparently believed that closing a curtain automatically renders any conversation completely silent to people standing outside the window, and blabbed it all. I confronted her, she admitted it, and then tried to get me to ask her out to dinner."

"Oh," Daphne conceded. "In that case, you did save his life."

"That's our first order of business, then," Val said. "You ring up your Scotland Yard pal, perhaps get us a few leads on how to start, and then we'll get to work."

"Aha!" Daphne said, "A cunning plan. The game is afoot!"

"Daphne," I said. "I like you. Please, never say the game is afoot again."

* * *

When I first met Inspector Hugo Drake, he was First Lieutenant Hugo Drake, an intelligence officer newly assigned to my section. I thought they'd mistakenly sent me a Boy Scout. But I soon learned that this baby-faced son of privilege had a quick and interesting mind and a knack for sizing people up. It didn't surprise me at all when he joined the police after the Armistice.

As I waited for the operator to connect us, I tried to predict how he'd react to Val's incredible story. I had rejected mere skepticism, moved past suspicion and landed on derisive laughter by the time he answered.

"Drake here."

"Report, Lieutenant Drake!" I barked.

He laughed in recognition. "Nothing to report, sir. Except that I'm on desk duty."

"Uh-oh, what's wrong?" I asked, "Has Scotland Yard finally realized you've misplaced your brain cell?"

"No, I've still got them fooled. But I have a broken ankle."

"How did you manage to do that?"

"It was a failed arrest involving a safe cracker named Lou the Seal, an errant constable with two left feet, and a rather inconveniently placed fire hydrant."

"Ouch. How long are you out of action?"

"It's only been three days. I'm desk-bound for a least another week or two."

"Oh, good," I said. "You're probably nice and bored by now."

"You wouldn't accuse me of being bored if you knew I was ignoring a raft of paperwork to read *Zoltan Szabo and the Puppet of Doom*."

"Then no, you're not at all bored. You're thrilled. Enthralled. Thrilled *and* enthralled. Thrilled, enthralled, and—"

He laughed again, "Yes, it's a good book. You're the best author on the planet. Every book should be written by you."

"Thank you for finally admitting that."

"But police time is supposed to be valuable, so what do you want? You never call unless you need my help. Has Zoltan apprehended Jack the Ripper? Does he need to know how long it takes for cyanide to kill a walrus? Do you need me to explain rigor mortis again?"

"Not at the moment," I replied. "But I'll get back to you about the cyanide. No, this time I'm reaching out to you about a real murder. Well, a *possible* real murder."

"A possible real murder," he repeated. "I know the words, but the sequence escapes me."

"I'm going to tell you about what we think is an actual murder, but I'm not making an official report. Can I talk to you off the record and get your perspective?"

"Griff," he returned, suddenly serious, "If we're really talking about murder here, not just one of your novels, then I can't play counselor. I have a duty to act on it."

"Hmm…" I thought for a moment. "Strike that. Forget I said it. I'm just going to go with a *hypothetical* actual murder."

"You're a writer, Griff. You know words. And you come up with a nonsense phrase like *hypothetical actual murder*?"

"Just be quiet and listen," I said. "Let's pretend that there's a titled family with a multi-generational curse that predicts the firstborn son of every heir will die before he inherits from his father."

"This isn't hypothetical," Drake observed. "It's Oedipus."

"It isn't Oedipus. You obviously don't know Sophocles."

"The Greek restaurant by Charing Cross Hospital?"

"How in the world did you ever graduate from university?"

"By studying as little as possible. Griff, you're not trying out an idea for your next book, are you? Because frankly, it sounds ridiculous."

"No, this is real. And hypothetical," I added quickly. "So, in this family… we'll call them the Smiths."

"Very imaginative."

I ignored him. "Since the 17th century, no eldest son of the

Smith family has ever inherited from his father. Every one of them has died."

"Please tell me you don't want me to investigate a three-hundred-year-old curse," he pleaded.

"I'm not asking you to investigate anything. Just listen."

He listened. And aside from a few sounds of disbelief, he didn't speak until I was finished.

"You're not pulling my leg with all this, are you?" He had the same tone of bewildered disbelief I'd heard in *my* voice when Val first told me the story.

"Nope. Sorry."

"Valentine Hatton-Haxley honestly believes his uncle has murdered his brother. Is that what you're telling me?"

I think my jaw literally dropped. It was the first time I'd ever experienced the whole jaw-dropping thing. I'd always assumed it was just a metaphor. But, no, mine dropped. Something popped when it did. It rather hurt. I don't recommend jaw dropping as a hobby.

"I didn't name any names!" I protested.

"Well, forgive me if I heard at the club that Valentine's brother died last week. Or for using my highly exceptional detective skills to deduce that you don't know anyone else whose brother died last week."

I sighed, "If you say *'Elementary, dear Watson,'* I'm hanging up."

"Good," he said. "Elementary, dear Watson. Now please hang up. I'm busy and would be more than happy to get back to not helping you."

"You're not busy," I pointed out. "You're hiding in your office, reading my book."

"It's a fair cop."

"So, what's the verdict? Will you help? After all, you owe me." Guilt was such a successful weapon against reluctance.

"I do? What do I owe you?"

"Drake, I have two words for you: Christine Peterson."

"That's a low blow," he groused.

"I know," I replied. "That's why it'll be successful."

There was a moment of silence on the other end, and I pictured Drake in his tiny, ruthlessly messy office. He'd be surrounded by piles of folders and a hoard of notepads, pencils, and dirty teacups. A chain-smoking squirrel gathering acorns of evidence to help grow the tree of justice... I stopped myself. I was beginning to sound like my colleague Mortimer O'Malley.

Drake sighed again. He was very eloquent with his sighs. "You're putting me in a difficult position," he said. "I'm supposed to investigate crimes myself, not act as house mother for a bunch of civilians."

"Hey!" I protested.

"Griff, you *are* a civilian. You and your detective are very smart, although I'm pretty sure you're not as smart as Zoltan. But if a crime has been committed, you need to involve the law. Officially."

"I will," I said. "But right now, we're not even sure if a crime *has* been committed. Once we know for sure that Erasmus really was murdered, I promise I'll hand everything over to the constables. We just don't want to drag in the local plod if Val is overreacting."

"I suppose I should object to that slur upon my rural brethren, but if there's a valid coroner's certificate, no evidence, not even a body to examine..." He sighed. "All right, Griff. What do you want me to do?"

"Bless you, my son. Just now I want you to find about a man named Gilbert Fitzhugh. Formerly a sergeant, now in service to Lord Sulpicius Hatton-Haxley. He's got a bad reputation and I'll kiss your goldfish if it turns out he doesn't have a record."

"Oh, please don't. He startles easily."

"So far, this Fitzhugh has our vote as the most likely candidate.

I feel like Val's uncle Sulpicius is behind the whole thing, but Fitzhugh was the one who killed Erasmus."

"Sulpicius and Erasmus," he mused. "Wherever does that family find those names? Right, I'll call you if I find anything. And I need your word that if you discover anything that might be evidence, you'll let me know. I'm walking a fine line here, Griff. I can't stay silent if I have knowledge of a crime. It could cost me my job."

"What crime? Everything I said was speculation, remember."

"Yes, well, I speculate that I am going to regret helping you. A murder allegation is no joke. Be careful, Griff."

Chapter 14

Val and Daphne had been quietly chatting, but stopped when I rang off.

"Well?" Val asked.

"Drake agreed to look into Fitzhugh. But he's not happy about me being involved in a possible crime. If this turns serious, we'll have to tell him everything."

Val nodded. "Yes, I know. I'm resigned to the fact that we will eventually have to go to the police."

I looked around the study, distracted by a portrait that Val identified as Great-grandfather Adjutor, standing on the ramparts of the Hall. For some reason known only to God and Great-grandfather, for I wasn't sure even the artist knew why, he was portrayed in the manner of an Admiral heroically surveying his fleet. He wore a vaguely nautical jacket with gold braid on the sleeve and a preposterously rakish, feathered hat. He was also holding a spyglass. This ridiculous prop was pointed at ships in a distant and wholly imaginary harbor.

I imagined the goal of all this pomp and circumstance was to gain in oil paint what gallantry he lacked in life. Unfortunately, the effect was more like a third-rate rep company's production of *H.M.S. Pinafore*.

Fortunately, some part of my brain suddenly lit up with a fresh distraction, saving me from my existing distraction.

"Excuse me for just one minute," I said to Val and Daphne.

"I need to make another call." I gave the operator the number and after an interval of clicks and buzzes, I was speaking with Archibald Mannering, one of the best one-armed jazz guitarists in the country. I was one of the few people to know that before he lost the arm, he was an extremely successful art thief.

In between putting down the thievery and picking up the guitar, he took his proceeds and invested in the markets. With great success. In fact, he owns a castle.

I had helped Archie not die in the war and he had returned the favor by telling me everything I got wrong in *Zoltan Szabo and the Curious Case of the Cursed Caravaggio*.

We exchanged our usual pleasantries. Or rather his was the usual, mine was infinitely more sanitized due to Daphne's presence. I got straight down to business.

"Archie, what do you know about the Megatherium crash?"

"Oh, good Lord, don't tell me you were in on that. What a bloody mess."

"No, nothing to do with me. But I think someone I know was."

"Friend of yours?" Archie asked, cautiously.

"Quite the contrary."

"Good. What do you want?"

"If I give you a couple of names, do you think you could possibly find out if they were investors?"

"I think so. There are a few people who owe me favors."

I gave him Sally and Nicky's names, asked after his mother, and promised a drink soon.

"You've got a bee in your bonnet about that Megatooth Trust thing," Val said as I rang off for the second time.

"No. But I think the *Megatherium* crash might be important. The timing is just too close for comfort."

"And even if it has nothing to do with the murder," Daphne said, "It would prove to the world what idiots they are. I wouldn't trust either of them with a thimble."

"See?" Val smiled. "She's the smart cousin. Erasmus always thought so, too."

"Tell me about Erasmus," I said, abruptly.

"What do you mean? You knew him yourself," Val protested.

"Not really. I spent some time here when I was, what, fifteen? Sixteen? I ran into him in London once or twice. But that doesn't mean I knew him. And I need to. And not just the good stuff, either. I need the juicy bits."

"Griff!" Daphne protested.

"Daphne, we're awfully short on evidence and clues here so let's at least have the story. Who might have hated him? Who might he have hated? Who benefits? Who would be capable, both physically and psychologically, of murder? Is there another motive for killing Erasmus other than the inheritance bingo?"

"He's right, Daph," Val said, glumly.

"So," I concluded, "let's go back to that day and go over everything again. Now, who was at breakfast?"

"I told you," Daphne sighed. "Erasmus and I, Uncle Sally and Aunt Jim, Aunt Elsie, Wulfie, Nicky. Oh! Oh, I completely forgot! Angela Astley was here."

"Oh, goody," I said. "Another new character. Who is she and when did she arrive?"

"Ah, the ghastly Miss Astley," Val said, and Daphne laughed.

"What makes her ghastly?" I asked.

Daphne looked at me with an expression of nauseating soppiness and batted her eyes. She adopted a breathless, brittle, little cut-glass voice and cooed, "Oh, Mr. Griffin, why I'm just *thrilled* to meet such an important man. I tried to read one of your books once and I had to put it down, it was so *thrilling*, too *thrilling* for a delicate little rosebud such as I. Why I was positively *thrilled*!"

Each time she used the word "thrill" she pronounced it as if it had five L's in it.

"Oh dear, one of those."

"Yes. She's the *soulful* type. Convinced every man she meets is either in love with her or just about to fall in love with her."

"Who is she?"

"She's sort of a goddaughter to Aunt Jim," Val said. "The daughter of an old school friend. Aunt Jim has made it her mission in life to marry Angela off to whichever one of my brothers was the Earl at the time. Invites her down for extended visits that last about a month, always tries to throw her and the Earl together. '*Erasmus, why don't you go riding with dear Angela, she needs some roses in her beautiful cheeks.*'"

"Just think, Val," Daphne said. "She's your problem now."

"That's evil," he protested. "As if impending death wasn't threat enough, you throw Angela at me."

"I'm sure she'd make a lovely Countess," Daphne teased.

"She'd make a better doorstop."

"You'll see for yourself, soon," Daphne said to me. "According to Aunt Jim she's arriving from London on the three o'clock train." I saw Val shiver.

"So, ghastly Miss Astley was here. But nobody said or did anything out of the ordinary at breakfast that day?" I asked. They shook their heads *no*. "Then let's move on to when you got back from your ride."

Daphne leaned back and closed her eyes, as if trying to see a film playing in her head. Her account of the morning was unchanged from the night before: She and Erasmus had returned to the stables at about ten, handed off their mounts, and returned to the Hall. They asked for tea in the morning room and afterwards Daphne said they needed to get ready or else they'd be late for the wedding. She went upstairs to change, with Erasmus saying he was just going to finish the last scone, and that he had something he needed to take care of in the study, and that was the last time she saw him.

"And later," I asked, "when you learned about Erasmus? You said you went to his room but didn't go in."

"Right, Sutherland stopped me. But I heard Lydgate and one of the footmen in the bath and I heard Fitzhugh in there, too. I could hear them talking, but I couldn't hear the words, if that makes sense."

"It does," I said, encouragingly.

"Mary was crying and I gave her a hug. That's where I was when Sally arrived. He walked right past me and went into Erasmus's room without saying a word to anyone."

"Was Aunt Ralph with him?"

"No. I never saw her upstairs at all. I didn't see her until later when we were all downstairs."

"And how did she react to the news, do you know? Was she upset? Crying, perhaps?"

She gave a sort of half-smile. "No, Aunt Jim doesn't cry. She doesn't believe in emotions. She was sort of pinched looking. The way she gets when her plans are upset."

There really wasn't much to say to that aside from a non-committal "hmm," so I *hmm*-ed and decided to change course.

"Tell me more about Aunt Elsie."

"Well, like I said," Val answered, "she came for a visit when I was about ten and has mostly stayed on ever since. Occasionally she would disappear for a few months or a year, having moved in with some other household, only to reappear again. Then one time she came back for good."

"And she lives here with Uncle Louise and Aunt Gregory?"

"She does," Val said, "but the boys spend most of their time in London. They have privacy there, and no Elsie. I don't think any of them like her very much."

"They think she's just plain mad," Daphne observed.

"Is she mad?"

"Not as mad as she appears," Daphne said.

"I've always thought that her persona was twenty percent for show and eighty percent legitimately gaga," Val added.

"You can't possibly consider her a suspect," Daphne said.

"No, not really," I mused. "But I'd like to know more about her. You've said you don't think she's dangerous."

Daphne answered instantly, "Oh, no. Elsie's eccentric, that's all. She really does believe in past lives, but in this life, she knows who she is. I mean she doesn't think she's Joan of Arc or Anne Boleyn. Not *now*, anyway. And she doesn't stick pins in dolls or have a lamp for a best friend."

"Val, do you think she's dangerous?" I asked.

"No," he said. "I don't think so. She's more than capable of causing morbid embarrassment, but I don't think she'd be capable of causing actual death."

"Uncle Sally and Aunt Jim, however, are a different kettle of stinky fish," Daphne commented.

"They seem like very uncomfortable people," I said. "How are they to live with?"

Val gave a silent laugh. "That whole branch used to live exclusively in the London house. It's part of the estate, but father always told Sally to think of it as theirs, and they do. But Sally and Jim came back here as soon as their three monsters launched into the world. They have their own wing."

"I think they prefer to live here because the Earl covers all the bills, so they save on essentials like vintage port and imported cigars," Daphne added.

I thought for a moment. "Did Erasmus mind that they were living here?"

"Certainly, he did," Val answered. "They are deeply unpleasant to have around. But there wasn't anything he could do about it. They have a legal right to live here."

"Does Elsie?"

"What? Have a legal right to live here? No. But as far as

I'm concerned, she has a *moral* right. My parents invited her to make her home here, so this is her home."

"That's sweet," Daphne smiled.

"I'm quite fond of the old bird. Besides, her presence annoys Aunt Jim, which is a fine reason to keep her around."

"Getting back to the crime," I said, "was Aunt Elsie upstairs when you went up to Erasmus's room?"

"I'm not sure. I don't recall seeing her there, but everything was so confused…" Daphne shook her head.

"Right then, one last time: both of you are convinced Aunt Elsie is innocent?"

"Oh yes," Daphne said. "She's harmless. She may have an interest in séances and tarot cards, things like that, but it's not as if she thinks she's a witch. Though I think she does honestly believe she can speak to the dead and that they tell her how people are going to die."

Val jumped in. "But she's never been right! Never once."

"So don't worry if she tells you that you're going to be run over by an ocean liner or mauled by a tiger. You're safe," Daphne said.

Val turned to me. "Has she predicted your death yet?"

"No. But I just met her yesterday. Maybe she needs to observe me before she pronounces sentence."

Daphne looked at me with mock sorrow. "I'm going to disappear. In Africa."

Val laughed. "Really? That's wild, even for her."

"I'm quite looking forward to it," she said. "I've always wanted to go to Africa."

"When you go," I said, "make sure you bring a good map."

"And a compass," Val added.

"Let's move on to the staff," I said. "What about Lydgate?"

Val said, "Lydgate, like Caesar's wife, is beyond reproach."

"But what do you know about him?"

Val thought for a moment. "Absolutely unflappable. If the

King arrived unannounced for Christmas dinner, he'd manage to turn out a feast without blinking an eye."

"I think we need to talk to him," Daphne said. "I doubt there's much that goes on here that Lydgate doesn't know about."

"And what about Erasmus's valet, Sutherland?"

"Again, Lydgate can give you all the details. Sutherland's only been here a little over a year, but the fellow seems to be capable and honest. I know Erasmus liked him."

"Did Sutherland like him in return?" I asked.

Val thought for a moment. "I think so. I never heard of any friction between them."

"Do you know how he came to work here? What happened to Erasmus's previous valet?"

Daphne answered, "That was Pagett. He married a woman from the village and the two of them took over the White Boar, one of the pubs. Her father's the landlord there. Sutherland came from the King."

"I was unaware that His Majesty sent valets out to work in the ancestral homes of his Peers."

Val chuckled. "The King Agency. It's an employment firm for household help."

"Ah. Now for the big guns. Tell me a bit more about the suspicious Mr. Fitzhugh."

Val answered. "He's a tough character with an intense loyalty to my uncle and, I should think, very few scruples."

"What about the rumors you mentioned? Theft and murder. Do you believe them?"

"I think there's a great deal of truth to them. As to the one about him killing that POW, I don't know but I wouldn't be at all surprised if it were true. I'd absolutely believe it of him."

"So would I," Daphne added. "I don't like him. I never have."

"For any specific reason?"

She shrugged. "Not really. To be honest, I've had very little interaction with him. It's just one of those instances where you get a bad feeling from someone but can't explain why."

"Do you know if he and Erasmus had any problems?"

"I don't know."

"None of us ever liked him," Val said. "Including Erasmus. Fitzhugh is Uncle Sally's man and sticks close to him. The rest of the family rarely sees him. You might want to talk to Lydgate, though. Being staff, Fitzhugh dines in the kitchen with the others. They'd probably be able to tell you more than we could."

"Do you know why he's so loyal to Uncle Suspicious?"

Val thought for a moment. "Money, probably, and power."

"Power?" I asked. "What kind of power does your uncle have?"

"Perhaps power isn't the right word. But I think Fitzhugh is the kind of soldier that likes the importance of rank. He probably felt lost when he was invalided out. But Uncle Sally came along and made him important again. Right hand to a lord? That's a strong inducement to someone like Fitzhugh."

"Val," I looked at him in surprise. "That's a very insightful answer. Are you feeling all right?"

"No. I'm suddenly overcome with a strong urge to hit my best friend over the head with a small log."

"I feel so loved," I said. "What about that doctor your uncle called in, Ridgeway? Do you trust him?"

Daphne responded, "I'm not sure. I suppose he knows his business. An old India hand, always talking about his glory days in Simla, when he apparently saved the Viceroy from certain death. But he's a snob and a gossip. Loves to name-drop about Lady So-and-so's gall stones and Lord Whatsits lumbago. He's thick as thieves with Uncle Sally. Sally used his influence to get Doctor Ridgeway posted as the local coroner, so he might feel obliged to do him a favor. And he *is* awfully fond of money." She paused. "Erasmus despised the man. I guess I do, too, if it comes to that."

"Did he?" Val asked. "Why?"

"Like I said, he's a snob. He'd drop everything to help Sally bandage a hangnail, but he wouldn't lift a finger to treat the poorer families in the village. Last year the child of one of tenant farmers nearly lost his leg after an accident because Dr. Ridgeway was playing golf with Sally and refused to cut the game short. When Erasmus found out, he reported Ridgeway to the General Medical Council."

"Did Ridgeway know about that?" I asked.

"Oh, yes. He was reprimanded, but nothing else came of it."

"Then Ridgeway had a reason to hate Erasmus."

"Absolutely." She paused. "Do you think he might have plotted with Sally?"

"Anything is possible," I said. "Especially where money or a professional reputation is at stake."

"That's true," Daphne said. "Wasn't there a crooked doctor who falsified an autopsy in *Zoltan Szabo and the Electric Scorpion*?"

"Good lord," Val exclaimed. "How many of these books have you written?"

"All of them," I replied.

"You know, we never really finished talking about Erasmus," Daphne observed.

"We never really began," I corrected.

"Well… Erasmus was nice," Val said. And then stopped.

"Nice?"

"Nice."

"That's all?"

"It's really the best way to describe him," Daphne agreed. "Erasmus was a nice man. Kind, considerate, polite. Perhaps not the sharpest card in the deck, but well-intentioned and extremely likeable."

"So, nothing like me," Val added.

"Nothing," I agreed.

Daphne continued: "But 'nice' also means harmless. I don't think he'd ever offended anyone, done anyone ill, made any enemies. Erasmus didn't seduce village maidens or steal from the church collection plate. He wasn't blackmailing a duchess or cheating at cards."

"Yet we have a pile of suspects," Val said. "My entire family and my uncle's pet snake. Maybe even Ridgeway, if we're feeling generous."

I looked steadily at Val.

"And *you*, of course."

"What?!" Val shrieked. I'd never heard him shriek before. I was impressed. It was a sharp sound, somewhere between a peacock and piccolo. "You think I killed Erasmus?"

"Not at all," I said. "And even if I actually witnessed you force feeding your brother a cat's-eye green bumfumbler—"

"Bumboozer."

"Whatever. Even if I saw you do it, I wouldn't believe you capable of murder. But it must be said that you did have one doozy of a motive. You're the Earl now."

"He didn't!" Daphne protested. "Val never wanted the title. He was so happy to have brothers standing between him and responsibility. And now that he's the Earl, you can see he's not exactly thrilled about it."

"Thank you, Daphne," said Val, slightly affronted.

"Was I only speaking inside of my head when I stated that I don't believe Val is guilty?" I asked.

"No, you said it out loud," Val said. "You just didn't say it loud enough."

"I'm sorry, who else should have heard me? Shall I open the window and shout it to the jackdaws?"

"What the hell is a jackdaw?"

"It's a type of crow," Daphne explained. "Haven't you ever heard of a jackdaw?"

"No." He turned to me accusingly. "Why are you making up birds? Why don't you just say 'crow'?"

"Forgive me," I replied, "I forgot that all the space in your brain is taken up with bumfumblers and the knowledge of how all your friends and relatives are going to die."

"I wonder if they have jackdaws in Africa," Daphne mused.

"Oh, this is getting us nowhere!" Val said.

I sighed. "I agree, and as much as I enjoy our witty repartee, we really must get down to investigating. Val, come talk to Lydgate with me. Just introduce us and assure him that you want him to answer my questions. Then get the heck out. I think he'll talk more freely if you aren't there."

"What about me?" Daphne asked.

"You mentioned being friendly with the staff. Maybe you could start with the maids. You know, woman to woman talk."

"Yes, of course," she said, drily. "I can ask them about their favorite shade of lipstick, segue into a discussion of matinee idols, and then subtly bring up the subject of family-cide."

"We all have a role to play," I said, sympathetically.

"What's mine?" Val asked.

"Comic relief."

"No, seriously," he said.

"Well, as the new Earl, I think you should go handle the Earl business."

"The Earl business?"

"Whatever Earls do all day. I imagine there's correspondence to write, maybe documents to handle."

"Documents?" He protested. "Just laying around? What kind of documents?"

"Don't ask me, I'm not an Earl. You are. But while you're at it, I think it would be smart to go through Erasmus's papers looking for evidence."

"Such as? I doubt we'll find a note from Uncle Sally reading,

'*Dear Nephew, you are hereby informed of my plan to kill you next weekend.*'"

"Hmm," Daphne agreed. "Probably not."

"No, but you should see if there's anything pointing to a motive for murder," I said. "Perhaps Erasmus called in a loan. Or prosecuted a poacher. Maybe a gardener objected to his plans for the north meadow, something like that."

"We don't have a north meadow," Val protested.

"It was just an example," I said.

"It's a stupid example," he grumbled.

"Forgive me," I said. "This is my first family massacre."

Chapter 15

Staying in someone's home does give you a sense of what the family is like. But if you want the full picture, you must look below stairs. Zoltan Szabo said that once in *Zoltan Szabo and the Strangeness at Midnight*. And at Tower Field Hall I learned Szabo was right. Talking to the staff was an eye-opening experience.

The Hall was run, as all such manors are run, by a small army of workers without whom most upstairs comforts would be impossible. Troops of kitchen staff, housemaids, lady's maids, footmen, valets, and a chauffeur. And outside the house there were gardeners and under-gardeners, grooms and stable hands, and a man who came in every spring and summer to make sure the tennis lawn was suitably verdant. All overseen by the estimable Lydgate and Mrs. Whiting, a housekeeper as-yet invisible to me.

Surprisingly, I found the staff's domain far more comfortable and infinitely more welcoming than the family rooms. We began in the warm and gloriously scented kitchen, a whitewashed room with bright leaded windows, a huge oak table worn smooth by generations of meals, and the sound of laughter echoing from a nearby room, something I'd rarely heard on this visit.

Lydgate rose quickly from the table as we entered, aghast at our invasion. The Earl was not a regular visitor below stairs. It was the first time I'd seen the butler in his natural element, and thus perhaps the first time I'd truly seen him at all. Even as I thought once again of my ear-pinching godfather, Lydgate became more human, somehow. He was a man of striking appearance, with an enviably erect spine and silvery hair. He was probably in his late fifties, and possessed the type of natural authority one usually associates with generals.

"May I help you, my lord?"

"Thank you, Lydgate," Val said. "If you don't mind, we'd like a moment of your time."

Lydgate inclined his head in a gesture befitting the king. "Of course, my lord. If you'll forgive the informality, may I suggest my pantry." At a nod from Val, he led us from the kitchen and down a short hallway and into his sanctum.

It was a pleasant room with a small desk in one corner and, along the opposite wall, a fireplace flanked by two welcoming armchairs. I had visions of the impeccable butler napping in his slippers here on a rainy afternoon, or perhaps enjoying a quiet cup of tea with his wife, the cook.

Some shelves ranged above the desk, weighed down by decades' worth of cellar records and shooting diaries. A solitary window looked out on the lush kitchen garden, where carrot tops and tomato frames were lined up like green and red soldiers.

"Lydgate, Mr. Griffin here would like to talk to you about my late brother. I would appreciate your cooperation."

"Of course, my lord," Lydgate said, the very model of formality.

"You may feel free to say whatever you wish to Mr. Griffin, even to repeat gossip or rumors if necessary. You understand? No standing on decorum. We need to know."

"Of course, my lord."

"Thank you, Lydgate," Val turned to me. "Good luck, Griff."

Val turned and left us, his steps echoing down the hall. Lydgate turned to me with an impassive expression.

"May we sit, Lydgate?" I asked.

"Of course, sir," he indicated the two armchairs.

Before I had a chance to begin, the butler astonished me by saying, "Forgive the liberty, sir, but I must say your books have given me many hours of enjoyment. Just last week, I was up late into the night because I couldn't put down *Zoltan Szabo and the Queen's Cipher.*"

If the man had reared back and punched me in the nose, he wouldn't have surprised me half as much. And I suddenly liked this man a whole lot more than I ever liked my godfather.

"Why, thank you, Lydgate. It's very kind of you to say so."

"Mrs. Lydgate is also a fan."

I wondered if he called her Mrs. Lydgate in private. Did he wake up, roll over, and say, "Good morning, Mrs. Lydgate?"

Shaking the thought aside, I took a breath and waded in. "Lydgate, I'm going to be frank with you. Lord Valentine has asked me to investigate the late Earl's death. He is under the impression that it may not have been an accident."

The man maintained a perfectly blank façade, as if he hadn't just heard me suggest a murder in his household. "Indeed, sir?"

"Indeed. And I have to admit that I share these suspicions, as does Miss Ferguson."

"I see, sir."

"May I ask if you also have some doubts?"

Lydgate was silent.

"Let me ask instead, if you think it could be *possible* that the late Earl's death may have been intentional?"

Again, he hesitated, and I began to realize that Lydgate was one of those men who always thought before speaking. In other words, he was nothing like me.

"Shall I say, Mr. Griffin," he began, "that yes, I believe it to be... *possible.*"

"Possible that Lord Erasmus was murdered?"

Lydgate winced a bit at my bluntness but inclined his head in silent agreement.

"I won't ask you to gossip about your employers," I said, and I could see Lydgate relax just slightly. "But I do have some questions about the sequence of events the day the late Earl died. Perhaps you could tell me in your own words what happened that day? And if there's anything you would like kept confidential, you have my word that I will not break your confidence. Unless such information leads to catching a criminal, of course."

The butler gave another of his wordless nods. It struck me that Lydgate had a great deal more natural dignity than Uncle Suspicious.

"Let's start at the beginning. Tell me about breakfast."

Lydgate's recounting paralleled Daphne's. Breakfast was laid out on the sideboard by eight in the morning. Lady Haxley, who was usually the first, came down at a quarter past the hour, followed by Erasmus at 8:30. Daphne and Elsie arrived together a few minutes later, followed by Uncle Suspicious, Nicky, and Wulfie. The mysterious Miss Astley came in just about the time the others were finished.

"Were you in the room that whole time?"

"No, sir, not all the time. I'm always in the dining room for dinner, but for breakfast the family serves themselves. I travel between the kitchen and the dining room to ensure the coffee and tea are always hot and that none of the dishes go cold or need refilling."

"Did you notice anything unusual?"

"No, sir."

"Do you remember what Lord Erasmus had for breakfast?"

"Yes, sir. His lordship always liked a large breakfast, especially before riding. Eggs and ham, porridge, coffee, toast, marmalade."

"And the others?"

"To the best of my recollection, sir, everyone breakfasted as usual and behaved quite normally."

I remembered the unknown quantity.

"What can you tell me about Miss Astley? Who is she?"

The butler hesitated again.

"I'm sorry, Lydgate. But I'm really not looking for gossip. It's important that I know who all these people are."

"Yes, sir. I understand. It's just rather awkward."

"Let me see if I can help. I've been told that Lady Haxley is a friend of Miss Astley's mother. I also understand that there has been a determined campaign to make Miss Astley the next Countess of Haxley. Is that so?"

Lydgate manfully tried to suppress a smile. "Indeed, sir."

"I've further been told that she's a rather *dramatic* young lady."

"That is an accurate description, sir."

"Do you think she might have had something to do with the late Earl's death?"

He was silent for a moment. "I honestly couldn't say, sir. I do know that the late Earl wanted nothing to do with her. He made that very clear. '*Hell hath no fury,*' as they say sir."

"Indeed, Lydgate."

"She is, if you'll excuse my saying so sir, a great deal harder than she appears."

"In what way?"

"Well, sir. With the family she appears helpless, delicate. One of those overly *womanly* women, if you'll excuse the phrase. But I've heard from two of the maids that she is…"

I came to his rescue. "Demanding? Rude? Difficult?"

"All of that, sir."

"Thank you, Lydgate, that's very helpful. Now, what happened after breakfast?"

"His lordship and Miss Ferguson left the room together and went to the stables."

"And the others?"

"Miss Armistad went out to her garden."

"*Her* garden?" I asked. "She has her own garden?"

"Yes, sir. She has an interest in home remedies, herbal teas, nostrums of that nature. She grows various medicinal plants."

Of course, I thought. "What about the others?"

"Lord and Lady Haxley went upstairs to their wing. I did not see either of them again until I was notified about the accident."

"And did you see Miss Armistad later that morning?"

"Yes, sir. At about eleven. I saw her going upstairs."

"What about Nicodemus and Wulfstan?"

"I didn't see Lord Nicodemus again until late in the afternoon. Lord Wulfstan left at half past ten to attend the race meeting at Bloomfield and didn't return until the early evening."

"I know that Lord Erasmus had tea and scones with Miss Ferguson after their ride. Did he eat or drank anything else? Was he perhaps taking any medicine?"

"I don't believe so, sir. But may I suggest talking to Sutherland, his valet. He would know."

"Thank you," I said. "I will. Do you know if Erasmus went straight up to his room after he left the study?"

"I understand from Mary—she's one of the maids, sir—that his lordship did stop by Miss Armistad's room first."

"Do you know why he was there?"

"No, sir. He often called to visit her."

"The Earl and Miss Armistad were friendly?"

"Oh, yes sir. Miss Armistad can be a little, well, eccentric, but the late Earl was quite fond of her."

"Yes, I've heard about her séances. And the way she predicts how people will… um… pass on."

Lydgate's impassive face cracked just the slightest hint of a smile before disappearing again in a blink.

"Yes, sir."

"*Et tu*, Lydgate?" I asked.

He glanced over at me. "A climbing accident, sir."

I was surprised. "Do you climb, Lydgate?"

"No, sir," he said, drily.

"Well, that should keep you safe," I observed.

"One can only hope, sir. My wife, I understand, will suffer from a putrid fever."

"Alas. Please give Mrs. Lydgate my sympathies."

In a mere five minutes, Lydgate had changed from being a sour stick, so much like my godfather, to an intelligent and droll individual. Thank God for good old Zoltan.

"How about Lord and Lady Haxley? Did Lord Erasmus get along well with them?"

Poor Lydgate, as he hesitated, struggled and failed to suppress a pickle-sucking expression.

"I have never known them to have words, sir," he said at last, diplomatically.

"Does that mean you've known them to have silence?" I asked.

"Sir?"

"Silence. Uncomfortable silence, where nobody talks and it's very cold and awkward."

He gave a sort of twisted smile. "Yes, sir, I might have known them to have silence."

It was time to change tack. "Would it be indiscreet of me to ask your opinion of Gilbert Fitzhugh?"

Again, a hint of a grimace. "I believe that Lord Haxley finds Fitzhugh to be an entirely satisfactory valet, sir."

"Do *you* find him to be entirely satisfactory?"

He hesitated again, so I went on. "Lydgate, I'm sorry to ask these questions, but we believe that somebody killed Lord Erasmus. Even if the guilty person is a member of the family, he, she, or they do not deserve discretion or protection. I respect your loyalty, but you also owe loyalty to the late Earl and to Lord Valentine, whose life may be at risk even now."

The butler sighed, but even through his professional passivity, I could see an acceptance that he would have to speak.

"No, sir," he admitted, "I find Mr. Fitzhugh to be entirely unsatisfactory."

"In what ways?"

"Firstly, sir, I do not believe he possesses the… er… correct moral character to be a gentleman's gentleman."

"Would you consider him to be immoral, then?" I asked.

"Not precisely, sir. Although when he first came here, I was obliged to have a word with him regarding his… um… behavior towards the female members of staff."

I filed away that little nugget to share later with Daphne. Perhaps she could draw some confidences out of the housemaids.

Lydgate went on. "I am also not entirely convinced of his honesty or his… er… sobriety."

"Does he drink?" I asked.

"Only to excess. Sir," he added hastily.

"Have you ever known him to lose his temper?"

The poor man shot me a look of utter distaste, as if he was mentally picturing awful Aunt Jim naked and sprawled on a chaise longue.

"Yes, sir, I'm sorry to say I have witnessed him in moments of, shall we say, unseemly anger."

I instantly both considered and rejected *Zoltan Szabo and Moments of Unseemly Anger.*

"Could you possibly elaborate?" I coaxed.

Lydgate sighed. I had to admit, he was one of the most eloquent sighers I'd ever encountered. "Last summer, the Vicar approached Lord Erasmus about getting up a Hall side to take on the village in a charity cricket match. But the village had what I believe is known as a 'ringer,' a young lad named Linus who was something of a whiz at bowling. A few nights before the match, Linus was drinking in the White Boar, one of the local pubs. He was teasing one of our grooms, Hawkes, about the match. Mr. Fitzhugh overheard and took exception to some of the things Linus said. That night, Linus was attacked while walking home. His arm was broken, and he missed the match. He never filed any charges, but it was generally said to be Fitzhugh."

"And do you believe that?"

"I do," he asserted. "I've had complaints of harsh words, some intimidation, from some of the younger members of staff. But Mr. Fitzhugh is absolutely under the protection of Lord Haxley, and there is very little I can do. It is… distressing."

"I see," I said. "He sounds like a thoroughly unlikeable man."

"Pardon me, Mr. Griffin, but have you not had occasion to meet the man yourself?"

"No, Lydgate, I've not had that pleasure."

"Ah." He paused for a moment in thought. "May I then say, sir, that I find Mr. Fitzhugh to be a cross between Bruiser Bochy, the Prime Minister's bodyguard in *Zoltan Szabo and the Chen Wang Brotherhood*, and Lady Arabella Duckworth in *Zoltan Szabo and the Sicilian Staircase*."

Even though both characters were created in my own mind, I could not immediately remember either of them. The man seemed to know my books better than I did, which made me like him even more.

I then asked Lydgate for his account of Erasmus's death, which added very little to Daphne's version. He'd been alerted to the tragedy by Sutherland, Erasmus's valet. Following Lord Haxley's instructions, he had rung up Doctor Ridgeway before coming downstairs to inform the staff. He and Mrs. Whiting then had to keep a gaggle of upset maids from further disrupting the household.

"Lydgate," I said, "I'm going to be blunt. Do you believe that Gilbert Fitzhugh is capable of murder?"

He threw another eloquent sigh into the conversation, this time followed by the tiniest and most reluctant of nods.

"And do you believe that Lord Haxley is capable of ordering Fitzhugh to commit said murder?"

Another slight incline of the head.

"Thank you, Lydgate." I paused again. "Do you believe that others in the Hall and in the village would agree with this assessment?"

"I'm very much afraid so, sir," the butler replied in a tombstone tone. "I think if you spoke to the locals, the general opinion would be that Mr. Fitzhugh is quite capable of anything, sir."

"I see. Do you know his movements on the day that Lord Erasmus died?"

"As I said, sir, I did go between the servant's hall and the dining room, so I can't speak to all his time. He came down for breakfast about seven a.m. At eight o'clock he took up Lord Haxley's tea. I remember because he chastised one of the maids for not putting the milk jug on the tray. Most inappropriate; it is not his place to correct the maids. Poor Lily was quite upset, and I was still calming her down when Fitzhugh came back with his lordship's laundry. He then spent some time in the morning down here, reading the newspaper." He sighed. "I find his idleness concerning, sir. It sets a bad example for the younger members of the staff."

"No doubt," I said. "So, was he down here for the remainder of the morning?"

"I'm afraid I don't know, sir. There were times when I went into the staff lounge, and he wasn't there. But his duties require him to be upstairs dealing with his lordship's needs. All I can say was that there was nothing out of the ordinary."

"And after Lord Erasmus was found?"

"I can't say for certain, sir. Things were, as I'm sure you can understand, confused. But I did see him several times that afternoon, either down here or going to Lord Haxley's room."

"Do you remember what he did in the evening?"

"Yes, sir. At half past six, we laid out a cold buffet for the family, so if anyone was hungry, they could suit themselves. I asked Fitzhugh to help set things up as a few of the maids were still quite distressed, sir. After laying out supper, he joined us in the hall as usual for the staff meal."

"Did he seem at all different or strange?"

"Not that I could see, sir. The atmosphere around the staff table was subdued and somber, so there was not much conversation. But he appeared to be his usual self. He sat in here with a book until about half past ten when Lord Haxley rang for him."

"I see. Well, thank you, Lydgate. You've been very helpful. If you remember anything else, or if a member of the staff mentions something we should know, please tell me or Lord Valentine."

"I will, of course, sir."

"Oh," I said, "just one more thing. Lord Valentine has told me about the family curse. Do you or the staff believe in it?"

He looked pained. "I cannot speak for the staff, sir. But I must admit that this family has had some extraordinary deaths."

"For instance?"

After some hesitation he began to tell the most remarkable stories of Hatton-Haxleys past, surpassing even Val. I really must find a way to work some of them into a book.

Chapter 16

In my experience, a man and his valet usually become a tight unit. Not exactly friends, not quite family, yet more than employer and employee. The relationship is unique. So, when Lydgate sent Sutherland in for our interview, I hoped that he would be as eager to solve this mystery as we were.

Within a minute of meeting him, I knew I'd found an ally.

Sutherland looked to be about my age. He was tall and thin, with arms and legs that seemed too long for his body, rather like a puppy who hadn't quite figured out how limbs work. He had a homely, likeable face and was obviously willing, even eager to do anything to help.

His story came tumbling out.

"I became concerned," he said. "It was nearly the time that his lordship said he wanted to leave for the wedding, and he was still in his bath. I knocked on the door and received no answer, so I went in and…" He stopped, obviously grief-stricken. I looked out Lydgate's window into the garden, giving Sutherland what little privacy I could until he'd gotten himself back under control.

"I'm sorry for your loss, Sutherland. And sorry to have to ask you these difficult questions."

He gave me a sad, appreciative smile. "Thank you, sir. If there is anything I can do to help…?"

"Let me ask you this. Do you think it possible that Lord Erasmus was murdered?"

He swallowed heavily at the word but nodded immediately. "Yes, I do sir."

"May I ask why?"

He hesitated, so I added: "Lord Valentine, Miss Ferguson, and I all think he was murdered, too. I was just curious as to why you do."

"There are many reasons, sir. The marble, sir. And the book. But mostly just because he is dead. His lordship was perfectly healthy. He wasn't sick, his heart was sound, how could he just die like that? It doesn't make sense that he would be his usual self, joking around, looking forward to seeing his friends at the wedding, and then suddenly... dead. I still don't understand it."

"We agree with you, Sutherland." I thought for a moment. "Please, if you don't mind, tell me what you saw when you entered the bathroom."

"Well, sir, I found his lordship slipped down in the tub, with his head under the water. And the book was floating on top."

"What was the state of the room?" I asked. "Was there water on the floor, as if he'd been splashing it?"

"No, sir."

"None at all?"

The valet looked at me with new awareness. I had apparently awakened his secret, inner Zoltan Szabo.

"No, sir," he said, slowly. "And whatever happened to him had to happen within the hour between when I drew his bath and when I found him. I was still in his bedroom when he first got in, laying out his suit for the wedding. I could hear him singing. He always sang in the bath, and always denied it afterward. I commented on it once and he looked at me like I was making it up."

"What was he singing?"

"He was singing a... well, a music hall song called *The Girl with Too Many Brothers*, sir."

Without thinking, I started singing:

She's the girl with too many brothers,
each one a chaperone.
She's really not worth all the bother,
I can't get that girl alone.

Suddenly, Sutherland joined in:

I took her and one brother to dinner,
I took her and another to tea.
Although she may look like a winner,
The girl's too much trouble for me.

We smiled and resumed the conversation with a new-found sense of camaraderie.

"Did you hear him stop singing?"

"No, sir. He had just gotten to the third verse when I walked out."

"Then you came back, when?"

"About forty minutes later, sir. It was past time for him to change for the wedding. I worried that he'd be late."

"So, you went in and found him under the water, with no signs of struggle. Were there…" I hesitated. "Forgive me, but were there any sorts of marks on his body? Any redness or bruises?"

"No sir, nothing."

"I'm sure you didn't look that closely, but did you happen to see any sort of mark on arms or his neck that might indicate a hypodermic injection?"

His eyes widened slightly. "No, sir. Nothing. After the doctor left, I… uh… I felt it was my duty to dress his lordship for the last time. It seemed undignified to leave him as he was found, you see. Not that I was examining his body or anything."

"No, of course not."

"But I think if there'd been any sign, I would have noticed. You're thinking his lordship was poisoned."

"I am. Would you agree that's a possibility?"

"I don't see why not, sir." He thought for a moment. "Would it help, sir, if I gave you a list of everything his lordship ate or drank that day?"

"Yes, it would. Lydgate filled me in on breakfast, so we can skip over that."

"Well, after his lordship and Miss Ferguson returned from riding, they had tea. That was shortly after ten o'clock. I saw one of the maids going into the morning room with a tray. There was one teapot and a plate of scones, with butter and a pot of jam. I know that both his lordship and Miss Ferguson have a partiality to scones with jam, so I'm sure both ate the same thing."

"Yes, I think we can clear the tea and scones. Did he eat or drink anything else that day?"

"Not to my knowledge, sir. His lordship went into his study to review some accounts and deal with his correspondence. He was there until noon."

"You're sure of the time?"

"Oh yes, sir. His lordship asked that I fetch him at noon. He often lost track of time. Then he stopped in to see Miss Armistad in her room while I drew his bath. He often did that."

"I see. Um… having met Miss Armistad, may I ask if she's ever told you…?"

The valet smiled, "Apparently, sir, I shall die from pneumonia when I am ninety-two years old."

"Congratulations on your long life."

"Thank you, sir. I shall endeavor to enjoy it."

"Let's return to breakfast for a moment. I understand that in addition to the family there was a Miss Astley there."

"Yes, sir."

"I've heard that Miss Astley was being pushed towards the Earl as a potential Countess. May I ask what his lordship's opinion of the young lady was?"

"Let me just say, sir, that any plans Lady Haxley had regarding Miss Astley and his lordship were held in vain."

"He wasn't getting the family jewels out of the vault, then?"

Sutherland laughed. "Oh, no. His lordship found her both difficult and unpleasant. But he was a kind, polite gentleman and did his best to gently dissuade her from the idea that a marriage between them was a possibility."

"Was she receptive to this gentle dissuading?"

"No, sir. She thought he was playing... well, whatever the masculine equivalent of 'coy' is."

"Oh, dear."

"Eventually his lordship had to be direct. Miss Astley's attempts to snare his lordship had reached a dangerous stage."

"Dangerous? In what way dangerous?"

Sutherland leaned back in his chair, discretion being no match for a juicy story.

"Well, sir. On the morning before the tragedy, at about seven, his lordship awoke when he heard his door open. It was Miss Astley, wearing only her nightdress. He believed she had the idea of sneaking into his bed, causing a scandal, and forcing him into marriage."

"Good lord!"

"Indeed, sir," said the valet, pleased at my shock. "He was angrier than I'd ever seen him. I was just coming down the hall with his morning tea when I heard him shouting. I'd never heard him raise his voice like that before."

"What happened then?"

"Fortunately, sir, she'd had no opportunity to shut the door before he began shouting. He saw me in the corridor and said, *'Aha, now there's a witness!'* He absolutely berated her, sir. Called her the most shocking name and ordered her out of the room. Told her, and I quote, sir, '*If you and I were the last man and woman on earth, then you and I would remain the last man and woman on earth.*' He also said that any man who married her wouldn't invite guests to his wedding, he'd invite mourners."

"Well, that's clear enough," I mentally added the ghastly Miss Astley to my list of suspects. "How did she respond?"

"Oh, she said something melodramatic and ridiculous. I do believe Miss Astley's exact words were, '*I'm never going to give you up!*'"

"Oh, dear."

"Yes indeed, sir. I believe his lordship had words with Lady Haxley about her protégé after breakfast, and they were not well received."

"Poor Erasmus."

"Indeed, sir, it was most uncomfortable."

"I imagine so. One last question, Sutherland. What is your opinion of Gilbert Fitzhugh?"

Once again, the seams of Sutherland's discretion cracked wide open. "To be perfectly honest, sir, I detest him. And I believe if you ask any of the other staff members in confidence, they will say the same."

"May I ask why?"

"He's just... not one of *us*, sir."

"In what way?"

"Below stairs, I mean. He doesn't interact with the rest of us. Doesn't make himself friendly. Doesn't join in our conversations or little jokes. And he..."

"It's fine, Sutherland. I know it's hard to speak ill of another."

He sighed in resignation, "He's sly, sir. Cunning. I find him not only unpleasant, but dishonest. Oh, he's loyal to Lord Haxley, as a valet should be to his master. But I believe he would have no problem stabbing anyone else in the back before throwing him to the wolves and then burning the bridge. The man is thoroughly untrustworthy."

"I believe you, but can you give me some examples?"

"Well, sir, I know for a fact he helps himself to the Scotch decanter whenever he wants. And his lordship suspected him of nicking small items around the house."

"A snapper-up of unconsidered trifles," I quoted.

"Sir?"

"Sorry. Shakespeare."

"Indeed sir. *A Winter's Tale,* I believe, sir."

"Bravo, Sutherland. Tell me, did the Earl ever threaten to prosecute?"

"No, sir. There was never any proof."

"Do you know if the Earl and Fitzhugh ever had words or if there were any specific problems between them?"

He considered for a moment. "About four months ago, sir, Lord Erasmus came home from the village in a temper. He went straight up to Lord Haxley's rooms, and they were heard to have words. His lordship later told me that Mr. Simmons, who owns the local garage, complained to him about Mr. Fitzhugh continuing to be forward towards his daughter, sir. Even after the young lady had made her disinterest plain. His lordship was outraged, sir. I believe he spoke directly to Fitzhugh as well."

Sutherland stopped abruptly and reddened a bit. I had the feeling he'd reached the end of his comfort in telling tales. So I let him go, and sat for a moment in Lydgate's cozy pantry, pondering.

Chapter 17

Upon leaving the servants' area, I had the great misfortune to choose the drawing room as a destination, thrusting me headlong into an unexpected *tête-à-tête* with Angela Astley. God help me.

I was certain of her identity the moment I saw her. She was blonde, sort of midway between a good Chablis and a bad Gewurztraminer. Unfortunately for her, I prefer reds. She had a bland, chocolate-box kind of prettiness, with perfectly applied makeup and a dress that seemed more suitable for a garden party than a bereavement. Sprigs of tiny pink roses bloomed across a floating silk creation of soft lavender.

Her intention was to look fetchingly feminine. Instead, she looked like one of the cheaper kinds of greeting cards. I was pretty sure hers would read, "*Sorry your brother is dead, but you can still marry me!*"

"Oh," she trilled, "you're the famous author. Why I was just so *delighted* to learn you were a friend of dear Valentine's. I, too, am an old friend."

I turned a laugh into a polite cough. Daphne's impression of Miss Astley had been uncanny, from the excessively genteel manner to the breathless little spurts that made her sound like an exhausted asthmatic. I assumed she thought it enticing.

"Oh, but I must confess, Mr. Griffin, I'm afraid I haven't read any of your books. But I'm told they're absolutely *thrilling!*"

I was wrong about Daphne's version of Miss Astley's speech. She hadn't put nearly enough L's in *thrilling*.

"Well, that's all right, Miss Astley. I don't expect everyone to read my books."

"Oh, I'm sure I would love them if I was only *brave* enough. I don't like to be scared; you understand."

"Of course, I understand. Although I do write murder mysteries and not ghost stories."

I made myself a bet that the next phrase she uttered would begin with an "oh." I won the bet.

"Oh, but you know how a lady's nerves are always so *delicate*. Why mine are right on the surface."

A surface protected with a thin sheet of steel, I thought. But I said, "That sounds painful. Have you seen a doctor? I don't believe the nerves are supposed to be right on the surface. They're supposed to be deeper."

That brought forth another nauseating giggle. I vowed to never make the woman laugh ever again.

"Oh, you *writers* are always so... well... so *professional* with your words."

"Yes, being professional with words is highly recommended for someone who makes their profession with words."

"See how clever you are?" She made it sound like an insult. "Oh, I was so pleased to learn you were here, Mr. Griffin. It's simply *thrilling*."

I wondered if everything was thrilling to her.

"Really? You surprise me. I would expect you to be so upset about Lord Erasmus that meeting a minor author, however professional with words, would pale in comparison."

Reminded of the circumstances, her expression changed instantly. Suddenly she appeared as heartbroken as someone without a heart can look, even brushing away a tear. Her ease in calling up tears was no doubt the result of a lifetime of pouting and imposing herself as the main character in all situations. It struck me that Angela Astley's greatest ambition, aside from marrying into great gobs of money, was likely to have an opera named after her.

"Oh, yes," she cooed with patently fake sorrow. "Erasmus. *Dear* Erasmus. We were very close, you know."

"Were you?"

"Oh, yes. He was *terribly* in love with me."

Yes, being in love with this woman would be terrible.

"You poor thing," I sympathized. "His death must be just devastating."

"Oh, yes. I'm just *shattered.*"

Somehow, she managed put even more A's into *shattered* than L's in *thrilling*. She had the most fascinating diction I'd ever heard.

Angela lowered her voice to a nauseatingly conspiratorial whisper. "Oh, he was terribly *passionate*, you know. Why, he almost *frightened* me. He could be so *primeval!*" She gave a delicious shiver. "But I'm afraid I just didn't feel the same way towards him."

"How sad."

"Oh, it *was.*" She nodded with pleasurable sorrow. "He was *heartbroken.*"

"Poor Erasmus."

"Oh, yes. In fact, I think that's why he did it."

"Did... did what?" She wasn't about to suggest... was she?

"Why he took his own *life*, of course."

Yes, she was. I blinked a few times.

"You... you think Erasmus *killed himself?*"

The invisible tears were back, and she dabbed them away with a practiced touch of her tiny lace handkerchief. "Oh, yes, that's the only explanation, really."

"Is it? The doctor said Erasmus drowned in his bathtub."

"Oh, yes. But I'm sure he took something dreadful and *romantic* to make himself drown. Perhaps what Juliet took."

"Juliet stabbed herself. It was Romeo who took the poison."

"Even better," she sighed. "Yes, like Romeo, dying for *love*."

"With a religious text for company," I reminded her.

She was silent for a moment before inspiration struck. "Oh! He must have been looking for solace in God's grace. Searching for warm comfort in a cold world, devoid of the love of the woman with whom he was *obsessed* with."

"There's an extra 'with' in your delusion," I observed.

"In my what?"

I didn't answer, concentrating instead on the wobbly feeling in the pit of my stomach as she fixed her eyes on me, earnest soulfulness ratcheted up to full force, and simpered, "Erasmus was a sweet, but I've always preferred more *intellectual*, *successful* men. Like... *authors*, for instance."

If only she knew how little was actually in my bank account at the time. I was no Earl of Haxley. Perhaps her ideal man was simply whoever was nearest. I was pretty sure that if Val walked in the door at that moment—and I prayed that he would—she'd turn her limpet personality in his direction and talk about how *thrilled* she was to be around a man of such status.

But neither Val, Daphne, nor a conveniently rampaging water buffalo came to disturb the scene. I couldn't spend another moment alone with the appalling creature, manners be damned. I stood, blurting, "Will you excuse me, please, Miss Astley, I must go feed my cat."

* * *

CATULLUS WAS FINE, of course. What I really needed was a quiet interlude to think, but my luck was out. As I headed towards my room, Aunt Elsie's door swung open.

I couldn't help but think of her as "Aunt." She had a very

aunt-y air about her. Today she was clad in another remarkable collection of skirts and scarves. She wore at least five. Scarves, I mean. Just the one skirt, an eye-searing yellow number that fell in a series of flounces, giving the impression of multiples. Amid the liquid folds and clumsy knots, I spied an impressive array of necklaces, ranging from what looked like a rather superior pearl choker to the childish acorn-and-string contraption I'd seen the previous evening.

As if all this weren't quite enough to make an impression, she also sported a set of glossy black rosary beads and two or three more scarves wound around her head in sort of makeshift turban, or perhaps a field dressing for a near-fatal head wound. The whole ensemble gave the appearance of a carnival fortune teller who had fallen head-first down the stairs of a convent.

Her eyes, however, were clear and lively and, unfortunately for me, glued to my face.

"Oh good, you're here," she exclaimed, coming forward and grabbing my hand. "You're late. I expected you over an hour ago."

"I… I'm sorry? Expected me for what?"

She leaned in close and peered myopically at my face. I felt like a fresh recruit enduring his first, terrifying inspection from a general. It didn't help that she listed off my features as if she were taking inventory.

"Nice, straight nose," she muttered. "Yes. Regular features. Brown hair… more mink than squirrel."

"Wonderful," I said, "I've always hoped people would see me as more mink than squirrel."

"Yes," she approved. "You are a very attractive man. And those eyes, of course. I'm so pleased that you've kept the bi-colored eyes. Very wise, quite striking. Of course, there was that one time they hung you as a witch because of them."

"Wouldn't I have been hung as a warlock?" I asked, unable to stop myself.

"My dear, what makes you think that you are always a man?"

"Um... Is there something I can do for you, Miss Armistad?"

"Please, do call me Elsie," she urged. "After all, we're old friends, aren't we?"

Not in this lifetime, I said to myself. She dragged me into her room.

Aunt Elsie's living quarters assaulted the senses in a riot of colors and a profusion of velvet, candles, incense, and books. The books were stacked everywhere, like a forest of colorful tree stumps.

In the center of the storm sat a quartet of bright chairs in clashing flower prints. Bright yellow sunflowers sat next to pastel pink roses, opposite sickly-pink hydrangeas and vivid purple pansies being attacked by gigantic ladybirds. It was the sort of mismatched décor of which writers often say, "*it should have looked garish but somehow it all managed to work together.*" In this case, those writers would have been wrong. It simply looked garish.

Once again, the ever-dubious Hatton-Haxley family art collection was on display, with much of the wall space covered by paintings, etchings, and a photograph of Queen Victoria. One surprisingly delightful work looked like an early Degas, depicting a group of dancers working at the barre, but it was hung alongside a triptych of incomprehensible pastel sketches that could have been characters from Shakespeare, or perhaps wanted criminals. There was also a series of drawings depicting sinister-looking occult symbols, including an upside-down pentagram and a dagger piercing a heart. I found none of them comforting.

Averting my eyes, I caught sight of a stunningly beautiful chess set on the table, carved from ivory and jade. A game was in progress. As I studied the play, I couldn't help but pick up a discarded pawn, enjoying its cool smoothness.

"By the way, James," she called over her shoulder. "You're not still friends with any those darned Etruscans, are you?"

I put the pawn down clumsily. The clatter distracted her.

"Be careful not to disturb the game," she warned. "I really think I've got him this time."

"Who is your opponent, Miss Armistad?"

"Oh, Voltaire," she said, casually. Adding, "He's a worthy adversary, but he will overuse the Queen. So ironic, really, coming from a Frenchman. But then, of course, he *did* live before all that nonsense with their Queen and her cake. I was playing with Lorenzo de' Medici last month, but he was such a bad loser. Now, do sit down."

She all but pushed me into the hydrangea chair and took the rose chair for herself. I would have preferred to sit in the pansy/ladybird chair, not because it looked more comfortable but because the giant flying beetles were rather unsettling and if I could sit on them, I wouldn't have to look at them.

Something on the sunflower chair moved, startling me until I saw that what I had taken to be some sort of striped cushion was, in fact, my own beloved cat.

Elsie followed my surprised gaze. "Oh, I hope you don't mind. Catullus wandered in, so I gave him some cream."

"How did you know his name is Catullus?"

"Why, he told me, of course," she said. "But Catullus and I are old friends."

Just when I thought the day couldn't get any odder.

"Oh? Did he get a medal at Waterloo, too?"

"Don't be silly," she chastised me. "He's a cat."

"Right. Miss Armistad, is there something you wanted?"

"I thought it was time we caught up," she said. "It's been ever so long."

"It has?"

"Not since Waterloo."

"Yes, of course. I'm sorry that I... um... died on you." Another sentence I never imagined saying.

"Well, I knew it was going to happen," she said. "Oh... *tea*!" She jumped up and crossed to a large screen painted with a Japanese scene of fishermen bringing in the nets at sunset. Moving the screen aside, she revealed an antique table set up with what looked like a laboratory. Bunches of dried flowers and herbs hung from white cords in front of shelves crammed with small glass bottles, fat ceramic jars, tins, and boxes. Most of them completely free of anything so mundane as a label. On the table sat a mortar and pestle, a wooden rack filled with test tubes, and a set of rather choice cut-glass decanters displaying a range of suspiciously colored liquids.

I felt a moment of unease as she lifted on tiptoes towards the highest of the shelves until I realized she was reaching for a small kettle, which she set down atop a sturdy spirit lamp. From amid the profusion of plants and packets she pulled down a tin which I recognized from my own mornings: *Colbert's Special Earl Grey*.

She spooned some leaves into a ceramic teapot shaped like a cabbage and resumed her monologue. I had no idea where the next few minutes were going to take me, but at least there would be tea.

"I know I say this each time we meet," she began, "but I really do want to apologize for 1676."

"Oh, well, no hard feelings," I said, politely confused.

"Really? Well, that's quite a relief. You're quite forgiving in this life." She finished making the tea and poured it into flowery china cups that managed to clash with all the other random flowers in the room. Elsie placed them carefully next to the chess set, then moved the table about three inches to her left for no reason before returning to the shelves. Retrieving a large tin labeled *King Rufus Dog Biscuits*, she opened the lid and offered the contents to me. "Biscuit?"

"No. No, thank you."

She shrugged and pulled one out. It didn't look like a dog biscuit. It appeared to be some type of shortbread. I sipped the tea. It wasn't Colbert's Earl Grey. It was pale, grassy-scented, and bitter. I coughed. She smiled.

"My tansy. Perfect for those prone to dropsy."

I wasn't sure what dropsy was but was pretty sure I wasn't prone to it. I put the tea down with a smile and resolved never to touch it again. Catullus stared at me, looking amused, as I turned my attention back to Aunt Elsie.

She had settled back into the rose chair and crossed her long, thin legs. I noticed she wore mis-matched shoes.

"Now, James," she said. "What have you been up to since 1815?"

How do you answer someone who asks how you spent the century before your birth? And who the hell was James? I fell back upon my right to stay silent.

"Are you married this time around?" Elsie pressed.

I felt a sudden urge to be married. Married with nine children. But I told her the truth. "No, I'm not married."

"Really?" Was that my terrified imagination or did she ask that question with a gleam in her eye? *Oh, God!* I thought, *Quick! Start a conversation. Any subject! Make something up. Just get her off marriage!*

"Tell me Miss Elsie," I stammered, desperately. "Were you close with Erasmus?"

"Oh, poor, dear Erasmus. Unlike you, he never forgave me for 1676," she said mournfully. "But do you remember when the three of us went on that picnic, just outside of Troy? It was the year before the war. You and he bet me that I couldn't strip naked and—"

"Haven't seen Erasmus in years," I blurted, desperately and loudly. "Not since I ran into him in London, ages ago. In the British Museum, surprisingly. By the Rosetta Stone. He was, uh, with a llama! And… and the Prime Minister!" I floundered.

She talked right past me, relentless. "Oh, and then there was that time when we three were in that geisha house—"

"Yes, it was a llama, the Prime Minister, and the Archbishop of Canterbury," I continued, pretty sure she wasn't listening to anything I said and determined not to engage with anything *she* said. "We had sardines and custard for dinner with the Prince of Wales—"

"—And those drunken samurai came in one night and paid us to—"

"—Then, after dinner we broke into the Tower of London, stole a Beefeater, and we all swam to China—"

"—Remove our kimonos and dance for them, and then—"

"—But pirates captured us before we reached China, and they took us to America—"

"—One of us poured sake while the other two—"

I was practically shouting by now: "So we went to Hollywood and made that movie where the llama kidnapped Rudolph Valentino!"

"Uh… Griff?" Thank the Lord and all his dead sainted brothers, I heard Val calling me from the hallway.

"Here!" I screamed. "I'm in here!" As if I was trapped in the rubble after an earthquake, frantically signaling to rescuers.

Rescue, in the form of Val, walked into the room. "Hullo, Griff, and greetings, Aunt Elsie. What are you two up to?"

"Oh, we were just catching up on old times, dear. So many wonderful memories."

Val looked upon me with pity, making it perfectly clear he knew what "*so many wonderful memories*" meant. I began to wonder just how long he'd been standing outside that door.

"Oh, I'm so sorry to have interrupted," he said, all mock innocence. "Shall I come back?"

I decided at that moment that I hated Val and would never speak to him again.

"No, thank you," I said quickly. "In fact, I'm afraid I really must get back to that very important, top-secret mission I am performing for His Majesty's government. Why don't you sit down, Val, and keep Miss Armistad company?"

"I'd love to," he said. "But I promised you that I'd help you with that... uh... top-secret thing. You'll excuse us both, won't you Aunt Elsie?"

"Of course. Of course." She waved her hand dismissively. "As it happens, I'm waiting for Mary and Daisy to join me so they can witness my new will. I need to make some changes now Erasmus has left us. Valentine, dear, you'll be pleased to know that I'm leaving all the sheep to you. James, dear, we'll finish catching up later."

"James?" Val asked. "Who is...?"

"And don't forget to watch out for the swans, dear," she said as we turned to leave.

"Swans?" Val and I asked at the same time.

"Oh, yes, dear, uh... well *this* dear one," she gestured vaguely to me, "will meet his end because of *swans*."

"I will?" How common was death by swan, I wondered.

"Mm. You must *always* be cautious when swans are about, James."

I said the only thing I could think of. "I promise I'll be careful. And don't you forget to stay away from... uh... people who juggle machetes."

As I scooped up Catullus and effected my escape, I heard Aunt Elsie lob one final grenade my way.

"By the way, James, did they ever find your other arm?"

Chapter 18

"Valentine Dunstan Jarlath, if you ever see me alone with your Aunt Elsie again, you come in and rescue me immediately or I will break your nose, have you arrested, and glue your golf clubs to the inside of your bag."

He laughed. Which didn't help.

"And then I'll tell her you said she was Attila the Hun in a past life, and lock you in a room with her."

He sobered instantly. "Now, that's mean!"

"I know. By the way, congratulations on inheriting all of Elsie's sheep."

"Thanks. I didn't even know she had sheep."

"Perhaps they're imaginary. She's mad," I said. "And I am very uncomfortable on her insistence that she and I have a long history as a couple."

"As a couple of what?"

"You're not doing yourself any favors, Val. Remember, you invited me here to get to the bottom of all of this. If you don't want my help, I can just get in my car and leave, and you'll be stuck here with one half of the family wanting you dead and the other half waxing nostalgic over the grand time we all had during the Black Plague."

"You're right, I'm sorry. Who would have thought someone with your war record would be afraid of one old lady."

"Look, I enjoy reminiscing about woolly mammoth hunts as

much as the next man, but your aunt is a menace. And believe me, it takes a lot to scare a man who was a hero at Waterloo."

"Fair enough."

"So, where are we going?"

"Over to Daphne's room," he said. "It seems she's discovered something interesting."

"I sincerely hope that whatever she discovered does not involve me and Aunt Elsie sailing on the Titanic. Because I'm pretty sure that one doesn't end well."

Daphne was billeted near the end of a long corridor in the guest wing, in the same room she'd used ever since she was a child. As he knocked on the door, Val peered at me with a mischievous expression and said, "I think you'll love the décor."

The door swung open.

Daphne's wallpaper was covered in swans. Big, white swans, wings spread in flight, swooping across the light blue sky of her walls. And fat, swimming swans, gently floating into my stunned consciousness like weird hallucinations.

"Oh no," I said, stepping back. "Non. *Nein.* Nope. Not here. We're going back to Val's room."

I turned on my heel and marched back to the family wing. There was a moment of shocked silence before I heard them following me down the hall. I got to Val's room, went in without waiting, and threw myself disconsolately into the chair by the fireplace. Aunt Elsie had put me in a mood.

Val and Daphne entered, laughing.

"Swans! Did Aunt Elsie really tell you to beware of swans?" Daphne asked between giggles.

"Yes," I said grimly. "She did. Swans shall be my doom."

"How do you think they'll kill him?" Val asked Daphne, mercilessly.

"Well, I suppose drowning is the obvious answer," she replied. "I vote for drowning."

"Ah, but you forget their fiendishly large wings. I think poor Griff will be flapped to death."

"I hate you both," I said.

"This is wonderful," Val said, fiendishly. "From now on, whenever I want to unsettle you, I'll just whisper '*swans,*' and watch you shudder in terror."

I returned his evil smile. "And I'll whisper, '*Aunt Jim's varicose veins*' and we'll be even."

The expression he flashed me was delicious.

"Aunt Jim's what?" Daphne asked.

"To each man his own demon. Val's demon apparently takes corporeal form as his aunt's varicose veins."

"She's covered in them; I just know it!"

"Well, that's understandable," Daphne said. "But *swans*?"

"You shouldn't laugh, Daphne," said Val, sternly. "It's a well-known fact that swans are responsible for tens of deaths every millennium."

I gave up. "Some are doomed to pestilence and others to war, while I shall meet my maker covered in down feathers."

Daphne threw a few cushions on the floor and sat with her back against the arm of Val's chair, handing out cigarettes as the rest of us spread ourselves comfortably about the room. Catullus settled into his new favorite lap.

"While you were walking down memory lane with Aunt Elsie, Daphne learned something," Val said at last.

"And what's that?"

"The day before he died," she said, "Erasmus had a huge fight with Uncle Sulpicius."

"Oh, goody," Val perked up. "Dirt!"

"Do you know what they fought about?" I asked.

"Oh, yes. Erasmus found out that Uncle Sally had gone to Mr. Eldridge about switching some family investments over to schemes recommended by and, of course, overseen by dear Nicky."

"Really? Did you overhear this fight?" I asked Daphne.

"No, I wasn't here, worst luck. I got it from Mary."

I grunted. That name seemed to come up a lot. "Mary. She's one of the maids, yes?"

"She's also a dear friend. We sort of grew up together because her father used to work for my family. We used to play at being brides and took turns marrying each other and then having sword fights afterwards."

"Not the usual family and servant kind of relationship."

"Exactly. She's not spreading gossip around, but she does tell me things that a member of staff wouldn't normally say to a guest. Do you see?"

I saw. "I see," I said.

"I just wanted Val to know that. I don't want Mary getting into trouble for spilling family secrets."

"Good God, no," Val said. "Mary's one of the few sane people in this house. Grand girl. Talk away."

Daphne smiled her thanks.

"Now tell us everything," I urged.

According to Daphne, Mary had been putting fresh flowers in the rooms and was walking past the Earl's study on her way to the dining room. The door was closed, but as she approached, she heard raised voices, loud enough that she could follow most of the argument.

Uncle Sally insisted that Nicodemus would have a brilliant career in finance if only he could show his superiors that he could bring in investments and manage them with his innate skill and expertise. But all the Hatton-Haxley investments were overseen by Erasmus and the trust, in the person of Mr. Eldridge. Sally suggested that a certain percentage of the accounts should be handed over to Nicky, who was onto a sure thing, guaranteed to turn a tidy profit. Not surprisingly, Erasmus refused.

Unfortunately, he refused in terms such as *"over my dead*

body," which was met with a menacing, "*That might happen sooner rather than later.*"

Followed by, "*Are you making a threat, Uncle?*" Which was countered with, "*I will do what's necessary to make sure my family isn't being cheated.*"

This apparently led to, "*I'm the one who's worried about being cheated, by that cheap bank clerk,*" which earned a "*Ha!*"

Then: "*When it comes to money, Nicky and I are far more qualified than you or Eldridge to make a decision.*"

Ending with an ominous, "*But I'm the Earl, aren't I?*"

I gave an impressed whistle. "Well, that certainly suggests a motive."

"By the way," Daphne explained. "Those weren't exact quotes. I wasn't about to write anything down. But Mary said she'd be happy to talk to you personally." She smiled at Val again. "Now that she knows it won't cost her job."

I turned to Val. "I'm still confused about something. The family money isn't controlled by the Earl directly, it's Erasmus—or now, you—*and* Eldridge?"

"Actually, it's the firm. Eldridge, Baker, Armstrong, and Eldridge. And all the partners are required to sign off on any substantial decision."

"All four of them have to agree?"

"No," Val answered. "Just three. Eldridge the Elder is dead."

"Ah, yes, I forgot. How sad," I murmured vaguely.

"Yes," Daphne said. "He was mauled by angry swans."

"Watch it," I growled.

"Sorry."

"So, Val, if you die, your Uncle Suspicious becomes the Earl and he takes control of the money, but with the prestigious firm of Dead Eldridge, Whoozits, Whatsit, and Undead Eldridge looking over his shoulder. Is that right?"

"Afraid so."

I could hear Catullus purring from three feet away. At least one of us was carefree and happy.

Val was next to report. The contents of Erasmus's desk had been perfectly boring. There were no death threats, poison-pen letters, or warnings of doom to be found. I told the others about my talks with Lydgate and Sutherland, then Daphne took the baton again and shared the rest of the dirt she'd uncovered among the staff, which mostly amounted to the fact that everybody hated Fitzhugh.

I turned to Val. "Say, do you know what regiment Fitzhugh was in? Didn't you tell me Geoffrey Fowler had served with him?"

"Right. Fowler was First Royal Warwickshire, I think?"

"Hmm." I thought for a moment. "First Royal Warwickshire was Fourth Division, Tenth Brigade. Under Wilson."

"How do you remember all this?" Val asked, surprised.

"It was part of my job," I answered. "They were with the First Princess Victoria's at Ypres. Isn't that where you said Fitzhugh was wounded?"

Val just nodded. I thought some more.

"Old Benedict might have crossed paths with him," I said at last. "He served with the Princess Vic's. Do you remember him, Val? Roger Benedict? He was about three years ahead of us at school. Had those gorgeous sisters that looked like a Rossetti painting?"

"Oh, really?" Daphne purred. "Tell me more about these sisters."

Val said, "Shut up Daph," without any heat. "Yes, I remember Benedict."

"I think I'll have a chat with him. It might help to get the story from someone who was there. I'll also try to get hold of Geoffrey Fowler. He may some regimental gossip. Mind if I make camp in your study, Val? By the way, are there any extensions in the house?"

"Oh, they've been extending the house for centuries," Val said.

"I mean to your telephone line, idiot. Is it possible I could be overheard?"

"Ah. No. Father hated telephones. Erasmus was indifferent. There's only one other phone and it's down in Lydgate's pantry. Nobody will listen in."

I hesitated.

"If it helps any," said Daphne, "I'm not sure Uncle Sally even knows where the butler's pantry is. I think he believes this house is run by elves and slaves."

I nodded. "Right, I'll give Benedict a call. Get his impression. I'm pretty sure I can track him down."

"Great," Val said. "And while you're doing that, I think I'll do something Earl-ish."

"Such as?" I asked.

"Well, it couldn't hurt to go through the recent history of the Hall more thoroughly. Check the estate records, that kind of thing." He sounded less than thrilled. "There may be something there that could point to a new suspect."

"And I can go have a chat with Alice, one of the housemaids," Daphne added. "She was one of the first of the staff to arrive at Erasmus's room. I'd like to get her version of what happened and who arrived when."

"Right. Well, troops, we all have our assignments. Let's meet up again before dinner, say six o'clock. Here?" I asked.

"And what's wrong with *my* room?" Daphne asked with an innocent smile.

"I'm not speaking to either of you," I said, and walked out.

Chapter 19

As I made my way through Tower Field Hall, once again I was struck by the eerie atmosphere of the place. It was, technically, a house of mourning, but the silence ran deeper than that.

As far as I could tell, only Val, Elsie, and Daphne were truly in mourning. Perhaps a few of the servants as well; Sutherland seemed quite shaken up, but the others showed little emotion. Then again, they'd all had a lot of practice at misplacing members of the Hatton-Haxley clan. Maybe they were simply numb. But the silence in the house felt hollow.

No voices echoed through the corridors. No laughter, no footsteps. There were no sounds of people going about their day behind the many closed doors. I couldn't hear the staff laying fires or making beds. No rattle of tea things or scrape of brush and dustpan. It was the quiet of an empty church, quite different from the sad quiet of grief, and the effect was unnerving.

I found myself, absurdly, rather hurrying to get into the study, like a child racing to their room to avoid the family ghost. Welcoming the relative normalcy of the study, I rang up the operator, got directory service for London, and was soon chatting with Roger Benedict.

I once heard Roger Benedict described as "unflappable." The word summed him up perfectly. I have never met a more peaceful or sedate individual. Nothing ever ruffled or upset him. Not the German army in Belgium, nor our excitable headmaster at school. Rumor had it that right before going over the top at Ypres, he brewed a pot of tea and clipped his fingernails. You could tell Roger Benedict that his nose was on fire and all he would do is ask for a glass of water.

We traded small talk for a bit before getting to the meat of the conversation. A noted historian with four books to his credit, Roger was leading a satisfyingly placid life. He had recently married, and I silently hoped the bride was not expecting passion. His Pre-Raphaelite sisters were well, and his work was highly regarded. In sum, all was right with his world.

"The reason I'm ringing you up," I said after the pleasantries had been observed, "is because I find myself in search of certain information which only you can provide."

"Indeed?" He asked the question without the least hint of curiosity, as if hearing from a minor acquaintance out of the blue for the first time in at least five years was not in the least unusual.

"I'm staying with Valentine Hatton-Haxley—"

"Ah. Did I just read in the *Times* that another of his brothers has passed away? Who was it this time? Something suitably odd for that family, I recall. Elphantine or Sausagius? Something like that."

"Erasmus."

"Oh yes, Erasmus. How that family must hate their sons to give them such ghastly names. So, what can I do for you two?"

"I'd like some inside, uncensored information about someone you served with."

"Hmm." I could almost hear him thinking through the soft crackle of the long-distance line. "I do hope you're not fishing for gossip. I served with some exceptional soldiers; I don't want to pour tarnish on any of my men. Who are you talking about?"

"Sergeant Gilbert Fitzhugh."

His momentary silence spoke volumes, then I heard him sigh.

"What's he done?"

"Why do you assume he's done anything?"

He gave a sort of *harrumph*. "I can't think of any reason anyone would contact me about Gilbert Fitzhugh unless he was in trouble or causing it. You would hardly be ringing me for a eulogy, or because he'd won a humanitarian award, or been elected Pope."

"It's because of Val's brother that I'm ringing. Fitzhugh is Val's uncle's valet. He was here last week when Erasmus died, rather mysteriously. I'm wondering if—"

"He did it," Roger interjected. However, being Roger, he interjected calmly. "Whatever it is, Fitzhugh did it. The man's a devil. Completely unprincipled and thoroughly reprehensible. Anyone who hires him as a valet is either a fool or equally despicable."

"High praise, indeed. I hate to ask you to tell tales but—"

"I don't mind telling tales about that bounder. If I'd had my way back in '15, he'd have been court-martialed and shot. Did you know he killed a German prisoner?"

"I'd heard a rumor."

"Oh, it's more than a rumor. A young neighbor of mine was there when it happened. He was a Private under Fitzhugh, and they were escorting some prisoners to an aid station when they stopped for a water break. Fitzhugh walked up to one man and demanded his watch and cigarette case. When the man refused, Fitzhugh shot him, point blank."

"Good God. Why wasn't he cashiered?"

"Because he was the ranking officer present, with only a few young recruits as witnesses. They were all terrified of him. His temper was well known and rightfully feared. He was known to strike subordinates, so most refused to cross him. One lad who reported him for robbing the dead after a battle showed up the next day looking like a slab of meat. He said someone had thrown a blanket over him from behind and beaten him senseless with a whispered warning to mind his own business in the future."

I mumbled an oath no vicar would approve of.

"Exactly," Roger agreed. "The brass knew he was rotten but could never gather enough evidence to bring charges. Nothing was ever said on the record. He also had a booming sideline in forged passes. Pretty convincing ones. He learned how to duplicate the Major's signature and made a fortune."

"And he wasn't arrested?"

"Nobody would shop him. His customers were hardly going to confess to paying for falsified papers. Speak plainly, are you suggesting Fitzhugh may have had something to do with Val's brother's death?"

"Yes, I am. The man he works for, Val's awful uncle, had a strong motive to want Erasmus out of the way. And has an equally strong one for getting rid of Val next."

"That's concerning," he said in the same detached tone in which he might order breakfast. "If Fitzhugh is about, then Val most certainly needs to watch his back."

"That's partially why I'm here," I explained.

"Good. Keep your eye on him. And do what you can to keep a watch on Fitzhugh. Are the police on the case?"

"Yes and no," I said.

"Elaborate, please."

"I spoke with Hugo Drake and asked him to see what he could, unofficially, find out about Fitzhugh. But the local police aren't involved. There's a dubious coroner's report calling the death an accident, and I believe Val is concerned that the actual guilty party could be a more trusted servant or a rather batty aunt."

"Hmm," Roger said. "Well, if he changes his mind and wants to go to the authorities, be careful. That man Fitzhugh is a thorough rat."

* * *

THE STUDY DOOR opened and Wulfstan strode in just as I was hanging up. He looked not at all happy to find me there.

"I need to make a call," he said, without a hint of apology.

"It's fine, I'm done."

At the door, I casually added, "I was merely checking in with an old friend of mine. He's a CID Inspector."

Wulfstan stopped and cleared his throat nervously, then switched to feigned nonchalance. "Oh, so you're chummy with fascist police stooges, eh?"

I paused at the door and turned. "Do you view all policemen as the authoritarian implements of a ruthless, ultra-nationalistic dictatorial government whose purpose is the forcible suppression of opposition?"

Judging by the look on his face, the only part of that he'd understood was "the." I hid a smile and mentally thanked Dr. Ellington's Political Theory seminar from my school days.

"I never conveyed my sympathies," I said. "I'm sorry about the death of your cousin. I understand you were here when it happened."

"Yes," was all he said to that. Then he looked at me. I knew his type, the kind that can't abide silence. After a few moments of me looking back at him and not saying anything in response, he caved. "I came down to research working conditions at the local… uh… mine."

"Oh, I didn't know there was a mine around here. What kind?"

"What do you mean, 'what kind?' The kind that goes into the ground."

"Yes, but what do they mine? Coal? Salt? Owls?"

Signs of desperate thought flashed across his face. Eventually, he set a slimy smile and said, "What difference does it make? You're clearly too posh to care about the plight of the workers."

"Well, then, it's a good thing you're not. The downtrodden workers deserve someone of common stock to care about their working conditions." I smiled.

Feeling he'd been insulted, but not understanding how, Wulfstan switched to the other opening I'd given him. "I… wasn't around much last weekend."

"No, of course not. You were down a mine. Of some sort. It's too bad promoting the cause of labor takes up so much of your time. I understand there was a race meeting nearby, that might have been a nice way to spend a day."

He glared at me but didn't speak.

"Were you here when the valet found Erasmus?"

"No. I was busy at the… er… mine, and then I headed back here. I was supposed to speak at the Hatton-Under-Tower Soviet Club that evening. I had to stand them up."

"And I'm sure both comrades of the Soviet Club were very understanding when they heard of the late Earl's death. Were you and Erasmus close?"

"Not really. We didn't have much in common. He wasn't an intellectual, like me. His mind was fixed on the selfish pursuit of status and wealth. No thought for the common man, the rights of the worker. Only on exploiting them."

I enjoyed tweaking the little rat, and he kept feeding me material, but it was time to stop fencing. I pounced.

"Do you think they killed him?"

"What? Who? What? Why?"

"You forgot 'when,'" I said. "I mean the common people. Do you think they killed Erasmus because he was exploiting them and too posh to care about the plight of the workers?"

The wolf pup just stared at me.

"After all," I continued, "it had to have been murder. You're too much of an intellectual to accept that your cousin calmly got into his bath, filled his mouth with marbles, and picked up an obscure theological work for a little light reading. Why, with your brains and knowledge of the world, you undoubtedly found the whole story fishy. You never did buy it as an accident, did you? You're too smart to be fooled."

"Uh, well, yes. Or... uh... no."

"Yes, you agree it was murder or no, you're not too smart to be fooled?"

"Uh, which..." I could almost hear the rusty wheels turning as he tried to decide how to answer. He swallowed. It had the unfortunate side effect of highlighting his freakishly large Adam's apple. It was even more prominent than Nicky's.

"Certainly, Erasmus's death was a little, uh, unusual," he stammered. "But I don't think it was murder. Who'd want to kill him? He was harmless."

"But I thought he was exploiting workers in the... what was it, a tin mine?"

"Well, no, he doesn't actually have ties to the uh... mine."

"So, which was it? Was Erasmus harmless or was he a brutal capitalist getting rich on the sweat of the workers?" I asked.

Wulfstan picked a lane, for better or worse. "Erasmus cared nothing for the plight of the masses," he blurted. "All he cared about was capitalist greed. Money and luxury. He was too selfish for more lofty pursuits."

"Well, he had a few lofty pursuits," I quipped. "For instance, I heard a rumor he was thinking about buying a sailboat. That's something only a selfish capitalist would do, don't you agree?"

I heard the door slam behind me.

Chapter 20

That evening was the family's official gathering in memory of old Adjutor, the dotty great-grandfather. As I bathed and changed for dinner, I kept thinking of that cruel and ridiculous will of his. What had Val called it? A *tontine*? Last survivor takes all? What a perfect way to set one's family against each other. It's a wonder there were any Hatton-Haxleys left.

Somewhere below, I knew the house was filling up with guests. But the corridor stretching from my room to Val's remained eerily silent. My knock seemed thunderous against his door.

"Come in," he called.

I walked in. "You did that wrong," I said.

"I did?"

"Yes."

"Which part? *Come* or *in*?"

"If you're seriously afraid of becoming the next late Earl, you should at least ask who it is before shouting to come in."

"You're right," he admitted. "Would you like to go out again?"

"Why? So, you can practice your '*who is it?*'"

"No, so I can barricade the door."

"Too late, I'm already in." I folded myself into one of the chairs by the fire with a long sigh. "Val, you're my best friend. And I'm sorry for casting aspersions in the direction of your relatives. But your relatives are horrible people."

"Yes, they are."

"How in the world did you grow up relatively normal around these ghouls? Each one I meet drives me closer to insanity. This is the worst family reunion since Henry VIII had all his wives over for tea."

"It wasn't easy."

"At least I've been spared Wulfie's poetry. I dread it. The only thing that could make that fake communist even more insufferable is iambic pentameter."

"Don't worry, cousin Wulfie can't count high enough for iambic pentameter."

"And isn't there one more delight to come?" I asked, "The youngest cousin. What did you say his name was? Flounderford? Thrumfluger? Saint Cyanide of Spitalfields?"

"Theobald." The sound that Val made next could only be described as a snort.

"Of course," I nodded. "Good old Theobald. I haven't seen him since Elsie and I went to that big bonfire with our old pal, Nero. What's he up to, these days?"

"He's the star player on Saint Gordon's Insufferable Little Wanker team," Val said, glumly.

"I can't wait."

"Theo's a monster. Likes to pull the wings off frogs. Invented paper cuts. Collects books on medieval dentistry. Was canned by his Headmaster once for arguing that Pontius Pilate had a point, and that Caligula has been slandered by history. He even prepared visual aids. Theo wasn't born, he was hatched from an egg like a snake-turtle-vulture."

"Is that one hellish animal or three?"

A knock at the door left that mystery forever unsolved. "Please God, don't let it be a cousin," Val grumbled.

It *was* a cousin. Luckily for us, it was the good one.

Daphne looked lovely in a dinner dress of rich turquoise.

She'd draped a dark blue wrap artistically around her shoulders and held it in place with a charming silver brooch in the shape of a dragon.

I stood and smiled in greeting, nodding towards the brooch. "I like your dragon. Family crest?"

"Oh, no," she replied. "The Ferguson family crest is a rampant chicken on a cracked shield against a field of three-humped camels."

I laughed, but an odd look in her eye stopped me. She was staring intently, her gaze flicking between my face and Val's. "Is something wrong?" I asked.

"Not at all," she said, not at all embarrassed at being caught staring. "I just realized that you and Val look even more like brothers than Val and Erasmus did. You have the same dark brown hair, straight nose, nice mouth. Why, you're both quite handsome, really."

"Yes," Val agreed. "But I'm handsomer. Griff is hideously scarred."

She turned to me. I lifted the fall of hair off my forehead so she could see the two-inch scar just at my hairline. "Fencing scar," I said.

"You have a fencing scar? Oh, how romantic and dashing. Was it a duel over a woman? Please tell me it was a duel over a woman."

"It wasn't a woman," Val corrected. "It was an actual fence. He tripped over a cat and fell face-first into a garden fence."

Daphne laughed. "There goes that image."

"So, what have you been doing with your afternoon?" I asked her.

"Not much," she replied. "I spoke with some more of the staff and had a poke around the house. Didn't learn anything new. Ended up in the attic."

"The attic?" Val mocked. "Are you crazy? The attic is the

haunted part of the house. They keep the bodies of Victorian children in the attic."

"How odd," I observed. "My family has always hidden bodies in the priest's hole."

"We use the old well," Daphne added.

"Mm. We'll have to figure out where to stash Val," I said.

"Ahem," Val interjected. "Here I am, facing death in a house full of maniacs, and my nearest and dearest are stirring up attic ghosts and cracking jokes."

"I'm sorry, Val," Daphne said. "But you'll have to excuse me. After all, I'm merely an unimportant outsider from the far side of the family. Unlike you, the Fergusons are not handed a black spot upon reaching majority."

"And I'm not even family," I added.

"Lucky you," Val sad, glumly.

"But I'll miss you."

"Stop that!"

"Sorry," I said. "It's easier to make bad jokes than to accept that we're actually looking for evidence that half your family murdered the other half. I mean, I'm convinced, but I still don't believe it. If that makes any sense."

"I'm sorry, too, Val," Daphne said.

"You know we're both on your side."

"I do know. Thanks."

"So," I asked, "what fresh horrors should we expect tonight?"

"Nothing too ghastly," Val answered. "A few more guests have arrived. Tonight, we toast my great-grandfather, then tomorrow we'll inter Erasmus. Or his ashes, at any rate."

"What actually happens tonight?" I asked. "Is it anything like *The Musgrave Ritual*? Will there be a secret ceremony? Do you have to swear a blood oath? Tell me there's a secret handshake at least. I love secret handshakes. In fact, there's one in the book I'm working on."

"Ooh," Daphne, enthused, "what's the title?"

"*Zeppo Ziggerjammies and the Exploding Wombat of Emperor Plotz*," Val replied.

That set us off again and it was several minutes before we actually got to talking about the ceremony.

"Nothing much happens, really," Val explained. "We do this every year and it's always the same. We gather with the family solicitor on hand to ensure fair play and drink a toast to the memory and wisdom of Great-grandfather Adjutor."

"Wisdom?" Daphne said. "If you ask me, Great-grandfather Adjutor has a lot to answer for."

"Amen," I said.

"But other than that," Val said. "It's just a big dinner. And I've arranged for each of us to sit next to one or two of our suspects."

"That should be fun." I had been hoping for another dinner with Daphne as my partner.

"We need to pay attention to everything said tonight."

"Right," Daphne agreed. "I'm going to bring up Erasmus as much as I can."

"Perfect," said Val. "Steer the conversation. Watch for reactions, listen to every comment. We need to be completely focused tonight on catching one of them out. Be obsessed. Be old Ahab hunting Moby-Dick."

"You know, most people spend country house weekends playing tennis and having costume parties," I observed. "We get to feel seasick on a whaling ship. And when have you ever read *Moby-Dick*?"

Just then, the dinner gong sounded. "Aha," Val said. "Thar, she blows!"

Chapter 21

If I manage to avoid swans for the next seventy years or so, and thus die of old age, I will still look back on the night of Adjutor's dinner as one of the oddest of my life.

To begin with, there were two new people to meet. Because of course there were.

First, the Bishop, who turned out to be John Snedly-Daniels, Bishop of Wickham. As far as I was concerned, he already had two strikes against him: his occupation and his name. I don't see how anybody can take a 'Snedly' seriously, let alone trust spiritual advice from one. But he was a friend of Uncle Sally (which I suppose makes three strikes) and had come down to preside over the funeral.

The Bishop was in his seventies at minimum, with tufts of snow-white hair that curled around his face like those bizarre sketches of animals in medieval manuscripts made by monks who'd never actually seen them, so you can't tell if they're meant to be sheep or goats, but they look both stupid and vicious and you'd rather avoid the beastly beasts entirely. That's *exactly* how the Bishop looked.

Gazing sourly around the room, he gave the impression that laughter was a mortal sin and we were all going to hell. Not that there was much to laugh about, but there were moments of levity in the conversation of which he clearly did not approve.

The other newcomer was the dreaded cousin, Theobald.

He was about sixteen years old, with carefully tousled mouse brown hair and matching eyes. I mean his eyes were also brown, not that they were tousled. Unlike his brothers, who had their mother's tiny features floating in faces full of skin, Theo had large features overrunning a face two sizes too small. He looked rather like a ferret, which, now that I write that, seems grossly unfair to ferrets. He was a small, frighteningly precious being with tiny, restless feet and furtive little hands.

"Griff, this is Theo," Val said, immediately leaving me to my own devices as he strode off to speak with the Bishop.

"Hello Theo," I said.

"It's *Theobald*," he insisted in a nasally whine.

That, as far as I'm concerned, finished him. Who would insist on being referred to as Theobald when you can so easily pass as a Theo?

"Right," I said. "Goodbye, Theobald."

I turned away, with the intention of joining Val and the Bishop. I mean, Snedly is a silly name, but it's better than insisting on being a Theobald. However, my attempted exit was foiled by Daphne. She joined us with a "Hello, Theo, how's life?"

"How come she gets to call you Theo?" I asked.

"She's pretty," he said.

"I'm pretty," she said.

"Hello, Daphne," the little blister said to Daphne's neckline, "How are you?"

Daphne, noting the direction of his gaze replied, "I'm up here."

He turned to me with a what could only be defined as a leer and said, "Daphne and I aren't actually related, you know."

"Which means he thinks he and I could marry," she said, "If only he were human."

Theobald laughed. "She's crazy about me, you know. She knows I'm the best of the brothers."

"That's rather like being the best way to die from a disfiguring disease," she said.

"She's just jealous because our family has money and hers doesn't."

"Theo, I'd agree with you, but then we'd both be wrong." She took my arm and led me towards her parents.

Again, I was welcomed into the tiny oasis of relative sanity that surrounded Lord and Lady Ferguson. They were kind. Nothing they said sounded like a threat. And it was so refreshing to participate in a conversation where I didn't have to decipher double meanings or come up with cutting retorts.

I was just beginning to enjoy myself, sipping atrocious sherry and chatting amiably with Daphne's parents, when Val cruised up to us. Daphne snagged him by the arm.

"Just out of curiosity, Val," she murmured. "Who's going to be my whale?"

"What? Your what?"

"Remember, be like Ahab? Which whale do I get for a dinner partner? If it's Theo or Wulfie, you won't have to worry about them killing you, I'll do it myself."

"You drew the lucky straw, my dear," he said. "You get the biggest of big fish: Uncle Sally."

"Yay, me?"

"That's cruel," I observed.

Val turned to me. "I'm sorry, do *you* want him?"

"Yay, Daphne!" I replied.

Val moved closer. "I wanted to make it easier for you to engage him in conversation, so I put Aunt Elsie on his other side. Sally would rather volunteer for a firing squad than talk to her. He'll ignore Elsie and you can be charming and witty."

"It's all right, I know how to work that man," she said with determination.

"And how's that?" I asked.

Val laughed. "Put a girl that's even halfway attractive and young in front of him and he instantly thinks he's a bit of an old dog."

"Don't say things like that right before dinner," I pleaded. I turned to ask Val who my whale was, but at that moment, dinner was announced.

As it turned out, I didn't get anything so simple as a whale. I had to steer between Scylla and Charybdis.

* * *

I DECIDED MY friendship with Val was over for the fifth or sixth time that weekend when I found myself seated between Aunt Jim and cousin Wulfstan. Either was marginally better than Angela Astley, I supposed, but it was cold comfort.

Within moments of the soup being served, I discovered that Wulfstan was the worst soup slurper I had ever met: noisy, ill-mannered, and disgusting. Turning away, I mustered all my courage and engaged Aunt Alfred in conversation.

"Tell me, Lady Haxley," I said, trying to tune out the song that Wulfie was playing on his soup, "I understand the Hall has quite a history. Exactly how old is it?"

She shot me one of her loathing glances, sniffed, and said simply, "Tudor."

Oh my, was it going to be a long evening. I tried again, this time with a conversational opening that I knew couldn't fail.

"I just met your youngest son, Lady Haxley. Val tells me he's quite the athlete." There, I'd put in a plug for Val speaking highly of one of her precious sons *and* given her a topic she could run with.

"Oh, yes." She nodded. "Our Theo is the star player on the Saint Gordon's football team. He also runs on their athletics team, plays rugby, is captain of the Saint Gordon's cadets, and is Head Boy of his house."

"Well, my goodness," I said, with the closest thing to sincerity I could muster. "However does he find time to study?"

"Oh, Theo is quite the scholar as well. Last prize day he took home awards for maths, geography, and English. And his recitation of *The Wreck of the Hesperus* has been known to bring people to tears."

"Yes, well, Longfellow often has that effect."

"Oh, no," she corrected. "It's the skill with which he recites it. *Such* pathos!"

I quoted:

O father! I see a gleaming light,
Oh Say what may it be?
But the father answered never a word,
A frozen corpse was he.

I smiled. "Never fails to brighten any gathering."

Beside me I heard Wulfstan snort. I turned, reluctantly, to him.

"And what about you, Wulfstan? What did you excel at in school? With your interest in politics, I imagine you studied something along those lines. Law, maybe? Or economics? Or did you forego university altogether to dedicate yourself to pursuing the dignity of labor? Perhaps you apprenticed as a factory worker or miner. I understand there are mines of some sort in the area."

Wulfstan shot me a look of near-hatred. "I read English. At Oxford."

"Wulfie is a highly regarded poet," his mother added.

"Really?" I asked. "I'd love to read some of your work. Where have you been published? Is there a volume or two I could purchase?"

Wulfstan's glare rose to an incandescent loathing, cementing my opinion that tweaking him was my new favorite pastime. Indeed, it was a hobby that everyone could enjoy. Fun for the whole family.

I turned my back on him, smiled at Aunt Jim, and, bolstered by a book on political philosophy Val had told me I could find in the library, rained down a nonsensical string of terms.

"Tell me, Lady Haxley, do you share your son's beliefs that we should all work towards the creation of a socioeconomic order structured upon the ideas of common ownership of the means of production and the absence of social classes, money, and the state?" While I was pretty sure I used the right words, I was equally sure I was using them in the wrong way. Not that it would matter with this lot.

The lady turned to me with a look of total confusion. "I'm not sure I understand the question, Mr. Griffin."

"Well, I'm sure your son could explain it much better than I. Wulfstan, why don't you tell your mother all about…" But the moment was lost. Before I could finish, Wulfstan had turned to Lady Ferguson and started a conversation about breeding Airedales, a topic about which neither appeared to have any knowledge or interest. In a dim part of my mind, I wondered what had prompted him to think of Airedales in that moment. But it meant I had no choice but to talk to Aunt Jim.

"The last time I visited Tower Field Hall," I said, "I remember having a wonderful game of chess with Erasmus." I'd never played chess with Erasmus in my life. For all I knew, he didn't even play chess. But it was as good an opening as any. "I'm really going to miss him."

She replied, with a total absence of emotion, "Yes. So sad. Such a waste."

"But I know that Val will do a fine job of following Erasmus's footsteps as the Earl of Haxley," I added.

This time there was emotion in her reply, but I couldn't figure out if it was anger, denial, envy, or boredom—if boredom is an emotion. "I'm sure Valentine will be thoroughly satisfactory."

Thoroughly satisfactory? I thought. How does one achieve the lofty status of being thoroughly satisfactory as an Earl? By managing not to lose the Hall at the roulette wheel? Successfully not marrying a burlesque queen? Giving the crown no reason at all to behead him for treason?

"Oh yes," I agreed. "Thoroughly satisfactory." Fortunately, the soup course came to an end and Wulfie's bowl was taken away before he could lick it. To be honest, it seemed like the persona of Comrade Wulfie came more naturally to him than being the grandson of an Earl. He may not have been a revolutionary, but he was surely revolting.

With Wulfie glaring at nothing on one side and Aunt Floyd absorbed by the fish course on the other, I realized that any further conversation was up to me. I turned to the aunt and steeled myself for another attempt, only to be flummoxed by the amount of food she managed to cram into her freakishly tiny mouth. She could really pack it away. And where did it all go? Lady Haxley was a tiny woman who gave the impression that she lived solely on tea and cucumber sandwiches. Yet there she was, eating like a Viking.

I glanced across the table at Uncle Suspicious, who was shooting affronted looks at Val. As the Earl, Val got to sit at the head of the table while dear Uncle was relegated to sitting with the masses. His displeasure was plain to see, although proximity to Daphne surely offered some compensation. I also noticed that instead of sharing in the delicious wine the rest of us were drinking, Uncle Suspicious had Lydgate fetch him a decanter of Scotch. Anyone who would drink Scotch with fish was obviously a madman.

I turned back to Aunt Jim and started again. "Were you and Erasmus close?" I asked.

She chewed, swallowed, and reloaded. Chewed, swallowed, and reloaded again. Finally, she replied, "I was, and am, fond of all my nephews." And reloaded again, indicating that was all the response I was going to get. Quite the little chatterbox, our Aunt Jim.

I gave it another go. "I know Val and his brothers are… *were*… older than your sons, but I imagine they had a lot of childhood adventures together. I know when I got together with my cousins, we always got into some mischief."

She looked at me with disapproval. "Young Valentine and his brothers often got into trouble," she said with a haughtiness that would have done Victoria proud. "But my sons have always behaved with absolute probity."

"Really?" I hoped my disbelief was masked by a veneer of teasing friendliness. "No muddy footprints? No sneaking a hedgehog into the house?"

"Of course not! *'He that is a companion of riotous men shameth his father.'* Proverbs, 28." She sniffed in indignation, scooped up more fish, chewed, swallowed, and continued.

"My boys have always been their mother's pride, and they continue to be." She was warming to the subject now. "For instance, even though he shouldn't have to work for a living, my Nicky has never complained and has, in fact, become a rising star in the financial world."

I could not, for the life of me, imagine Nicodemus *not* complaining about having to work for a living.

"My Nicky," she continued, with a disgusting overabundance of maternal blindness, "has always been a prodigy. So brilliant. And you should hear him sing! The voice of an angel. One of the strong, warrior angels, I mean. Not one of those fat Italian baby angels." She introduced yet more fish into her disturbing mouth, and I wondered if she'd received an extra portion when I wasn't looking.

"Oh, of course not," I seconded.

"He's quite the sportsman, too. Nicky can ride like a centaur!"

"Do centaurs ride? Don't they just, well, gallop?"

She ignored me and plowed on. "And he speaks perfect French. Why, when we spent Christmas with the Duc and Duchess de Fourcade, they said my Nicky could pass for a genuine Frenchman! I do believe his accent improved while we were there, but then he did spend so many hours conjugating with the Duc's daughter."

I coughed and reached for my water. This she took as an invitation to continue.

"As it happens, Nicky's biggest problem when he was at university was deciding what to study. He began with law and would have made a brilliant barrister. Then he took up architecture. Had he continued, I'm sure he would have been another Christopher Wren."

Only a mother, I thought, could look at a sticky cove like Nicky and see another Christopher Wren. Lady Haxley really did love her horrible offspring and spoke with genuine pride—along with, I was sure, a great deal of blindness. But what surprised me even more was her sudden garrulousness.

By this point I was finding it so difficult to restrain my laughter that I was getting cramps. So, I cut her off and asked point blank, "Tell me, Lady Haxley, do you believe in the family curse?"

Aunt Jim, having reduced her fish to a skeleton, daintily applied her napkin to her tiny mouth. By way of answering me, she quoted.

"*Have nothing to do with Godless myths and old wives' tales; rather train yourself to be Godly.*" She turned to look me in the eye. "Timothy 1, verse 4."

With that, she happily moved on to salting the roast beef that had arrived in front of her. But as I returned to Comrade

Wulfie, I spied her discreetly taking up a pinch of salt and tossing it over her left shoulder. So, then. For all her Biblical quoting, Aunt Arthur was superstitious.

Back to business. "You know, Wulfstan," I said, "I grew up with sisters, and they were great fun, but I always wanted brothers. The three of you must have had some memorable times growing up. You must have been good friends."

"*Humph*. My brothers are unbearable," he said. "Nick cares only for himself. And Theo is a precocious imp of Satan with all the brotherly feeling of Jack the Ripper's pet rat."

"Sounds delightful," I commented drily. "I look forward to not getting to know them better."

Wulfie snorted. "Take my advice and ignore them both. You'll be happier that way."

At that moment there was a lull in conversation, and I half-heard Aunt Elsie mention Erasmus. But the moment passed. I turned back to Wulfstan. "Miss Armistad is an interesting woman," I said. "She told me today I was going to die in a swan attack."

At that, I heard the first real laugh I'd ever heard from his side of the family, a true hearty guffaw. "She's batty. Has she told you about your previous lives?"

"Oh yes. I died at Waterloo, apparently."

"Oh, then you're much younger than I am," he said, "I died at Marathon."

"May I ask how you're going to pass this time around?"

He took an immense swallow of potato and said simply, "Snakebite."

"Ah. Do you spend a lot of time around snakes?" I asked.

"Nope. But now I'm terrified of them."

"I thought she was always wrong."

"She is. But I absolutely refuse to be the one time she's right."

"Oh, the woman is mad," Aunt Jim said. "She should be

locked up. I can't tell you the number of times I've felt that she might be dangerous. It's quite frightening."

"Really?" She was bewildering, to be sure, but I couldn't imagine daffy Aunt Elsie being truly frightening. "Has she ever threatened you? Or caused anyone harm?"

"None that we can prove," she replied. It was the kind of needlessly cryptic response that shows the speaker wants the listener to beg for details.

I didn't. Instead, I turned to Wulfie and, trying to change the subject, said the worst thing possible: "You know, we have writing in common. I am also an author." I nearly bit my tongue, but it was too late. That "also" would cost me.

"Oh yes," he said with a fascinating combination of envy and disgust. "You write *popular fiction*, don't you." He spat it out, as if I wrote pornographic nursery rhymes.

"Yes," I happily agreed. "I do write popular fiction. It's nice, being popular. You should try it."

"I believe you write so-called mysteries," he observed.

"Yes," I smiled. "And you write so-called poetry. Tell me, what exactly rhymes with manifesto?"

He ignored that. "Who is your publisher?"

It was clear where this was headed. "Catesby and Ratcliffe," I said, naming one of the biggest publishers in the country. "But they only publish *popular fiction*. They surely can't compete with poetry and political discourse, or the more academic publishing houses you transact with. Who is *your* publisher?"

Wulfstan turned away to yell across the table at Nicky, asking about a mutual friend. I smiled to myself and continued dinner.

* * *

SOMEHOW, WULFSTAN AND I made it out of the meal alive, which was a testament to my restraint. I had never met a less convincing communist in my life. At one point I asked for an opinion o Leon Trotsky and Wulfie thought I was talking about a racehorse.

At a signal from Val, we all rose from the table, and a new ordeal began. The moment the men reached the billiard room, Theobald began to grill me about Daphne. That's when I realized I hadn't had nearly enough wine at dinner.

"Are you and Daphne dating?" Theo asked without preamble. "Because I just can't see it." He looked me up and down as if I were an uppity peasant.

"Are you the annoying cousin I've heard about?" I asked in reply. "Because if so, I can absolutely see it."

"I don't like you," he declared.

"Okay." I walked away. He followed.

"Hey!"

"What, hey?" I asked. "Hey, what?"

"I wasn't done speaking to you."

"Well, I was done listening." I kept walking. And he kept following.

"I want to talk to you about Daphne."

I hauled up all my condescension and smiled at him.

"No."

We did the *I walked, he followed* thing again.

"Would you stop walking away," he hissed. No, really. It was an actual hiss.

I stopped and pretended to think it over.

"Hmm… No, I find I rather like walking away from you. In fact, I think it's my new hobby." I demonstrated by, once again, walking away.

"But…"

I kept on walking and joined Val at the cue rack. "Game?" I asked. He nodded and we chose our weapons. Theo followed like a lost puppy with a title. I looked at him, wordlessly. And it pleased me no end to see he had no idea what to do.

Val looked at Theo. Then me. Then Theo. Then me again.

"Why is Theo following you?" He turned to Theo once more. "Why are you following Griff?"

"Because he walked away from me!"

I grinned at the brat, then turned back to Val. "Would you like to break?"

Val broke, sunk absolutely nothing, and we began to play. Theo stood there for another minute or so like a confused fish; that is, if a fish could stand. And if, indeed, a fish could be confused. His mouth gaped and a look of absolute stupidity settled onto his face. We ignored him. Finally, out of options, Theo wandered off.

"Well, Griff? Have you learned anything?" Val asked.

"Yes. I've learned that your family is horrible."

"That isn't news, even to you."

"No, but it's relevant nonetheless." I sank a couple of balls before continuing. "Seriously, Val, your cousins are awful. And that miserable little tick Theo has an unnatural fascination with Daphne."

"I know," he said glumly. "He has this weird fantasy that he's going to marry her someday."

I made a sort of choking sound, missed a shot, and Val took the table.

"Really," he said, "what did you learn during dinner?"

"Nothing," I admitted. "But I asked your aunt about the curse, and she evaded me. Have you really never talked with her about that? Not even once?"

"Good Lord, no! That would require a conversation and I avoid those with anybody who shares my surname."

"It's a good thing you plan on staying single, then, because that would be a terrible rule to have with your wife."

"Well, hopefully, if I ever got married…" He stopped.

"She'd keep her maiden name?" I suggested.

"No, it would be to someone who…" He stopped again.

"Who would never speak to you?"

He gave me what I believe they call the "evil eye."

"That's it!" Val declared. "Tomorrow night, you're sitting between Theo and Angela."

"Oh dear, I think I'm suddenly coming down with a case of diphtheria," I warned.

"Good, you can give it to them." Val shot and missed. "I give up. What's the billiards equivalent of toppling your own king in surrender?"

"You could cry 'Uncle,'" I suggested.

"I'd rather not, he might come over."

We re-racked our cues and headed to the drinks. Ignoring a decanter of port, we both opted for Scotch and found a pair of leather chairs at far corner of the room.

"Why are you so interested in whether Aunt Jim believes in the curse?"

"If she does, it might mean she's not a threat," I murmured. "As much as she might want to be the Countess of Haxley, I don't think she'd risk her beloved Nicky."

"And If I die, Sally becomes the Earl and suddenly precious first-born Nicky is in the cross-hairs."

I looked over at Uncle Sally, who was trouncing Nicky at billiards. Then at Wulfie, who was laughing at his brother's impending defeat. A thought occurred to me.

"Tell me something, Val: do you think number-two son Wulfie is despicable enough to kill Erasmus? And then kill his own father and older brother to become the Earl?"

Val went wide-eyed for a moment. "That's a devil of a thing to say, that anybody would kill three people just for a title and a pile of money. But honestly, I wouldn't put it past Wulfie. He *is* one of the world's foremost experts in unscrupulousness. Another being Nicky."

"Hmm. And tell me, just how much of a financial wizard *is* Cousin Nicky? You haven't been putting him down just for my benefit?"

"Hardly. He really is an idiot. And a sly, miserable little huckster on top of that. A man who would foreclose on his own grandmother's orphanage." Val smiled. "You know, I seem to have a flair with words. Perhaps I could help you write your next book."

"No."

"Why?"

"I depend upon selling these books to buy food, you know." I looked at my watch. "Have we spent enough time on manly pursuits to join the ladies again?"

"I suppose so."

"Well, you're the Earl," I reminded him. "If you think it's time to seek better company than we have here, the ball is in your court."

"Ah, so being the Earl does have one benefit," he sighed. We made a move for the door.

* * *

THE DRAWING ROOM once again felt like an oasis after the overloaded masculinity of the billiard room. It was bright and comfortable, and I felt better in the company of the lovely Daphne and her refreshingly normal mother. Even Elsie, perched delicately upon a piano bench, had her own sort of bizarre charm; as there was no piano nearby, I could only assume she'd been rearranging the furniture again.

Discussion of Erasmus's upcoming funeral soon dampened the atmosphere. Val had finalized the arrangements while I was interviewing and telephoning, and I felt a little badly that I hadn't been there through what was surely a painful and disagreeable business. On the other hand, I was relieved that I hadn't been there through what was surely a painful and disagreeable business.

Daphne filled me in as I joined her on the sofa.

"Val has decided to proceed with the funeral tomorrow. With the bishop presiding."

"Well, that sounds like a lovely send-off."

"I wish we could postpone," she said. "At least until we knew more."

"Daphne, there's nothing we can learn from a jar full of ashes."

"I suppose not, but I just heard something very interesting from Aunt Elsie."

"Oh, what's that? Did you go to gladiator school together?"

"Of course, we did," she replied. "But this is a little more pertinent."

"Tell me."

"That copy of *The Gospel of Nicodemus* was hers."

"What?" I couldn't have been more surprised if she'd slapped me. "How did you find out?"

"My mother and I were talking with her, and the subject of books came up. Aunt Elsie loves talking about books. She said she'd been reading *Nicodemus* recently but had mislaid her copy, so now she was revisiting Miss Austen."

"But... She knew Erasmus was reading that when he died. When I first met her, she told me some nonsense about watching him read it in her crystal ball!"

"Oh, she knows it was found with him. But it vanished before then and nobody ever returned it to her."

"That's odd. The whole thing is odd. You don't think...?" I stopped.

"No! Of course not. Aunt Elsie loved Erasmus. He was her favorite. They often had tea together in her room and he loved her stories of past lives. He even had a favorite."

"What was it?"

"Oh, she signed the American Declaration of Independence."

"Really? Well, that's impressive. Who was she? John Hancock? Benjamin Franklin?"

"Button Gwinnett."

"Buh… Who in the name of Thomas Jefferson is… No, never mind, we're straying from the subject."

"What *is* the subject?" Val asked, coming up suddenly.

I looked to Daphne. It was her news, after all. "The subject is that the copy of *The Gospel of Nicodemus* found in Erasmus's bath belonged to Aunt Elsie."

"The who what now?" Val said incoherently.

Daphne outlined the details: "According to Elsie, she had been reading it on Friday morning in her room, put it down at lunchtime, and when she came back, she couldn't find it. At the time she thought she'd simply been careless and that it would turn up. She never suspected it would turn up with Erasmus."

"But why would someone steal Elsie's book and toss it into Erasmus's bath?" I asked.

"You don't think—"

"Of course not!" Daphne and I replied in tandem.

"No. Neither do I," Val admitted.

"But can either of you think of a reason why her book would have been found where it was?" I asked.

"Someone was trying to frame Elsie," Val said. "Sally and Jim hate her. They want her gone."

"Setting Aunt Elsie up as Erasmus's killer does have a kind of twisted logic, I suppose," Daphne agreed. "She can make people uneasy."

That was true enough.

"I'm going to my room," I sighed. "My brain is full. I'm no closer to understanding what's happened than I was two days ago. It's increasingly clear to me that I'm only good at solving my own crimes. Er… The ones I write, I mean."

I excused myself, made the necessary good-nights, and went upstairs.

As I was coming down the hallway, I noticed that the door to Elsie's room was open. And there was Catullus once again, dashing out, tail twitching as he played with some object he'd stolen from the room. I sincerely hoped whatever it was, it was neither poisonous nor valuable. I bent down to pick it up.

It was a cat's-eye green marble.

Chapter 22

In movies, funerals are always held on gray and rainy days, with the mourners huddled under a flock of umbrellas as the deceased are meteorologically baptized into eternal rest. It's fitting. Yet nothing on this strange weekend wanted to follow the script, and that extended to the funeral of the late Erasmus Hatton-Haxley, 16th Earl of Haxley. Erasmus's final farewell came on a splendid day of dazzling beauty and warmth.

When I awoke at about seven, a line of bright sunshine shone between the curtains and across my bed, illuminating Catullus, who sat upon my chest. My cat and I regarded each other like conspirators. "*Bonus dies, domine,*" I said in my usual morning greeting. Catullus responded with his usual morning greeting: lifting his back leg to begin his daily grooming. It was not an elegant pose, but I forgave him his awkwardness.

A knock on my door revealed Sutherland, of all people, bringing morning tea for me and a plate of sardines for my furry Hastings. I wasn't sure if cats had little gray cells. In fact, I was often convinced that Catullus had no brain at all, but he had certainly earned his fish this morning. Finding the marble had surely been a master stroke of detective work.

"Good morning, Sutherland," I said. "Thank you for the tea. I certainly didn't expect you to bring it up."

"Good morning, sir. I was awake early, sir, and rather at a loss. It was comforting to have something to do."

I remembered with a shock that Sutherland had just lost a dear master and, I was certain, a friend. This would be a difficult day for him.

"The service will be at eleven, sir," he continued. "Down at Saint John's in the village."

I gave a small laugh. "With all the names in this family, I'm rather disappointed that the local church has one as normal and dull as John."

"If it helps, sir, Lord Erasmus…" he swallowed and then continued gamely, "Lord Erasmus thought the inside of the church was quite fussy and distinctly unattractive, so he referred to it as St. John the Atrocious."

I laughed. "Yes, I like that better."

"You'll be able to judge for yourself, sir."

"I'm afraid I won't, Sutherland. At least not today."

"Sir?"

"I will not be attending the funeral."

"Sir." The lone word was spoken with perfect professionalism, but I could hear both a question and an assessment in it.

I dropped my voice conspiratorially, to indicate I saw him as a comrade in arms. "I can't think of a better time to search the rooms of our various suspects than when they're all out of the house and otherwise occupied."

I'd thought the matter through overnight. It might raise eyebrows, but Erasmus and I hadn't been close, so it wouldn't be an insult if I didn't go, especially if I was out to avenge his demise. And Daphne, who did know him well, would be there to support Val. It was the perfect opportunity.

"I see, sir," he said. Again, perfectly professional, but did I detect a hint of approval this time?

"Tell me, Sutherland, will the staff be attending?"

"Most of us, sir. Mrs. Lydgate and a few of the kitchen maids will be busy preparing the luncheon."

"What about Fitzhugh?"

He paused. "I don't know, sir. But he'll be in the kitchen soon to get Lord Haxley's tea. Perhaps I should state my opinion that everyone not required to provide for the guests should attend the funeral, out of respect for the family. I believe I can enlist Mr. Lydgate to support me. In fact, I believe Mr. Lydgate would make it an order."

We shared a smile. "I think that's only proper, Sutherland."

* * *

HALF AN HOUR later I was washed, shaved, dressed, and starving. Catullus had followed his sunbeam across the bed and was sound asleep in its center. I watched him for a moment, wondering how he kept getting out. I wouldn't be surprised if he wound up attending the funeral in my stead.

I left my room just as Elsie was leaving hers. Perfect timing. "Good morning, Miss Armistad."

She turned to look at me, and I bit back a grin. She wore a long black skirt of a pre-war vintage, topped with an amazing confection of velvet and lace in deep purple with gold *fleurs-de-lys* down the sleeves. A scarf in eye-watering yellow was woven into her steel gray hair, accented by a gay, bright-green border of what looked like dead frogs. The top portion of Aunt Elsie looked like an electric canary. With electrocuted frogs. The bottom portion was Queen Victoria.

"My dear James, we're old friends," she said. "I think you can call me Elsie."

"I'd be pleased to," I said. "But my name is Gideon. Gideon Griffin. My friends all call me Griff."

"I know they do, James." She smiled abstractedly at me. I went up to her and she took my arm. I briefly had the nauseating thought that she was remembering us walking down the aisle at some point in her many pasts. I quickly chased that thought away.

"I hope Catullus hasn't been bothering you," I said as an easy conversational opener as we went down the stairs. "I can't figure out how he keeps escaping my room."

"Oh, no," she said happily. "Young Catullus and I are friends. As for his getting out, well, cats have a way of getting what they want, don't they?"

"I suppose so. By the way, I apologize for him. I found him coming out of your room last night."

"Oh, James, there's no need to apologize on his behalf. He already has."

Naturally, I thought. He'd also probably spent many a happy hour reminiscing with her about the glory days at the court of the Virgin Queen. I wondered if they were humans or cats back then.

"I'm afraid he stole something from you," I added.

"What was that?"

"A marble." I waited for a reaction. There was none.

"Oh, that's fine. I have plenty."

"You do?"

"Certainly. Nice things to have around, aren't they?"

"Marbles?"

"Yes. So pretty, in a glass bowl. And they feel so nice when you stick your hand in the bowl and roll them around."

"I'm sure they do. Do you play with them?"

For the first time, she looked at me seriously. "You may think it silly, but Erasmus and I would often get on the floor and play. We'd drink the good Scotch, the stuff we hide from Sally, and we'd shoot marbles and chat. I'll miss that."

The rest of the trip to the breakfast room was made in silence, and I was happy to see that Val and Daphne were already there. Happier still to see nobody else was.

As Elsie served herself, I walked over to the others for a quiet word.

"I just want to let you know that I won't be going to the funeral with you."

"Why not?" Daphne asked.

I explained why not and earned their joint approval.

"Great idea," Val said, "though I'll miss your company. What will you be looking for?"

"I have no idea. And it's unlikely anyone would be stupid enough to keep evidence around for this long. But we've got to be sure."

"Anything we can do?" Daphne asked.

I told them about Fitzhugh and trying to make sure he attended the service. Val nodded. "I'll make sure he goes."

"One more thing. If I don't finish before everyone returns, I may need your help. Either in searching or in keeping people occupied."

"If you don't find any evidence, I swear I'm going to plant some," Val murmured. "I'm not letting Fitzhugh get away with this."

"Let's leave compounding a felony until *after* I search. I'd like to start with Erasmus's room."

* * *

AFTER A RASHER of bacon and approximately half a loaf's worth of toast, Daphne, Val, and I headed upstairs, to the door three rooms down from my own.

"Neither of you need be a party to this if you don't want to," I said. "I can tackle this on my own."

Val just shook his head, but Daphne responded, "No, we want to help. We owe it to Erasmus. Squeamishness doesn't trump justice."

"Say, you should use that in a book!" Val said.

"God, no, that was awful," Daphne said. "Let's go in."

The curtains were drawn tightly, casting a funereal gloom

over everything. But when I opened them, sunlight flooded in from three arched windows to reveal a gorgeous room in tones of peacock blue, dark greens, and purples, overlooking a splendid view of Tower Field Hall's gardens and odd fountains. It was a suite befitting an Earl, and I wondered briefly if Val would move in now that he held the title.

"Has the room been cleaned since…?" I asked. There was no need to finish the thought.

"No," Val assured me. "Lydgate offered to have one of the maids take care of it, but Sutherland insisted it was his duty. Lydgate told him it could wait until after the funeral. It hasn't been touched."

"Including…?" I nodded to my left, indicating the doorway to the bath where Erasmus had bathed his last.

"Including," Val confirmed.

"You can leave the bath to me if you don't want to go in there," I said. Val nodded his thanks, then moved towards a huge Jacobean bureau that stood facing the vast, Earl-sized bed. Daphne crossed to the opposite wall near the windows and inspected a writing desk.

"Searching is a lot harder when you don't know what you're looking for," she said.

"Well, a note reading, '*I am going to kill you until you are dead*' and signed with the murderer's name might be nice," I said.

"Not helpful," Val observed.

"Sorry. But honestly, I feel like if we knew what we were looking for, we wouldn't need to look for it, if that makes sense."

"It doesn't," Said Val.

"Yes, it does," Daphne argued. "But I can't explain it any better than Griff can."

They silently returned to their searching. I started towards the bath but was distracted by the bedside tables—two beautifully made walnut pieces with drawers and small cupboards inlaid with ivory and rosewood in a geometric maze. I opened one but paused, reluctant to search through a dead man's things. I was no policeman. But the police weren't here, so it was up to us.

My examination revealed that Erasmus was a surprisingly orderly man who kept nothing but the usual items beside his bed. On top of the first table lay a silver valet tray holding a keyring and billfold, a box of Croft Caramels which contained two pieces, and a few books including, rather surprisingly, *Zoltan Szabo and the Vanishing Whippet*. I felt rather unsettled by this discovery and found myself wishing he'd chosen something else. Anything else. The fact that he died with one of my books next to his bed made me take Erasmus's death personally. Highly egocentric, I know, but it was also honest.

I picked up the book, noting a leather bookmark stuck in only about twenty pages from the end, which seemed terribly unfair. Poor Erasmus had died never knowing who was responsible for shooting Maestro Jean-Juan Jorgensen, along with his wife, his mother-in-law, and his horse.

The other bedside table held little of interest. There were a few handkerchiefs, an old newspaper with the crossword halfway done, incorrectly. A pen and notepad.

I gathered my courage and strode into the bath. It was green and white with a lovely, tiled floor and the aroma of fresh pine. I was vaguely jealous. My bath was an ugly beige and smelled like me. But then again, I wasn't an Earl. But then after that, I wasn't dead. I supposed I had it better, after all.

The bathtub itself was unremarkable. I don't know what else I had expected. Sharp pointed spikes on the bottom? Or a wire hooked up to the electric outlet? It was an elegantly curved but perfectly normal bathtub. And there was nothing else about the bathroom that looked out of place or suspicious. Another nice view from the window. Some dazzlingly white towels.

I checked the shaving cabinet above the wash basin and

found a razor, a bottle of aspirin, toothbrush and paste, and a comb. None of it appeared poisoned, not that I'd have any way of knowing unless I popped some of the aspirin or tasted the paste. Neither seemed appealing, or relevant. I closed the cabinet and returned to the bedroom.

Val had moved on to a small bookshelf and was fanning through volumes, occasionally raising his eyebrows as his gaze fell on a spicy passage. Apparently, Erasmus's infamous taste in reading matter had not changed much over the years, *Zoltan Szabo* aside.

"Now, this is interesting," Daphne called out. She turned from the writing desk, holding a large green marble up for our inspection.

"That's a bumboozer!" Val took it and looked closer. "Yes, it's Erasmus's bumboozer. I remember it from when we were kids."

"How can you possibly remember a marble from twenty years ago?" I asked.

"Easy. Here, look. Erasmus's was the only bumboozer—"

"Oh, good lord, please stop saying that ridiculous word!"

"Very well, Erasmus was the only one of us who used a cats-eye green bum… shooter. The rest of us used blue or red. We'd trade them. Erasmus never traded his."

"Huh." I told the others about Catullus's find from last night, and my discussion with Elsie this morning.

Daphne smiled. "Elsie and Erasmus played *marbles* together? That's delightful."

"That's weird," Val disagreed.

I glanced behind her at a pile of papers she'd unearthed from the desk. "Anything in there?"

She gave a sad sigh. "Nothing. Just normal letters from friends, invitations, that sort of thing. Nary a threat in sight."

"Ditto," said Val. "This room's clean as a whistle. Except for those books, I mean." He gave a mock leer.

"Well, let's hope for better luck in the other rooms. Val, before you go, could you please draw me a map?"

"Sure. I'll have to ask Lydgate where Fitzhugh sleeps. I'm not up on staff geography."

"Thanks. His is the room I'm most looking forward to searching. Oh, that reminds me. What does he look like? In case I run into him in the halls."

"Sort of beefy, short hair, squinty eyes. Could win a blue ribbon for looking the most like a potato at the next village fete. But he wears exceptional suits."

"Great, I'll look for a potato in a Savile Row suit and that'll be him."

"I bet you'll find something wildly incriminating in his room," Daphne said.

"I rather bet I won't."

"Eh? Why not?" Val asked.

"Because the man may be a blighter but he's not an idiot. He's hardly likely to write, '*don't forget to murder the Earl*' on his desk blotter."

"No," Daphne sad sadly. "Probably not. But if you don't find anything that ties him to murder, will you at least lie and tell me he wears pink silk underwear or collects dolls or something?"

"That's a promise."

Chapter 23

Once the last of the attendees left for the service and I had the house pretty much to myself, I felt hopelessly overwhelmed. The three horrid sons. Aunt Elsie. Sulpicius and Jim. And Fitzhugh. That was a lot of searching. I decided to try Sulpicius and Fitzhugh's rooms first. They were the ones most likely to have anything of interest.

Val had acquired the house keys from Lydgate, so locked doors wouldn't be a problem. Sure enough, it turned out Uncle Suspicious's door was locked. Who locked the door to their own bedroom in their own home? But then again, this wasn't his home. His family was just occupying a wing. And sure enough, someone was snooping while his back was turned. I pushed that line of thought aside and entered.

The room was overstuffed in the extreme, crammed with centuries of furniture and dubious *objets d'art*. It was as if Val's uncle couldn't bear for anyone else to have access to the Hall's treasures. His quarters resembled an antique store more than a bedroom.

Worse, most of it looked like the handiwork of evil dwarves in the Black Forest. Sulpicius's huge poster bed looked like a stand of trees, holding up a tapestried canopy of virulent reds and blues. The mattress was so high off the ground that an upholstered stool sat by the side, making it easier for massive Uncle Sally to climb into to his ornate nest. I imagined him imagining himself one of the great kings of old every time he lofted himself into dreamland.

A pair of marble-topped bedside tables held unfortunately matching lamps. I say "unfortunate" because even one would have been a mistake. Two constituted a deliberate violation of taste. They were wrought in gold like grotesque statues. At first glance I took them for depictions of a satanic orgy, but closer inspection revealed grimacing cherubs entwined in a disturbing ballet of impossible proportions and questionable anatomy.

Around the room, three massive, mismatched bureaus stood like dolmens against walls papered in gold brocade. A pair of overstuffed armchairs in a mistaken shade of green squatted in front of a fireplace the size of a small cave, capped by a white mantel from which a huge faux-Chinese vase of glorious vulgarity threatened to topple on unwitting visitors. I couldn't imagine a better lair for Uncle Suspicious.

Searching the most obvious places revealed only that he had abysmal taste in neckties. I moved on to the attached private bath. His medicine cabinet was crammed with bottles and jars, most of them unremarkable. One small, unlabeled bottle hiding behind the iodine looked promising, but it was merely smelling salts. Another bottle beckoned, marked simply: *Tonic to be taken before meals and at bedtime.*

I pulled out the stopper and rather cautiously took a sniff, then chastised myself. The stuff smelled terrible, but how would I know what an actual poison smelled like?

After the bath, I tried Uncle Sally's study. Luckily this room was more restrained than the bedchamber, although a heavy, ancient, rigidly-ordered desk took up a good quarter of it. Atop the desk lay a spotless, perfectly aligned blotter, along with a handsome sterling pen holder and letter knife. Two framed photographs sat on either side. One, a grim family photo of all five Hatton-Haxleys looking miserable in each other's company.

The other, a hunt meeting of some sort. Uncle Sally's bulk took up most of the photo, as he proudly showed off a hideous trophy. Aunt Jim, looking bored, stood at his side. What a depressing pair of images.

In a sterling box placed in the exact center of the desk, I found bills, personal letters from many thoroughly dull people, and various correspondence on business matters. The man spent a fortune on cigars and liquor and seemed to have no actual friends. So much for that.

In the top right-hand drawer, I found Uncle Sally's check ledger. I hesitated before opening. Zoltan Szabo frequently went through people's possessions and read their private correspondence, but I had never realized how much nerve it took to do so in real life. It all felt terribly invasive, even immoral. But Daphne's words swam up in my mind: *squeamishness doesn't trump justice*. I silently cursed her for permanently planting that phrase in my consciousness and opened the ledger.

Sulpicius Hatton-Haxley maintained a healthy bank balance. So healthy it made me wonder if the amount listed was honestly earned, secretly inherited, or if an inventory of Val's estate might perhaps reveal a few valuable items were nowhere to be found. I couldn't think of many other possibilities. Surely even Uncle Sally wasn't stupid enough to take investment advice from Nicky.

But then I found something even more interesting.

As a writer, I've had cause to research quite a few things that had nothing to do with my real life. Because of my books I know how to make *coq au vin*. I know which drugs can be used to feign death. I know the name of Rembrandt's mistress, but I'll never tell why. And even though I have never had a valet myself, I know their yearly salary is about £750.

So why had the new Viscount Hatton-Haxley written a check for £3,000 to Gilbert Fitzhugh?

"He certainly did three thousand pounds worth of *something* for you, Uncle Suspicious," I muttered to myself. But what? Murder? What else could Fitzhugh do to merit that much money? Given Fitzhugh's character, or lack thereof, blackmail also wouldn't be out of the question.

So, there were two obvious possibilities, and I liked them both. Either Sulpicius paid Fitzhugh to kill Erasmus, or Sulpicius killed Erasmus and was paying for Fitzhugh's silence.

Still, I had to be honest. Those theories were fun, but the ledger proved nothing. Fitzhugh was being exorbitantly overpaid by a man who had more ready cash than I would have expected, but that was all.

Closing the desk drawer, I returned to the bedroom and finally turned my attention to the giant bed itself. And then I found a third option, something that Sally really *would* pay to keep quiet.

With all the ingenuity of a six-year-old, Sally had chosen the world's most obvious hiding place for things he probably should have burned. There were three of them, right under the mattress.

The first spilled out of its envelope with a whiff of perfume:

Dear Sally,

It's been two days, and your roses still make the dressing room smell like a garden. I will never forget this weekend. My first trip to the Ritz, my first lobster, my first dance with you. I hope your back doesn't hurt too much after the other first of the weekend.

The next 10 days will seem like a year.

Your Kitten

The second continued the theme:

> *Dearest Sally Cat,*
>
> *How is my silly boy? Do you miss me? Or have you forgotten all about your little Kitten? London is lonesome without you, and your kitten hasn't had any petting since you left. Please come back soon so I can show you how beautiful your latest gift looks around my throat. It's been weeks and your Kitten is missing her Sally Cat. I shall purr so loud when he comes back to me.*
>
> *Meow, meow,*
> *Your Kitten*

And the nauseating final act:

> *Sweetest Sally Cat,*
>
> *I'm still dizzy from your visit and the plans we made. Shall we start our new lives in Paris or New York? I don't care. The show ends at the end of the month, we can leave the very next day.*
>
> *Kisses from*
> *Your Kitten*

Val was going to love hearing about this.

Chapter 24

Behind stairs, Tower View Hall felt like an entirely different house than the sections in which the Hatton-Haxley family lived. The atmosphere was lighter. And the art, surprisingly, was a significant improvement.

I knew nothing of servants' halls, but I wouldn't have thought collections of fine art were common. Yet looking at the walls and furnishings, I had the fanciful notion that Lydgate was a secret connoisseur, keeping all the best objects for the help while leaving the family with the dregs.

There were no three-handed Zeuses or leprosy-afflicted garden nymphs here. Instead, I found a gorgeously realistic Landseer spaniel, all spotted coat and soft eyes. Nearby was a lovely Rembrandt etching of Diana at her bath. Farther along the wall, a magnificent Hepplewhite gateleg table held pride of place, topped by what looked to be a Limoges flower bowl full of golden mums.

I counted off the doors and tried the door to Fitzhugh's room, half expecting it to be locked, like Sally's. Yet it opened without fuss. He was evidently feeling more secure than his employer. I strode inside.

* * *

When we'd gone through Erasmus's room, I felt guilty. When I'd searched Uncle Sally's suite, I felt like a burglar.

I felt no such qualms about riffling through the notorious life of Gilbert Fitzhugh.

The room was perfectly neat. Not a thing out of order, and entirely devoid of comforts. After the stately elegance of the corridor, that raised a question. I went back outside and knocked on the door directly opposite Fitzhugh's. Hearing no answer, I peeked inside. That sunny little room was equally tidy, but furnished in quality and style, with old but comfortable-looking things likely used by the family in prior generations. So Lydgate and the Hatton-Haxleys had no objection to making the staff's bedrooms feel homey. Therefore, Fitzhugh's lack of creature comforts was intentional. His choice.

I went back to Fitzhugh's room and took in the scene. An iron bedstead with a plain white comforter. One bedside table with a lamp. A plain but serviceable dresser, one armchair in faded blue, one wardrobe and a washstand. That was all. Some of the places I'd stayed in during the war were more welcoming.

The room was entirely without personality. No photos. No books. Nothing on the walls. Nothing to show who the occupant was. But that, I soon realized, was the key. Fitzhugh still saw himself as a soldier, and a soldier keeps his kit neat. *Ready for inspection, sir!* The man was wallowing in Spartan martyrdom when he could have kept his clothes in a Hepplewhite bureau.

The table with the lamp also held an empty silver tray, where I assumed he kept his watch. Next to this was the first sign of individuality in the room: a bottle of cologne bearing the ridiculous name *Gladiateur*. I uncapped it and took a whiff. It lived up to the name, smelling like a blend of Roman sweat, sandalwood, and death by trident.

Just as I thought I had Fitzhugh figured out, a quick glance through his wardrobe revealed that this Spartan gentleman's gentleman wore handmade Italian leather shoes and bought his suits in Bond Street. Val hadn't been kidding. So, no aesthetic comforts, but vain in his appearance. And he could afford to pay for a bespoke wardrobe. I thought again of Uncle Sally and his £3,000.

Moving to the dresser, I found a wooden box holding a rather choice collection of cuff links, including a nice pair in onyx, a gold set engraved with his initials, and one of flat silver that had lost its mate. There was also a pair made from what looked like the strike ends of two German dum-dum bullets. Hardly typical for a valet. Nor, I thought, at all in good taste. But, like the bottle of *Gladiateur*, it fit.

Next to the box sat a second silver dish containing loose change, along with a fat white candle in a small pewter stand and a folding knife engraved in German. I suspected he'd taken the latter from a prisoner of war.

I put everything back as perfectly as I found it, mentally thanking my exceptionally tidy mother and a series of martinet COs for teaching me all about surprise inspections. Still, the time it took to search Fitzhugh's room was only slightly longer than the average sneeze.

There had to be more. I began to knock on the walls, looking for secret panels like the hero of a penny dreadful mystery. I poked around what furniture there was, pressing on joints and looking for catches and hidden compartments. I even got down on my hands and knees and looked under the bed, but there were no shameful secrets there, not even a dust bunny.

Remembering something Zoltan Szabo did in one of my early books, I began feeling around under the chair, a move that seemed hilariously melodramatic. Or was it? My fingers knocked into something small and hard, tucked away under the upholstery. And a small slit cut into the fabric.

The glass vial I pulled out was only about two inches high and about as big around as my thumb. A glass stopper with a rubber seal kept it closed tightly. And it was partially filled with a colorless liquid that I was pretty sure wasn't water. I mean, who would hide a vial of water in the upholstery of their armchair?

Zoltan Szabo would have known what to do next. As the creator of Zoltan Szabo, you might imagine I would know, too. But I had no bloody idea.

There were two options, both bad. Removing the vial would alert Fitzhugh to the fact that someone had been in his room. Leaving it there meant it could be destroyed.

Fortunately, two more thoughts arose: First, that I'd seen similar vials in Aunt Elsie's room, and second, I should go get one.

I dashed down the back stairs and into the family wing, having no earthly idea why I was running. The funeral service probably hadn't even started yet. I knocked on her door and, hearing nothing, went in.

Once again Catullus was there, this time having a wash on the hydrangea chair. The Japanese screen was in place across what I thought of as Elsie's laboratory, and I moved it out of the way. There was the rack full of identical vials, none labeled, but all managing to look contradictorily innocent and suspicious at the same time. And in front of the rack was one empty vial, sitting on a piece of Tower View Hall notepaper on which was written:

Dear James,
I thought you might need this.

"Who the hell is James?" I wondered, until I remembered that *I* was James, at least according to Elsie. Perhaps it was James who won the medal at Waterloo. But I had more important things to ponder, starting with: *How on Earth had Elsie known I was going to come in here and steal one of her little bottles?*

I picked up note and vial, decided not to think any more until I got back to Fitzhugh's room, and crossed to the door. I paused to ask Catullus, "*Porta aperta vel clausa?*" He didn't answer, so I closed it. Apparently, he could let himself out anyway.

The Hall was still empty and quiet as a tomb in a library for the mute, and I was back in Fitzhugh's room in moments. Then I had a moment of detective confusion. Exactly how much poison is required to test for poison to see if someone who was poisoned died from poisoning? A few drops? Half a bottle? Better to take too much than too little. After all, I'd look like a git to call in every favor I'm owed to get Scotland Yard to run a few tests only to have them laugh me out with a "you idiot, we need at least a pint and a half to test for cyanide!"

I decided to simply switch the bottles.

A little exploration in the corridor revealed the servant's loo, and I filled the vial so kindly provided by Aunt Elsie to the same level as Fitzhugh's vial. I put the bottle of water under the chair and let myself out.

When I returned to my room, Catullus was sleeping on the bed.

The gears turned quickly in my mind: I had the house to myself. Less than five minutes had passed since I'd left Catullus in Elsie's room. I had closed the door to that room. The door to my room was also closed when I arrived. Yet there he was.

I was beginning to fear my cat.

Catullus opened his eyes a fraction as I opened the bureau, intending to hide the vial of maybe-poison in my shaving kit, and let out a scolding "meow." Startled, I turned, and I swear some sort of cosmic interchange passed between us. Understanding dawned: *Not here, you idiot.* Maybe he really was smarter than I.

"*Cogitatio bona,*" I said, and took the vial downstairs to the library.

* * *

AFTER THE JUICY revelations of Uncle Sally and Fitzhugh's

rooms, all expectations were off. Had I mined all the family secrets or were Aunt Jim and her three awful offspring harboring even more?

Auntie had an impressive jewelry box, but it was relatively barren of impressive jewelry. I had done enough research while writing *Zoltan Szabo and the Emerald Idol of the Ruby Queen* to recognize what is real and what is fake. What was in the box wasn't fake, but it was hardly top-drawer quality. I made a mental note to ask Val if there were any safes in the house.

Tucked away amid silk blouses and expensive-looking shoes, I found a surprise: a deck of tarot cards. Did the Bible-quoting aunt have a secret side order of paganism to go with the superstitious streak I'd noticed at dinner?

Young Theo had nothing of interest in his room except for an incredibly lewd book, complete with pictures, that would have made even Erasmus blush. It was purportedly about the secret lives of French actresses, but I suspect "actress" was a euphemism. Theo also had a box of cigars and a bottle of Scotch squirreled away, both likely stolen from his father's stores.

After that, I expected little from Nicky's room, but I was in for a shock. The room was pink. All pink. Everywhere. He had a pink rug. Pastel pink walls. Pink upholstery on the chairs. A pink duvet adorned with tiny pink roses. Nicky's pink-heavy wardrobe was one thing. But this room was like walking inside a guinea pig.

It took me a moment to realize some of the furniture was *not* pink, but it nevertheless completed the theme of "ugliest bedroom in the history of sleep." A tall dresser infected with an over-abundance of curls, rosettes, and flourishes dominated one wall. The opposite wall proclaimed Nicky's devotion to the family tradition of hideous art. There were two paintings, one depicting a Wagnerian maiden standing atop an alp and apparently complaining loudly. The other was a sentimental study of a broad-shouldered knight taking leave of his fair-haired sweetheart who, if she rose from the awkwardly rendered chair, would be about three feet taller than the castle behind them.

Nicky's desk was a study in confusion, with mail, pens, books, papers, a box of golf balls, two ties, half a muffin, and a framed photograph of the whole family, looking bored, nauseous, and terribly posh. A pink Royal Doulton vase crammed full of wilting pink roses and a pair of matching candlesticks holding mismatched fat pink candles—one of which leaned and bulged awkwardly over a small puddle of pink wax—completed the mess.

The rest of Tower Field Hall had been impeccably clean, but this desk was downright slovenly. Perhaps the staff was under orders not to touch it.

Opening the desk, I found a stack of papers topped by some confusing and, I suspected, shady financial records. I noted a few questions Val might want to raise with the family solicitor.

In another drawer, a letter from someone signed Maurice mentioned some very large numbers along with carefully worded phrases like "deny any foreknowledge" and "upcoming quarterly audit." He was also told he better show up the following week with more customers or his parents would receive several slips of paper bearing many numbers and Wulfie's aristocratic autograph.

Nicky's mess of papers was impressive, but when I moved down the hall to my old pal Comrade Wulfie's room, I found something nearly as good: a missive from someone named Milray, reminding Wulfie of a considerable debt. Wulfie was instructed to "stump up soon," or else he could expect a personal visit from one "Mr. Havana." This was intriguingly unfriendly. I wondered how he'd wound up in such a precarious position, but all became clear when I found a rolled-up copy of the racing news in one of Wulfie's jacket pockets, complete with check marks indicating that he had no idea how to pick a winning horse.

Wulfie also provided me with a humorous moment. The

copy of *Das Kapital* on his bedside table was, in fact, a copy of *My Man Jeeves* wrapped in the paper dust jacket of Marx's manifesto. For the first time, I hoped I would eventually have to come clean about this ethically questionable search. The idea of asking Wulfie what he thought of Gussie Fink-Nottle was one I relished.

I glanced at my watch. The family had been gone about an hour and a half by this time, and I doubted they'd be away much longer. Val had said that after the mass, everyone would come back to the Hall to install his urn in the mausoleum, at the far end of the grounds. I likely wouldn't even hear them until they were back in the main house. So I went downstairs and made myself comfortable in the library, pulling down a copy of Dickens's *Pickwick Papers* and letting my mind take a break from clues, motives, and the question of what side Elsie was on during the Wars of the Roses.

A quarter of an hour later, Daphne found me there. I could see she'd been crying and felt another pang of guilt for playing detective instead of being with my friends.

"Why are you in a room with no alcohol?" Daphne asked. "Today, there should always be alcohol. There should have been alcohol at the church."

"Worry not, there is." I handed her my flask. "How was it?"

"Right up there with the top three funerals I've ever attended," she said with a sigh. "It was awful. The Bishop gave the eulogy for a total stranger. Nothing he said suited Erasmus. I'm sure Aunt Jim gave him his instructions, but he just kept rambling on about what a devout Christian Erasmus was. How good and kind."

"Wasn't he good and kind?"

"He was. But he was hardly a paragon. This made it sound like he'd never committed a single sin in his entire life."

"Sorry I missed it. Where's Val?"

"Being a good host. Did you find anything?"

"Several things. Can you grab him? There's something here I need you both to see."

In a few minutes, Daphne returned with Val, who looked shattered. Without a word, I gave him my flask. He took a grateful swig. Daphne intercepted it for a second go as he passed it back. I took one of my own to complete the set.

"I understand it was quite the tribute," I said. "One that made Erasmus sound worthy of his sainted namesake?"

Val gave a humorless laugh. Daphne said, "Oh yes, he fed the hungry, rescued orphans from burning buildings, and donated half the Hatton-Haxley fortune to help fallen women."

"That last part might be true," Val observed. "Just not in the way you implied."

She elbowed him in the ribs. "Sorry," he said. "So, what did you find?"

I explained to them the record in Sally's check ledger. I was immensely gratified by their stunned appreciation.

"Well," Val said, "that makes both of them look guilty of… well, something."

"Fitzhugh certainly did something to make your uncle part with £3,000. Murder is one possibility," I said.

"Why else would Sally give Fitzhugh that much money?"

"Hard to say," I said. "Fitzhugh could have demanded it. Given his character, or lack thereof, blackmail wouldn't be out of the question."

"True. But what would he be blackmailing my uncle about?"

"Off the top of my head," said Daphne, "I'd say murder tops that list, too."

"And there's another possibility, but I'll get to that. First, have a look at this." I strode across the room to a set of Shakespeare volumes that looked like they had sat untouched for centuries and came back with the vial in my hand.

"What's that?" Daphne asked.

I set the scene of Fitzhugh's room, describing in vivid detail how I found the vial, and my ingenuity in hiding the bottle here, in the library. At the risk of sounding boastful, I believe I did justice to all my storytelling powers. My friends were rapt.

"But... Why here?" Val wondered. "Why not just keep the dashed thing in your room?"

Daphne was quicker on the uptake. "Because if Fitzhugh somehow discovers that the vial in his room has been switched with water, he'll look for the person who did it. Now, who was not at the funeral and had lots of time to wander around the house, unobserved, and free to steal hidden bottles of poison from the rooms of highly suspect servants?"

"Exactly," I said. "I'd be mad to put it in my room. But hidden among thousands of books that nobody ever reads? It'll never be found. I put it behind *King Lear*."

"Good, my relatives can't even *spell* Lear. Anything else?" Val asked.

I pulled out my notebook, cleared my throat, and began to read: *"Dear Sally Cat..."*

* * *

By the time I'd finished reciting the third gruesome letter, Daphne looked a bit green. Val was trying to hold back a laugh.

"Good old Uncle Sally," he wheezed. "I wonder if Aunt Jim knows?"

"That really is blackmail material," Daphne observed.

I shook my head. "It would be if somebody other than Sally had the letter in their possession. But it's still in his room, which makes me think nobody knows about it."

"Careless of him to leave it around," Val observed.

"Yes, it is."

"So, what's next?"

"I call Drake and find out how to get this vial analyzed. Then I need to talk more to Athos, Porthos, and Aramis. They're not leaving today, are they?"

"No, thank God," said Val. "And that's the first time I've ever said *that*. The reading of the will is tonight. Everyone is staying on."

"Good. Just keep talking to everyone you can. At this point, any information could be of use, no matter how incidental it seems. The more we know about… well, about everything, the better off we are."

"We should rejoin the gathering," Val said. "People will notice if I'm gone too long."

"Right," I said, as I gently pulled *Lear* back off the shelf and replaced the vial. "By the way, did anyone comment on my absence from the funeral?"

"Oh, yes," said Daphne. "Aunt Jim made one of her sniffy comments. '*I don't see Mr. Griffin here, isn't this why he came?*'"

"Damn. How did you reply?"

"I said that you came to support Val, but that funerals were against your religion."

I snorted in laughter. "Daphne, I think I love you."

"Alas, my heart belongs to Douglas Fairbanks."

"By the way, Val, I took a quick look at your aunt's jewelry box," I said.

"Aunt Elsie? I imagine you found two or three Faberge Eggs and a length of popcorn on a string," he observed.

"Undoubtedly, but I mean the other aunt," I corrected.

"Eww. You went through *her* things? Better you than me."

"It wasn't too bad. Once I shot her three-headed guard dog with a poison dart, the coast was clear."

"Well, then, you must not have looked into her mirror. I'm told it can turn men to stone."

"It worked on her," I said. "But I couldn't find anything of value in there. Are there any precious family pieces that might be in a safe here? Or perhaps at the bank?"

"There's a safe in the study. And we do have a few rather nice pieces in there that I remember my mother wearing. Some impressive pearls, a few rings, one or two very nice bracelets and such."

"Oh, there's a gorgeous ruby and diamond brooch I remember her wearing every Christmas," Daphne added. "I always admired that."

"Come on, I'll show you." Val led us down the hall and into the study and indicated yet another of those hideous paintings which the Hall seemed to have in endless supply. This one was a dramatic seascape with surprisingly realistic water, but no sense of proportion or perspective. A lighthouse four hundred feet tall teetered on a speck of a rock, guiding a ship about the size of a postage stamp into a cramped harbor full of tiny men and towering carts pulled by gargantuan… horses? Dogs? Weasels? I gave up.

Val took the painting down, revealing an ancient wall safe just like the ones one reads about in books like mine. I turned away politely as Val turned the dial a few times, and a moment later the Hatton-Haxley family jewels lay before us. Rather nice ones, too.

My own family's heirlooms were limited to my mother's drab wedding ring and an old watch with no minute hand, no number seven, and no winding stem. Basically, it was just a face and some spare parts. But Val's family had proper gems that sparkled and everything.

Val handed over a few velvet boxes that Daphne and I opened with due reverence.

"I'm not sure what to look for," she murmured.

"Don't look for anything," I said. "Look for evidence of something *missing*."

Val was the one who found it. Or didn't find it.

"Oi!" Val exclaimed. "What's this?"

Daphne and I glanced over to see Val holding up a square box in blue velvet. The lid was open, and the interior displayed a beautiful, jeweled brooch. Or at least half of one. It had a lovely, filigreed setting and dozens of tiny, brilliant diamonds ringing the edges. But there was no center stone.

"Where the hell is it?" Val asked me.

"I have no idea," I said. "*What* the hell is it? What's missing?"

"A ruby," Daphne said. "*The* ruby. The one I was talking about. It's huge. About the size of my thumb."

"Goodness. What's it called?"

"What?" Val wondered.

"What's it called? Don't large stones always have a name?"

"A name? It's a rock, not a pet!"

"Come now, it's got to be the Eye of Something or the Heart of Something," I insisted. "They always have names in books."

"I don't think associations with body parts are necessary for a whopping great stone to be stolen," Val sniped. "But if it makes you feel better, call it the Uvula of Saint Ursula."

"That's the spirit. Any idea what the old uvula's worth?"

Val looked aghast. "You aren't supposed to ask questions like that!"

"I have to ask if we're going to solve a murder. And now, apparently, a robbery as well."

Val grumbled and pulled a fat envelope out of the safe. He examined the contents for a few moments before answering.

"According to the insurance documents, the ruby was last valued at…" He coughed. "Twelve thousand pounds."

"And we thought three thousand was either a motive for murder or payment for murder," Daphne observed.

"Indeed. Val, who has the combination to this safe?"

"Everybody in the family, most likely. Uncle Sally, certainly.

And Aunt Jim. Those two tell Nicky everything, and he probably told his brothers, just to show off."

"And nobody told me?" Daphne protested. "I bet I'd look wonderful in rubies."

"You'd look wonderful in anything," I said, surprising myself. Daphne colored prettily. Val made a rude hand gesture.

Chapter 25

The Tower View Hall staff put on an impressive post-funeral buffet for their late Earl, with wonderful food and plenty of champagne. Some fifty guests came up from the village and a few more traveled down from London to toast Erasmus's trip to the afterlife, so I mingled on the fringes, unashamedly eavesdropping.

The sudden death of yet another Hatton-Haxley was seen as odd by many in attendance, but nobody mentioned foul play. Still, I wasn't alone in my dislike of the cadet branch of Val's family. While everyone was carefully aware whose home they were in, and spoke with the respect befitting a funeral, it was easy to pick up on the fact that while Val and his brothers were looked upon fondly, no such sentiment was felt towards his cousins.

I made a parlor game out of reading between the lines. When one local matron referred to Aunt Jim as "a woman of *high* standards," the implication was "*she's a pompous, judgmental snob.*" A round man who looked like a politician in an old Punch cartoon said of the cousins, "They obviously all take after their father," leaving me to imagine the rest of the sentence: "*…every one of them a criminal.*" Of course, my own prejudice might have been inventing subtext for perfectly innocent comments. But I don't think so.

I had wandered onto the terrace and was sitting on the stone wall, squinting at the nearest fountain, which depicted either a water nymph with an amphora or Prince Albert with a goat on his back, when dear Uncle Suspicious oozed over in my direction.

"May I join you, Mr. Griffin?"

I hadn't heard him walk up, being too engrossed in the nymph. Or the prince. "Of course, Lord Haxley," I said. "I was just admiring your gardens."

"Yes, they're quite extensive. And that fountain is spectacular, don't you think? It's my favorite."

"Is it?" Despite the invitation, I restrained myself from saying what I really thought. "Yes, it's quite… something. I was trying to figure out what it depicts. Something from mythology? Venus, perhaps? Or a river goddess?"

He looked at me with surprising hostility. "Saint George and the dragon."

"Oh, yes. Sorry, I'm color blind."

That made little enough sense to leave him speechless for a moment. I needed to do more of that. Alas, it didn't last.

"Lady Haxley and I were surprised at your absence from the funeral."

"I hope I gave no offense to you or Lady Haxley," I said. "But I had never intended to go."

"And why is that?"

"Oh, didn't Lady Haxley tell you? My religion forbids me to attend funerals." I silently thanked Daphne for the line.

"And exactly what religion is that?"

"I'm sorry, but my religion forbids me from discussing my religion. But you have my deepest condolences. You and Lady Haxley must be grief-stricken. If there's anything at all I can do for you at this unhappy time, you need only ask."

He knew I was insincere. I knew he didn't believe me. That made us equals. But he could hardly say anything except what he said: "Thank you. Lady Haxley and I are naturally very upset."

I wouldn't say there was anything natural about either of them, except for born-in-the-bone awfulness.

"It must be a great comfort to you both to have your sons with you," I said. "You must be very proud of them." I practiced my insincere smile, the one I put on whenever someone asks, "where *do* you get your ideas from?"

"Yes, of course. Lady Haxley and I are very proud of all three of them."

I wondered if he was going to work his wife into every response, the better to remind me I was speaking to the ever-so-very-much-important *Viscount* Hatton-Haxley. Yeah, he probably was.

"Young Theo seems to be quite the star at school. Does he have any idea what profession he might like to pursue?"

"Yes, my son, the Honorable Theobald, is regarded very highly at St. Gordon's. The headmaster, Dr. Inglethorpe, told me just last month that Theobald was the brightest pupil he'd ever had the honor of teaching. And Dr. Inglethorpe has taught the sons of some of the finest families in the nation. In fact, both the Duke of Wenham and Lord Luceby, the cabinet minister, have sons at Saint Gordon's."

"Didn't Lord Luceby's son get arrested for trying to steal a zebra from the London Zoo?"

Uncle Suspicious didn't succeed in stifling a snort of laughter. "Yes, he did."

"Well, I'm glad to hear that the illustrious Dr. Inglethorpe, who has taught the sons of so many important men, thinks that the Honorable Theobald is brighter than a zebra-stealer."

He was silent.

I looked back up at the house. "You have a truly beautiful home, Lord Haxley."

"It is not, exactly, *mine*. In that sense."

"Ah, that's right. It all belongs to Val now." *And my, what a big vein you have pulsing above your ugly eyes, grandma.* I kept smiling my bland smile because it seemed to infuriate him so much. "I'm sure Val will do an excellent job now that he's the Earl. It must be reassuring to know everything is in such good hands." I swear I could hear Sally's teeth clenching.

"Yes, no doubt Valentine will handle things adequately."

"Adequately? That's not very high praise, Lord Haxley."

"Forgive me, Mr. Griffin, but I fear not everyone shares your confidence in my nephew."

"Oh? Do you and Lady Haxley have your doubts?"

"We do. As do our sons. And there are others who share our feelings."

"I see. I happen to know Val rather well, perhaps I can help allay your concerns. May I ask what worries you?"

"He has no experience at being the Earl."

"May I point out that you do not, either. Nor do your sons."

"No, but my father was the Earl, and I learned a great deal from him."

"And may I also point out that Val's father was also the Earl and I'm sure Val learned from him."

"Yes, but Val was never intended to be the heir."

"Forgive me, Lord Haxley, but would you prefer me to keep shooting down your arguments or would you rather just stop saying foolish things?"

"How dare you!"

"Oh, I assure you, it takes no daring. It's rather fun. Now, down to business. Do you think Erasmus was murdered or do you truly believe he just spontaneously burst into drowning all on his own?"

"You... He..."

I decided that stammering isn't a good look on a Viscount.

"Tell me, Lord Haxley, did you like Erasmus?"

"He was my nephew!"

"I'm clear on the relationship. I asked if you liked him."

"That's none of your business," he huffed. He puffed out his massive chest like a monstrous penguin. I think it was supposed to be intimidating.

"I'll take that to mean, no?"

"You can take it whatever way you want." He turned to go back into the house.

"Oh, by the way," I called. "I spoke with a friend who served with your valet, Fitzhugh, during the war. You might want to keep an eye on him. I'd hate for you to be nursing a viper in your aristocratic bosom. I've heard he's quite a dangerous character. Why there's even a rumor that he killed a prisoner." I smiled. He glared. "I just wanted to give you a friendly warning."

He turned away with as much dignity as he could muster—which wasn't all that much—and marched inside. I imagined he was heading straight upstairs to have a talk with Fitzhugh. I decided I should do the same with Val, and that both of us should watch out for the man.

What I had just done was either daringly clever or abysmally stupid. Perhaps I should have thought before showing my hand, but being passive wasn't getting me anywhere. Instead, I had come right out with the fact that we suspected murder and done so in an extremely rude way. That was intentional, as I wanted to see how Uncle Maude reacted when he was angry. At the very least, he would likely try to toss me out on my ear. But since Val had the title and I was Val's guest, he could protect me from eviction. And it occurred to me that if one of our chief suspects knew he was suspected, he might be less likely to try any more murdering in the immediate future. Maybe.

A titter of laughter broke my train of thought. There, sitting behind the corner of the terrace, was Aunt Elsie.

* * *

"Oh, that was fun, James," Elsie said. "And I'm glad you said what you did, because Fitzhugh killed dear Erasmus and it was that horrible man who told him to do so."

Since coming to this house I'd been confused, surprised, and more confused. I'd also been stunned into near immobility. But nothing had thrown me quite like hearing vague Aunt Elsie speak so coherently about murder.

"You… *you* think Sulpicius Hatton-Haxley had his nephew murdered?"

"Of course. Don't you?"

"Yes. Yes, I do."

"And I imagine Val and dear Daphne agree with us?"

"Yes, they do."

"Good. Now what are we going to do about it?"

"Um, pardon me Miss Armistad, but—"

"Please, James, call me Elsie."

"Thank you, Elsie, and please call me Griff. Not James."

"Of course, dear." She smiled vaguely. "Since you took the bottle that I left for you, I assume you found the poison. Who had it? Fitzhugh or Sally?"

"How did you know…?"

"Because I knew a clever man like you would find poison. Hemlock, perhaps. There's some missing. Or nicotine."

"Hemlock?!"

"Yes, *conium maculatum*. I had a distillation of it on my shelf and it went missing a few days before Erasmus died. And that very afternoon as I was coming upstairs, I saw Fitzhugh leave the corridor where my room is. He has absolutely no reason to be in that part of the house. His duties extend to the east wing, exclusively."

"Hemlock?" I repeated, dumbly. Honestly, the woman had flummoxed me.

"Perhaps. It can take effect in as little as fifteen minutes; pure nicotine can kill even quicker." She frowned a little. "With a pure alkaloid of nicotine, only a few drops can kill almost instantly. And it's odorless, colorless, and tasteless."

"Murder is always tasteless," I observed. "But are you saying you keep nicotine alkaloid around?"

"Yes. I've made it often. It's good for roses."

"Nicotine. Hemlock. On your shelf."

It was highly surreal, sitting in the afternoon sunshine having a conversation with a kindly yet bizarre old lady about which poisons worked the fastest.

"Do you think the marble and the gospel were meant to implicate me?"

Who was this suddenly sensible woman?

"I suppose they wanted it to look like Erasmus had a stroke or something, fell unconscious, and drowned in the bath. But then they realized people might not believe that, so they might as well make it look like murder. That way if anyone asked questions, they could point the finger at the batty old dear who talks to dead people and ship me off to the local asylum. Killing two annoying birds with one marble, so to speak. Besides, who else in the household knows how to distill poison? I'm the perfect suspect. Aside from having no motive, of course."

"Miss Elsie, you stun me."

She smiled. "My dear, I'm not nearly so much a fool as I look."

"But why…?" I stopped.

"Why am I always talking about past lives and moving chairs? Why did I play marbles with my grown-up nephew?"

"Well… Yes."

"If you had to share a house with Sally and Jim, your favorite hobby would be annoying them, too. The more outrageous I am, the more uncomfortable they get. A woman has to have some fun, after all."

And then she winked at me. She *winked!*

"I am very confused," I said.

"Oh good. I love having that effect on people. I remember once in Russia... well, never mind."

"Miss Elsie, forgive me. But I have no idea who you are right now."

"Oh, that happens to me quite often, James." She gave me a look of teasing humor, telling me she knew perfectly well that my name wasn't James. Who was this woman? "So, where *did* you find the poison?"

"In Fitzhugh's room. It was under a chair, in a slit in the upholstery."

"How clever. I'm afraid it didn't occur to me to look there."

"*You* searched Fitzhugh's room?"

"Of course! I loved Erasmus very much. He was a dear, sweet man. I knew right away that he'd been murdered, and I knew it was Fitzhugh at Sally's orders. I just didn't know how to prove it. But surely you do."

"I'm at a loss," I said. "I don't know how to obtain a conviction for murder. Not unless I lay all the clues myself, so they point like a blinking neon arrow at the guilty party."

"I wish you could point at Fitzhugh with a big arrow. A big, very sharp arrow."

"You seem to have no doubts," I observed.

"Not a one. Besides, I know what happened. Erasmus told me."

"He... excuse me, he *told* you?"

"Yes, that very night. I consulted the planchette, you see, and he told me all."

So, the sensible old woman was gone, and batty Aunt Elsie was back. I had thought she was merely eccentric. But could she be mentally ill? Was I a fool to listen to anything she said?

"I'm not crazy," she said, as if reading my thoughts, which I found highly disturbing. "Erasmus told me that he'd eaten a caramel in his bath, that it tasted a bit funny, but he thought perhaps it was old. A minute later he felt faint, leaned his head back, got a sudden pain in his stomach and that was it."

"He *told you* this?"

She smiled indulgently. "I said I'm not crazy. I didn't say I wasn't different. So, now that you have the poison, what's next?"

"Well, I have a friend in the CID, so I'll ask him about getting the vial analyzed."

"You should also analyze the caramels."

"The caramels that a dead man, by means of a Oiuja board, told his eccentric aunt tasted funny?"

"Yes. Erasmus loved caramels. He always had a box of his favorites in his room. I'd check them if I were you. If they're even still there. Erasmus said there should be two left."

I was being out-thought by a woman who believed I died at Waterloo. But she was right. Every detail needed to be looked into, regardless of the source. "Hmm... I do remember seeing a box of caramels on Erasmus's bedside table. And, come to think of it, there may well have been two pieces left."

"Talk to Sutherland," she advised. "He'll be able to tell you if anything's amiss."

"That's a good idea."

"Don't sound so surprised," she said. "I have them occasionally, James." She smiled her non-vague smile, which was noticeably different from her vague one. "Since you've looked through our rooms, I'm assuming you've seen Sally's check book?"

My jaw dropped again.

"By the way, you do believe that I saw Fitzhugh leaving the family part of the house?"

Well, that was an awkward question. Unfortunately, my momentarily silence conveyed my doubt.

"So, I suppose there's no point in telling you I actually saw him leaving Erasmus's room on the morning of the murder?"

"Miss Elsie, *are* you telling me that?"

"Not if you won't believe me."

I changed the subject. "Miss Elsie, our agreeing Erasmus was murdered is one thing, but acting on it is another. I'm hoping to talk Val into calling in the police. Perhaps you could have a word with him as well."

She sighed. "I'm very much afraid they'll get away with it even if Val does call the police."

* * *

It seemed more important than ever to get the contents of that bottle analyzed, so I waded through the mourners with the intention of calling Drake and finding out what to do. But before I could reach the study, I happened to run right into the one man I most wanted to talk to.

"You're Gilbert Fitzhugh, aren't you?" I said, stopping him in the corridor.

"Yes."

As I waited for the accustomed "sir," which did not come, I found myself studying his face and not much liking what I saw. He had a heavy brow and a prominent forehead, rather like something I'd once seen in the museum of natural history. His eyes were small and so dark brown they almost looked black. His hair was cropped short, like a soldier. Or a convict. But his suit was impeccable. It was the suit of a gentleman, not a gentleman's gentleman. In fact, it was nicer than mine.

"I believe we have a mutual acquaintance," I purposely did not say "friend." "Captain Roger Benedict?"

He said nothing, but his tiny eyes got even smaller.

"I understand you served together."

Again, no response.

"I should probably extend my sympathies for the death in the family. Did you have much to do with the Earl?"

"No." Again, no "sir" followed it.

"Oh, that's right. You work for Val's uncle Sally."

His beady eyes squinted in disapproval. "I am employed by *Viscount* Hatton-Haxley," he said, as eager to remind me of the new title as his employer had been.

"Indeed. He must be heartbroken to lose another beloved nephew."

Nothing.

"Mr. Fitzhugh, could you please stop talking for a moment so I can get a word in edgewise?"

He squinted again. I was beginning to think his entire vocabulary was made up of squints.

"That's better," I said, smiling. "Let me ask you something, and if you can limit yourself to a one-word answer, that would be great. Do you think that Lord Erasmus was murdered?"

Silence.

"Really?" I said, as if he'd spoken. "Because we rather do. 'We' in this case being the new Earl, Miss Ferguson, and I. But you disagree?"

Squint.

"Wow. That's a good point. I didn't think of that. But why would Lord Sally want to kill his nephew?"

He squinted so hard I wasn't sure he could see me anymore.

I laughed as if he'd said something hilarious. "Wow, you got me with that one. Well, it's been great talking to you. We must do this again sometime." And I headed to the study, leaving him squinting after me.

Chapter 26

Well, now I'd really done it. I'd brazenly shown my hand to both of our chief suspects. After that display, Val wouldn't be the only one who needed to watch his back. I'd be lucky to get out of Tower Field Hall alive.

Hugo Drake picked up on the third ring and listened patiently while I explained what I'd found. He wasn't entirely happy.

"Griff, do you realize you have tampered with evidence? This is serious."

"What was I supposed to do, leave it there?"

"Yes! Suppose we test that vial and find poison. There was no witness present when you found it in Fitzhugh's room. Indeed, there's no proof it was ever in his possession. One man's word against another's doesn't usually result in a conviction."

"What about fingerprints? Wouldn't his fingerprints on the vial prove something?"

"Yes, it would prove that at some point he touched it. Did you at least wear gloves?"

"Uh… No."

"Fine. So, there's as much evidence against you as against him."

"Right. Very well, I'm an idiot. Let's accept that and move on. Can you arrange to have this stuff analyzed?"

He gave an exasperated sigh. "Let me make a few calls. The local village will only have a local constable. Where's the closest police station, do you know?"

"Danforth, I think."

"Give me an hour and then take that bottle to the Danforth police station. I'll tell them to expect you."

"Thanks."

"But Griff, this is it. If there's poison in that bottle, no more fun and games. We'd have a duty to open an investigation. Make sure Val knows that once you do this, there's no going back."

"I understand. Thanks, Drake. I owe you."

"Damn right, you do." He hung up.

Dealing with people is much easier in a book than in real life. Or perhaps it's just that I deal better with my own fictional creations. Regardless, I'd had enough of impromptu inquisitions for a while.

Back in the drawing room, I stole Daphne away from her mother, pulling her aside for a quiet word.

"Where's Val?"

"I have no idea," she said. "I haven't seen him in a while. Why?"

"I need to speak with you both. I'm going to retrieve that bottle from the library. Could you please find him and meet me in my room?"

"Of course. Is anything wrong?"

"Aside from the fact I let both Uncle Suspicious and Fitzhugh know I'm looking at them as murderers, no, not a thing."

"What? Why on earth would you do that?"

"I'll explain. See you soon."

* * *

REMINDING ME WHY we were friends, Val showed up carrying a bottle of champagne.

The bubbly helped me deal with my frustration at having no witness to swear that the bottle was hidden in Fitzhugh's room, and the uncomfortable knowledge that I'd confronted both suspects way too soon.

Val and Daphne were discouraged by Drake's comments. But it was my conversation with Elsie that really caught their attention.

"What do you mean '*she made sense*'?" Val asked.

"Just what I said. She's not nearly as batty as people take her to be."

"She admitted that she does all that just to annoy Sally and Jim?" Daphne laughed.

"And their sons, yes. I believe she is genuinely fond of Val's family, though. And she loved Erasmus. You can tell by the way she speaks about him."

"I can't believe this," Val said. "We've always thought of Aunt Elsie as, well, mad."

"She has some unusual beliefs, but she's not crazy. Well, not entirely," I amended.

"This makes me love her even more," Daphne said.

As if on cue, there was a knock on the door, and the woman in question came in.

"Ooh," she smiled. "It's a *champagne* costume party. May I join you?"

"Certainly, Miss Elsie," I said. We'd all stood when she entered, but she motioned with her hands to sit down. I pulled a chair forward, but she shook her head and joined us on the floor, folding her skirts under her and smiling at us with the excitement of a little girl stumbling upon a tea party.

"So, I suppose dear James has told you all about how I'm not really all that crazy," she said, smiling as Catullus made himself at home on her lap.

"James?" Val asked.

"That's me," I explained.

"Of course. Forgive me, James," Val said.

"Hey, only she can call me James. You can't," I protested.

"She can?" Val asked, surprised. "How come?"

"Because I'm not sure how to stop her."

"Now," Elsie said, ignoring me. "How do we get Suspicious Sally and his horrible henchman for killing Erasmus?"

"That's it, Aunt Elsie," cheered Daphne. "Let's get right to it."

"We have the bottle," Val said, "but it doesn't prove as much as we thought it might."

"I have muddled things considerably in not wearing gloves or having a witness to the discovery of the bottle," I explained to Elsie.

"But even if we can't prove that you found the bottle in Fitzhugh's room, wouldn't the presence of poison be some sort of proof?"

"If it does contain poison," I said. "We don't know that yet."

"It does," Elsie said with surprising certainty.

"It must," Daphne agreed. "Otherwise, why hide it?"

"And what about the check that Sally wrote to Fitzhugh?" Val added. "I can't think of any legitimate reason why he'd pay that much to his valet."

"Should we take Uncle Sally's check ledger for safekeeping?" Daphne asked.

I shook my head. "We shouldn't tamper with any more evidence. Besides, even if he gets rid of the record, his bank can verify the check."

"A bottle and a check," Elsie said. "It's a start, but not enough."

She turned to me. "James, you're a writer. If you were writing this as a book, and planned on Fitzhugh being revealed as the killer at the end, what other evidence would you use to convince your readers? Footprints? Cigar ash? A signed confession?"

I laughed. "Miss Elsie, you're a wonder. And that's a fascinating way of looking at it. Those things are all very useful, but we don't have them. And this isn't a book. We can't go back to chapter three and insert a threatening note or invent an eyewitness."

"But the ingredients aren't so different," Daphne observed.

"I suppose not." I thought for a minute. "Traditionally, the key to finding a killer in a murder mystery is to look for someone with means, motive, and opportunity. When you've figured that out, it's time to stop throwing in clues and move right to the denouement."

"*De-nude-ment?*" Val asked.

"It's a literary term that means the part when everything happens," Daphne explained. "It's usually at the very end."

"Ah. That explains why I don't know the word. I rarely make it to the end of books."

"You rarely make it to the beginning of books, either," I said. "But mysteries usually end with a sort of two-part resolution. The first part is the revelation of the guilty party, and the second part is the detective's explanation of how he reached the solution. But again, in a book my goal is just to make an interesting story. I'm not trying to win a conviction in a court of law."

Val reached out and refilled my glass, topping off everyone else as well.

"So, all the evidence we have is circumnavigable?"

"Circumstantial, yes."

"And I can't just go to court and say that I saw Fitzhugh pour something into Erasmus's martini?" Val asked.

"Absolutely not! Ever heard of perjury?"

"Sure. Ever heard of Perkin Warbeck?"

"What?" I was confused. Again.

"Perkin Warbeck," Val said, smugly. "Pretender to the throne. He said that he was one of the princes in the—"

"I know who Perkin Warbeck is. What does he have to do with this?"

"Nothing. I just learned about him the other day and wanted to work it into a conversation. I'll have you know that I am one of the great thinkers of the day."

"I'm sure you are," I humored him. "I, however, am stunned into stupidity by the revelation that you have heard of Perkin Warbeck."

"I have heard of a great many famous dead people," Val said, grandly.

Elsie leaned over towards Daphne and said in a stage whisper, "I honestly don't know why people think *I* am the crazy one in the family." Then, rising: "I'm going to go back to my room and take a nap. And rewrite my will."

I moved to open the door. As she passed by, I said, "Miss Elsie, I must ask. Who was Sally in a previous life? Did you know him?"

She smiled at me. "Sulpicius is now, and always has been, a worm."

Chapter 27

It was a relief to get away from the Hatton-Haxley madhouse for a while, even if it was only an hour. I saddled up Lucille the Lagonda and enjoyed the short, sunny drive to Danforth. At the police station, a young constable with absolutely no sense of curiosity took the vial and said that someone would call me when there was anything to report. And that was that.

I momentarily considered not returning to the Hall. If I left immediately, I could dine in London that night, leaving murders and mystery far behind. But I couldn't leave Catullus in such a perilous situation. Nor could I abandon Val and Daphne. Or even Aunt Elsie, who was quickly becoming a new addition to my "favorite people I've ever met" list.

My new favorite person waylaid me once again as I passed by her room on the way to my own. This was becoming a habit.

"Oh good, James, you're here." She opened the door to invite me in but turned away to speak to someone inside. "You were right, he was home. How clever you are!" She meant Daphne or Val, I assumed. I should have known better. She was, of course, talking to Catullus.

"Do you know that I tried speaking to Catullus in Latin, but he told me that he would only speak Latin with you? I thought that was very sweet."

"How did you know I speak to my cat in Latin?"

She gave a me a pitying look.

"Now," she began as if we were continuing a conversation from thirty seconds ago, "About those caramels."

"The ones that Erasmus's spirit told you were poisoned?"

"Exactly. Well, I asked Sutherland to take another look at that box. And it's empty."

"What? Is he sure?"

"Positive. He remembers being in the room with Erasmus not long before he died and checking the box of caramels to see if it needed to be replaced. There were three pieces left. Erasmus told me he took one into the bath, so there should be two remaining. But they're all gone."

"Damn. Oh! Pardon me, Miss Elsie."

"Oh, that's perfectly all right, James. You always did have a salty tongue."

I was terrified by the places *that* conversation might lead, but Elsie mercifully stuck to the subject at hand. "I can only assume Sally or Fitzhugh took the remaining caramels because they were tainted as well, and they were removing the evidence."

"Miss Elsie, I'll say it again. You're a wonder."

She smiled. "James, I want you to help me. Convince Val to hold a séance tonight."

"A… a what? I was thinking more along the lines of fetching something off a high shelf? Or maybe running into the village to buy you some sugar cubes."

"Sugar cubes? Why should I want sugar cubes?"

"Because you… Never mind."

"No, we must hold a séance. Tonight. And I want everyone to be there."

"Why?"

"So we can confront Sally and that man with everything we know and see how they react, of course."

"But Miss Elsie, we don't know anything."

"*You* may not know anything, but *I* do."

I was silent, and a bit lost.

"Think about it, James. It can't do any harm. I don't expect a full confession, but if we succeed in getting a reaction out of either of them, we gain something. And if we don't, we're no worse off than we were."

"But how on earth would we get Suspicious and Fitzhugh to attend a séance? You know they'll refuse."

"Perhaps. But we have a jack up our jumper."

"Do you mean an ace up our sleeve?"

"We have a card secreted in our clothing," she compromised.

"And that is?"

"Why, Val of course."

"Val? He's the queen in our corset?"

"You'd be surprised what people will do if someone with power and money tells them to do it."

"That's a good point. But not a good idea."

"Why not?"

"Well, for one thing, if you're right and you confront them with the clue of the caramel box then they have a reason to want you out of the way. And I don't want you to put yourself in danger. I've got myself in hot water that way as it is."

"James, that's very sweet of you. But I insist."

"Will you let me talk it over with Val first?"

"Certainly."

"Thanks. I'll go find him." I looked over at Catullus. He was asleep again. "I think Catullus wants to stay here."

"That's fine. We still have more to catch up on."

"Naturally."

* * *

I COULD HEAR voices from Val's room and knocked, gingerly. He bade me come in and I found him drinking tea and laughing with Daphne.

"What's the joke?"

Daphne giggled. "We were reminiscing about when we were kids and Medard locked Erasmus and Val in the attic as a joke and then forgot about them. They had to spend the whole night up there."

"I told Medard if I died, he could eat me to stay alive," Val said.

"That was very generous of you."

"How did things go with the police?" Val asked.

"Fine. They said they'd call with the results. Probably not before tomorrow."

"That's it?" Daphne wondered.

"That's it. Oh, and Aunt Elsie wants to hold a séance tonight."

"Good lord, why?"

I told them about the box of Croft Caramels, and her plan to confront them with what she thought she knew.

"Who is going to conduct this séance?" Val asked.

"I'm assuming Elsie will," I said.

"Oh dear," Val mused. "Can't we at least get a professional charlatan?"

"Well, it can't happen tonight!" Daphne said.

"Why not?"

"Tonight, you may recall, is the reading of the will," Val answered. "Just another happy family event."

"It's just an endless carnival around here," I said. I was about to say more when we were interrupted by a knock on the door. Val called out and Sutherland came in.

"Excuse me, my lord, but I found something that I think might interest you."

"The man of the hour! Come in, Sutherland, and join the discussion. What have you found? We've already heard about the missing caramels."

He reached into his pocket and handed a small metallic object to Val, who held out his palm so Daphne and I could see.

It was a flat silver cuff link. The twin to the one I'd noticed atop Fitzhugh's dresser.

"Where did you find this, Sutherland?" I asked.

"Under Lord Erasmus's bed," he answered. "This did not belong to him. And it wasn't there when I straightened the room last week. I found it just now while putting away Lord Erasmus's belongings."

"It wasn't under the bed when we looked either," I added. "So how did it get there and who put it there?"

Chapter 28

For two days, I'd been making myself unpopular with the distaff side of Val's family. As we gathered for drinks before dinner on the night after the funeral, I discovered I wasn't the only one. Uncle Sally, his fleshy face full of fury, accosted me with great indignation.

"That thing you brought down with you is a dangerous, vicious creature!"

"The Lagonda? My car is not in the least vicious."

"Not your car, your cat! I was just walking past your door when the beast came out of nowhere and sunk its claws into my leg."

Well done, Catullus! I thought. But I wondered what Sally had really been up to. Catullus rarely scratched anyone, and never without reason. I murmured some sort of insincere apology.

"It should be put down," Sally exclaimed, putting the last nail into the coffin of my hatred for him. *It?* My faithful cat was not an "it." And he was going to live for at least another twenty years unless he caught rabies from Uncle Suspicious.

"The wound was extremely painful. My man must have used a half bottle of iodine on me before we got it wrapped up. Kindly keep that damned monster in your room and remember that you are only a guest here due to my nephew's poor judgment." With that he stomped away.

I knew Catullus could look after himself but decided it

would be wise to keep a closer eye on him, regardless. If Sally and Fitzhugh would poison Erasmus, they'd have no scruples at all about a cat.

I looked around for Elsie and Daphne, but at that moment dinner was announced. As my partner, I had to escort the ghastly Miss Astley. Even worse, Nicky was seated on my opposite side.

Dining with Angela Astley was like trying to swim through a vat of treacle. She was so tooth-achingly romantic that she made it impossible to enjoy my food.

To begin with, she insisted on staring at me with a sort of adoring-puppy look. I never wanted to see anyone look at me like an adoring puppy again. I hated it so much that I needed to come up with a new simile because the whole thing was putting me off adoring puppies. And I like adoring puppies.

Angela's gushing appreciation of my genius talent was so hilariously over the top that I had a hard time keeping a straight face. Shakespeare had nothing on me. I was once again deemed *thrilling*, with an absurd surplus of L's. Angela was one of the most unabashed gold diggers I'd ever come across, and her naked attempts at flattery were about as inconspicuous as a fan dancer in a Chekhov play.

"Oh, it's so *thrilling* to meet such a *famous* author! And so talented! And successful!" Angela trilled. "I heard a rumor that they might make a film from one of your books. How exciting! *Hollywood* calling!"

I swear her favorite punctuation was the exclamation point.

"Oh, just think," she mused. "*Your* words and characters up on the screen! You know who would be great as Zircon... uh... Zardoz?" She tried again. "You know who would be great as your detective? Douglas! Fairbanks! Junior!"

"All three of them?" I asked.

She unleashed a thoroughly sick-making giggle. "Oh, you. But you must admit that he is very handsome."

"Who? My detective?"

"Oh, Douglas Fairbanks, silly. So handsome."

"As handsome as Erasmus?"

The effect of the deceased's name was instant, and not even remotely believable. Angela blinked away the tears that weren't springing into her eyes and tried to look prettily tragic. "Oh, poor, *poor* Erasmus. I shall *always* wonder if I should have accepted his proposal. It might have given him something to live for."

"I'm sorry Miss Astley, I didn't know Erasmus had actually proposed."

"Oh yes, *several* times. Many times. More than once."

When she stopped trying to count, I said, "In that case, I am remiss in not offering you my sincere condolences."

"Oh, how *very* kind of you," she simpered.

She paused. I waited for another "oh" to warn me of the next outburst of blather.

"Oh, I'm sure a sophisticated man of the *world* such as yourself understands what I mean when I confess that I have had my share of *unfortunate* love affairs."

I was glad she was so sure I understood her. I understood nothing at all.

"Oh?" I asked. *See how you like it*, I thought.

"You see here before you, Mr. Griffin, one of those women *fated* to find that love is often tragedy. A woman who knows that *beauty* may be a curse as well as a blessing."

It was well she admired her beauty enough for both of us. It spared me the necessity of pretending.

"Oh, Erasmus was not the first who…" She sighed and sniffed, implying the sentence was too painful to finish.

"The first who…?"

"No, no, some secrets simply cannot be shared." I imagine she meant this insipid melodrama to be appealingly Garbo-esque. Sadly, she was more "grot-" than "Garbo-."

"Oh, but if *you* asked me for my life story, I'm sure it would make a *thrilling* book! Oh yes, if you asked me about my life, I just wouldn't know *how* to begin." She beamed at me, damply yet eagerly.

"How about with '*oh*...?'" I suggested helpfully.

That left her nonplussed for a moment, but she soon returned to my future brilliant career in America. "So, *has* Hollywood called, Mr. Griffin?"

"No. And I'm not sure I'd pick up the phone anyway."

She laughed out of all proportion to my response. "Oh, I suppose I should be grateful. After all, It would be *tragic* to meet you like this, only for you to run off to America. Why, we'd be just like two ships passing in the *night*." The puppy eyes were back.

"The *Titanic* and the *Lusitania*?" I offered.

She didn't react, and I suspected she'd never heard of either ship. "Oh, *Hollywood!* When they do call, I imagine they'd pay a great deal of money to get you to go to Hollywood."

I pretended to consider that. "Perhaps. And I must admit, it would be nice to be able to give more to the church."

She wrinkled up her face. "The... the church?"

"Yes. You see, when I left the priesthood, I decided to keep my vows of poverty and chastity. Most of my royalties are paid straight into the Vatican coffers."

I somehow managed to maintain a straight face. But she looked mildly ill and confused, rather like a nauseous sheep.

"You're... a Catholic?"

"No. Why, are you? Would you like to be? I can make that happen. I think I remember all the right words." I smiled blandly.

"But you said you were a... *priest*," the epileptic sheep bleated.

"Yes, but only for a decade or so. This wine is delicious, have you tried it?"

"And you give *all* your money to the church?"

"Of course. In fact, the proceeds from *Zoltan Szabo and the Dragon in the Snow* built an orphanage in Africa, and *Zoltan Szabo and the Haunted Clarinet* paid for three priests to bring Catholicism to Finland."

"Finland?" She asked as if she'd never heard of the place.

"Yes, Finland. You know. That country that lies in between Canada and Mesopotamia."

"Oh. Um… Yes. *That* Finland."

"Yes. In fact, despite my fame and success as an author, I'm almost completely broke."

"*Broke?*" Angela hiccuped.

"Yes. But I retain enough for my studies. Would you like to know about topsoil? I just read the most fascinating book about topsoil."

She discovered her plate at that point and didn't speak to me again for the rest of the meal.

Feeling flush with success, I turned to Nicky.

"Nicodemus, what did you think of the Chancellor of the Exchequer's comments about devaluing German gold? Do you think the Swedish minister's response was fair or did he go too far?"

Nicky swallowed too much food in his panic and began to choke. After several satisfying slaps to his back, I smiled and waited for his answer.

"Uh… that's a complicated question. I'm not sure I can explain all the intricacies to a layman," he croaked.

"Oh, but please try," I urged, eagerly.

"Uh… well… you know I speak from a position of…" He paused to clear his throat. "So-called privilege and there are certain things I'm not allowed to tell the public. But it has to do with earnings ratio, inheritance taxes, and the… uh… American market."

"I see," I said, enjoying his obvious discomfort. "Tell me,

what are your views on old Crackenthorpe's proposal for aid to Caspinstan?"

He looked perplexed. No surprise given that I was pretty sure there was no old Crackenthorpe, and quite certain there was no Caspinstan.

Nicky became interested in his plate for longer than the plate deserved. Finally, he cleared his throat again and eventually landed on the face-saving comment of, "I would prefer to not discuss the... uh... Craptanistan business at the moment. A bit disrespectful of the family mourning, don't you think?"

I nodded admiringly. "Bravo. That's a nice tactic. *'Not befitting the occasion, old boy.'* Full marks."

"Mr. Griffin, you are—"

"Yes, I know I am. Let's keep it friendly. How about I give you, right now, one hundred pounds if you can tell me the name of the Chancellor of the Exchequer."

He stared at me and looked so lost at sea that he might as well be the Flying Dutchman.

"And if you don't mind a personal question," I added with a smile, "I was wondering if you know anybody who lacks your financial genius and, therefore, may have lost a pile on the Megatherium Trust."

Now I had two guests who refused to speak to me for the rest of the meal, which suited me fine.

After dinner, it was time for the family to deal with Erasmus's distribution of property. But first we were offered our choice of sherry or port, which Uncle Sally declined with his usual grace: "Damn you, Lydgate, you know I hate port! Give me my ruddy Scotch." For once I envied the man. I hated port, too.

As the family and Mr. Eldridge, the aged lawyer, trooped off toward the library, I took the opportunity to whisper to Val, "Good luck. I'm going to miss you." He punched me in the arm.

That left me alone with Daphne, her parents, Elsie, Miss

Astley, and the Bishop. Even with the latter two on hand I considered I got the best of the deal, compared to poor Val dealing with all those grim details in the library.

Daphne walked up to me and whispered conspiratorially, "How did you enjoy dining with Angela?"

"She's very interested in money, isn't she?"

"I imagine she's already toting up how much an author makes and deciding whether or not to ask you to join her in a walk to the summer house tomorrow."

"She did her toting at dinner. But I don't think I'm in her financial league."

Daphne batted her eyes and did her best impression, "Oh, but Mr. Griffin, it's so *thrilling* to meet you. I'm already half in *love* with you already. Why I'd love someone as *brilliant* as you even if you were *poor*. I wouldn't *marry* you, but I'd still *love* you. You aren't poor, are you?"

My snort was fortunately covered by the sounds of everyone else settling into chairs and talking amongst themselves.

I eyed a nearby stack of magazines and a chess set that the Bishop seemed keen to try out but joined the ladies at the card table instead. I sat opposite Aunt Elsie and wondered if the two of us had set up bridge signals in some previous life, perhaps killing time while waiting for the Great Fire of London to start.

"Miss Elsie, forgive me, but shouldn't you be in the library with the rest of the family?"

"Oh, no dear. Tonight is official estate business. I have no place in the line of succession for the Earldom. But Erasmus's personal will shall be read tomorrow, and he says I should attend that."

In the silence that followed, Lady Ferguson dealt, Elsie looked at her cards and made a truly outrageous bid. I looked at my hand and wondered if Elsie knew that clubs were the black shamrock-y things. Daphne bid next, and I was staring without much hope at my hand when we heard a commotion coming from the library—one shrill scream, a few masculine shouts, and the sound of running feet.

I leapt to attention and heard a loud clatter as Lord Ferguson and the Bishop rose from their chess game, knocking over the pieces. Daphne looked with concerned confusion at her mother before tossing her cards down on the table and running to my side. Aunt Elsie picked up Daphne's hand and looked at it.

"Griff! Griff!" I heard Val yelling from down the hallway. I dashed towards the library and met him halfway.

"Val! What's happened?"

"He's dead!"

"What? Who's dead?"

"Uncle Sally!"

Chapter 29

The inhabitants of the library were posed theatrically, like a *tableau vivant*. Sulpicius was bent over in his chair, head down as if staring at his shoes, his thick arms hanging limp by his side. Lady Haxley stood like one of the Trojan Women, her hands clasped, face distorted in a grimace that may have been grief or distaste.

Nicodemus stood behind his father, one hand on the back of the chair, the other rubbing his chin in a nervous gesture that suggested he was afraid he had syrup on his face. Wulfstan and Theo sat next to each other in mis-matched chairs. Wulfie appeared stunned into immovability, but Theo just seemed excited. Eldridge stood, murmuring "dear, oh dear" over and over in an inane litany.

I approached Sulpicius's chair slowly. He certainly looked dead, but for some reason I felt the need to check for myself. I felt for a pulse, ignoring the offended cries from Nicky and Jim as I dared to lift his wrist. Oh, yes. He was dead.

Sounds from the doorway drew my attention away from the body. I locked eyes with Daphne. She looked shocked, but calm.

I turned to Val. "What happened?"

He swallowed heavily before speaking, "I don't know. I was walking behind Uncle Sally, and I noticed he was sort of shaky on his feet. But I didn't think anything about it. Then we took our seats and Mr. Eldridge began reading. About three or four minutes later, Uncle started moaning and clutched his stomach. Someone, I think it was Nicky..." He looked over at his cousin, who nodded. "Nicky asked him if he was okay, and he just started convulsing and retching. He moaned loudly and then fell forward. It... it was only a few seconds and then he just... stopped moving."

The Bishop had reached Sulpicius by this time and began muttering over the lifeless body, *"Depart, O Christian soul, out of this world..."*

"The fear of the Lord prolongs life, but the years of the wicked will be shortened." Lady Haxley quoted in her odd, deep voice. "Proverbs 10."

There followed a moment of awkward silence, as we tried to follow her meaning. But she burst out again with: *"For he sees that even wise men die. The stupid and the senseless alike perish and leave their wealth to others.* Psalm 49."

Even in the face of personal tragedy, the woman came across as a sanctimonious harpy.

I was steeling myself for her next dismal pronouncement when Lady Ferguson crossed the room and put her matronly arm around Lady Haxley. "Come, dear, come with me." She began to lead the new widow out of the room, but I stopped her.

"I'm sorry, but I think everyone should stay here for just a moment." I nodded towards the library sofa which, thankfully, faced away from the body. "Lady Ferguson, perhaps you could take Lady Haxley over there." I noticed the drinks cart in a corner of the room and looked over at Daphne. "Some brandy for Lady Haxley, Daphne, if you would."

Nicodemus spoke for the first time. "I say! I don't appreciate you ordering us about like this. I think my mother should be allowed to leave the room."

"And I don't particularly care what you think," I returned in a commanding voice. I'd mastered that tone terrifying young soldiers during the war. "None of you is to leave the room for the moment. I believe we all need to have a chat."

Nicodemus held my gaze in a test of will, but I'd had my share of those in the war, too. He folded quickly. I thought for a moment. There had been a certain degree of Boy's Own Adventure about the whole mad weekend thus far, but seeing awful Uncle Marge dead in his chair had a sobering effect. It was past time to end this.

Elsie sat down next Lady Haxley and Lady Ferguson and gave an animated explanation of what Lord Haxley was doing and where he was going now that he had left us. Her babbling was neither comforting nor possible. Wherever Sulpicius was headed, I seriously doubted he was "*gliding with joyous feet upon the verdant pathways of the heavenly kingdom.*"

Elsie smiled radiantly as she reported each implausible detail. I suppose for a woman whose hobbies are predicting other people's deaths and rewriting her will to prepare for her own, witnessing one becomes a gratifying event. But her insistence on recounting how poor Lord S had passed on in each of his previous incarnations was not helping the situation. I wondered if she could turn Crazy Aunt Elsie off for the night.

"I think his most beautiful funeral came after he was killed at Thermopylae. Remember, my dear Captain?" Elsie looked at me with the sparkle of a fond memory and I looked at Daphne with the fear of a trapped man. But Daphne, thank goodness, was able to hush Elsie up and led her to the far side of the room.

I turned to Val, grabbed him by the arm, and led him to the opposite corner.

"Val," I said, "we need the Earl."

"But... *I'm* the Earl," he replied.

"No," I disagreed. "At the moment you are Valentine. We need you to be the Earl of Haxley."

"Griff, in the immortal words of Julius Caesar, '*quod* the heck?'"

"Look, you sainted idiot," I began in that sort of insistent whisper usually reserved for stage villains. "Nicky was right, for once in his life. I have no authority here. I can't start issuing orders and expect them to be followed. But *you* can."

"I... can?" Val asked, dubiously.

"No, Val," I said with steadily dwindling patience. "*You* can't. But the Earl of Haxley *can*. If you want me to take charge, then you need to take charge first. Your uncle is dead, one of the people in this room may be responsible, and it's time to for you to step up. Stand up for your brothers."

I both saw and heard the gulp, but then he looked at me with more determination than I'd ever seen in him before. "What do you want me to do?"

"I want you to act like the man in charge."

"Oh, he said," sarcastically. "Just *act* like the man in charge. No need to actually *be* in charge?"

"No," I said. "I'm to be in charge. Per your own wishes, remember?" He nodded. I continued. "But you need to come out as the head of the family and the owner of the Hall. Assert your authority and tell them what to do. Specifically, inform them that I have your confidence to investigate this matter and they are to cooperate with me. You will further inform them that if I do not get their cooperation, there will be consequences."

"Consequences? What kind of consequences? Will they be forced to read *Zeppo the Zebra and the Exploding Siamese Triplets*? Do I threaten them with the rack? Or endless pots of Aunt Elsie's famed duck-tongue tea?"

"Threaten them with whatever you want," I replied. "Just make it strong. Forceful. This is your Saint Crispin's Day Speech."

"Crispin? Crispin was my great-grandfather's cousin. He's been dead for about fifty years. Why are you bringing him up?"

"Not him," I corrected, wearily. "*Saint* Crispin. The speech. Before Agincourt. Henry V?"

"What does Henry V have to do with it? I'm pretty sure he's on the list of people with unimpeachable alibis, along with the King, Charlie Chaplin, and me. Unless you don't think I have an unimpeachable alibi. In which case I officially dis-invite you from this weekend."

"Val, you're not making sense. Are you hysterical? Is this you actually being hysterical?"

"Hysterical!" Val squeaked. "Why would I be hysterical? I'm only six feet from a dead uncle. At a distance and in a condition at which most uncles are measured vertically, not horizontally."

From somewhere behind me, I heard one of those coughs that people in rooms always make when they want you to remember that they *are*, in fact, in the room. I was aware that pretty much everyone was staring at us.

"Val, listen to me. For once in your life, stop being a charming young ass and do what needs to be done. If you can't take charge for real, just act like you can. Remember when you wanted to go on the stage?"

He nodded. "Yes, but that was only because actors get to kiss actresses in public. Ten shows a week."

"Well, here's your chance to be an actor. If you can't be the Earl of Haxley, then be Henry V. Be Julius Caesar. Be Ahab!"

"Ahab?"

"Last night, you urged us to be Ahab hunting Moby Dick, remember? Here's your chance. Be Ahab. Take charge of your ship."

"Right," he said. "Be Ahab. I'm Ahab. I am Ahab and this is my ship. I can be Ahab."

And then, before I had a chance to prepare myself, Val stepped forward.

"All right," he roared. "Everyone, listen to me!" My friend's transformation was sudden and stunning. I was so proud. Val clasped his hands behind his back and began to stride—no, *limp*—across the floor. Oh my God, he was actually limping! Val's transformation into Captain Ahab was complete. And hilarious.

"This situation is dire," he said. "But Mister Griffin is here at my request."

Limp.

"I asked him here because, quite frankly, I am not satisfied that Erasmus's death was an accident."

Limp.

"And now we have yet another death in the family. Rather suspicious, don't you think?"

He limped, turned… and began limping on the opposite leg. But at least everyone was listening.

"I should go to the police with my suspicions."

Limp.

"But until we know more about who might have done these dreadful things, I'm not willing to risk the scandal."

Limp, turn, switch legs.

"Mr. Griffin has my permission to take full charge of this situation. And since we all want to get to the truth of these events, I know I can count on you to answer his questions truthfully and to cooperate with him entirely."

Limp.

"If any of you chose to be difficult, I should be inclined to take it as an indication that you have something to hide."

Suddenly, to my horror and delight, he stopped limping and adopted a most peculiar accent, sort of a cross between an American cowboy with a head cold and a Teutonic majordomo. Who was he trying to be now?

"Lydgate!" He barked in a weird sort of guttural drawl. "Please call Doctor Ridgeway, tell him he is needed here at once." The butler stared at Val as if looking at a stranger. I didn't blame him.

Val turned to me. "Griff, I'll set you up in the study. Please let me know how you want to proceed. Everyone else, back to the drawing room. For once in our lives the Hatton-Haxleys are going to behave like sensible people. Shall we?" He indicated the door.

As Val locked the library and pocketed the key, I decided then and there, with great daring, that we could remove dear Uncle Sally from our suspect list.

Chapter 30

Like reluctant but obedient school children, the crowd trooped off to the drawing room. Val cornered two footmen who'd been drawn by the commotion, instructing them to stand outside the library door and not let anybody in.

We let the rest get ahead of us before Val stopped and grabbed my arm.

"Griff, Uncle Sally is dead!"

"I know. We were just talking about it."

"He's dead and I was Ahab!"

"Yes, you were Ahab. You were a wonderful Ahab," I said, feeling distressingly like a proud uncle patting a favored nephew on the head for surviving his first hangover.

"I didn't know I had it in me," he admitted. "That was rather enjoyable, actually. Aside from the dead uncle and all."

"I always knew you were more than just a pretty face."

He smiled proudly. "I'm looking forward to Ahabbing at the cousins some more. Those monsters deserve some serious Ahabbing."

Val was reveling in his newly acquired Ahab-ness, but I was confronted with the terrifying prospect of having to instantly become a serious and competent investigator.

I stopped in the doorway of the drawing room to survey the scene. Daphne's mother was comforting Aunt Jim, who sat in a sort of dry-eyed mope on the sofa. Wulfie and Nicky were raiding the drinks cart while that little wart, Theobald, sat looking as bored as any son can who has just watched his father die.

Aunt Elsie sat near the abandoned bridge table, only her chair had moved about four feet away. She munched on sugar cubes as if they were bonbons, with a placid expression on her face.

Mr. Eldridge and Lord Ferguson stood uneasily by the unlit fireplace, clearly at a loss for what to do. The Bishop was speaking to them, but neither appeared to be listening.

Miss Astley and Daphne sat in armchairs facing the sofa, the former in a rigid example of perfect posture, the latter glancing around the room with a sort of eager suspicion, trying to deduce who might have just committed murder.

As the others became aware of our presence, I noticed a general straightening of backs and various resentful looks. Val cleared his throat as if to speak, but I immediately turned and left the room again.

"Griff, wait, what's wrong?" Val yelped.

"We need to take a closer look at late Uncle Suspicious before I start talking to people. Come on."

We headed back to the library, and I reached out to Val for the key. He hesitated. "Uh… you don't want me to actually come in with you, do you?"

"Yes, I do. This time I will have a witness to everything."

"Damn," he said under his breath.

* * *

Suspicious Hatton-Haxley looked even larger in death than he had in life, a gargantuan mass of ex-uncle. But it was the first time I had been in his presence without wanting to punch him in the nose. Just below his chair was the glass he'd dropped, with a small amount of liquid still inside. I wrapped my handkerchief around it and picked it up.

"Should you be touching that?" Val asked.

"I just want to make sure the dregs don't spill out. I assume we're both thinking the same thing?"

"That even while we're talking, you're writing the plot of *Ziggy the Zeppelin and the Dead Uncle in the Library*?"

"No. That Sally was poisoned. That's really the only thing that could account for such a sudden death."

"That was my first thought, but now I don't know. He was hardly a fit specimen. Wouldn't a stroke or a seizure be more likely?"

"You saw the whole thing," I said. "Did he seem to have any kind of seizure?"

"No. He just started choking and then he was gone. It only lasted a few seconds."

"That sounds like what Elsie claims happened to Erasmus. It's got to be poison. The question is: was it in this drink? It might have been something he ate at dinner. Or even earlier."

"Really? How long do poisons take to work?"

"It depends on the type of poison. Cyanide can kill instantly. Strychnine can take a while, especially if the victim has had a large meal. There are some, like taxine, that can take hours. But I think we're safe in assuming whatever the poison was, it was given to him today."

With much reluctance, I sniffed at the glass. And with even more reluctance, I sniffed at Suspicious.

"What in the name of all that's holy are you doing now?" Val exclaimed.

I answered without looking up. "Exactly what it looks like. Seeing if I can smell anything."

"Eww. Like what?"

"Like almonds," I replied.

"Why would you care if my uncle smelled almonds?"

I stood up. "Val, you really are thick sometimes. Cyanide

smells like almonds. I was checking to see if I could detect the scent."

"And can you?"

I shook my head. "No. I can't smell anything except some rather eye-watering aftershave."

I moved around and checked his neck for any marks. "Now what are you looking for?"

"Just checking to see if he might have been injected with something. But frankly, I doubt I'd recognize a hypodermic mark. Plenty of moles and whatnot, though."

I stood up and looked at Val. "We're going to need to pin everyone down on anything they may have seen. And I believe we should search everyone."

"That should be fun," Val said, glumly.

"I probably should have done that before I let everyone leave." I shook my head at my mistake. "But let's search here for now. Look for anything that could have held poison. A small vial. Maybe a bit of folded paper."

"Griff, do you have any idea how hard it's going to be to find a folded bit of paper in a library? All someone would have to do is slip it inside a book and it's gone. You hid that vial you found in here precisely because nobody would find it."

"True," I agreed. "But think back, did anybody wander around looking at the books? Or did everyone just walk in and sit down?"

"Everyone walked in and sat down."

"Who sat where?"

Val pointed out where everyone was. "Fine," I said. "Let's just look around these areas. Check under cushions, look around the tables. If something was hidden, it would have to be quick and surreptitious."

Val pulled the cushions off the sofa. "You know, you talk like a writer."

"I am a writer," I observed.

"I know. Only a writer would use a word like 'surreptitious.'"
"Precisely. I'm a writer. I know all the words."
"Well, I must confess I'm confuddled."
"No, you're not," I said.
"How do you know?"
"Because that is *not* a word."
"See? That proves I'm confuddled!"

While Val continued searching around the various chairs, I returned to the dead man and began searching his pockets, although it seemed extremely unlikely that I'd find anything.

Imagine my surprise when my fingers closed on a scrap of thick paper, folded over twice.

Unfolding the paper carefully, I found no powder or other trace of poison. But there was a note. It was written in black ink with an awkward, nearly incomprehensible scrawl, and comprised only one sentence:

You must pay for your crimes.

Chapter 31

Wordlessly, I handed the note to Val. He read it and looked up at me.

"I suppose this is what one would call a clue?"

"Yes, it is. Do you recognize the writing?"

"No," he replied. "But then I probably wouldn't. We're not a very writerly family. It's not like Aunt Jim sent us lovely, chatty letters when we were away at school. *'Dear Valentine, so far only the one death this year, my hasn't it been hot? Love, Aunt Jim.'*"

I looked at the note again. "The writing is atrocious. It's almost illegible."

"Do you think it's from the killer?"

"Don't you?" I asked.

"I'm not sure. Uncle Suspicious was certainly the type to have more than one enemy."

"One who might be capable of murder?"

"I should think anyone who met Uncle might be ready to murder him within minutes of making his acquaintance."

"I can't argue with that," I agreed. "I certainly took an instant dislike to the man."

"Maybe you killed him, then," Val said.

"You're right, I admit it. Case closed."

"I always knew you'd come to a bad end."

"Or a bad weekend, at any rate. This note suggests to me that

Sally killed your brother and tonight's murderer decided to save the His Majesty's Courts a long and expensive trial."

Val looked at the note again. "No, I don't recognize this writing at all."

"We should check your uncle's room for a sample of his hand."

"Why?"

"Because the other possibility is that he's the writer, not the recipient. And while we're there, we should also see if he's received any other threats."

"Threats?"

I looked at him, "You don't think this note is a threat?"

"I suppose." He paused. "But don't you think if it was a threat there would be an actual… threat?"

"You don't think him ending up dead is enough of a threat?"

"Yes, of course. But the note doesn't actually threaten anything. It doesn't say, '*stop or I will kill you until you are dead*'—"

"Val, the man *is* dead. And we're losing time."

Val opened his mouth, shut it again and said, "Right. Let's go."

* * *

Sally's chambers looked even more hideous at night: cold, unwelcoming, and sinister. I was glad Val was with me. But I attacked the massive desk with far less delicacy than on my first visit.

I was looking for the incriminating check ledger. Instead, I got waylaid by an unfinished letter to someone named "Winker" that referenced risqué rumors about a Sir Foster Denominator and an apparently infamous (and highly flexible) dancer with the glorious name of Honeygold Pagan. It was with difficulty that I stopped reading the words and, instead, concentrated on the handwriting.

The letter wouldn't win any awards for penmanship, but it

looked nothing like the threatening note. It seemed unlikely that Sulpicius had written both.

I pulled out the ledger and showed Val the record of the check to Fitzhugh, since he hadn't seen it himself.

"That payment can't be for anything innocent," he said.

"I agree."

Val looked around the room. "Where did you say you found that suspicious bottle in Fitzhugh's room?"

"It was in the upholstery on the underside of his chair."

"Hmm..." Val knelt beside a comfortable-looking armchair. I saw his arm disappear underneath.

"Uh... Griff? *Ta-da!*" With a magician's flourish, Val withdrew his hand, displaying a small glass vial between thumb and forefinger. It was a twin of the bottle I'd found in Fitzhugh's room, probably nicked from Aunt Elsie's supply.

Val sat back on his heels and looked triumphant. But I was utterly confused. Why would *both* men have vials of poison in their rooms, hidden in the exact same place?

"Put it back!" I yelped.

"Why? It's evidence."

"Exactly! I already got spanked once by Drake for tampering with evidence. I'm not making that mistake twice."

"You're not," Val said, wrapping the vial in his handkerchief and pocketing the find. "I'm making that mistake for the first time. Besides, this time there's a witness. We can both attest to the fact that we found this here."

I wasn't sure I'd count as a valid witness in the eyes of the law, but the damage was done. Val's prints were on that vial now, just as mine were on Fitzhugh's. I sighed and picked up the check register. We might both be doomed when the police found out, but at least no more evidence would conveniently "disappear" like Erasmus's caramels.

As we took a last look around, the echoing ring of the front door sounded from somewhere below us.

"That's probably the doctor," said Val. "He lives all of five minutes from here."

"Let's go down. I'd like to intercept him before he has a chance to talk to the others."

"Why?"

"Because somebody down there just killed your uncle, and I'd rather that person not have a chance to collude with the local medico."

* * *

We arrived just as Lydgate was escorting the doctor through the front hall.

Doctor Ridgeway was a silver-haired man with a prodigious nose and snooty expression that gave the impression of an arrogant camel. His rounded, well-fed look marked him as a successful country practitioner, and I got the idea that the suit he was wearing had been made for him several large dinners ago. He carried the requisite black bag of his profession. But I remembered Daphne's story of how the doctor delayed treating an injured child to complete his golf game. Besides, he'd been friends with the late, unlamented Uncle Sally. That alone marked him as a man of incredibly poor judgment.

"Hello doctor," Val said as we reached the ground floor. "Thank you for coming."

"Good evening, my lord," he said in sepulchral tones. "This is a tragedy. Horrible, horrible. What happened, exactly?"

"We're not sure," I replied. "That's why we called you."

The doctor looked at me curiously, and Val performed the introductions. "Griff, this is Doctor Gerald Ridgeway. Doctor, my friend, Gideon Griffin."

We shook hands brusquely, like two boxers sizing each other

up. I rather liked that. I fantasized about punching him in his prominent nose.

"Uncle is in the library," Val said, and led the way. He had the key out of his pocket and was moving to unlock the door when I stopped him.

"Just a moment! Doctor, if you wouldn't mind waiting a moment? I must speak with the Earl. Val, would you join the others in the drawing room?"

"What? Why? Are you trying to get rid of me?"

"No, not at all," I murmured to Val. "I'm trying to make sure the rest of your family doesn't either run off or collude to get their stories straight. We've left them alone too long. I'd feel better if you could keep an eye on things."

He nodded. "Good idea."

"And can you send Mr. Eldridge to join us, please."

"Why?"

"The doctor was one of your uncle's cronies, and his actions when Erasmus died were suspect. I'd like Mr. Eldridge there as a witness to whatever happens. I also get the feeling that we won't get the truth out of the doctor about Erasmus unless we put the fear of God into him."

"You're going to put the fear of God into him?"

"I'm going to try."

"Ooh," Val said, and headed away, towards the drawing room. I envied his chance to be in the same room as the drinks tray. The doctor huffed impatiently but said nothing.

A moment later Mr. Eldridge joined us, accompanied by Val.

"You were supposed to watch your family."

"Yes. But if you're doing Fear of God, I don't want to miss it. Daphne and Aunt Elsie will watch the others."

"Oh good," I said. "Elsie can distract everyone from Sally's death by reminiscing about the good old days when they all used to roll hoops together in the Hanging Gardens of Babylon."

I opened the door and we entered. The doctor stood just inside the room, looking at dead Uncle Suspicious with a sort of dismayed surprise. "Good lord," he observed. "What a tragedy. Poor Lord Haxley."

"Yes, indeed," Eldridge agreed.

"Tell me what happened, my Lord," Ridgeway said, meaning Val this time. He nodded at Eldridge. "Edmund, I want your account as well."

Val and Eldridge began to explain the events leading up to Sally's death, but the doctor soon cut them off.

"His heart. Or perhaps a stroke or seizure. No, it was definitely his heart." The idiot was determining the cause of death before he'd even touched the man. Surely that violated some oath.

"I'd prefer you provide an examination before the diagnosis, doctor," I said politely. "In fact, I rather think we are standing in front of murder."

"*Murder*?" He goggled like something out of a Mack Sennett comedy and repeated the word, with several implied question marks after it.

"Murder," Val confirmed. "Right, Griff?"

Doctor Ridgeway interjected: "Surely, you're not serious… uh… Griff?"

"I am serious, and don't call me Griff."

The doctor replied with a sort of beached-guppy gulp.

"The circumstances *were* highly unusual," Eldridge added with judicial understatement.

"But what possible reason could you have to suspect this is… uh… not natural?" The doctor looked as if he'd just sucked on a lemon.

"Well, let's start with Erasmus. You said *his* death was an accident. A perfectly healthy young man, dropping dead in this house under circumstances so bizarre that a wet envelope would be sharp enough to suspect something."

Gulp, went the doctor.

"Drowning in a bathtub, while reading a gospel, with a giant marble in his mouth? Didn't that make you even the tiniest bit suspicious? But you signed off on accidental drowning in mere minutes."

Gulp.

I was enjoying myself far too much under the circumstances, but he kept gulping, so I kept talking.

"Or let's take the long view. I'm not saying the so-called family curse is real, but this family does have more than their fair share of freak accidents, suicides, and other calamities, wouldn't you say?"

Gulp. Gulp.

"Why in just this one family, entire branches have been pruned off by falling gargoyles, avalanches, electrocution. As well as, I have recently been told, a toboggan accident and a fatal snakebite—that one in Cornwall, no less. Topped off with one accidental beheading, two intentional beheadings, and a single case of death by a large pig."

"Oh dear," muttered Eldridge. "He's right, you know."

The gulping doctor looked a shade less healthy than Uncle Sally by this point.

"However," I plowed on, "the leading cause of death in this family goes to the cellar steps, which over the centuries have claimed three men and a dog named Crumbly. How many of those deaths did you personally sign off, Doctor? How many led to an investigation?"

That was met with one more *gulp* and an audible swallow.

"I should also point out the astounding coincidence that this particular family has a title, property, and money. And the people who die so mysteriously in this family are usually either the title holder, or next in line and rightful heir to that money and property. Correct?"

I paused. He didn't gulp. I was vaguely disappointed.

"So here we are, gathered for the funeral of the party of the first part, the 16th Earl of Haxley, dear Erasmus. Hymns have been sung. Toasts have been made. Then, in less time than it took you to blubber 'oh, his heart' in your blinkered ignorance, yet another Hatton-Haxley dies in yet another suspicious circumstance."

"Indeed, young sir!" Eldridge seemed to approve of my little tirade. He almost clapped.

"Now to me, Doctor, anybody who can add all of that up and instantly proclaim 'heart attack' is either a fool or a suspect. So, Doctor, which are you?"

I suddenly wanted a cigarette.

There was a gratifying moment of silence while the doctor recovered. Then he cleared his throat and tried to save face. "Well, of course there will have to be a postmortem under the uh... circumstances."

"I'm glad you agree that *'the... uh...circumstances'* warrant some caution. After all, we only want to find justice if these men were, in fact, murdered."

"Uh... Yes." Oh good, the gulp was back. "Of course, yes. Justice. For... for the family. I will, of course, be as considerate as possible towards the family. I've known them all for years, you know."

He turned and smiled ingratiatingly at Val, who flashed him a clownish grin in return.

"I've known them for years as well," I said. "And since Lord Valentine is a gentleman and I am not, I'm telling you that whatever deal you had going with his uncle is over. We want the truth, doctor. Not just about Sulpicius but, most especially, about Erasmus. And if we don't get the truth, we will know." I smiled.

Gulp.

I nodded, happily. "Now, as you've seen the body and agreed to a postmortem, shall we join the family?"

Val shot me an amused look and led the way, followed by the red-faced doctor. I took up the rear. As Eldridge passed by me on his way out of the room, he murmured, "I quite enjoyed that."

Chapter 32

The atmosphere in the drawing room was grim with a touch of melodrama.

As soon as I entered there was a general outcry from the family. I ignored them all, except for Daphne. She came to greet us with the report that Val and I had truly set the cat among the pigeons by excluding the cousins from the doctor's examination. Of course, he hadn't made any examination, but they didn't know that.

I turned to Val. "Be prepared to Ahab at them again if they won't cooperate."

Behind me, I heard Doctor Ridgeway give an offended huff as he made his way over to Lady Haxley, who sat at attention on the sofa. I nearly laughed when the doctor made a great show of reaching for her wrist to check her pulse; that one act was more attention than he'd given to her probably-murdered husband. Daphne's mother sat beside them, offering comfort that, in my opinion, Lady Haxley didn't need. The widow was perfectly dry-eyed and looked more bored than grief-stricken.

Athos, Porthos, and Aramis looked equally unconcerned. For three sons who had just watched their father die, they were all rather depressingly un-depressed. It gave me the distinct impression that as bad as I had found Lord Haxley to be, he may actually have been worse. Neither his wife nor his sons seemed to care a whit.

The position of chief mourner seemed to be held, oddly enough, by Angela Astley. She cried with such perfect tears and such an absence of blotching that I suspected she was faking again. But it was a good fake. At least she was trying.

I poured myself a fortifying dose of Scotch before turning to address the room. It felt like the last-chapter-but-one in my books: the one where Zoltan Szabo gathered all the suspects together to identify the murderer. Perhaps I merely wished that it was one of those scenes because it would mean I had solved the case. Instead, I was just this side of hopelessly confused.

Still, if Angela Astley could fake it, so could I. Since Val had found so much success in Ahabbing the family, I decided to Prospero them: give them an act mysterious enough to confuse, while simultaneously convincing them that their inability to understand things was their own fault for being stupid. Hey, it worked for Shakespeare.

I began by addressing the group in my "Major Griffin" tone.

"So far, I've only heard Lord Valentine's version of what happened to his uncle. I'd like to hear from someone else. Mr. Eldridge, would you please describe what took place in the library? And the rest of you, if you disagree or have something to add, please feel free to interject. I want to get a full and clear picture."

"Excuse me," said Comrade Wulfie. "But who put *you* in charge here?"

"The Earl of Haxley," I said. "You were there, remember? Any objections?"

"Yes," he said. "You don't belong here. I don't see why we should answer to you."

"I agree with Wulfstan," added Nicky.

"Well, it's either me or the police," I said politely. "Which shall it be? Your choice."

That raised the temperature in the room a few degrees. Then

Val, resuming his role as Ahab, turned it up a bit more. "We've had two sudden deaths in a week. Does anybody think this is a tragic coincidence? Because I certainly don't. I think that they are connected and that they are suspicious. Now, in addition to being a celebrated mystery novelist, Mr. Griffin was also a decorated Intelligence officer in the war and has experience in this type of thing. I have asked him to investigate because I think we'd all rather avoid a public scandal."

"But again, it's your choice," I added, smiling at Wulfie. "If you still have a problem with me, I have an old friend up at Scotland Yard who I'm sure would be happy to undertake a formal investigation."

"No," Lady Haxley said in her dry, commanding way. "No."

That one word was enough to silence the room. Nobody said anything for several moments, until Mr. Eldridge gave the dusty cough of a man who has spent decades breathing in old wills and dry contracts.

"*Ahem.* May I begin, Mister Griffin? Very well. I had just started reading the late Earl's will. All the required family members were present in the library, and Lord Haxley was sipping a drink. Scotch, I believe, that was his usual."

"Was anybody else drinking?"

"I believe everyone there had a glass, either in hand or nearby. But there was much business before me, so I didn't pay much attention to that. I did not have anything to drink as I, in fact, am habitually abstemious."

I held back a smile and determined my next novel needed a dull-as-dust solicitor who used the phrase "as I, in fact, am habitually abstemious." I made the mistake of catching Daphne's eye and had the uncomfortable feeling that she knew exactly what I was thinking.

"I had just completed reading aloud the declaration and revocation of prior wills—the standard preambulatory matter, you know—when I became suddenly aware of Lord Haxley... er... coughing. Explosively."

"It was more of a gasp than a cough," Nicky said.

"With a moan," Val said. "A sort of *gasp-cough-moan.*"

"A gasp-cough-moan," I repeated.

"Yes, that's it," Val said. "A definite gasp-cough-moan."

"I thought it was more a groan than a moan," Wulfie said.

"What's the difference?" Val asked.

"Well, a moan is sort of *uuuggghhhh*, you know," Wulfie demonstrated. "*Uuuggghhhh*, like that. But a groan has more of an *ooohhhh* to it."

"No," said Theo. "A groan is sort of an *uurrrggh*."

Nicky chimed back in. "Eh, I think what he did was closer to an *aaarrrgh*."

"Good show! *Aaarrrgh*. That was it."

"We get the idea," I growled. "Can you please stop doing impressions of your dying father?"

"Sorry," mumbled one of them. I didn't know which one.

I turned back to Eldridge, figuring at least he wouldn't demonstrate what he thought a gasp, cough, moan, or groan sounded like. "Please, sir, go on."

"Oh yes, of course." He cleared his throat again. "Well, there was... a noise. I stopped reading and looked over at Lord Haxley. He was doubled over, clutching his stomach."

"Did he say anything?"

"No. Well, he sort of coughed and—"

"Moaned," someone said.

"Yes, yes, I think we've covered that. But did Lord Haxley say any actual words?" Silence. "Very well. Who was sitting closest to him?"

"I was," Nicky said. "But I didn't hear anything. Or at least nothing worth repeating."

"So, he did say something?"

"Yes, but it was just something like '*Aaarrrgh*—'"

I glared at him.

"And then, 'Oh, God.' Nothing else."

"Right. And then what, Mr. Eldridge?"

"Well, he... uh... Lord Haxley... died."

If I had been writing this scene, at that point the grieving widow would burst into a heart-wrenching sob of overwhelming sorrow. But because this was real life involving Aunt Jim and not a work fiction about a woman who possessed emotions, there was no reaction. Not so much as a whimper from Jim, Angela Astley, or anyone else. There was, instead, another awkward silence.

"I see. Does anybody else have anything to add?"

Nobody did. I turned to the doctor. "Doctor Ridgeway, what is your procedure here? Will you notify the police now?"

"Not necessarily. I could... I mean I have the authority to declare..." He trailed off as I looked sharply at him. He tried to meet my look with defiance, but it melted instantly under my glare. "Ah, in this instance, I think that we would be best served by alerting the police."

"And holding a postmortem," I added.

"Er... yes."

"Then I suggest you call the authorities immediately and begin the official proceedings."

"What?" Wulfie objected. "You said you wouldn't notify the police!"

"No," I corrected. "I said you could choose either me or the police. You chose me, and now I choose the police. Doctor, I'll leave the formalities to you. Please begin immediately." I turned to Aunt Jim. "Lady Haxley, I am very sorry for your loss. Excuse me, everyone." I turned and left the room.

I had only gone a few steps when Lydgate stopped me in the hall.

"Pardon me sir," he began. "There was a telephone call for

you, but I took a message." He handed me a piece of paper, gave a quick nod, and walked away.

I unfolded the note. It read:

> Contents: nicotine alkaline. That makes you marginally less annoying.
> Drake.

Chapter 33

Loyal Catullus, curled in the exact center of my bed, raised one sleepy eye and regarded me with a haughty, judgmental look. I wished I had thought to bring my glass of Scotch with me. Or better yet, a whole bottle.

I had successfully put the fear of God into Dr. Ridgeway, and the discussion in the drawing room went better than it might have. But I was glad my part as Zoltan Szabo by way of Prospero was over. There was still much to be done, but now it would be in the hands of the police, where it had always belonged.

I kicked off my shoes and lay down on top of the bed, within neck-scratching distance of my cat. "*Haec est fatum domus*," I said, expressing my poor opinion of Tower Field Hall. Catullus gave a soft "mew" of agreement, stretched, and jumped off the bed, looking expectantly at the door. A moment later there came a soft knock. I called out a welcome and, to my pleasure, Daphne entered.

"Hello, Catullus," she said, lavishing affection on my fickle cat, who wove love knots around her legs. "I bet you already know who the killer is, don't you?"

"Probably," I said. "But he refuses to tell me unless I give him a whole salmon."

"Will he settle for some kippers and a tummy rub?"

"If you're providing the tummy rubbing, then yes." I looked

at the door, which Daphne had closed behind her. "Should you be here?"

"What do you mean?"

"Well…" I suddenly felt as if I were doing something caddish. "We are in my bedroom, with the door closed."

She laughed. "Are you afraid of your reputation?"

"No, yours."

"How Victorian of you, Griff. I think my reputation can handle a private conversation or two. Besides, Catullus is here to see we don't get up to anything illicit."

"Oh, I wouldn't depend upon his virtue," I cautioned. "I have a sneaking suspicion that I have grand-kittens all over Chelsea."

"Well, Val will be joining us soon," she added. "He's just gathering some refreshments."

"Not cocoa again."

"No, whiskey."

"Thank God."

"That was a very impressive display downstairs. You handled everyone beautifully."

"I didn't handle anyone," I protested. "I just got the story."

"And what do you think?"

"I think we have two unsolved murders."

"And two murderers?" Val asked, entering the room without knocking.

"No. Maybe? It seems unlikely, doesn't it?" I asked.

Val gave a laugh that denoted anything but humor. "Well, at least the second murder has one less suspect than the first."

"So, what do we do now?" Daphne asked before I could.

I filled them in on the message from Hugo Drake as the much-needed alcohol was passed.

"Nicotine?" Val asked, incredulous.

"Nicotine," I affirmed. "And I should tell you that your Aunt Elsie—"

"Oh, you don't think…!" Daphne protested.

"No, I don't. I just wanted you both to know she can distill it and she keeps a supply. In case the police ask about that."

Val suddenly looked worried. "What should we say if they *do* ask? How do we keep Elsie safe?" I found his protectiveness very endearing.

"We tell the truth."

"Really?" Daphne asked.

"Yes, really. That's what we're all after. And we all agree that Elsie is innocent, so there's nothing to hide."

"True. But we know her. And *like* her. To anyone else, a batty old aunt looks tailor-made for the crime. What if the guilty party tries to put the blame on her?"

"Then you leap to her defense. You're far more powerful than the murderer."

"How do you know?" Val protested. "We don't even know who it is yet! I don't fancy my chances against Fitzhugh in a fight, even with his gammy leg."

"He doesn't mean that way," Daphne explained. "You're the Earl of Haxley, idiot. Your word outweighs everyone else's."

"Oh. Huh."

"By the way," I wondered. "How does one become an Earl?"

"Haven't you been paying attention to the plot of this book? Brothers. All dead. Remember?"

I looked at Daphne, "You're right, he is an idiot. I mean is there a ceremony? Maybe a small, tasteful affair at Westminster? Or are you officially an Earl as soon as someone says, '*The Earl is dead, long live the Earl*'?"

"Oh, you ignorant commoner, you know nothing of how such things are done. There *is* a ceremony, but it's at Saint Paul's. It's a large and lavish affair to which you will not be invited."

"Don't worry, I'll bring you as my escort," Daphne said.

"Well, if we need to keep the current Earl alive until Saint

Paul's, I think it's time to call Drake, tell him about the latest, and ask if he can come down and handle things before whoever Ridgeway calls in bungles it."

"Good idea," she said. "I have my doubts about the local police. One time I reported to Sergeant Brightfellow that our Christmas wreath had been stolen. He noticed another wreath hanging on the door of the rectory and accused Father Sullivan of the crime."

"Oh, fine," Val said. "He'll probably arrest Catullus."

Catullus shot up his rear left leg as a silent insult and began grooming in protest.

"Val, I'm sorry but this could get ugly. You may take some heat for not calling the authorities over Erasmus."

"If you do, we won't let you stand alone," Daphne vowed. "We were all in agreement. If we did wrong, we'll all take responsibility."

"Well then, let's just hope the authorities see things our way."

* * *

"Griff, for God's sake. It's eleven o'clock on a Sunday night. Can't you leave me alone?" Drake moaned when I finally reached him at his flat.

"I'm sorry, Drake, but things have taken a turn for the worse down here."

"Oh Lord, what now? Has Val's fifth cousin once-removed confessed to being Jack the Ripper?"

"Almost."

"Before you tell me the grisly details, did you get my message?"

"Yes. Nicotine."

"Yes," he confirmed.

"So, we finally have some proof?"

"Not really, I'm afraid," he said. "You found a vial of nicotine alkaloid, which is dangerous but not illegal. You claim it was found in this man Fitzwilliam's room, but that is also not a crime, even if you could prove it, which you can't."

"Fitzhugh," I corrected, glumly.

"Whatever," he said. "And you have no evidence that it was given to Erasmus."

"No," I said glumly. "And with Erasmus having been cremated, there's no evidence left."

"Cremated?" Drake sounded intrigued.

"Yes. Suggestive, isn't it? According to Val, Erasmus would never have wanted to be cremated. Yet according to Val's late uncle, cremation was Erasmus's fondest last wish."

"*Late* uncle?"

"Yes."

"How does a late uncle relay the last words of a nephew who has only been dead a week?"

"The late uncle does so by *becoming* late about a quarter of an hour ago."

"Hang on, another suspicious death?"

"And another suspicious bottle."

"You didn't touch that one too, did you?"

"Val did."

"Yes, of course Val did." He sighed. "Who was the uncle?"

"The man I'm pretty sure killed Erasmus. The late Viscount Sulpicius Hatton-Haxley."

He gave a windy sigh, "Griff. I'll go pretty far for a friend, but I won't break the law or my vow to uphold it. If your theories are even close to correct, by not reporting Erasmus's murder you may have contributed to another one."

I was mildly alarmed at what little regret this bald statement of fact caused me. Hell, my morality was disintegrating fast in this atmosphere.

"Look," I replied, "I've already asked the local doctor to ring up the police and hold a postmortem. But I was hoping you could come down and take over the case. Apparently, the local guy is a yobbo with all the detecting skills of a wooden plank."

"I couldn't come down there even if I wanted to. Which I don't."

"Why not? It sounds like an interesting case."

"Good Lord, Griff. The CID doesn't just ride into a country crime scene, trample over the locals, and yell 'what's all this, then?' There are procedures for these things. It's up to the Chief Constable of the county to request our help. Unless and until, my hands are tied."

"Damn."

"Besides," he continued with some justified heat, "I don't want to be involved any further in this affair. I just hope nobody finds out that I ever knew about your so-called *hypothetical actual murder*."

"I'm sorry, Drake. You have my word; I won't involve you further. I owe you for this."

"You can start to make amends by telling me who the killer is in your book."

"What book?"

"*Zoltan Szabo and the Puppet of Doom.* I've been reading it, remember? Only I left it at work, and I was on the last chapter. Tell me, who did it?"

"Oh, uh…" I had to think for a minute. "Ah, yes. It was the Russian magician."

"No, it wasn't."

That took me by surprise. "What do you mean, no? I'm the author, I should know who my killer is."

"Yes, one would think so. However, in this particular book, the Russian magician is most assuredly *not* the murderer."

"How would you know? You haven't finished it yet."

"I know because the Russian magician is the *victim*, Griff."

"It was suicide."

"Being stabbed in the back by a sword in a disappearing cabinet is a form of suicide?"

"Yes. Well, thanks for your help, Drake. Tell Alfred at the club to put a bottle of port on my tab."

"How generous. You don't belong to my club, and we don't have an Alfred. But listen. Tell Val that once the local police have started their work, he could ring up the Chief Constable in Danforth and ask that CID be brought in, that might persuade them. By the way, what's the rest of Val's family like?"

"In a word, horrible. There's a fake communist, a financial con artist, a public-school horror, and a gold-digging harpy who makes your Christine Peterson look like Jane Eyre."

"Please don't call her *my* Christine Peterson."

"Sorry. It's a mess, Drake. Oh, and there's an eccentric aunt who may or may not be crazy and may or may not have witnessed our chief suspect leaving Erasmus's room on the morning of the murder. And who has warned me that I shall die from swans."

He laughed. "You're making that up!" I protested my honesty, but that just made it seem even more outlandish.

"How exactly will these swans kill you? Smothering? Pecking? Or perhaps they, too, are armed with vials of nicotine?"

"Stop speculating about my demise."

"I don't need to. Swans are etched by the Heavenly Host onto the tablet of your doom."

He hung up before I could blaspheme.

Chapter 34

Sergeant Herbert Brightfellow was the most poorly named man I'd ever met. He was a complete idiot. A certified, award-winning, world champion idiot.

Brightfellow was a well-fed oaf whose overstuffed uniform sported a prominent gravy stain. A mop of red hair and an abundant red mustache divided his face into upper and lower hemispheres that seemed, somehow, mismatched. It was as though his head receded towards two different vanishing points somewhere near his nose.

I emerged from the study just in time to receive a full blast of onion-scented attention from this local copper who, to my regret, turned out to be a huge Zoltan Szabo fan.

"Ah, Sergeant Brightfellow," said Val, who had switched from Ahab to some sort of Dickensian official for this part of his performance. "This is my good friend Gideon Griffin, whose work you may know."

"Indeed, I do!" Brightfellow enthused, wringing my hand as if trying to squish all the liquid from a turnip. "I am a *rabbit* fan."

I swallowed a laugh.

"It's always a pleasure for Griff to meet his rabbit fans." Val smiled.

"Why just last month I enjoyed *Zoltan Szabo and the Island of the Secret Flowers*, and I figured out in chapter three that Dr. Vestuvian was the killer."

"No, he wasn't," I said. I'd endured many conversations like this and always kept my rogue's gallery ready to hand in my mind. "Dr. Vestuvian was the killer in *Zoltan Szabo and the Parchment of the Ar-du-Mahk*. The killer in *Zoltan Szabo and the Island of the Secret Flowers* was the Prime Minister's cousin's husband."

"I believe you're mistaken, sir."

"I'm sure you do, Sergeant," I said, losing all hope. "But I can assure you that it was the Prime Minister's cousin's husband. He imported that entire flock of sheep just so he could—"

Val, for once the voice of reason, coughed in an unmistakable statement of reproach. *Right*, I remembered. *Dead uncle*.

Dickensian Val explained in short, simple sentences what had transpired that evening. The Sergeant's response of "oh dear, oh dear, oh dear" had the unfortunate effect of making both Val and I burst out into thoroughly disrespectful giggles. I didn't know policemen actually said that.

We apologized, saying we were very highly wrought under the circumstances, and led Brightfellow into the study. He got out his notebook, licked a thumb, and turned to a blank page. "Now then, can you tell me who is in residential at this time?"

I bit the inside of my cheeks, trying to avoid a second outburst of giggles. I think Val was doing likewise, as he began reciting the list of guests in a high-pitched, wavering voice that sounded like a parody of refined nobility. So much for Ahab. But it still fit Dickens.

The Sergeant then asked us to take him to the "scenario" of the murder and told me his favorite book of mine was *The Shroud of the Baskervilles*. I lost the will to live.

The doorbell sounded once again, and Val dispatched me to see who it was. I reached the entry hall as Lydgate was admitting a tall soldierly-looking man who was either the local undertaker or, please God, someone superior to Brightfellow.

Our luck was in.

* * *

INSPECTOR JACK PARRISH of the Danforth station impressed me instantly by possessing a brain and inquiring about the deceased rather than "the descendant." I informed him that Brightfellow was in the library with Val, examining the body.

"If I know Brightfellow," Parrish said, "he's probably spilling biscuit crumbs all over the corpse and telling Lord Valentine that he's a 'creditor' to his family line."

I laughed, relieved. "Oh, thank God," I said, fervently. "I was beginning to wonder—"

"He's the Chief Constable's brother-in-law," said the inspector, shaking his head glumly.

Val was standing just inside the doorway of the library, as far from his late uncle as he could get. Brightfellow was bending over the body as if preparing to pick up a sleeping drunk.

"Brightfellow, get away! You've been warned about that," the Inspector said in the tone of an exasperated father.

Inspector Parrish shook hands with Val and guided him once more through the events of the evening, asking intelligent questions that reassured us we weren't entirely at the mercy of the blind.

I stood back with the others, which unfortunately left me right next to Brightfellow. He insisted on talking to me more about my books. Or somebody's books. Or perhaps somebody's weird fever dreams about a world where books don't exist, and you have to explain the concept to a herring.

"What was the book you wrote where the dead artist wasn't actually dead, his sister wasn't his sister, the killer didn't kill him, and there were all those badgers about?"

"Why, Griff!" Val broke off from the Inspector and turned to me with mock excitement. "You didn't tell me you wrote a book all about badgers. What's it called?"

"*Mr. Babbington and the Slathering Badgers of Hell,*" I grumbled.

"Ooh, it's a stuporious book, Lord Earl," said Brightfellow, with genuine enthusiasm. "Especially at the end when you find out that Chinese butler wasn't speaking Chinese after all, he was speaking Dutch."

"Because Chinese and Dutch sound so much alike," I sighed.

"You've said a morsel-full there, Mr. Griffin!" I was thankful Val was there to bear witness to this event, otherwise nobody would believe me.

"Right." The Inspector turned, having completed his notes. "The rest of my people will be here shortly. Lord Valentine, is there someplace where I can interview everyone privately? I'd like to start with you, if I may."

"Of course, Inspector. Everyone is gathered in the drawing room, but the little sitting room should suit your needs. I'll show you."

"Thank you, my lord. Brightfellow, please escort Mr. Griffin back to the drawing room and stay there until you are called."

"Yes, sir."

"And Brightfellow?"

"Yes, sir?"

"Don't say anything. To anybody."

"Yes, sir."

Not ten seconds after this vow, he was telling me how much he enjoyed *Zoltan Szabo and the Murder of Lord Peter Ackroyd*.

Once in the drawing room, I cut off the Sergeant from speaking and informed everyone of what had happened over the previous twenty minutes, ending with the fact that they'd be called one by one to speak to the authorities. I was greeted by looks of loathing from the family, who protested that they had been cooped up for an absurd amount of time already while I apparently had the run of the house. Daphne, her parents, Elsie, the Bishop, and Eldridge simply nodded their calm acceptance.

Miss Astley was somewhere in the middle, both geographically and emotionally, wiping away another in her endless supply of ready-made tears.

Aunt Jim rang for coffee. Nicky expressed a desire for stronger fare, and for once I had to agree with him. Lydgate opened a fresh bottle, and I drank because this night called for Scotch. And plenty of it.

Eventually Daphne and I found a quiet corner.

"Well," she said. "Finally, a mysterious death is being taken seriously around here. We're sure to find the killer now that the police are questioning everyone."

"It does create a problem though," I observed.

"Does it?"

"We all thought Uncle Sally and Fitzhugh were behind it all. Well, with Sally dead that just leaves Fitzhugh. And I can't see him doing away with his master."

"I can. Maybe that check bounced."

"Points to you. That hadn't occurred to me."

"It's pretty unlikely though," she admitted.

I nodded. "I'm afraid so."

"Have you told the police about the check? Or the poison bottle?"

"Or the other bottle that may also be a poison bottle?"

"I will when the Inspector interviews me."

"What's he like?"

"The inspector? He seems a sharp enough man," I said. "But Sergeant Brightfellow over there is an unbelievable idiot. You really should find an excuse to go speak to him. You'll enjoy the experience."

"Really? I could do with a distraction. I think I'll offer him some coffee." Daphne wandered away towards the door.

I welcomed the prospect of a few minutes alone but just then the Theobald creeped over. I wanted desperately to shoo him away, but the poor kid *had* just lost his father, so I decided to do the decent.

"Theo, I'm sorry about your father."

"It's Theobald."

So much for civility. "Were you and your father close?"

"No, I was about six or seven feet away."

Sigh. "I mean, did you have a close relationship?"

"Oh. Not really. He was awful."

What I thought was, *that's the pot calling the kettle...* What I said was, "What was wrong with him?"

Theobald took the Scotch out of my hand, swallowed a good dram, belched, and tried to pass it back. I let him keep it.

"You met him," he said, taking a second swig and giving me a sour look. "Don't pretend he was anything other than an absolute bastard."

"I take that to mean you don't believe he died of heart failure," I observed.

"Father?" He snorted and swigged the last of the Scotch. The way he swallowed without batting an eye suggested Saint Gordon's School was swimming in contraband liquor.

"I always figured someone would do him in. Surprised it didn't happen ages ago." The hand that wasn't holding my erstwhile Scotch snapped out and stole my cigarette. "By the way, what do you have on dear cousin Val? Opium? Dirty photos? Do I have a score of little bastard cousins running around the more picturesque corners of London?"

I looked at the little horror in genuine confusion. "What in the hell are you talking about?"

"You and Val, in the library earlier. He was being his usual dithering moron self until you pulled him aside. A few words from you and he was swaggering around the room like Kitchener's idiot brother. You must be holding something juicy over him to get him to do your bidding like that. How about cutting me in? I could do with a bit of the ready, you know."

He handed back the empty glass with the half-smoked cigarette marooned on the ice like a limp flagpole. "Think about it," he whispered. And then, louder, "Thanks for the drink." He slouched into a distant armchair and closed his eyes just as Daphne returned from her *tête-à-tête* with Brightfellow.

"Well?" I asked.

"He's like something out of a Restoration comedy. He said I was very pretty, and I reminded him of his favorite Anjou."

I blinked. "You mean he has a favorite pear? Or did he mean like Margaret of Anjou?"

"Neither," she said, laughing as decorously as possible, but still earning a stern glance from her mother. "I think he meant *ingenue*."

"Oh dear. Better than Adolphe Menjou, I suppose."

"I saw you having a quiet chat with Theo," she said. "Horrible, isn't he?"

"Dreadful. And so broken up by watching his father die that he could barely finish my Scotch."

"Sometimes I think he's the worst of the brothers," she said. "Nicky and Wulfie are self-centered, dishonest, and generally unlikeable. But Theo has a touch of the truly repellent about him."

"Like father, like son," I observed with a laugh, earning me my own disapproving look. Daphne's mother was good at disapproving looks. "Your mother is really good at disapproving looks," I said.

"I know. She's a wonder. It comes in handy sometimes. Whenever the vicar gets a bit too wordy on a Sunday, if he ever makes the mistake of catching mother's eye, she can usually bring the sermon to a conclusion. Sometimes even before the poor man gets to the point of the lesson. I recall one time she flustered him so badly he ended his sermon with the words, '*Oh Lord, please make her stop.*'"

The following laugh earned us each another look.

"Oh," Daphne said, as if just remembering. "It may interest you to know that Brightfellow has a wonderful idea for the plot of your next mystery novel."

I groaned.

"In it, your detective, whose first name he is certain is Sven, is trapped on a zeppelin with a German spy, a Greek jewel thief, and a lion on its way to a zoo in China."

"I've never written a book without my detective's name in the title, and he still gets it wrong. Wait… he's taking a zeppelin to China with a spy, a thief, and a lion?"

"And he has a mid-air affair with a French nurse on her way to be a missionary because her Danish lover was killed on the Somme."

"The Danes were neutral in the war."

"That's what you focus on?"

"It's the easiest."

"Just be warned, he's waiting for his opportunity to explain it to you."

"I'm doomed."

She laughed, then stopped herself, even without one of Lady Ferguson's disapproving looks. "We shouldn't be laughing. Poor Uncle Sally…"

"No," I said, "don't start 'poor Uncle Sally-ing.' He may be dead, but that doesn't mean he's suddenly respectable. His own wife and children aren't upset about it."

"It's all a bit overwhelming, I suppose." She gave me a sort of half-smile. "What should we say to the Inspector?"

"What do you mean?"

"Well, obviously we should tell him what we know, but should we share our suspicions about Sally and Fitzhugh?"

"I intend to," I said.

"But what if we're wrong?"

"Then we're wrong. Inspector Parrish seems to know his business. He'll take note of our suspicions, and hopefully he'll investigate. But he's hardly likely to march Fitzhugh out in handcuffs just because we don't like his cologne."

"Ugh. You've noticed it, too? Explosive, isn't it?" She ventured. "Would you believe it's called *Gladiateur*?"

"It would be."

Chapter 35

I made a bet with Daphne that the Inspector would either call me in second, which is to say right after Val, or as the very last witness. I was last.

The second slot went to Nicky, which surprised me until I remembered that he had suddenly become the new Viscount Hatton-Haxley. Poor Aunt Jim, meanwhile, had sped from Lady Hatton to Viscountess Hatton-Haxley to Dowager Viscountess in seven days flat.

Time dragged as the drawing room slowly emptied over the next hour, then seemed to stop entirely when I found myself alone with the ghastly Miss Astley. I decided the police could use someone like her. Five minutes locked in a room with Angela Astley would be enough to break anyone.

"Oh, isn't this *awwwwful*," she said.

I agreed that it was, indeed, awwwwful.

"Oh, I'm sure this will just *ruin* my plans," she said, petulantly. "I was supposed to leave tomorrow to join the Arbuthnot sisters at their place in Cap d'Antibes."

Was she serious?

"If I'm not there in time, I'll miss seeing Pongo and Bunty before they leave for Venice."

"I thought Pongo and Bunty were going to Spain," I chimed in, wondering who on earth would voluntarily go through life with a nickname like Pongo.

"Oh, no," she replied, oblivious to my sarcasm. "Pongo and Bunty always go to Venice this time of year. But Chubby and Pips are off to Spain next month."

"Are all your friends named after dogs?"

"I beg your pardon?"

"Nothing."

"Oh, I do *hate* it when my plans are ruined."

"I'm sure Lord Haxley would be very upset to learn his death has inconvenienced you so much."

"Oh! First poor, dear Erasmus, and now this."

"Yes, it *has* been a busy week, hasn't it?"

"Although I'm going to be just the teeniest bit *naughty* and say all of this is rather *thrilling*."

I noticed that she only put the requisite number of L's into her thrills this time, no doubt out of respect for the solemnity of the occasion.

"I've never spoken to a *policeman* before. Oh, I suppose it's too much to hope that he'll be a gentleman. I mean, what if he asks me about Erasmus? A rustic bumpkin would never understand what *love*, deep *love*, can do to a man. Especially when it's not returned."

She shot out her hand towards me in a gesture I'd only ever seen in a melodrama and put on what she no doubt thought was a look of female helplessness. I suspected she was about as helpless as a hammer.

"Oh, Mr. Griffin, do intercede with the police on my behalf. Make sure they know I'm not to blame for Erasmus. Please, I *appeal* to you."

"No, actually, you don't." I said it with a smile, so the slight went right over her Gewurztraminer-colored curls.

I could have kissed Brightfellow when he came to collect her, but I settled instead for a large brandy. Probably not the best idea on top of all that Scotch. I may have hallucinated

Brightfellow's excited idea for a new book. It wasn't the one Daphne had warned me about, though. This one was some nonsense about sparkling teenage vampires.

I murmured something incoherent to the poor man and joined the Inspector, not in the least surprised to see Catullus in possession of the little sitting room's most comfortable chair.

"Ah. Thank you, Mr. Griffin," said the Inspector. "Sorry to keep you until last. I've heard some very unusual stories in the past hour or so and your name crops up in most of them."

He smiled as I picked up my cat and took the chair.

"I understand the excellent Catullus here is your animal?"

"There are some who would assert that I am his."

"That's in the way of cats," he observed. "I also understand that Catullus found a clue."

"You mean the marble he found in Aunt... er... In Miss Armistad's room?"

"Yes. Interesting woman." He paused and I swear I caught a twinkle in his eye. "Forgive a personal question, Mr. Griffin, but may I ask how you are going to...?"

"Join the choir invisible?"

"Just so."

"Would you believe, swans?"

"Swans?"

"She told me to beware of swans. I have no idea what that means."

He laughed. "When I get home, I must reassure my wife that I shall do the decent and go down with my ship. Presumably, sometime after I join the Navy."

"Rule, Britannia."

We both indulged in a tension-breaking chuckle before getting down to the grim business at hand.

"Now, sir, could you please give me your version of tonight's events?"

I explained what I could, pausing to answer the Inspector's many questions. I had little of value to add to the immediate investigation, not having been in the room when Sally died, so we quickly moved on to Erasmus and what Val, Daphne, and I had been up to the past few days. I started with Val accosting me at the club and ran through everything in chronological order. Laying it all out like that, I had the vague notion it might make for a mildly amusing but utterly nonsensical novel.

"I see," he said, when I had wound down. "You tell a very clear story, Mr. Griffin. But then again, telling a clear story is your business, isn't it?"

"It is. But as I've learned, it's easier to invent an imaginary murder than to solve a real one. I assume both Miss Ferguson and Val... Lord Valentine, I mean, have told you their versions of the same events. Hopefully we make some sort of sense."

"Let's just say it's... interesting." That wasn't the word I wanted to hear, but at least he didn't look at me like I was a moron.

"Have you spoken with Gilbert Fitzhugh yet?" I asked.

"No, sir. I started with eyewitnesses and now the other guests. I'll get to the staff soon."

"I can put you in touch with the man I mentioned, Roger Benedict. The one who served with Fitzhugh."

"Thank you, sir. I'd appreciate that. And we'll also check in with the War Office for his service record. I'm not personally acquainted with your friend, Inspector Drake, but I'll apply to him for a copy of the analysis of that bottle, which we can compare to this second one you say you found. If you'll excuse me, sir, but you shouldn't have taken those."

I blushed, which was decidedly uncomfortable and made me feel like blushing even more. "I know. It was a stupid idea. But I thought having some evidence in hand was better than none."

"It is better. If," he stressed, "and *only* if, that evidence is found and handled in the right way. The proper, legal way. Not passed around by friends and family of both the victim and the supposed murderer."

"You're right. I'm sorry."

"Ah well, nothing to be done now. But from now on, you must leave everything to the professionals. No more searching bedrooms or tampering with evidence. Am I clear?"

I nodded, feeling as though I was back at school getting called on the carpet by the headmaster for smoking behind the chapel.

"Now, Mr. Griffin, I'm afraid I'm going to ask you to be indiscreet, but it can't be helped. Tell me, if you will, what you know of the family. They seem a rather, um, unusual lot."

"Yes, the Hatton-Haxleys are... unique."

"Forgive my lack of familiarity with titles and names, Mr. Griffin. But I notice we have Hattons, we have Haxleys, and we have Hatton-Haxleys. I don't suppose you could explain how that all works, could you? I asked Lord Valentine, but it was even more confusing afterward."

"I tried asking him about it, too. I'm sorry, Inspector. I find the first names hard enough to understand without worrying about how many H's appear in anyone's monogram."

I reached into my jacket for my cigarette case, lifted an eyebrow in question and, having been motioned by the Inspector to go ahead, lit up before answering.

"So, the family. I only know Val, really. We were at school together. He's one of my oldest and, I must say, closest friends. I've stayed here at the Hall before, and casually knew his family, but that was years ago."

"A very nice gentleman, the Earl," said the Inspector before continuing shrewdly, "Looks like a fool but is not nearly so foolish as he looks."

I laughed. "A perceptive observation, Inspector. Val is one of those charming and disarming individuals who is easily underestimated."

"I can assure you, sir, I make it a point to never underestimate anyone." He opened a small leather notebook and uncapped a pen. It made me instantly feel like sweating. "What can you tell me about the rest of the family, sir?"

"Not a lot, I'm afraid. I'd not met any of them before this weekend."

He shot me a knowing glance. "Mr. Griffin, you are a writer and writers observe the people around them. You were also in intelligence in the war and you're no fool. Please, I'm not asking for facts, just your observations. Lord Haxley, for instance."

"Well, I didn't like him. And I wasn't the only one."

"Oh, forgive me," the Inspector said. "I didn't make myself clear. By Lord Haxley I mean the new Lord Haxley. Lord Nicodemus."

"I suppose he is the heir now, isn't he?" I stopped, something occurring to me. "Inspector, have you heard about the family curse?" Just hearing those words coming out of my mouth made me want to squirm, but the Inspector didn't blink an eye.

"Indeed, sir. Lord Valentine told me about it. And I've heard it mentioned by others. Why?"

"Well, suppose we say that Nicky believes in the curse. If Erasmus dies, then his father, and then Val, Nicky becomes the Earl."

"You believe him capable of killing three members of his own family?" He said it without inflection, but I could feel the incredulity.

"I believe him capable of killing the whole village if there's enough money in it. But no, the point is that if he wanted the estate and the title, he would make sure to do it in that precise order, so that his father died before Val. Because if Val had died and Sally come into the title, that would have made Nicky the heir as eldest son and put the family curse squarely on his own head. But if Val dies *after* Sally, Nicky is in the clear, curse-wise."

The Inspector stifled a laugh and said, "That sounds right. But you don't actually believe in this curse, do you?"

"No, of course not. But some of the family members do. Only I can't figure out which ones."

"Let's leave that aside. Tell me, Mr. Griffin, do you believe whoever is behind the death of Lord Erasmus is also behind the death of Lord Haxley? And mind you, I see little evidence of either being murder yet. But if we accept your theory that both men *were* murdered, do you believe we are looking at two different killers?"

I chewed on that for a moment. "I suppose one murderer in the family is easier to accept than two."

"Indeed. And in that case, you must admit sir," the Inspector observed, "that Lord Haxley, the late Lord Haxley, was unlikely to be behind the death of Lord Erasmus."

"Not if he was acting alone," I agreed. "But he could have been part of a conspiracy, only to fall out with his partner."

"And you think that partner was Gilbert Fitzhugh?"

I nodded.

"Meanwhile, you've talked yourself into finding it plausible that Lord Nicodemus might be ruthless and cunning enough to murder his own father in an attempt to gain the title without risking running afoul of the family curse."

"I'm just speaking out loud, really," I admitted. "But I'm struggling to come up with anybody who had a motive for killing both Erasmus and Uncle Suspicious. And I'm not finding anybody."

This time the Inspector couldn't hold in his laughter. He coughed out a snort. "Uncle *Suspicious*?" He laughed again.

"Sorry, Inspector. It isn't as funny as it used to be." I felt like a cad for joking about the man.

"So, about these suspicions you, Lord Valentine, and Miss Ferguson apparently shared. Have you told anyone else in the house about them?"

"Er... Yes. We've spoken to Lydgate the butler, and also Sutherland, Lord Erasmus's valet. And I believe Miss Ferguson has discussed it with one of the maids. Mary, I think." I saw his eyebrows rise just a little with each name.

"And did you tell them that you suspected any particular party? Or did you merely put forward the suggestion that Lord Erasmus's death was murder?"

"When I spoke to Lydgate and Sutherland, I can't recall if I mentioned any names, but even if I didn't, they'd have had little trouble figuring out who I suspected from the questions I asked."

"I see. Anyone else?"

"Well... Just today I rather showed my hand to both Sally and Fitzhugh."

The eyebrows fell into a scowl as he looked at me sharply. "Was that wise, sir?"

"No," I said. "But it was fun."

"It was *fun*," he repeated. "Lord, save me from amateur detectives."

He stood then, in an unmistakable gesture of ruler dismissing a courtier. I stood too, dislodging an affronted Catullus. "Thank you for your time, sir. Don't leave the premises, and the library is off limits, as I've told the Earl. Once the mortuary people are done, I will lock the room and keep the key. Otherwise, you may move about the grounds as normal. Now get some sleep, as I'll have more questions tomorrow."

"Excellent. Good night, Inspector."

We thus parted on amiable terms, despite my many missteps. I headed upstairs assured we were in good hands.

Chapter 36

The Inspector's suggestion of sleep had its appeal, but my mind was buzzing. I wanted to have a long talk with my friends. But as had happened so many times before, the door to Elsie's room opened just as I was approaching, allowing Catullus to slip past me and run inside. To my surprise, though, it wasn't Val's favorite aunt beckoning for us to enter.

"Griff, thank goodness," Daphne said, grabbing my arm and all but yanking me into the suite. "You've been ages."

"The inspector saved me for last," I sighed. "You owe me a shilling."

Val was seated in the hydrangea chair, a brandy glass in one hand and a pained expression on his face. Elsie sat in serene repose, very upright and sipping some spirit in an outrageous shade of blue from what looked like a test tube.

Val shot me a weak smile and gestured to the decanter at his side. "Pour yourself one. You're going to need it." Something in his tone told me that one wasn't going to be enough. I poured myself a generous slug and took the ladybug chair, nipping in scant seconds before Catullus could claim it.

"And why am I going to need this?" I asked, warily.

"Because my Aunt Elsie and the Honorable Miss Daphne Ferguson want to hold that séance they were talking about. Right now. To contact either Erasmus or Uncle Sally."

I was silent for a moment. Of all the ways I might have

pictured this day ending, holding a séance mere hours after a shocking death would not have made the list.

"Sally hasn't been dead very long," I tried to argue. "Doesn't it take some time for him to get fully to the other side? He's probably busy getting measured for his forked tail."

But Elsie, bless her, didn't take up my sarcasm and said it was "very thoughtful" of me to consider things from his point of view.

"You know," she added, "this will be the first séance I've hosted without Erasmus in years. I hope he'll come tonight."

"Erasmus?" Val sat up, stunned. "Erasmus and you used to hold séances? Together?"

"Yes dear," she said, placidly. "We spoke with all the boys after they passed. All except Medard, that is. But then again, Medard and I never really got along. The dear boy was a bit too rational. The rigorously sane have such a difficult time coming back for a visit."

"Aunt Elsie," Val said, hesitatingly. "Would you mind if Daphne, Griff, and I had a private word?"

"Oh, of course not, dear. I'll just start gathering the materials." Elsie stood and went into the adjoining room.

"What's she going to do, unwrap a new box of ectoplasm?" Val said. Daphne "shushed" him. But as soon as Elsie was gone, he started again. "Why in the world would you agree to a séance?"

"Because it will bring her comfort," Daphne said. "It can do no harm and we might even learn something."

"Like what? Whether or not Erasmus thinks Saint Peter needs a haircut? If Uncle Sally is having cocktails with Vlad the Impaler?"

Daphne punched him in the arm. "She really wants this. It will make her feel better and she may let something slip that she is not aware that she knows."

"That makes no sense," he argued.

"Yes, it does," I said. "Elsie may know something that she

doesn't realize is important. I assume that's what happened with those caramels. She was playing with her Ouija board, suddenly remembered something she'd seen before and forgotten about, and imagined it was Erasmus who told her. If a séance frees up her mind like that, what have we got to lose?"

"Perhaps our sanity?" Val ran his fingers through his hair in frustration. "This family is so mad, I'm afraid we're just one séance away from getting a special group rate at the local laughing academy."

Elsie floated back in with an armful of candles and a sort of triangular plate. "I thought we'd use the planchette," she said. "It's what Erasmus liked best."

"Who or what is the planchette?" Val asked.

She smiled at me, "I think James knows, don't you?"

I nodded. "I used one in *Zoltan Szabo and the Vengeance of the Venetian Virgins*." I heard Val snort. "It's a heart-shaped thingy on wheels, with a hole in the center. You set it on a sheet of paper, put a pencil in the hole, and everyone places a finger—"

"Two fingers," Elsie corrected.

"—Two fingers on top. It's used for automatic writing."

"Automatic writing?" Val asked.

Daphne nodded. "You ask questions, and the spirits use your energy to write out the answers."

"Well, then, there's no point," Val said. "Erasmus had the most illegible handwriting ever. Dead Erasmus's handwriting must look like a ransom demand from Satan."

Elsie smiled. "James, could you please move that little table over here?"

There was a small round table by the French doors. Val moved it to the center of the room while I slid the chairs into position.

"Should we have more than four people?" Val asked. "What's the quorum for a séance? I would have thought we'd need thirteen or something."

"And who would you prefer to join in our séance?" I asked. "Your Aunt Leroy? Nicky? I'm sure Miss Astley would find it simply *thrilling*."

Val shuddered. "Good point. Four is more than enough."

Elsie looked up from her preparations. "Would you please open the door to the terrace, dear? Spirits dislike enclosed rooms. They're more likely to come if we leave a door or window open."

I had no idea who "dear" was in this context, but I was closest, so I opened the door, taking a deep breath of the cool night air. I stepped outside briefly, looking at Elsie's plants and wondering which one was hemlock.

"Right, everyone," Elsie said brightly, like a teacher calling her class to order. "Let's take our seats and begin."

Elsie lit candles and placed them around the room, so that when she switched off the electric lamps, there was still enough shifting light to see everyone. I noticed she had thrown a black lace scarf over her head, making her look a bit like a fortune teller and a lot like an Italian widow.

She laid a few sheets of the Hall stationary on the table, covering most of it, and placed the planchette in the center. It was made of some rich, honey-colored wood with Celtic symbols spiraling out from a small, round hole in the center. Into the hole, she placed a thick pencil.

At Elsie's signal, we each put two fingers on the device.

"Everyone put your other hand on the table. That way the spirits can see we have no hidden weapons," she said.

Hidden weapons? I thought. They're dead. What do they have to be afraid of? Are they simply paranoid? Do ghosts only show up at these things so they can *finally* hear what people are saying about them behind their dead backs?

"James, please stop looking so seasick," Elsie scolded. "You'll put me off." I murmured an apology. Yet as bizarre as the whole thing was, I was becoming rather glad that Daphne talked us into it. Poor Elsie might be batty, but she had lost a beloved nephew and it looked as if this diversion might provide her some comfort.

"We start by greeting the spirits and inviting them to visit," Elsie intoned. "I shall speak on our behalf."

That was a relief, since I wasn't sure I could pretend to talk to one of Val's dead, sainted brothers with a straight face.

"We are gathered here with open minds and welcoming hearts to speak with anyone who wants to converse with us. Come, spirits, for you are among friends."

"Doesn't that rather depend upon who shows up?" Val asked. "I mean, if the Spanish Inquisition burst in, I'm not sure I'd be very welcoming."

I chuckled. "Why, are you expecting the Spanish Inquisition to show up?"

"*Nobody* expects—" Val was cut off by a stern *shush* from both Daphne and Elsie.

Elsie waited a moment for everyone to settle down, then continued. "We invite you to use our energy, to draw from our life force and join us here tonight in communion."

I began to feel uncomfortable again. "Miss Elsie," I said, "I'm not sure if I agree with inviting random spirits to draw from my life force. I prefer my life force intact. After all, I am still using it."

"I don't want to run out of life force, either," said Val. "Can't we invite them to draw from someone else? Theo, for instance? The world could easily do without him. Whatever remains after his life force has been sucked out by some random dead person is more than enough for me."

"Hush," Daphne scolded.

"Behave," Elsie chastised in a school mistress voice I wouldn't have expected from her. I studiously avoided catching Val's eye because I knew it would send us both into fits of laughter.

Our hostess began again in a warm and encouraging tone. "All are welcome here, and we mean you nothing but good. But we would especially like to speak to Erasmus Hatton-Haxley. Erasmus, my dear, I've done as you asked. Now would you please come speak with us? I'm sure dear Valentine has a great deal to say to you. All the things he couldn't say while you were alive. Valentine?"

Elsie turned to him encouragingly, and I saw panic cross his candlelit face.

"What?"

"Go on, say something to dear Erasmus. You must have left some things unsaid," she encouraged.

"No. Not in the least. Nothing unsaid. I have absolutely nothing not unsaid to say to Erasmus."

"I think that's a double negative," Daphne observed.

"I think it might be a rare triple negative," I said.

"Are you positive?" Val asked.

Elsie ignored us all and plowed on. "Tullia Calpurnia, dear, are you there? Can you guide Erasmus to us, please?"

I whispered to Daphne, "Who is Tullia Calpurnia?" But before she could answer, Elsie smiled at me.

"Tullia is my spirit guide. She was married to a Roman legionnaire in Gaul. Poor soul, died during childbirth. Very sad."

"Wish I'd known," Val said. "I'd have sent flowers."

Daphne kicked me in the shin. "Ow!"

"Sorry," she said. "I was aiming at Val."

"*Children!*" Elsie said, reducing us all to six-year-olds.

"Sorry, Aunt Elsie," Val murmured. "We'll be good."

There followed a few minutes of silence that felt much longer. But before I could think of something to say that would break the tension without offending Elsie, the planchette began to move. I was not the only one to jump.

"Welcome," Elsie said. "Is this Erasmus?"

i have come back

I blinked. But the writing was still there.

"Oh, how lovely," Elsie said. "Welcome, Erasmus. Are you well, dear boy?"

"Doubtful," Val said. "After all, he is dead."

shut up val

That succeeded in shutting him up.

"Oh, my goodness," Daphne whispered.

hello daphne nice dress

I was struggling to read the words, as they were written upside down from my perspective. Then I started focusing on Elsie's right hand, as I was pretty sure she was directing the spectral conversation.

Elsie smiled at Daphne. "Say hello to Erasmus, dear."

Daphne swallowed, "Um. Hello, Erasmus."

i'm all dead

"Yes, we know, dear," Elsie said. "I'm so sorry."

me too

"He's all dead as opposed to being only partially dead?"

"Val, please," Elsie urged. "Say something to your brother."

"Do I have to? Can't I just sit here and not believe?"

don't be an ass

"Oh great, I'm being insulted from the other side."

if the shroud fits

I must note here that the appearance of automatic writing is a slow and frustrating process. God only knows how many minutes we spent waiting for the messages to emerge, one scrawled word at a time. But as the séance went on, I found myself increasingly enthralled by the suspense, and eager to see what would be written next.

"Go on, Val," Elsie urged.

Val said, "I'm sorry you're all dead."

it was sally

"Yes, dear," Elsie said. "We know."

candy poison

"He poisoned the candy?" Val asked.

duh

"Sorry," Val grumbled. "I didn't know death had such a destructive effect upon grammar."

amo amas amat

"Oh great, now he's speaking to your cat. In life he found English a challenge but dead he sounds like Cicero."

do you want to be haunted

"Sorry," he said.

Elsie smiled at me. "Go on, James, say hello."

Feeling like a total fool, I joined the exchange.

"Uh... hello, Erasmus."

hello james

Val laughed. "Great, Aunt Elsie's got him calling you James."

griff

"That's right," I said. "Sorry you got murdered, Erasmus."

"We think it was Uncle Sally," Daphne added.

sally not here

"Sally isn't with you?" Elsie asked.

other place

"I think he's trying to say he's in Heaven and Sally's in Hell," Elsie interpreted.

hell

"Good," she said with an approving nod. "That's just where he belongs."

"He's only been dead for ten minutes," Val objected. "It takes longer to drive into the village than it takes to get to Hell?"

he didn't drive idiot

I watched Elsie intently but couldn't see any signs of effort on her part, no pushing or pulling on the planchette, although she had to be doing it all. Calling me James was the clincher. I had to hand it to her, though. She was an extremely skilled séance-faker.

Val suddenly took his fingers off the planchette and sat back. "Look, I'm not entirely convinced that this is really happening," he said. "But even if it is, how can we know this is Erasmus? Maybe it's a dead Erasmus impersonator."

"Now there's a limited career," I murmured.

"Fingers back on, dear," Elsie instructed. He obeyed. "Now, why don't you ask him something that only Erasmus would know, something that I could not know. That way James won't think I'm controlling the planchette."

I opened my mouth to deny the accusation, then closed it. It occurred to me that Elsie may have been one of the most perceptive people I'd ever met.

"Oh, I know! Is Aunt Jim covered in varicose veins?"

"Val, that's awful!" Daphne protested.

"Indeed, it is," Elsie agreed. "Val, he's dead, not a peeping tom. Ask him a serious question this time."

Val thought for a moment and then asked, "What was our nickname for Mister Folliott?"

"Who?" I asked.

Daphne answered, "he was the vicar when we were little."

mister falls a lot

"Hmm." Val nodded. "Which one of us locked Nicky in the attic overnight?"

medard but we blamed servatius

"One more," he said. "When the barn cat had two kittens, who named them Oxford and Cambridge?"

you

"Well, that's certainly spooky," Val observed. "I'm talking to my dead brother."

"Are you sure?" I asked. "Am I the only one who doesn't believe in any of this?"

yes

"Lovely," I said.

ask me

"Ask you what?"

"I think he wants you to ask him something so he can prove to you that he is real," Daphne explained.

"Unfortunately, Erasmus and I didn't have any secrets that only he and I knew."

calico jack

"Who is Calico Jack? Someone you served with during the war?" Daphne asked.

"I doubt Griff served with pirates," Val said. "You didn't, did you? Perhaps I was asleep when you told me about the night Lieutenant Long John Silver and Private Blackbeard stormed the German trenches."

"Calico Jack was a dog my family owned when I was a kid," I answered, confused.

thumb

"OK, that's it," I said. "I'm done. I'm not here. I'm in bed, asleep. Dreaming. All a dream. In fact, I'm not even here. I'm asleep in my own bed. In London. I'm not in this room talking to a dead man. La-la-la."

"Who is thumb?" Val asked.

"Thumb isn't a who, it's a what."

"Fine, what is thumb?"

"My thumb. On my hand. One time I was playing tug of war with Calico Jack, and he bit my thumb."

"Erasmus bit your thumb?"

"No, the dog bit it, you ninny."

lily

"And by way of apology, he gave you a lily?" Val said.

"No, Lily was the name of my mother's cat."

"Really? What did she bite?" Val wondered.

"Nothing."

"Well? Are you convinced?" Daphne asked. "Nobody else here could have known that."

"Erasmus couldn't even have known that!" I shook my head, trying to think clearly. "No. I must have mentioned Calico Jack and Lily to someone this weekend. I refuse to believe this. It's not happening."

"How about me?" Daphne asked. "Erasmus, can you tell me something that only the two of us would know?"

lisping hamlet

She burst out laughing. "All right, I'm convinced. This really is Erasmus."

"What the heck does 'lisping Hamlet' mean?" Val asked.

"I'll never tell. But only Erasmus would know."

"Oh, this is insane," I said, with a mixture of discomfort and disbelief.

"It's all right, dear," Elsie smiled at me, "It takes some people longer, but you'll come around."

"That's what I'm afraid of."

Daphne, entirely convinced, cut to the heart of the matter. "Erasmus, we're trying to find out what happened to you. We know about the caramels, but they're gone. Can you point us to any evidence that Sally or Fitzhugh might have tampered with your caramels?"

nicotine

"Yes, we know," Daphne said. "Griff found a bottle of it in Fitzhugh's room."

"And I found another one in Sally's room!" Val interjected.

how much

"How much nicotine did he use?" Val asked. "I have no idea."

no how much

"He's a bit dull after death, isn't he?" Val said.

how much money

Elsie caught the drift first. "You mean, how much did Sally pay Fitzhugh to kill you?"

There was no reply, which she apparently took as a yes. She looked at me.

"Three thousand pounds," I said, still feeling like an idiot.

worth more

"Yes, dear boy, you were worth a lot more."
"Did Fitzhugh also kill Sally?"

frame

"Framed?" Val asked.

set up

"Any idea what he's trying to tell us?" Daphne asked.

I shook my head. Postmortem conversations were proving to be frustrating.

Our hostess turned back to the invited guest. "Erasmus, dear, we're having trouble understanding. Is there anything you can show us?"

get up

Nobody got up.

get up val

"Uh, Val? I think he wants you to get up," I said.
"Why? What does he want me to do?"
"How should I know? None of *my* previous séances were choreographed by the dead."

Val got up. "I'm standing up, Erasmus. Now what?"

bookshelf

"Val, dear," Elsie said. "I believe Erasmus wants you to go to the bookshelf."

"Which one? This whole room is basically a library," Val observed.

third shelf red leather under painting of romeo juliet

Elsie smiled and pointed to the "art" in question. Val walked towards it. "That's Romeo and Juliet? I always thought it was Tristan and Isolde."

Daphne chimed in, "I thought it was Heloise and Abelard."

"You're all wrong. It's the Marriage at Cana," Elsie corrected.

not romeo

"No, Erasmus. Cana."

I got up and joined Val in front of the painting in question, looking at it with amused interest. Like all the other art outside the servants' wing, the painting was awful. "I'm sorry Miss Elsie, but this can't be the Marriage at Cana."

"Oh? Why not?"

"Because there's a walrus lounging by a swimming pool in the background." Both women got up and joined me.

"You're right," Daphne laughed.

"How odd. I've never noticed that before," Elsie mused.

"Why did you think it was the Wedding at Cana, Aunt Elsie?" Daphne asked.

"Why the wedding party. And Jesus Christ, of course."

I peered more closely at the work in question. "What wedding party, Miss Elsie? I don't see one."

She pointed. "There, of course."

"Wedding party? I think that's a horse and cart," Val said with a laugh.

"And where is Jesus?" Daphne asked.

Elsie pointed again. "That's the walrus," I said.

Elsie got about one nose away from the little painting and

squinted at it. Then she whirled around. "Oh dear, how rude of us! We've left poor Erasmus all alone at the table."

Daphne and I followed, but Val had not forgotten the reason why we were all at the bookcase. He pulled a red leather volume from the third shelf and read the title aloud: "*Christian Saints, Prophets, and Martyrs.*"

"Eh? That's not one of my books," Elsie said. "It belongs in the library downstairs."

"Are you sure?"

"Yes, of course. It's one of the books the family uses to come up with names."

Val nodded. "Of course. I've seen this book my whole life. Aunt Elsie, maybe you borrowed it and forgot?"

"No, I'd remember," she said. "Someone else must have put it on my shelf. I have no idea why."

I took the book from Val and examined it. The aged tome showed generations of use, and many notes were scribbled in the margins. One page, marked with a piece of folded paper, was of special interest.

"I think I know why this book is here," I said. "Listen to this."

> St. Erasmus of Crete
> *9th century A.D.*
>
> *A blacksmith (some accounts report that he was a sword maker) from Heraklion who became a Christian after hearing St. Stefanis of Philippi preaching the word of Christ. After his baptism, he abandoned both his family and his smithy and became a mendicant preacher throughout the Greek isles.*
>
> *After converting several members of the army, who then abandoned their posts, local authorities*

> *arrested him. He was banished from Crete on two occasions but returned both times.*
>
> *Erasmus was martyred under the orders of the governor. He was bound with a gospel tied around his neck as a sign of his Christianity and his mouth was filled with stones to weigh him down and prevent him from praying aloud. He was then thrown into the sea, whereupon he drowned. Erasmus of Crete is the patron saint of blacksmiths, arsonists, and burn victims. He is also the patron saint of people named "Erasmus."*

"So, all that ridiculousness with the gospel, the marble, and the bath does have an explanation," Val said.

"Or at least a source," I corrected.

"But it's still crazy," added Daphne.

Val looked over my shoulder at the book. "Is planting the book here in Aunt Elsie's room part of an attempt to frame her for Erasmus's death?"

"I can't think of another reason. They weren't subtle about which page to look at." I indicated the paper bookmark. "But look here, there's something written on it."

I unfolded the paper and immediately began to laugh.

"What? What is it?" Daphne asked.

I cleared my throat theatrically and read:

Dirge for the Great Unwashed

Factories belching smoke
Vomiting on the proletariat

I'm an ass in a capitalist yolk
They are labour's Judas Iscariot

I march with my comrades in misery
I stand with my fist in the air

I fight with sorrow and injury
My heavy heart, it is heavy with care

"What in blazes was that?" Val asked.

"I'm pretty sure it's an example of Wulfie's so-called poetry. By the way, he spelled yoke as Y-O-L-K."

"Holy wobbling Wordsworth, that's even worse than I'd imagined," Val said. "And I can imagine vast quantities of worse."

"Things just got a lot more interesting," I muttered to myself.

"May we please get back to poor Erasmus now?" Elsie begged. "We have been *terribly* rude."

Obediently, we resumed our places. Elsie put a fresh sheet of paper under the planchette, and we each put two fingers on top. But my brain was abuzz and I interrupted once more: "Elsie, have you ever seen Wulfstan reading this book?"

"I didn't even know he could read. Has the brains of a bar of soap, that one."

good one auntie

"Thank you, dear."

In the excitement of finding the book and the poem, I had almost forgotten our drunken party not only included my best friend, his crazy aunt, and his attractive distant cousin, but also his number fourth dead brother.

"Thank you for finding the book, Erasmus," Elsie continued. "Is there anything else you can tell us?"

"Yes," Val added. "For instance, who killed Uncle Sally?"

i heard

"What did you hear?" Val said.

they talked

"They? You mean Sally and Fitzhugh?" Daphne asked.

no they talked after

"You heard them speaking afterwards about what happened?" Apparently, Elsie was fluent in ghost, because she seemed to have no problem interpreting these frustrating messages.

guilty no proof

"You know that they're guilty but there isn't any proof?" Elsie said.

killed me

"So they *did* kill you?" Val asked.
"Erasmus," Daphne said. "Do you know who killed Sally?"

deserved it

"Yes, I'm sure he did," Elsie agreed. "Don't worry, dear, we'll make them pay."
"Him," Val corrected. "It's just a 'him' now, not a 'them.' Sally's already dead."

no not them

"Not them?" I asked, frustrated. "What does that mean?"
"Patience," Elsie urged. "Erasmus, dear, could you perhaps tell us more, please?"

not them no proof

"Are you saying that Sally killed you but there's no proof?" Val asked.

there are two

"Any idea what it... He is trying to say?" I asked.

there are two

Val said, "I'm going to go out on a limb here and suggest he's saying there are two."

not helping

I laughed. Dead Erasmus made little sense, but he was funny.

there was one there was another one

"Erasmus," Daphne persuaded, "could you be a little more coherent? Please?"

no sorry

"We'd like to help you, Erasmus. But you're not making much sense."

"Erasmus," Elsie's tone was firm. "Who killed Sally?"

There was no response. I stared at the planchette, but there was no movement. Elsie repeated the question. The planchette remained still.

"Erasmus, dear, are you still there?" Elsie looked up as if she expected to see him hovering above the table. "No, he's gone. Poor thing. It takes a lot of energy for the spirit to communicate with those of us who are still waiting for the great change."

"The great change?" Val asked.

"I think she means those of us who are currently non-dead," I explained.

"Oh, James, you are so very wise." Elsie grinned.

I turned to Val. "See? I am very wise."

He said something unprintable.

"At least we learned something," Daphne said.

"What did we learn?" I asked.

Elsie looked surprised. "Well, we learned that Sally and

Fitzhugh killed Erasmus. I think that means we have an open and dry case."

"I think you mean cut and shut," Val corrected.

"Whatever. We have learned that."

"No, Miss Elsie, I'm afraid we haven't learned that," I said.

"But Erasmus said—"

"I'm sorry, Miss Elsie. But even if testimony from ghosts was admissible in a court of law, the fact remains that Erasmus did not, in fact, say that Sally and Fitzhugh were the ones he overheard speaking."

"You're right," Val agreed. "He never actually named names, did he? We just interpreted what we thought he was saying."

"And when I asked him outright if it was Sally and Fitzhugh whom he heard speaking, he never said yes or no. He said… well, nothing useful," Daphne said, discouraged.

"Well, I still think it was Sally and that horrible henchman of his," Elsie asserted.

"Perhaps," I said. "Well, Miss Elsie, you got your séance, and I found it quite… something. How did it rank in terms of best and worst séances you've held?"

She put her head on one side and regarded me with a smile. "The best would have to be when Erasmus and I spoke with Machiavelli. He was surprisingly whimsical. And the worst would have to be the time where I accidentally contacted Harry Houdini and he wouldn't shut up. He was with me for nearly a week. It was awful."

Elsie looked at me with the bright, clever gaze she'd showed earlier. "There's another thing we've learned, or confirmed. It appears someone wants very badly to frame me for murder. Should I be worried?"

"No, Miss Elsie. We know you didn't do it. And anyone who says otherwise will have to deal with all three of us."

"You know the whole idea of my killing anyone is lunacy.

If I were the murderous type, Sally would have been bumped off ages ago."

"You could be in trouble if the cause of death turns out to be voodoo, Miss Elsie."

"Oh, don't worry, the doll and the pins are well hidden. I planted them in Jim's room."

I prayed she was joking.

A clock softly chimed three times, and Elsie yawned. "My children, this old lady is tired. I love you, now go away."

We rose. Val and Daphne each kissed her on the cheek. As I bent to kiss her hand, Elsie leaned in close and whispered, "Erasmus and I are counting on you, Griff."

She called me Griff!

Chapter 37

Val and Daphne were waiting for me in the corridor outside Elsie's room.

"Well?" Daphne said. "What did you think?"

"That was easily the best séance I've ever attended."

"We pride ourselves on our séances," Val said.

"There are certainly enough prematurely dead people to talk to," I quipped. "Is the Hall haunted?"

Val stopped in his tracks. "Good God, no. You don't believe in ghosts now?"

"No. It just struck me that with everything else around here, curses and séances and whatnot, it's odd that Great-great-great-grandfather Petrolius doesn't go bump in the night, moving candlesticks about."

"You're right," Daphne agreed. "It's not a real country weekend experience without the terrifying spectre of a headless horseman prowling the grounds."

"Poor Uncle Guthlac," murmured Val. "I need alcohol. Join me?"

He opened his door and peered in as if expecting to see a guillotine where his desk used to be.

"You didn't lock your door?" I asked.

"Why would I lock my door in my house?"

"Because you're terrified of Nicky becoming the third Earl of the week? Because you made me turn the place upside-down looking for poison dart booby-traps?"

"Good point."

Once in, he headed straight for the decanter. He lifted the stopper, sniffed, shrugged, and poured out three brandies.

"I can't recall an evening when I've indulged in so much drinking," Daphne admitted. "If there are any more deaths this week, I may become a dipsomaniac." She pulled a cushion off one of the chairs and curled up on the floor. Val and I joined her.

"Val, I can see something under your bed."

He instantly looked alarmed. "What? Is it a bomb? A booby trap with a sword? Two swords? Something worse than two swords? A badger? Angela Astley?"

"No," I said. "It's my cat. See what happens when you leave your door unlocked?"

Catullus slid luxuriously out from his hiding place, glanced with exquisite boredom around the room, and surprised me by passing up Daphne's lap for Val's.

"*Quod erat demonstrandum*," he said, greeting my cat with a scratch behind the ears. Catullus slitted his green eyes in ecstasy. I smiled fondly at the pair.

"What now?" Daphne asked.

"Now we listen in rapt silence as Val goes over his interview with Inspector Parrish."

"Why?"

"Because Parrish knows how to run an investigation. Knows the right questions to ask. Tell us what he wanted to know, and it'll help us see what he's looking at."

"That's a very clever idea," said Daphne.

"It is," agreed Val. "Give me a cigarette and I'll tell you."

As it turned out, Val, Daphne and I had all had similar interviews. The inspector focused on the Hatton-Haxley family, giving the impression that he was inclined to exclude the guests of culpability.

"Oh wonderful," Val moaned. "Even if I manage to survive

this weekend, I may end up as a suspect in my uncle's murder. Perhaps I'll join the Foreign Legion. They'll never find me there."

"I thought you were trying to avoid dying."

"Hmm... Very well, I'll open a diamond mine in Africa."

"You don't like hot weather," Daphne countered.

"And besides," I added, "you don't just open a diamond mine. You have to discover one."

"And after you discover one, you open it so you can get the diamonds out," he explained, patiently.

"Getting back to our quiet weekend here at Mayhem Manor," I said. "What do you both think about Sally's death?"

"I'm still thinking poison," said Val. "He obviously wasn't shot, stabbed, or bashed. That big body of his had to give out eventually, but not like that. Poison's the only thing left."

"Plus, there's that suspicious vial you found in Sally's room," Daphne added.

"Which matches a bottle we *know* contained poison and was probably used to kill Erasmus. But are we assuming two murderers or one? If two, did they just happen to use identical methods? If one, would they dare use the same poison twice?"

"I don't see why they wouldn't," Daphne said. "After all, it worked once."

"Yes, but if you recall when I so infamously rifled through Fitzhugh's room and ruined the evidence, I substituted water for what was under the chair. So that couldn't have been used to poison Sally. There must be two batches of poison."

"We might have better luck asking who had a motive," said Val. "But it's not going to be easy. Sally was universally disliked. But I don't believe he was killed just because he was a horrible person. There must be a specific reason to kill him now."

"*Cui bono*," I said.

"Are you talking to your cat again?" Val asked.

"No. *Cui bono*. To whose benefit is the crime."

"You talk to your cat in Latin?" Asked Daphne.

"Yes. I tried speaking to him in Welsh, but he found all those L's confusing."

"*Koo bono*," said Val. "Right. Aunt Jim and my horrible cousins certainly benefit monetarily. I don't know their finances, but we all saw that check book. Sally's money would give a quick and large influx of cash for anybody who needed it."

"And now Nicky is the Viscount and heir to the title, so he benefits even more," said Daphne.

"And the Viscountcy comes with a generous allowance from the estate, which gives Nicky a triple motive," said Val.

"Are you sure about that?" I asked.

"I should know. It's what I've been living on for years."

"Good point. But what about the others? Your aunt, Wulfie, and Theo. How does this affect them?"

"Well, aside from the blessed sense of freedom that must come from being Sally-free, I'm not sure. No doubt his will and testament follows the standard form, making Nicky his heir and ensuring a substantial income for Aunt Jim. Wulfie and Theo would benefit because his family would have more money at their control."

"Do you think the sons are capable of killing their father?" Daphne asked.

He thought for a moment. "Not really. That takes courage and the move to action, and none of the boys have either. I can imagine them committing all sorts of sordid crimes, but not cold-blooded murder."

"But your aunt may be a different story," I said. "She's most definitely cold-blooded."

"An alligator in alligator pumps," he agreed. "But the motive is thin. I could see her having a motive if she cared about… well, anything beyond superiority and righteousness. But she doesn't. I've been around these people all my life and I've never once spotted any sign of affection between the two of them, nor any other emotion, come to think of it. The most impassioned thing I've ever heard Aunt Jim say to Uncle Sally was 'take your umbrella.'"

"I'm surprised she didn't quote scripture and tell him 'getteth not thou wet,'" I said. "That woman has a definite crucifixation. Why does everything she say sound like it should be stitched onto a sampler?"

"She probably thinks that if she appears to know the Bible backwards and forwards, people won't notice she lacks a soul."

"Let's get back to the murder," Daphne interjected. "Jim may not have loved Sally, but she might still have been offended and angry if she learned about his affair." The memory of those *Dearest Sally Cat* letters made me shiver.

"I imagine she had a long list of grievances against him, even if she never let them show."

"And let's not forget Fitzhugh. He's still got to be considered a prime suspect," said Val.

"But why would he kill your uncle?"

"Who knows? A falling out between criminal partners? We know he has an explosive temper."

"And as Sally's valet, he had every opportunity to administer poison," added Daphne.

"As did your all your cousins and aunts," I pointed out. "Any of them could have gotten at Sally's personal Scotch bottle when nobody was looking."

Daphne sighed. "This isn't getting us anywhere."

"Maybe not," I said. "But thinking out loud always helps me see things more clearly."

"Then I hope you don't mind if we eavesdrop while you talk to yourself."

"The only people I can see having a motive to kill Erasmus are the same people who had a motive to kill Sally," I said. "Except for Fitzhugh. I don't think he had a motive for Erasmus, but I can believe him killing for a commission."

"And £3,000 is a lot of commission," said Val.

"Please gentlemen, may we call it a night?" Daphne suggested. "It'll be morning soon. I'm tired, drunk, and my mind is going in circles."

"Mine, too," said Val. "But that's not unusual."

"Shall I walk you to your room?" I asked Daphne. "Or at least stagger?"

"I think I can make it without incident."

"Are you sure?" Val asked, warily. "What would you do if Theo pounced out at you with felonious intention?"

"Laugh, probably."

Ten minutes later I was lying in bed, wide awake, and fighting with my cat for ownership of the covers. There was a murder. *Two* murders. And a jewel theft. And a casual midnight chat with my friend's dead brother. And a mess of suspects and clues and motives, none of them quite adding up. If I were to be clear-headed in the morning, I needed sleep. But I couldn't shut off my brain.

In desperation, I picked up one of the books from my bedside table. I was pretty sure that *A Short History of Cricket* would drop me out in about twenty minutes.

It took five, at most.

* * *

THE NEXT THING I knew it was eight o'clock and Sutherland was bringing me my morning tea, opening drapes to let in the bright sun, and declaring it a beautiful morning. By all rights I should have had a pounding hangover, but I felt clear-headed—or as clear-headed as one could, given the confusing circumstances.

Catullus wound his way through Sutherland's legs with a purr that could be heard in France. I soon saw why as Sutherland set down a small plate of kippers, scratched Catullus behind the ears, and became my cat's new favorite human.

When he stood up again, Sutherland regarded me with the air of someone who has something to say but doesn't quite know how to begin.

"Is something bothering you, Sutherland?" I felt like an idiot because, of course, something was bothering him. A great many things, no doubt, starting with his dead employer and ending with the dead uncle.

"Um… Well…" He stammered until he apparently decided to just get it over with and said in a rush, "Did you know, sir, that he… that Lord Haxley and Mr. Fitzhugh argued on the day of… the day when his lordship died?"

"Could you be more specific about which lordship's death you are talking about? Your pronouns have defeated me. Do you mean the day Lord Erasmus died, or yesterday when his uncle died?"

"I am referring, sir, to the day that Lord Erasmus died. Later that evening, after… all that… well, I was walking past Lord Haxley's room and overheard them."

"Really, Sutherland? Well, then I'm going to be very impolite and ask you to tell me everything."

He sighed. "I rarely have a reason to go into the part of the house where the Viscount has his rooms. But things were understandably disorganized after Lord Erasmus was found, and Mr. Lydgate asked me to deliver a telephone message to Lord Haxley. As I neared the door, I heard voices."

"Could you hear what was being said?"

"Some of it. I heard Lord Haxley say, 'how could we predict the crisis' and 'it was just a book.' And that's all I could hear, sir."

"Could you hear what Fitzhugh said?"

"No sir. I could hear his voice but couldn't hear any words. Not until the end when I heard part of a sentence."

"And what did he say?"

"All I caught was, 'you should have let me handle it, you fool.' Then Lord Nicodemus came around the corner, so I moved on."

"And what time was this?"

"About seven o'clock that evening, sir."

"So… six hours after the body was found? Hmm. Thank you, Sutherland, that's helpful."

"I wasn't sure it was worth mentioning, but after all that's happened this weekend… Oh, there's one thing more, sir. When I saw Lord Nicodemus in the hallway that evening, I noticed he had what looked like a black eye."

Interesting. "*Looked* like a black eye? Was it a black eye?"

"I suppose so, sir. I noticed it again the next day. It wasn't bad, just a slight bruising."

"Thank you again. That is very interesting."

"I'm pleased I could be of assistance, sir," he said sincerely. "Will there be anything else?"

"No, thank you. And Catullus thanks you for the kippers."

Catullus took a moment from washing his paws with his fish-scented tongue to meow politely.

I drank my tea, cleaned up, and headed downstairs to see who might have died in the night.

* * *

I NEARLY FLED on discovering Lady Haxley alone in the dining room, but hunger conquered cowardice.

"Good morning, Lady Haxley," I said. "Let me say again how sorry I am about Lord Haxley." I would have said more, but she looked up from her plate, fixed me with her basilisk stare, and my mind went blank. I sought refuge in the toast rack.

I had to admit, for a woman who had lost her husband only twelve hours earlier, she was entirely composed. Not a hair out of place. No red eyes or signs of copious weeping. And her grief-induced lack of appetite manifested itself in a huge plate of bacon, eggs, and kippers. Only the unrelieved black of her dress gave the slightest hint of mourning.

We ate in non-companionable silence while I ran through and rejected several conversational gambits. Just when I was afraid that the awkwardness would compel me to that last gasp of polite desperation, a comment on the weather, I was rescued unexpectedly by the lady in question.

"Have you spoken with Valentine this morning?" The question came at me so suddenly that I dropped a splat of strawberry jam onto the exact middle of my napkin. Hurrah for napkins.

"I'm afraid not, Lady Haxley. Would you like me to find him for you?"

"No, that's not necessary. Thank you." She staunched her sorrow with another huge forkful of eggs, chewed thoroughly, and asked, "Do you know when that inspector will be back?"

"No, Lady Haxley. I don't. But I could ring him up if you need to speak with him."

"Not necessary."

Once again, Lady Haxley struck me as one of the coldest women I'd ever met. She was so emotionless that it almost put me off my toast. Perhaps she'd warm up if I asked about her progeny.

"Your sons must be very upset," I observed. "If there is any way I can be of assistance to you or to them, please let me know. I lost my own father not so long ago, so I understand what they're feeling."

"Do you really?" She put down her fork and glared at me over the expanse of white linen and Wedgwood. "Was your father murdered, too?"

Oh, yes. Cold as an iceberg.

"Do... do you believe Lord Haxley was murdered?"

"Oh, don't play stupid, Mr. Griffin, it doesn't become you.

Certainly, he was murdered. And as soon as the inspector gets here, I will tell him who the guilty party is."

"Um... Perhaps you could tell me, as well?" I knew she wouldn't, but I had to try.

"No, I couldn't."

"No, of course you couldn't," I said with exquisite politeness.

"But I believe we may avoid a scandal by dealing with the matter privately. And medically."

Ah. Of course, she was referring to Aunt Elsie. Probably already had a room reserved under Elsie's name at Dr. Wiggle's Home for Wealthy and Insane Aunts.

"I wonder if Nicky, Wulfie, and Theo agree with your choice of chief suspect. Or perhaps you haven't compared notes."

"Nicodemus. Wulfstan. Theobald."

She enunciated dramatically and with just the right cadence to make it clear I wasn't fit to discuss her sons at all, never mind giving them nicknames. "And I have not discussed their father's death with them. This will upset them terribly. Especially Nicodemus. He feels things."

Don't we all? I wanted to ask. "Was Nicodemus particularly close to his father?"

She put down her fork and glared at me. *"A wise son brings joy to his father, but a foolish son brings grief to his mother.* Proverbs 10:1."

"I'm sorry, Lady Haxley, but I have no idea how that answers my question."

"All my sons brought true joy to their father. And none has ever brought grief to their mother. They are all heartbroken. But Nicodemus, even more than his brothers, feels such deep emotions. He may seem strong and stalwart, but his heart is heavy with care."

She stood to leave. I rose also, to open the door for her. She looked at me with the condescension of Lady Catherine de Bourgh, and observed in a voice of sandpaper and vinegar,

"Perhaps if you spent more time reading the Good Book and less time writing bad ones, you might come closer to understanding my sons."

She was halfway out the door when I called her name: "Lady Haxley." She turned and I quoted, *"Whoever of you loves life and desires to see many good days, keep your tongue from evil and your lips from telling lies.* Psalm 34."

She didn't react, and I stood for a moment in thought after she left. After all those years, the one time I pulled Dr. Bloom's lectures on Christian ethics out of my brain was to insult a brand-new widow. I searched my feelings to see if I felt badly about that. I didn't, so I had more toast.

A minute later, the door opened and Lydgate came in.

"Pardon me, Mr. Griffin."

"Good morning, Lydgate. How is the staff dealing with this latest death?"

"We are doing our best to carry on as usual, sir," he said. Which I took to mean, *nobody is terribly upset and we're all fine.*

He continued, "Apologies for interrupting your breakfast, sir, but there's a Mr. Mannering on the telephone for you."

I rose. "Thank you, Lydgate. By the way, do you know where Fitzhugh is?"

"Yes sir. He's down in the staff kitchen. I believe he is reading what would have been Lord Haxley's *Times*, sir. Shall I fetch him for you?"

"No, not at all." Although we were alone, I still lowered my voice when I asked, "Lydgate, is there any way you can make sure that he stays down there for the next quarter of an hour? I want to check something in his room and don't want him to interrupt me."

Lydgate's eyes widened. "Sir, as the butler here I must say that the staff have rights, and such a search should only be undertaken by the police."

He was right, of course, and I felt my face flush a little. Still, that was disappointing. "So, you won't help me, then?"

"Oh, no, sir, I shall be happy to assist you. It's just that as the butler here I had to say it. I shall head downstairs now and should have no problem keeping the bounder occupied."

"Thank you, Lydgate."

I dashed into the study and in a moment was speaking again with Archibald Mannering, the former art thief turned financial wizard. "Good morning, Archie, you're up early."

"Actually, I'm up late," he laughed. "I wanted to call you before I crashed. As it happened, at a party last night I ran into exactly the right man to give me the inside blather you asked for, about the Megatherium Trust."

"Wonderful. Did he know anything helpful?"

"Absolutely. The winner of your stupid investor contest is one Nicodemus Hatton-Haxley, who was apparently into the fund for close to £15,000."

I whistled. "Indeed," he agreed. "And I am told there is good reason for supposing that most of the money he invested wasn't his."

"Any idea where it came from?"

"Well, here's where we get into a dicey area. You know how much I enjoy poking my nose into other people's money. My sources tell me this Hatton-Haxley bloke works for the Sheffield Commercial Bank."

"Yes. Does that mean anything?"

"It might. This is ultra-secret, Griff. I'm probably skirting some laws here. But I heard something. It hasn't been publicly announced yet, but Sheffield Commercial is merging with Gordon and Burns, which means that Sheffield's annual audit will take place next month and not in January. So, if anybody was concerned about what a surprise audit might find, they're probably sweating rivers right now."

"Well now, isn't that interesting?"

"Mmm. I thought so. Oh, my source also says that the merger was agreed to three weeks ago. Most of the employees probably know about it by now."

Including, I was inclined to guess, Nicodemus.

"Mannering, you're irreplaceable. I owe you one."

"You owe me about fifty, but who's counting? Ciao."

I glanced at my watch and dashed upstairs, praying Lydgate hadn't lost track of Fitzhugh. It had occurred to me in the night to wonder if the vial of water I'd put in place of the poison under Fitzhugh's chair was still there. Not that either its presence or absence would tell me anything definite, but for the sake of curiosity, I wanted to know.

The room was as pristine as it had been before, with no indication that the death of Fitzhugh's master had in any way caused a break in his routine. I stopped for a moment to look for the mate to the cuff link that Sutherland had found. It was still there, on top of his dresser. The German pocket-knife was also there, next to the tray of spare change and the lumpy pink candle. There was also a full bottle of tawny Port which I knew by reputation was quite rare and expensive. I'd have to ask Lydgate to check the Hall's cellars.

Dropping to one knee, I checked the underside of the chair. I found the slit in the lining, but not the vial. Which meant… Actually, it meant nothing. I had no idea who had put it there in the first place, and no idea who might have removed it after I switched bottles. But I was tempted to declare Uncle Sally not guilty by reason of becoming dead.

I scanned the room one last time and then went downstairs to call Drake.

As soon as I identified myself, my old friend cursed me.

"What have I done this time?"

"That cockamamie book of yours."

"Which one?"

"*The Puppet of Doom.*"

"Oh, yes. What about it?"

"I bought another copy because I'd left mine at the office. And I stayed up reading past two this morning, only to find out that the Russian magician wasn't murdered at all! Committing suicide so his wife could collect on his insurance to pay for her operation? That makes no sense! What a horrible book!"

"Not one of my best, I grant you. But I wrote it in a month, so I'm actually rather proud of it."

"Why in the world would you only spend a month writing the damned thing?"

"I needed the money. I wanted to go to Africa. Can we get on to the important question of whether Gilbert Fitzhugh has a record?"

"Only a very long one. Mostly pub brawls, but nothing more serious than penalty notices, a few small fines. Apparently, the man knows his limits. He's been connected to some thefts, a few burglaries, a few knife fights in which he usually came off the victor. And reputed to be a casual debt collector for a few of the more unsavory gangs, but no serious charges pressed."

"An unsavory character, but nothing surprising."

"No, but there is something that I think *will* surprise you."

"Oh?"

"He's not the only one in that house with a police record. Have you ever heard of the Milray Club?"

Chapter 38

Inspector Parrish sat on the big leather sofa in the study and regarded me over a cup of Mrs. Lydgate's special Earl Grey. His expression gave nothing away. I imagined he'd make a first-rate poker player.

I had been speaking for some time. When I finally wound down, he said nothing for a few moments. Then he smiled like he was trying desperately to hold back a laugh, making me feel about nine years old.

"I really must read one of your books," he said at last. "I have a feeling I would find them most entertaining."

I wasn't sure if that was a compliment.

"Tell me, Mr. Griffin, what interpretation do you put on finding this bottle missing while searching Mr. Fitzhugh's room, mere hours after I instructed you explicitly *not* to do anything of the sort?"

"I'm not entirely sure what it means. But I do think that Lord Haxley was poisoned. Don't you?"

"I shall reserve judgment until the results of the postmortem come back. Although I can say that we tested everything in Lord Haxley's rooms and found nothing suspicious."

"How about the contents of his medicine cabinet?" I asked.

"There, too. Nothing out of the ordinary. Everything was true according to the labels."

"He had some sort of tonic…" I recalled.

"Yes. A harmless bromide to aid in digestion. And only the deceased's fingerprints were on it."

"Only Sally's fingerprints?" I sat forward. "Are you sure?"

The Inspector narrowed his eyes and studied me. "Yes, of course I'm sure. Why?"

"Because my fingerprints should have been on that bottle, too. I opened it when I searched his room yesterday, during the funeral."

The Inspector sighed, touching a hand to his forehead.

"Yes, of course you did. And without gloves, I presume?"

"No, I was an ass. Again."

His look agreed with me. The Inspector was a master of pitying looks and uncomfortable silences. They were a wonderful interviewing technique, one I had used myself in the past few days, but now it was being used against me. And it worked. The more the Inspector stared at me, the more I was tempted to talk. I resolved to make Zoltan Szabo adopt a bit more silence.

"Mr. Griffin, Is there perhaps something important in that bundle you are cradling in your lap like a prize Persian?"

I realized I had been silently broadcasting to Parrish that I had found something important. "Well, yes, there is."

"Are you going to make me guess what you have there?"

I loosened my death grip and placed on the table between us a white hand towel. This I unfurled with great delicacy.

He looked at the object inside, and then at me. "It's a candle," he observed mildly.

"It's a *pink* candle," I pointed out.

"Yes. It is a pink candle." He looked mildly irritated.

"It's a *lumpy* pink candle."

He sighed again. "Mr. Griffin, is there any reason why you are merely describing this object rather than explaining why you brought it to me?"

"Sorry. Did Val tell you about the missing ruby?"

"Yes. It's not often two murders and a jewel robbery occur in one house in a single week, so of course he brought it up. We're looking into it. Why?"

"Why? Because I believe I know where the ruby is." The note of childish triumph in my voice was unseemly, but I didn't care.

"And where is it?"

"In a lumpy... *pink*... candle."

The Inspector let loose yet another of his sighs. It was the kind of sigh usually reserved for schoolmasters who have just lost their last nerve. "Right." He paused and visibly counted to ten. "A few questions, Mr. Griffin, if you don't mind. So, where did you get this? What makes you think the ruby is in this lumpy pink candle? And please, oh please, tell me you have *not* tampered with evidence *once again*, or else I will also have to ask why I shouldn't place you under arrest right now."

Oh dear. I was hoping I'd have the chance to explain my brilliance before having to justify my actions. "Well..." I cleared my throat. "In order of your inquiries, my replies are: It was in Fitzhugh's room. I think the ruby is there because what else could explain a lumpy pink candle in an immaculate home like this? And yes, I'm afraid I did tamper with the evidence again. But I had a reason. I had to take it before Fitzhugh came in and found it. Because I'm pretty sure it was planted in his room. That room is like a monk's cell; he'd spot it immediately. And he'd destroy it the moment he found it. Well, except for the ruby. He'd keep that, of course."

For the first time the Inspector displayed an emotion other than polite interest. He was intrigued. I could see it in the slight raising of one eyebrow. I had always envied people who could raise one eyebrow. It manages to be simultaneously interrogative and condescending. Zoltan, of course, could raise one eyebrow, and often did.

"You see, Inspector, when I did my first illegal search..."

I paused because I thought I heard him whimper. "My first *perfectly innocent* search, I mean, I found this lumpy pink candle."

"In Fitzhugh's room, you just told me."

"No, Inspector. I found it in *Nicodemus's* room." The other eyebrow shifted ever so slightly, which I took as a show of appreciation for my minor triumph.

"You noticed a candle?" He seemed skeptical.

"Because it's lumpy. I always have Zoltan notice the small details. Why would a candle be lumpy? Candles are known for their lovely properties of standing up and being smooth and candle-shaped. So why is this one so grossly misshapen? Was there a sudden attack of bee pox affecting the wax and causing swollen glands? Candles don't have glands, Inspector."

To my intense surprise, the Inspector gave out with a roar of laughter. It took, in fact, more than a few moments for him to collect himself.

"Begging your pardon, sir," he finally wheezed out, wiping a few tears away. "But I really must read one of your books. '*Candles don't have glands, Inspector!*'"

Suddenly we were both laughing.

When we regained our composure, Inspector Parrish picked up the towel and took a closer look at the candle.

"But if the ruby is in here, why would Lord Nicodemus put it in Fitzhugh's room?"

"I'm not sure it was Lord Nicodemus who moved it. I think someone else may have planted it there to frame Fitzhugh."

"To frame him for stealing the ruby?"

"That," I agreed. "And other things."

"Such as?"

"I think they might be trying to frame him for murdering Uncle Suspicious."

"They?"

"Oh, yes. *They.*" I looked at the Inspector. "Nicky may have a swelled head, but it contains the brains of a very small duck. He couldn't plot a sneeze, let alone a murder."

"Then what do you think is going on? And who are you counting as 'they?'"

"The problem is I have strong suspicions, but weak evidence. However, I'll tell you what I think and…" But then I couldn't think of an "and," so I just stopped talking.

"And?" The Inspector prompted.

"And I've shown great restraint in not cutting open that candle. I didn't want to do anything without a police officer present."

"Makes a change," Parrish murmured. I ignored that.

"So, now that you're here, how about we cut it open and see what a bright boy I am."

"No."

"No?"

"No. Mr. Griffin, unlike your fictional detectives, we real detectives have procedures that must be followed. You've already made our job more difficult by tampering with multiple pieces of evidence. If you really believe the ruby is in this candle, the proper procedure would be for me to take custody of the candle in the presence of the Earl of Haxley and provide him with a receipt. I would then take it to the station where, before several witnesses, none of whom are *you*, a qualified forensics expert would crack open your little wax egg."

He paused just long enough to tell me this next bit was important for me to listen to and that I probably would not like it.

"But remember, Mr. Griffin, we only have your word as to where this was found, just like everything else. So as evidence it's lost whatever usefulness it may have had. For all I know, you stole the damned ruby yourself, you put it in the candle, and you are the one trying to frame Fitzhugh. I don't believe that, but if push comes to shove, I'll follow the evidence, which is currently covered in *your* prints."

My shoulders slumped as he chastised me. I felt positively wormy. "I may be a pain in your official neck, Inspector, but I'm only guilty of being overly enthusiastic, perhaps. Let me say again how sorry I am. Do you despise me too much to grant me one favor?"

"I'll grant you three favors," he replied. "The first is that I am not arresting you, though it's your final warning. Secondly, I promise to call you when we have the results of the operation."

"And the third favor?"

"I'll try not to hold it over your head that you have apparently overlooked an important clue."

"I did? What?"

The Inspector turned the candle over and held it out for my inspection. I looked. "Oh," I observed quietly. "Oh, holy cats."

"Now," he said, calmly, "walk me through it again. Tell me, as coherently as possible, what you think happened, who did what to whom, and why."

I leaned back into my chair, looking for the most comfortable spot from which to tell a most uncomfortable story.

Chapter 39

While I spoke to the Inspector, Val and Daphne had holed up in a corner of Tower Field Hall I'd never visited before. The south-by-southwest-parlor-by-living-room, I assumed. I wouldn't have been able to find them at all if Lydgate hadn't spotted me wandering around like a lost goldfish and pointed me in the right direction.

They were working out a crossword puzzle together. Daphne sat in a purple armchair so huge it made her look like Alice in Wonderland, while Val lay smoking on a matching chaise longue, posed like some spoiled Italian prince. It was a good look on him. Between them, owning a rather nice Bokhara rug, Catullus lay coiled into a perfect comma.

"Oh, Griff, perfect timing," she said. "What's an eleven-letter word for a Basque folk dance?"

"I have no idea," I replied. "Ask a Basque."

"That's only ten letters," Daphne smirked.

"We think it begins with F-D-B," Val added.

"Highly doubtful. So, the family is dropping dead one by one and you two are doing a crossword puzzle?"

"Lacking your brilliant detective mind, we're rather at a loss for what to do," Val said. "Consider the crossword a warm-up for our brains."

"Well, my brain is practically overheating. I've just come from speaking to Inspector Parrish."

"Oh, yes?" Val sat up and regarded me with interest. I had to smile at a rogue lock of hair that fell upon his forehead in the shape of a question mark.

"Oh, yes. I presented him with a theory and a new piece of evidence."

"Will you share with us this theory?" Daphne asked. "Or shall we go back to our puzzle? We're also stumped for a seven-letter word for a sea snail. It ends with D-C-L. I really should enlist Mary. She could solve this with both eyes tied behind her back."

"Eww," said Val.

I flopped into a seat opposite them. "Have either of you ever *done* a crossword puzzle before? Nothing in the English language begins with F-D-B or ends in D-C-L, unless you're trying to do long division with Roman numerals."

"I can't even do long division with English numerals," Val reflected.

"Well, don't keep us waiting," Daphne said from the depths of her oversized chair. "Tell us what you've discovered."

"I found the Adenoid of Aunt Aphrodesia!" I exclaimed.

"The... what of who?" Val asked.

"The stolen ruby. The lost family jewel. The blood red treasure of your forebears. You know, the Adenoid of Aunt Aphrodesia."

"Oh! He means the Uvula of Saint Ursula!" Daphne chirped.

I was looking at her, so I was unable to block the cushion which Val lobbed at my head. I responded with the sort of stern look that used to send troublesome Privates into fits of efficiency during the war. It had no effect on Val, who merely smiled.

"You're both mad," he said. "Fortunately, so am I."

"Okay," I said. "Let's try that again. I found the fabled missing stone which, I think, helps point out who is guilty. Or, rather, who is innocent."

"You're talking in riddles again. Did you write this?" He waved the crossword puzzle at me.

"Where was the ruby?" Daphne asked.

"It's hidden inside a candle. Someone softened the wax, pushed the ruby into the candle, and tried to smooth it out again. But they botched the job, and I noticed that the candle was lumpy."

"A lumpy candle?" Val asked.

"*Very* lumpy," I confirmed. "And, as I pointed out to the Inspector, candles do not have glands."

"Is that supposed to mean something?" Daphne asked.

"Sure," Val said. "It's the name of his next book, *Zoltan Szabo and the Glands in the Candle.*"

"Shut up," I said mildly.

"May a confused person ask where you found this lumpy candle containing Aunt Aphrodesia's glands?" Daphne said.

"In Fitzhugh's room."

"Aha! I knew it," Val exclaimed. "This proves he's guilty."

"No, actually. I think it proves he's innocent."

"What?!"

"Would you like to try that word again without sounding like a little girl?"

Val cleared his throat and repeated "what" in such a deep, raspy tone that he sounded like his Aunt Jim.

"But I think I know who did it?" I said, with a concerning lack of conviction.

"That's wonderful!" Daphne enthused.

"Well, aren't you just all that and a Yorkshire pudding?" Val said. "So, who is it and what happened?"

I sighed. The prospect of having to explain everything to my friends after explaining everything to Inspector Parrish and before explaining everything to everyone else, suddenly seemed exhausting. Better to do it all in one go.

"Not now. I think we need a Marmalade Magpie," I said.

"Is that a cocktail?" Val asked. "If so, I second the motion."

"Third!" Daphne chirped.

"Alas, it's not a cocktail. It's the term I use inside my head for the scene at the end of every book when Zoltan gathers everybody together and explains what the marmalade magpie is."

"Oh, you mentioned that before! But I thought you called it a… de-nude-ment?"

"*Denouement*. And yes, it's pretty much the same thing."

"But what *is* a… marmalade magpie?" Daphne asked.

"In cheap pulp novels, the dying man always gasps out something mysterious, like '*The marmalade magpie!*' And then he dies without explaining himself. So the rest of the book is about solving the mystery. Finding out—"

"What the heck the phrase 'marmalade magpie' means?" Val finished. "What a ridiculous notion. And this only happens in cheap pulp novels, you say? Yet it's also your pet phrase? How many times have you used it?"

"Only once!" I swore. "And I swear I felt guilty the entire time I was writing it."

"What was the book?" Daphne asked.

"Well… It was *Zoltan Szabo and the Marmalade Magpie* actually. But the big scene at the end happens in every mystery novel, and it's a pretty good phrase."

"It is not a good phrase. You honestly make money doing this?" Val sounded incredulous. "People actually *pay* to read your books?"

I looked over at Daphne, "Honorable Miss Irregular, would you like to be my new best friend? I find I have an opening."

"Look, Griff," Val said. "This is crazy. If you gather what's left of my family in one room and start throwing around ugly secrets and accusations and marmalade ruddy magpies in some crazy de-nude-ment, the only person left alive after the explosion will be your damned cat."

Catullus meowed in protest. Val muttered, "*Mea culpa.*"

"You think it's a bad idea?" I asked.

"I think it's the worst idea since you trotted off to Waterloo."

"You're probably right. But I think a Marmalade Magpie is the only way we'll get the guilty party or parties upset enough to betray themselves." I turned to Daphne. "What do you think?"

"I also think it's crazy, but I've always wanted to see one of those scenes in person."

"I must confess, I've always wanted to lead one. Zoltan does it all the time, I think it'd be interesting."

"But what about the police? Shouldn't they have a say in this?"

"Don't worry, I won't leave them out. Inspector Parrish already knows exactly what I think."

"And he's letting you proceed with this? Wow, for once I'm the voice of reason," Val said. "I'm on the side of wisdom, and I don't know how to feel about that."

Daphne regarded him, "I think wisdom looks good on you, Val. Don't you agree, Griff?"

"Yes, he's positively glowing with wisdom. In fact, I may need dark glasses just to look at him."

Val lobbed another cushion at me.

"So, when do we tell the suspects to gather?" She asked.

"Soon. Once Inspector Parrish calls me back with the answers to two questions, then I'll be ready."

Chapter 40

I spent the remainder of the afternoon second-, third-, and fourth-guessing myself. A routine that only got worse once the meeting began. What if I was wrong? Oh hell, I probably was. But if I completely embarrassed myself, at least I wouldn't have to see any of these people again. I could always get a new best friend.

Once the call came in from Parrish, there was no more putting it off. But the moment I walked into sitting room the severity of the situation struck me like a runaway train. Many pairs of eyes turned toward me with varying degrees of curiosity, suspicion, or outright hostility, stripping me bare.

I had never realized how much brash courage it took to stand up in front of a room full of suspects and say, "I know who did it." Writing a scene like that was one thing, because Zoltan was always right, which meant I was always right. But now, trying to make sense of real crimes, without the ability to revise or throw away the parts that didn't fit? Terror. Sheer mouth drying, voice-cracking, sweating and shaking terror.

Val was right, calling these monsters together was the worst idea I'd ever had. Worse than when I volunteered to be Aunt Elsie's favorite boatman back in ancient Egypt. Waterloo was a cakewalk compared to this.

I stared back at the assembly, unsure of how to begin. But surprisingly, Val took the lead. "Ahab" was back as Val assumed a dramatic pose against the mantelpiece, half going down with his ship and half waiting for John Singer Sargent to rise from the grave and paint him. I wondered if Aunt Elsie could arrange the commission.

"I thought it was time," Val declared, "that our family take the tremendous step of behaving respectably for a change. Mr. Griffin, who, once again, has my full confidence, has a few things to say and probably quite a few questions. You will all cooperate with him."

Nicky objected, as expected. "Mr. Griffin may ask all the questions he likes. But I, for one, have no intention of answering. He's no copper."

Wulfie stood up. "And I refuse to submit to the bourgeois false authority of—"

"Oh, do shut up," Val growled. Wulfie shut up and sat down.

"I, too, refuse to participate in this mock tribunal or whatever it is you're playing at," Aunt Jim said. "Mr. Griffin, you have no authority here."

"But I do." Valentine Hatton-Haxley, the 17th Earl of Haxley, spoke calmly yet firmly, commanding instant respect. It was a whole new side of the man. "Go on, Griff."

"Well, it's true that I have no constabulary authority," I said as casually as possible. "But I have spoken with Inspector Parrish, and he will be—"

The door swung open with movie-perfect timing, and all heads swiveled as Lydgate announced the arrival of the Inspector. The sudden looks of confusion and worry pleased me to no end.

Parrish and Lydgate smiled politely back. Following in their wake were Fitzhugh, Sutherland, and a lovely, dark girl with beautiful brown eyes. This, I was to learn later, was the maid, Daphne's chum, the oft-mentioned Mary.

"You can't honestly expect the *servants* to be a part of this," Aunt Jim protested.

I looked at Wulfie. "Isn't this the point where you lecture your mother about the evils of class difference and say that including the staff in this discussion is merely an example of natural equality?"

Wulfie looked like he was sucking on a goldfish and said nothing.

Val invited the newcomers to take chairs, which they did very much in keeping with personalities. The Inspector casually strolled in as if he were a regular visitor and stood beside an empty seat off to the side of the room, where he could keep a ready eye on everyone. Fitzhugh cast a universal glare at the company and sat stiffly at attention. Sutherland sank with an air of apology onto the very edge of the most modest chair, while Mary, following a motion from Daphne, sat next to her friend on the loveseat.

Val nodded at me to begin, like I knew what I was doing. I didn't. But before I could make an ass of myself by blurting, "*I've called you all here to name the murderer,*" Inspector Parrish began speaking.

"I want you to know that I'm not here to make an arrest, conduct interviews, or to explain any of my thoughts in this matter. I'm here solely because the Earl has very kindly invited me to join him as his guest for the evening. I fully accept that this is highly unorthodox, so I would like to reiterate that I am not at all here in an official capacity." He paused to look around the room. "That said, Mr. Griffin has rather persuasively explained *his* thoughts to me, and I am naturally curious to see what transpires." His manner was an odd mixture of authority and amusement.

He sat down at this point, nodding in my direction with a warning look that said, *be careful what you wish for.*

The floor was mine at last. And I still didn't know what to say. But after several seconds of scowling and trying to do that raising-one-eyebrow thing, the silence became unbearable, so I burst out with the first thought that came into my mind. Or rather the second thought, since the first was "*run!*"

"Your family certainly dies a lot," I said.

Someone, either Val or Parrish, snorted. Not an auspicious beginning. I cleared my throat and tried again.

"When Val first told me about this family, I admit I was a bit skeptical. I don't mean to mock a tragic history, but the combination of a family curse, a *tontine*, and a centuries-long series of suspicious deaths does sound unbelievable."

"It does," Val agreed.

"Look, I'm a writer. And I would *never* have the courage to stuff a single book with all the plot devices that exist in this family. Only a writer who was out of her mind would come up with a plot this confusing and nonsensical. Why, it would be practically unreadable."

"I wouldn't read it," Val said.

"You won't read *any* of my books. But at least they make sense," I observed. "I mean, what idiot author would cram in a curse, a family full of dead saints, a man who died with a great ruddy *bumboozer* in his mouth, a mysterious poisoning, possibly a *second* poisoning, a jewel theft, a séance, swindlers, an eccentric mystic aunt who predicts people's deaths, a multitude of absurd wills, enough family secrets to make the Tudors look like Quakers, and one fake communist?"

"Hey!" Wulfie objected.

"Shut it, Wulfie," Val said again. "You are about as believable a communist as I am a Vestal Virgin."

"Ooh, I was a Vestal Virgin once," Aunt Elsie said, and then thoroughly flummoxed the Inspector when she turned to him and asked, "*Remember?*"

The thread was getting away from me already. I scrambled to get back on track. "Right, so. While this sounds like the terrible first book of a delusional author, in this case it's all true. And confusing enough to cause actual pain."

"Oh, good, I thought it was just me," Val said. "Anyone got an aspirin? One without poison, please."

"However, I have come at last to one important conclusion."

"That you're barmy?" Theo asked from behind his hand. That earned him a chuckle from his brothers and a loud *shush* from his mother.

"That what we have here is three crimes. And also three perpetrators."

"What?" Val moaned. "You couldn't have given me a warning so that I knew to drink enough Scotch to make all this bearable? Are you going to make me face *three* murderers, killers that I share a name with, while sober? That's just cruel."

"Val," Daphne soothed, "don't be difficult."

"Sorry. But really, Griff, you think we have three killers?"

"No, I think you have two killers and one jewel thief."

"Oh, right! The old Adenoid of Aunt Aphrodesia! Or was it the Uvula of Saint Ursula? I've lost track," Val said, sparking general confusion.

"He means the Indian ruby," Daphne explained quickly. "Griff thought it needed a name and… oh, never mind. Griff?"

I continued.

"First off, I have to say that the Gordian knot would be easier to untangle than all the secrets in this family."

"The… what?" Val asked.

I turned to him. "Did you sleep through *every* class?"

"Possibly."

Aunt Elsie piped up, "You know, it's that lovely story about Alexander the Great. In fact, he once told me…"

Val abandoned his position as Ahab at the mantelpiece and moved to sit next to Elsie.

"Aunt Elsie, perhaps you could tell us about Alexander later.

Right now, Griff is going to point the finger at somebody, or maybe at three somebodies, and I, for one, am on the edge of my seat. And at the end of my wits."

I plowed on. "I also have to say that I have very little actual proof for my solution…"

From the corner of my eye, I saw the Inspector shift uneasily.

"*However*," I continued. "I believe the authorities do possess all the evidence needed to validate my theory."

"Then why don't you let them handle this and you can go back to your tripe-y novels?" Nicky asked with excruciating snottiness.

I called his snottiness, raising him one sneer.

"You're absolutely right, Nicky."

"*Lord Nicholas*," Aunt Jim corrected. I scattered a sneer over her as well.

"Yes, well, *Lord* Nicky, if you aren't interested in finding out who the killers are, please don't let me keep you. I'm sure you have new stationery to order. Go on. After all, none of you are prisoners. Yet."

There was a moment of silence and then Aunt Elsie surprised everyone by suddenly standing and crossing to the door. Val made a strangled noise that might have been "Wait!"

The silence deepened until Elsie stopped near the wall, picked up a small end table and moved it two feet to the left. She then turned with a beaming smile, said, "There, that's better," and returned to her seat.

I took this as my cue to resume.

"So, as I say, we have three crimes, three criminals, and secrets galore. Your family history is like something out of an old penny dreadful."

"Oh, I say!" Wulfie protested, and something in me snapped. I couldn't help it. Despite the situation, I burst into laughter.

"*Oh, I say?*" I wheezed. "*Oh, I say, Comrade Stalin, are we wearing cravats to the revolution?*"

"Now, Griff, that's not fair," Val commented. "You know it says in the *Factory Worker's Fashion Manifesto* that no true party member should wear a cravat after Dignity of Labor Day."

A discreet cough from the general direction of the Inspector was enough of a scold to end this latest diversion. But I did not apologize. I thought Wulfie was an appalling tick.

"Anyway, the one incontrovertible fact in the whole bizarre backstory was that Erasmus was dead. Val doesn't believe it was an accident, and neither do I. We're pretty sure he was murdered. And I'm pretty sure most everyone else in this room thinks the same."

"I certainly do," Daphne said. "And so does Aunt Elsie."

"Oh, well that settles it, then," said Theo, sarcastically.

"*Theobald*," his mother's intonation turned the word into one of extreme displeasure. Turning her attention to me, she added, "Nobody in this family would want Erasmus dead."

"Really? Not even your two eldest sons, both of whom have a serious case of empty pockets?"

"How dare you!"

"Jemima, dear, please stop interrupting the conversational flow. Some of us are enjoying this," said Elsie, drily.

Val, with his newly grown spine courtesy of Captain Ahab, turned to Nicky. "Dear me, cousin, what *have* you been up to?"

"Three guesses," I said.

"Well one thing he's been up to is getting fresh with certain members of the female staff," Daphne declared. She and Mary each shot him the evil eye.

"I deny that!" Nicky leapt to his feet, probably intending to look dramatic and commanding. But all he got was farce, as his sleeve caught in the arm of the chair.

Daphne also stood, far more successfully, and motioned for Mary to step forward.

Mary was a lovely girl with the sort of cream complexion that other women could only get out of a jar. She was a tiny thing, not much over five feet. But her dark, fierce eyes suggested a great deal of force.

Daphne turned to Val. "Val, I promised Mary that you wouldn't fire her for this. If you do, *I'll* settle the question of who the next Earl will be. You behave."

With her burning eyes locked on Nicky's panicked ones, Mary said with great poise, "Last week, I decided that I'd had enough of Lord Nicodemus always trying to kiss me or drag me into the linen cupboard."

"Aha! *You* gave him the black eye," I exclaimed with a laugh. Once again, I felt guilty for finding humor in all this, but I wasn't alone. Both of Nicky's brothers laughed, too.

"So, Nicky, not content with forcing unwanted financial advice on people, you force unwanted attentions on the maids as well?" Val asked, as angry as I'd ever seen him. I didn't blame him. Odd how we could both joke about his brother and uncle's murders, but the idea of an appalling cousin imposing himself on a member of staff was too much for us.

It was good news for Nicky's posterior that he hadn't moved away from the chair when he made his ridiculous attempt at standing, for he now took an equally ridiculous fall. His face turned the color of an expensive parchment with only queasiness written on it.

"I absolutely deny doing anything improper towards this young lady," he said, without much conviction. "No doubt she's attempting some sort of blackmail plot."

I was just in time to grab Daphne's arm before she could lunge over and punch him in the nose. I wouldn't care if Nicky had a broken nose, but I didn't want Daphne to get into trouble with Parrish present.

"Besides," Nicky continued, "it's just her word against mine. Who are people going to believe, me or her?"

As if arranged by a choir director, Daphne, Val, Elsie, and I, aided, surprisingly, by Wulfie and Theo, all said "Her."

"It's completely false!" Nicky persisted.

"I see," I said. "What if I were to tell you that if you actually were with Mary at the time in question, it would give you an alibi for Erasmus's murder?"

I assumed Nicky was thinking because he screwed up his face in a sort of grimace usually reserved for embarrassing bodily functions. He cleared his throat and squirmed a bit before replying.

"I... may have asked this, um... Mary to help me find some... er... missing pillowcases in the linen closet. And while reaching up to the... pillowcase shelf, I may have slipped and accidentally bumped into her."

"With your eye?" I persisted.

"Oh, very well, yes. I tried a little *noblesse oblige*."

"I believe the term is *droit du seigneur*," Elsie clarified. "Back when King Aethelbald..."

Val reached for her hand and hushed her again.

"I'm sorry about that," Nicky said, sounding anything but. "But at least now you know I couldn't have killed Erasmus!"

"Oh, you still could have killed him." I smiled.

"B-but you said..."

"I said, '*what if I were to tell you*.' Purely hypothetical."

Val burst into a peal of laughter. "Don't take this the wrong way, but I think I love you, Griff."

"Now, having covered one of Nicky's inappropriate behaviors," I resumed, "allow me to inform you of another bad habit: spending other people's money. Nicky, I have two words for you... *Megatherium Trust*."

Nicky looked as if he was wearing a suit made of stinging nettles. "Well then, I have two words back for you," he replied, stupidly. "I have no idea what you're talking about."

"Nick, you really are an idiot, aren't you?" Wulfie sneered. "Are you guilty of exploiting the—"

"Oh, stuff it, comrade," Val said. "I wouldn't be so quick to join the Casting Stones Brotherhood. You're hardly a paragon of honesty. And you've got your own awkward money situation, haven't you?"

"Now, just a moment!" Wulfie objected.

"Wulfie, we know you've always been hopeless," Theo said. "You couldn't pick a winner in a one-horse race. You should let me advise you. Last term I ran the school betting shop and came home with three hundred pounds clear profit. *And* a taxidermy beaver."

"He might have done better consulting you," I admitted, "as apparently he is very much in debt to some very bad men."

Wulfie turned almost as pink as his shirt.

"For both of you, one less person standing in the lethal line of succession would be a great help in solving your financial problems," I pointed out. "With Erasmus dead, your father became the Viscount. The next in line. That meant a far larger share of the family money. Perhaps even enough to cover a shortfall at work, or a rather dangerous debt."

"I refuse to listen to this any longer," said Jim, rising. "I shall call my solicitor and instruct him to file a complaint against you for slander."

"Excellent idea, Jemima," Elsie said, switching back to her sensible voice. "Perhaps after we solve two murders and a jewel theft, we can get on to the more serious crime of someone insulting your moronic sons."

"Aunt Elsie!" Daphne exclaimed with a laugh.

I smiled at the old woman and said, "Remind me to marry you next time around."

"Again? It's a date, James," she said with a wink.

The dowager Viscountess was in full flounce when I stopped

her with, "Of course, your sons aren't the only ones with a strong motive for murder, *are* they Lady Haxley?"

Her eyes grew huge in her tiny face. "You dare stand here, in *my* house, and accuse *me* of murder?"

"Ah, but it's *not* your house, Auntie. It's mine," Val said with the impressive new air of leadership that looked so well on him. "So please stop prancing about like a poodle and sit down."

"Have you no respect for my bereavement?" The line would have been more effective if she'd been able to knock out a few tears. But I could not imagine this woman shedding a tear in public. She'd rather take out her own appendix with a warm spoon than show weakness.

"Well, I can't speak for Val," I said, "but honestly, no. I'm sorry, Lady Haxley, but I *don't* have any respect for your bereavement. I know it's absolutely outside the rules of a polite society, but I simply cannot pretend any more. This is a house built on secrecy, resentment, betrayal, and greed. I'll admit to fostering a parlor game atmosphere here, but only because the whole situation is so absurd."

"I don't blame you," Val smiled. "We are definitely horrid."

I nodded. "The Hatton-Haxley clan is a fascinating mix. Fiendishly clever and yet brain-chuffingly moronic."

I heard the Inspector moan quietly, but he made no move to stop us. I think we was secretly enjoying it a little.

"Now, back to Erasmus's death. One thing that made this overly complicated situation slightly less complicated was the realization that there many suspects, but only one real motive. Money."

"Money," repeated Val. "Erasmus was a dear man and a decent Earl, killed because somebody in this family is a greedy, murdering bastard."

"Valentine!" Aunt Jim objected.

"Oh, hush, Jemima," Elsie said. "The word 'bastard' is in the

Bible. But if it'll make you feel better, after we deal with this trifling matter of a murder or two, we can strongly chastise Val for his language. Perhaps he can write '*I shall not say bastard*' five hundred times on a slate or he won't get pudding."

I bit the inside of my lip. "Go on, Griff," Elsie instructed.

There was something about Miss Elsie referring to me by my real name that gave me a warm glow inside. I smiled at her before continuing.

"Val is right in saying a greedy, murdering bastard killed Erasmus. Perhaps it was to avoid a public scandal and possible imprisonment…" I looked at Nicky, then turned to Wulfie. "Or maybe to cover a few gambling debts."

"But there was still a glaring problem. Why was Erasmus's death so obviously staged to look like a murder? Drowning in his bath, with a giant marble in his mouth? Improbable, to say the least. And I don't think anybody who knew Erasmus would believe him choosing to relax with *The Gospel of Nicodemus*." I looked at Nicky, "No offense to your namesake, but even by religious standards it's excruciatingly dreary."

"That is blasphemous!" The expected objection came from the expected source. I ignored Aunt Jim and plowed on.

"My point is, most murderers would take pains to disguise their crime, trying to make it look like an accident or suicide. The only reason for Erasmus to die holding a big sign reading '*Hello, I've been murdered*' is so the murderer could implicate someone else."

"Nicodemus, obviously," Theo chirruped. "The book was meant to name the killer. Or, wait… maybe Nicky *really was* the guilty party and Erasmus used it as a way of pointing the finger!"

"I object!" Nicky said, rising.

"Sit down, Nicky," I said. "This isn't the Old Bailey, and both those theories are absurd anyway. There's no way the killer would point to himself, and Erasmus couldn't very well have gone out looking for a book that just happened to bear the name of his killer after he was dead."

Jim stood again. "I find all this to be highly insulting and I do not see why my sons and I should be forced to listen to this so-called writer spin fabulous tales."

"Aunt Jim," Val said with chilly politeness. "Mr. Griffin is not a so-called writer. He is an author of some renown and considerable talent."

"How would you know?" Theo asked. "You've admitted to not having read any of his books."

"Don't be an idiot, I've read everything he's written," Val said. He turned to me. "Did you actually believe I didn't read them?"

I suddenly felt very pleased, and relieved. And stupid for also having believed him.

Val continued, "Now, as the head of the family—" I boggled at his ability to make that statement with a straight face. "—It is my wish that we all shut up and listen to what Mr. Griffin has to say."

"Thank you. As I was saying, *The Gospel of Nicodemus* wasn't meant to implicate Nicky. I rather believe the idea was to frame somebody else entirely. Two somebodies, in fact. I also think that by not anticipating that the Gospel could point the finger at Nicky, Erasmus's killer was, in a way, responsible for his own death."

"So, you know who killed Erasmus?" Val asked.

"I'm afraid I do. It was your Uncle Sally."

"That's preposterous!" Jim protested.

"No, Lady Haxley, it is not preposterous. It's what Val and I suspected all along."

"And I," said Daphne.

"And I as well," added Elsie.

Lady Haxley turned on Elsie and growled, "You're only saying that because *you* killed Erasmus. You're mad, you should have been locked up ages ago, and now you're trying to implicate my family. My husband was a fine man, the sort described in the Bible as…"

She paused, trying to think of the right phrase, but Elsie once again surprised the company by getting there first.

"*Proud, arrogant, abusive, ungrateful, unholy, heartless*," Elsie said with a smile of perfect innocence. "2 Timothy, verses 3 and 4."

And thus did Elsie secure her place in my life as one of my favorite people ever. She used the Bible to insult an enemy. And a dead enemy at that.

"What complicated the situation for Sally," I continued, "was that in trying to frame someone else, he ended up framing three people. Two intentionally and one unintentionally."

"I'm sure I speak for many of us here," Val said, "when I ask if you could possibly translate that into English?"

"Your uncle took steps to make us suspect both Miss Elsie and Mr. Fitzhugh."

I looked at Fitzhugh. This could hardly be a surprise to him, but he played it up.

"He did what?" Fitzhugh stood and glared at me. "That bloody ass tried to set me up for murdering Lord Erasmus?"

"Now, now, Fitzhugh," Val said mildly. "Language. Just because a statement is true doesn't mean it's appropriate for polite company."

"He did try to implicate you," I said. "But he didn't succeed."

"Wait just a minute, Griff!" Val called. "Stop the presses! Stiffen the Prussian Guard! Do you mean to tell us Fitzhugh here is *innocent*?"

"Of killing your brother? Oh, yes. As innocent as a newborn lamb in the spring, *tra-la*."

"But… but he makes such a good suspect." Val actually seemed disappointed.

"Yes, he does. Which is probably why your uncle picked him as a possible fall guy."

"And I'm the other possible fall guy?" Elsie offered.

"Precisely. Your book and your marble were placed at the murder scene, in hopes that if murder were suspected, any investigators would search your room, where they'd discover you keep poisons. He planted some more circumstantial evidence, too, but I'll get to that. It was all quite stupid."

Elsie clapped her hands like a small girl. "How exciting! I've never been a murder suspect before. Unless you count the Princes in the Tower."

I smiled at her. "I've always suspected Henry VII of that one."

"Oh yes," she agreed, "horrible man, and *so* disappointing as a lover."

"Can we please get back to this century?" Val asked.

"Yes, sorry. Anyway, Sally apparently thought…"

"Mr. Griffin, I must object to the late Viscount being referred to in such a disrespectful manner. Especially when you are also slandering him as a murderer. His correct title is—"

"Jemima, do shut thy mouth," Elsie said.

"Here, what about me?" Fitzhugh growled. He moved from the back of the room where the rest of the staff was lingering and made his way closer to the action. "What did he try? How did he try to set me up?"

"Well, there's a check somewhere for £3,000, and it's made out to you."

I could see Fitzhugh thinking quickly, concocting a story on the fly. I wondered if he'd deny ever receiving such a princely sum. Instead, he said, "That has nothing to do with this. It was a private business deal between Lord Sulpicius and me."

"Oh? What sort of business deal?" Val asked.

"I was… uh… planning to leave his service," he said, warming to his excuse. "I've got a chance to go in with an old friend as partners in a pub in... uh... Doncaster. The check was a gift. A reward for years of faithful service."

"So, you have given notice?" I asked.

"Yeah."

I turned to Lydgate and Sutherland, sitting fascinated at the back of the room. "Did either of you know about this?"

"No, sir," they said together.

Lydgate added, "The late Viscount would have informed me immediately, so I could start the process of finding a replacement."

I turned to Jim. "Viscountess, did your husband mention to you that his servant was leaving his service?"

"He did not."

"Well, uh..." Fitzhugh continued, "we were keeping it quiet. Until after the Earl's funeral, you know. We thought it would be inconsiderate to distract a house of mourning with such a minor domestic issue."

"Say, wait a second," Theo said slowly. "If Father wrote that check, it couldn't just be to frame Fitzhugh, because it would prove the two of them were in cahoots, partners—"

"*Theobald!*"

"Sorry, Mother."

"Ah, but the check was only the beginning," I said, explaining about the vial of nicotine I found under Fitzhugh's chair and the cuff link placed in Erasmus's room.

"What's that? You searched my room?" Fitzhugh squared his shoulders. "Who the bloody hell do you think you are?" His hands clenched into fists as he took a step forward. I saw Inspector Parrish stir.

"Yes, I did. And you should be *glad* I did, because finding that vial was the first step in realizing you were being framed." That calmed things down for the moment.

"Why?" Fitzhugh asked slyly, suspecting some kind of trick.

"Because unlike most of these people, you are not an idiot.

If you really had poisoned Erasmus, you wouldn't leave the evidence in your room. This is a huge house, it was a tiny bottle, and there are about a million hiding places in the Hall that wouldn't implicate you. But only one place that would."

"Damn right. But you said that was the first step. What was the second?"

I looked away from him and stared at Nicky. "The pink candle in your room." I was pleased to see the arrow hit. Nicky flinched and shot a panicked look at his mother who was too busy staring daggers at me to pay attention to her eldest.

"What pink candle?" Fitzhugh demanded. "I hate pink. Pink is for ponces."

"Yes, but there is someone in this house who loves that color. Which brings me to the one non-lethal crime of the week. The theft of your family's ruby. I'm told it's worth rather a packet."

"That's an extremely uncouth remark," Aunt Jim said.

"As we're investigating the crimes of murder and theft, I don't think I'll lose sleep over it."

"And he's right," Val added. "It *is* worth a packet."

"At first, I wasn't sure if the theft of the ruby had anything to do with Erasmus's murder, but it was one more mystery that had to be investigated. And the trail led back, once again, to Mr. Fitzhugh."

"I haven't stolen anything!" The fists were back, and he looked ready to use them.

"Well, you haven't stolen the ruby, in any case," I agreed. "But somebody wanted us to think you did. Along the way he made a capital mistake; one quite common in my business."

"Paper cuts? Writer's block? Incorrect use of the pluperfect tense?" Daphne asked.

"Close. No, Sally's problem is that he couldn't decide who he wanted the murderer to be. Was it Fitzhugh with the murder weapon hidden in his room? Or was it Elsie who made the poison, had a bowl of marbles in her room, and owned a copy of *The Gospel of Nicodemus*? And then there was the other piece of evidence he planted, that book Erasmus pointed us to, detailing how Saint Nicodemus died."

"Hang on," Wulfie said, warily. "*Who* did you say pointed you to this book?"

Val glossed over the answer to that uncomfortable question. "You know that huge book in the library listing all those obscure saints and the weird ways they died? Someone planted it in Elsie's room."

"And a passage was marked," I added, "describing how Saint Erasmus of Crete was martyred. He was drowned with a mouth full of stones and a Bible tied around his neck."

Someone whistled at that, probably Theo. But I looked at Wulfie. "And the bookmark used to direct our attention to this page contained an unsigned poem. Something about belching smoke and Judas Iscariot."

Wulfie blushed about fifty shades of mortified.

"In trying to cloud the whole thing in misdirection, he did too much. He was unsuccessful in really implicating either Elsie or Fitzhugh, while also stupidly pointing the finger at two of his sons. Nicky, through the gospel, and Wulfie with the poetry bookmark."

"Gosh, I feel left out," Theo commented.

I turned to Val. "*Nil nisi* and all that, but your uncle really wasn't the smartest assassin ever."

Any objection the widow would have made to that statement was forestalled by the arrival of Catullus, who, apparently summoned by my use of Latin, strolled in without a care in the world and took up residence in Elsie's lap.

"You see," I continued, "I believe both of these acts were sheer thoughtlessness. I think Sally stole a religious text at random from Miss Elsie without considering its implication.

It just needed to be a gospel. And he had to mark the page in that book of saints, so he used the first scrap of paper he found in the library. I don't believe he ever intended to cast suspicion on his sons. But because he did, he has now, as the phrase goes, joined the choir invisible."

"I don't follow," said Val. "How does that work? Who killed Uncle Sally?"

"Ah, you've gone too far. I'll get to that. Erasmus's murder is first, and Sally's murder comes last. But there's also the theft of the ruby. That's the potted fish spread in your murder sandwich."

"Eww!" Theo moaned.

"Hmm. Yes, that was bad," I admitted. "Sorry."

"Well, then, who stole the ruby?" Daphne asked.

I opened my mouth to speak, but was beaten to it by Aunt Elsie saying, "Oh, please, allow us."

I was so surprised that it took me a second to realize that she was currently bending down and whispering into the ear of my cat. Catullus promptly hopped down, padded across the room, yawned, stretched, and sunk his front claws hard into Nicky's leg, earning howls of protest from the victim and his mother, and the instant good wishes of everyone else.

It was all too much. Even Inspector Parrish burst into peals of raucous laughter.

Chapter 41

Once we'd recovered our breath and wiped the tears from our eyes, I paused to wonder what Daphne's parents, Miss Astley, Eldridge, and the Bishop were doing, considering I hadn't seen any of them since Chapter 35. Then I coughed and forgot them again.

The wretched Nicodemus, squealing like a seven-year-old girl, was instantly fussed over by his mother like Mary Magdalene at the cross, only with iodine and talk of a lawsuit. Catullus, unharmed and untroubled, returned serenely to the safety of Elsie's chair. She scratched his head and whispered, "Good show."

In the interest of sanity, I asked Sutherland to fetch a drinks tray and allowed the group a ten-minute breather.

"How am I doing?" I murmured to Val as I gulped a whiskey. "I hope this isn't completely incoherent."

"I can't speak to your performance, but I am having a lovely time watching Nicky squirm. Did he kill Sally?"

"Wait and see."

At the end of the intermission, I walked towards the mantelpiece, then changed my mind. The detective standing by the mantelpiece was such a cliché. I moved over to the sofa and leaned negligently against the armrest.

"Before our little interlude, Miss Elsie, my cat, and I all accused Nicky of stealing the family ruby."

"I didn't," he said, unconvincingly.

"Say nothing, Nicky," Wulfie instructed.

Nicky said nothing.

"And while I do say he stole the ruby I must also give him credit for astonishing creativity. And a demerit for unbelievable slovenliness."

"Oh, please explain," said Elsie, sipping sherry and stroking Catullus like he was a prize-winning Persian.

"I'm not sure if it was Nicky's idea or Sally's, but together they came up with a plan to borrow a bit of money from the family coffers, and anywhere else Nicky could get it, to invest in the Megatherium Trust."

"You keep saying those words," Val said. "What the hell is a Megatherium Trust?"

"That's the great question. Nobody seems to know," I said. "I certainly don't. It's an investment swindle that broke, and a vast amount of money went with it."

"Is that the one where the owners fled to Brazil?" Wulfie laughed.

"Don't laugh at your brother, Wulfstan," his mother snapped. She resumed tending to her beloved Nicodemus.

"Don't worry," Daphne soothed. "He's not laughing at Nicky. He's laughing in triumph that no workers were exploited in this naked pursuit of capitalist gain."

"Whatever the trust is, or was, doesn't really matter. What matters is that Nicky's employers at the bank recently decided that their annual audit will take place in a few weeks, and not early next year."

"That information is confidential!" Nicky protested. The outburst might have carried more weight had he not squeaked while uttering it.

"And I believe that the directors of the Sheffield Commercial Bank will find a significant shortfall in the Nicodemus Hatton-Haxley department."

"Aha," Val said. "The plot thickens."

"That's libel!" Nicky squeaked again.

"No, actually," I corrected. "It's slander. Except it isn't. It's only slander if it isn't true. And what *is* true is that Nicky dumped £15,000 into the trust."

"Impossible!" His mother asserted. "Where would he get money like that?"

"Mother," Theo said, "Were you listening? Do you want him to say it again?"

"And, of course, Nicky isn't the only one with money worries, is he, Wulfie?"

"I don't know what you're talking about," he said, "Trust you to come down hard on me because of my political beliefs."

"Oh, stuff it, Wulfie," Elsie said. "Two years ago, you were a Primitive Methodist and last year you were a vegetarian. If you're a communist, then I'm Mae West."

"You tell him, Mae," Daphne said.

"What Wulfstan is," I explained, "is an extremely unlucky gambler who owes a great deal of money at the Milray Club, a private, hole-in-the-corner gambling hell in Soho. It was raided, by the way, about a month ago. And that left Comrade Wulfie in a cell for a few days and owing a substantial fine."

"Wulfstan Vedast! Is this true?" His mother growled.

"Wulfstan Vedast?" I couldn't help myself. "His name sounds like a Romanian curse."

Wulfstan Vedast, showing a surprising grasp of priorities in one so thick, said "Mother, Father just died, remember? Maybe we could deal with my debts later."

"Oh, we will, Wulfstan Vedast," I said. He scowled and mouthed something unprintable. "We'll deal with your debts because they give you a motive for killing your father."

"I did *not* kill my father!"

"Maybe. Or maybe not. We'll get to that in a minute. Right

now, we're discussing how your brother stole the Indian ruby, your family treasure, trying to cover his embezzlement."

"Do you mean that little weasel stole from both his employers and his family?" Elsie asked.

Jim turned like a very tiny, very poisonous snake and snapped, "This doesn't concern you. You are not family. I've had enough of this nonsense."

My cynical heart swelled with pride to see that Val no longer needed Ahab to give him strength. He turned to Jim and said, "*She* is family. *You* are an in-law. And if you don't want to become outlaws, you and your sons will sit still and listen."

"My goodness, Valentine, that was magnificent." Elsie smiled. "I haven't seen you that authoritative since Thermopylae."

Val smiled back. "Thanks, Auntie. That's one of my all-time favorite battles."

"Leaving Thermopylae for now," I resumed, "we come back to Nicky doing his best imitation of Raffles. He took the ruby from the family safe and, needing a safe hiding place, heated up one of his bedroom candles. When the wax was soft enough, he simply pushed the stone inside."

"That's actually rather ingenious," Theo admitted. "I'll have to remember that." I noticed he'd taken advantage of everybody's preoccupation to help himself to another Scotch.

"It was ingenious," I agreed. "A very clever idea ruined by lack of attention to detail. He shoved the ruby inside and then just blodged it over, trying to smooth it out with his fingers."

I looked at the Inspector. I had been glancing his way from time to time, and throughout the dialogue his expression had veered between *I can kiss my pension goodbye* and *they'll never believe this at the next policeman's ball*. But this time he simply looked alert. I raised my eyebrows in a silent question, and he nodded the answer.

"The result of these shenanigans was an obviously misshapen

candle. Instead of a clever hiding place, he left a clue that stood out like a pink, waxy thumb. Not only that, but in reshaping the wax, he also very generously left his fingerprints imprinted all over it."

Someone, Fitzhugh I guessed, snorted.

"When I searched your room, Nicky…"

"You searched—" Nicky started to protest.

"Yes. Yes!" I addressed the crowd. "For God's sake, I searched *all* your rooms. Now I can be discreet about it, or I can use my photographic memory to recite all your belongings here to the rest of the group. May we accept that I snooped and move the proceedings along?"

"Oh, James," Elsie blushed. "That means you found my—"

"I first saw the candle," I interrupted loudly, "In Nicky's room. Today when I went into Mr. Fitzhugh's room again, it had relocated there. A lumpy pink candle in Mr. Fitzhugh's clean, precise, white room? I couldn't miss it. Nobody could."

"You tried to set me up for stealing the ruby?" Fitzhugh stood again and took one step towards Nicky, his signature move.

"Only very amateurishly. And I don't think the idea was his." I turned to Jim. "I think the idea was yours, Lady Haxley."

"How dare you," she said, but quieter this time.

"You know something, Val? This side of your family says, 'how dare you' a lot."

"I know. It's a three-part family tradition. Part one, kill a relative. Part two, act indignant when accused of doing it. Part three, repeat parts one and two."

"You mean *she* tried to set me up, too?" Fitzhugh muttered.

"Well, Lady Jim needed somebody to take the fall for her husband's murder. The ruby was a convenient development, and, as Val said, you make *such* a good suspect."

"Wait," Theo said. "Am I following this right? Are you accusing my mother of murdering my father?"

"Perhaps. Or she knows who did. But we'll get to that."

"Huh."

"But why would she want to kill Father?" Wulfie asked.

"Why wouldn't *anyone* want to kill Father?"

"Theo!" Nicky objected before his mother could.

"Oh, come on. He was a horrible man. We all thought that."

"I didn't," Nicky asserted.

"Then why did you say he was a horrible man to me last night when we were talking about his death?"

"No, you misheard. I said *honorable* man."

"Boys, boys," Val interrupted. "Let's not fight over who hated your father more. We can award the prizes later. Right now, I want the motive."

"Yes, the motive! I love motives!" Elsie said.

"Elsie, such enthusiasm is highly inappropriate." Jim corrected. Apparently even being accused of murder took second place to feigned politeness in her eyes.

"Oh Jemima, this whole scene is highly inappropriate. James may be a wonderful writer, but not even he can make all of this make sense. Go on, James. The motive."

I turned to Theo, who seemed to be the one most acquainted with the truth. "Theo, I don't suppose you and Wulfie ever looked at Nicky and thought, *golly but my parents treat him like he spits diamonds?*"

He snorted. "Oh, sure. He's always been the golden angel. Wulf and I aren't even in the race."

"Indeed. It's been obvious since the moment I arrived here. They'd do anything for him, don't you think?"

"Wait," Theo glared at me. "Are you trying to say I killed Father because of Nicky?"

"No, Theo. I'm trying to say that your father killed *Erasmus* because of Nicky."

"Wait. What?" Nicky sprang to his feet. As soon as he did

so, Catullus, from the comfort of Daphne's lap, hissed at him. Nicky sat down again. Quickly.

"He knew you were in pretty deep trouble," I pointed at Nicky. "In fact, I think the plan to embezzle from your bank was probably his idea. Plus, he stumped up some money of his own and, I'm fairly certain, some money of yours, Val."

"What the... oh, you mean money from the estate," Val said.

"Yes. But when news of the upcoming audit broke, both your uncle and your cousin panicked. If they couldn't repay the money, they were both facing ruin and prison. Killing Erasmus was the easy way out. It moved your uncle up to Viscount and increased his allowance."

"Griff," Daphne said. "This is ridiculously complicated."

"Well don't blame me," I protested. "I didn't write this plot. Nobody sane would."

"But you did write *The Woman in White*," Elsie said, smiling.

"So. Sally kills Erasmus," I said, "But they're still not sure they'll have enough money in time. Then Nicky here gets the bright idea of stealing the ruby. That would bring in enough to pay off the debt and maybe make some fresh investments, too. But I think you did that all on your little lonesome. Even Sally didn't know. And when your mother found out about it, she was less than pleased."

"Oh, dear, Jemima," Daphne said. "It seems you didn't do a very good job of teaching your boys their morals. *Thou shalt not steal thy family's heirlooms*."

Aunt Jim pursed up her lips and sniffed.

"Well, if Uncle Sally killed Erasmus, and Nicky stole the ruby—"

"I didn't!"

"Then who killed Uncle Sally?" Val asked.

"Well, we're down to Nicky, Wulfie, or your Aunt Jim, aren't we?" I asked, blandly.

The boys shouted denials over each other while their mother added her share of indignation. I ignored all of them and began talking to Val as if we were alone.

"It really can't be anyone else," I stated. "They all had such wonderful motives."

Val looked at me curiously for a moment. "Do they? Tell me again. Nicky stole from his bank. And Wulfie…?"

"He got pinched in a raid on an illegal casino. One, by the way, where some of the slots on the roulette wheel have been enlarged and the cards very slightly roughened."

"No, really? Do tell."

"One of the ways a young gentleman in debt to the Milray Club can help avoid the unpleasant physical consequences of that debt is to encourage their friends to become members. So that they, too, can lose large amounts of cash at crooked games. It's quite a scheme."

"Astonishing."

"So, Nicky and Wulfie both did very stupid things. The problem is that they are both just *so* stupid." I sighed. "I suppose I'll just have to figure out which is the least stupid. I'm sure I could pin the crime on him."

"It could go either way, really," Val said. "Each of them has the brains of a table."

"How dare you!" Aunt Jim said again. When was she going to learn that didn't work on me?

"Yes. Was it the moronic financial so-called genius who stole from his employers and invested the lot with a bunch of swindlers? Or the comic communist turned gambling shill with all the poetic talent of diphtheria?"

"Spoiled for choice, really," Val agreed.

"One is facing prison; the other is facing gangsters. Desperate times, and good motives for anything. Then again, we're also looking for someone truly evil. I mean it *is* pretty wicked to kill your own father. That's some Greek tragedy, one-way trip to the underworld type sinning right there."

"Oh, I see what you mean," Val, the perfect foil, said. "So, which of them is both stupid and wicked?"

"I think both are both. But yes, which one?"

"And didn't you mention something about Aunt Jim being a suspect?"

"Yes, it's time we looked at all this from her perspective. First, her idiotic husband convinces Nicky to steal from the bank. Then when they find themselves in danger of getting caught, her husband murders his nephew and manages to implicate both of his sons. To top it all off, there's the fact that your uncle was having a bit of naughty with a woman who sickeningly refers to herself as 'Kitten' in the third person."

Catullus made a sound that caused me to fear he was about to lose his kippers on the rug.

Aunt Jim leapt to her feet. "I've had enough of this farce. Neither I nor my sons will say anything further without the advice of our solicitors."

I ignored her and returned to chatting pleasantly with Val.

"Again, look at it from your aunt's perspective. She knows her husband has killed Erasmus. She's discovered he has a mistress on the side who, according to the letters, he was almost ready to start a new life with. But she knows his pride in his reputation would mean divorce would be out of the question. Where does that leave her? What would prevent him from offing his wife to make that new life possible?"

"Aha! So, either in anger at him for jeopardizing her sons, or in revenge for his affair, or out of the fear, real or not, that her own life might be imminently in jeopardy, she sent Uncle Sally off to his just rewards," Val summed up.

"Exactly. So, Viscountess Haxley. Who is more wicked? You, or one of your precious sons?"

Elsie made a small noise and I looked at her. "Ah, Miss Elsie, do you have any idea which of them it was?"

"Well, whichever one, they have committed evil in the sight of the Lord and, as it says in the Psalms, '*The wicked is snared in the work of his own hands. The wicked shall be turned into hell.*'" She looked across the room. "Isn't that right, Jemima?"

Aunt Jim stood, looking rather scarily like Clytemnestra in those Collier paintings, all righteous vengeance and disdain.

"My sons may have transgressed, but they have not earned eternal damnation. They did not kill their father. I did."

"Yes, Viscountess," I said. "I know."

Chapter 42

The rest was a blur.

The Inspector, who everyone had forgotten in all the loops and whorls of my explanation, rose from his chair and invited Aunt Guido and all her awful progeny to accompany him to the Danforth police station in order to "assist with the inquiry." I had to admit that after all the nonsensical blathering I had been doing, it was an immense relief that the Inspector agreed with my theories, or at least had heard enough from the main characters to haul them all away.

Lydgate and Sutherland quietly made their escape, no doubt to inform the rest of the staff of the evening's many shocking developments. Fitzhugh tried to follow on their heels, but I intercepted him.

"That check," I said quietly. "Three thousand pounds is a lot of money. I know he didn't pay you to kill Erasmus. And I doubt he suddenly decided to invest in a pub. So, what's the deal?"

He gave me his cold shark look and said, "What do you think?"

"*Dearest Sally Cat*," I mused. "I think perhaps the late Viscount didn't want the Viscountess to know about that."

"You're smarter than you look. Maybe I should read one of them books of yours." His face creased into what passed for a smile.

"Yet somehow, she found out anyway."

"That's as may be. What now? You going to stop me cashing that check?"

I shook my head. "That's up to you. You're a piece of work, Fitzhugh, but you didn't kill Sally or Erasmus, and you didn't steal that ruby, so that's where my investigation ends. I was merely curious."

"Heh. You're a better fake detective than most real ones." He turned to leave, tossing me a rude salute at the door.

* * *

"Griff, how much of that was blather and how much was real?" Val asked.

"Most of it was blather," I admitted. "I had a lot of hunches, a few clues, and almost no proof. I said so at the start. But I was pretty sure I knew who did each crime. And I knew the only way to catch Jim out was to keep attacking the sons, especially her precious Nicky. Eventually she had to break, either to point out that neither were stupid, or neither was wicked."

"But how did you know it was her?" Daphne asked.

"Little things. Sutherland overhead a conversation between Sally and who he thought was Fitzhugh. He said Sally mentioned something about 'how could we have predicted it' and 'it was just a book.' That seemed to suggest whoever he was speaking to knew all about Erasmus's murder. But then the other person said to Sally, 'you should have let me handle it you fool.' Fitzhugh would never call Sally a fool to his face."

"No. That sounds condescending," Val observed.

"It is condescending," I said. "And the only person in the house with enough power to put Sally in his place, was Jim. She has a very deep voice. When we met, I thought it was oddly masculine. Besides, at the time this conversation was taking place upstairs, Lydgate swears Fitzhugh was in the kitchen."

"How did she do it?" Elsie asked.

"Poison. The autopsy should show what the stuff was. But you might want to conduct another inventory of your garden laboratory."

"Yes, but *how* did she do it?" Daphne pressed.

"She put it in his tonic bottle. He took it before every meal. It was in his bathroom cabinet. I handled the bottle when I searched his room. Even opened it. Yet when Inspector Parrish tested it for fingerprints, the only prints on it were Sally's. So, she took the bottle sometime after I searched, added the poison, wiped off the prints, and put it back. Sally took his pre-dinner dose, and his fate was sealed. It was just macabre timing that whatever it was kicked in during the very dramatic tribute to St. Grandpa Whoozits."

Val furrowed his brow. "Say, what about that note? *You must pay for your crimes*. Who wrote that? Was it Aunt Jim? Fitzhugh?"

Daphne imitated Val's expression. "And that vial under Sally's chair. Was it the one that had the water in it or was it more poison?"

"How should I know?" I said, exasperated. "You can't expect me to solve everything! Parrish will figure it out."

"Do you think the inspector can actually make a case from all this?" Val asked.

"I think so. Remember, Jim confessed in front of Parrish and a dozen other witnesses. We did find a good deal of evidence, even if it was all circumstantial. No doubt the police will uncover more."

"You know," said Elsie. "I think Jemima may be more religious that I gave her credit for. I always figured all that dreary piety was for show. But now, I think if the inspector harps on about justice and righteousness and retribution and all those horrible Old Testament virtues, she'll confess to everything."

We were silent for a moment before Elsie went to the drinks cart. It was only as she was passing around cocktails that I realized the maid, Mary, was still in the room with us. Val seemed to notice her at the same time.

"Ah, Mary," he said. "Thank you for your help tonight. And I wish to sincerely apologize for the behavior of my cousin. He won't bother you again."

"Thank you, my lord."

She sat there still, on the loveseat, with Daphne's arm tight around her shoulders.

"Uh... that's all," Val said. "You can return to your duties now." Mary made to stand but Daphne tightened her hold.

"Oh, don't be stupid, Val," Elsie said as she handed Mary a drink. "Mary isn't here as a maid, she's here with Daphne. And we're very glad to have her, aren't we."

We agreed politely and all but fell into our drinks.

"I must say," Daphne commented after a moment or two of silence. "This all feels both unreal and anticlimactic."

"I know what you mean," I agreed. "None of anything that happened before this moment was real. It was some kind of group hallucination. And now that we've sobered up it feels like we climbed the Matterhorn, but it was completely fogged in, and we weren't rewarded with the view."

"Oh James," Elsie patted my hand. "You've always been such a poetic and droll soul. Do you remember when you helped Aristophanes write *Lysistrata*?"

"Actually, Miss Elsie, I'm afraid I don't. You plied me with so much *raki* that night that I don't remember anything after the turtle races." We all laughed.

"So, now what?" Daphne asked at last.

"Now Griff and I go back to London."

"Val's just eager for his date. He's wanted to go out with Miss Hyacinth Throgmorton since the Armistice," I joked.

Elsie, queen of surprises, had one more.

"Oh, James, now *you're* being stupid. Val wouldn't date

Hyacinth Throgmorton. Homer Throgmorton, maybe. But Hyacinth? Never. Homer is far more his type."

And having dropped that bombshell, she calmly reached for the decanter, took a sip, and her face brightened with a sudden thought.

"Oh, wouldn't it be lovely, Val, if you and Homer and Daphne and Mary went on a double date?" Val and I gaped at her and then looked towards Daphne and Mary, now holding hands and beaming smiles of outrageous joy.

"Wait... wait." I think my brain was in danger of exploding. "Daphne. You... and... Mary...?"

Daphne beamed at me, kissed Mary on the cheek, and then said simply, "Yes. You don't—"

"Oh, no, not at all. Good show," I murmured. But then the remainder of Elsie's dynamite exploded what was left of my brain as the fuse of my confusion met the match of... oh, the hell with it. I looked at Val. Really looked at him, for the first time in maybe ever. He looked very white and couldn't quite meet my eyes.

"Val, is this true? Is *Homer Throgmorton* really your type?"

He cleared his throat a number of times and then squeaked a bit when he finally answered. "Well, uh... I mean, not *him* particularly but... er... well, yes, he's *much* more my type than... um... Hyacinth. I'm sorry."

"I'm not."

The grandfather clock suddenly began to tick very loudly. Val shot me a grin so brilliant that my brain lit up again, and I did the only thing I could think of. I kissed my best friend.

"Oh my," said Elsie. "I certainly didn't see *that* coming."

—::—

Lisa Dornell was born in 1485 into a family of circus trapeze artists. Shunning the family business, she instead became famous for inventing envelopes and burlap. She is one of the world's leading collectors of Caesar Romero memorabilia and once worked as Harry Houdini's babysitter.

Today, Lisa lives in palatial splendor with one husband, two cats, and a great deal of residual Catholic guilt for the sins of her ancestors.

She is very sorry and it will never happen again.

Printed in Great Britain
by Amazon